## "GENTLEMEN, PLEASE. THERE'S A LADY PRESENT."

All eyes pivoted toward Megan. None appeared particularly happy about the intrusion.

"Oh, don't mind me," she blurted. "I'm a prospector too, and such talk is gettin' my hands all itchy."

A moment of stunned silence was followed by uproarious laughter. The way they were acting, she expected to be patted on the head and sent back to the punch and cookies like a wayward child. She set her chin defiantly, daring anyone to try.

"Lady, you're too sparse to heft a pick, much less swing one," the gent sputtered between chortles.

"You don't say." She grinned slyly and crossed her arms at her chest. "I'll grant I'm short on husky, but I'm powerful long on stubborn. We'll see which pays off by-the-by."

**"Megan O'Malley feels as real as Annie Oakley and Pocahontas ... utterly absorbing."**
**—Frederic Bean**

**"The plot intertwines fascinating history with clever fiction.... Suzann Ledbetter is a talented spinner of tales."**

**"A vivid portrait of th**

# TRINITY
# STRIKE

## Suzann Ledbetter

A SIGNET BOOK

SIGNET
Published by the Penguin Group
Penguin Books USA Inc., 375 Hudson Street,
New York, New York 10014, U.S.A.
Penguin Books Ltd, 27 Wrights Lane,
London W8 5TZ, England
Penguin Books Australia Ltd, Ringwood,
Victoria, Australia
Penguin Books Canada Ltd, 10 Alcorn Avenue,
Toronto, Ontario, Canada M4V 3B2
Penguin Books (N.Z.) Ltd, 182–190 Wairau Road,
Auckland 10, New Zealand

Penguin Books Ltd, Registered Offices:
Harmondsworth, Middlesex, England

First published by Signet, an imprint of Dutton Signet,
a division of Penguin Books USA Inc.

First Printing, January, 1996
10  9  8  7  6  5  4  3  2  1

For Nellie Cashman, a helluva gal,
and for the helluva fellow scribe
who guides my journeys—
every word of the way.

# PART ONE

# Chapter One

*January, 1884*

A saloon's plinkety piano rendition of "Camptown Races" drifted clear to Boot Hill, insulting the somberness of the occasion. Even the funeral service for two of Tombstone's finest didn't warrant a few moments of respectful silence.

"The Lord is my shepherd; I shall not want—"

The pair of wooden caskets lay side by side beneath the blazing Arizona sun. Dry-eyed, a rosary clutched in her fists, Megan O'Malley willed herself to endure Preacher Hiram Roe's droning eulogy.

"Yea, tho' I walk through the valley of the shadow of death—"

Flies clinging to Megan's black veil buzzed irritably, then flew away when the fabric billowed in the breeze. She smelled the salty musk of her own perspiration, yet her skin felt taut and brittle. That morning, she'd seen the fine lines grief and guilt were etching on her face.

"Thou preparest a table before me in the presence of mine enemies—"

She stared at the coffins, unable to truly comprehend that the men she'd loved most in the world lay inside them, hands clasped on their chests, eyes closed for all eternity.

"Surely goodness and mercy shall follow me all the days of my life: and I shall dwell in the house of the Lord for ever. Amen."

Bless them and keep them, Lord, Megan prayed silently. Forgive them their only sin . . . loving me.

The child within her stirred. She placed a hand on her swollen belly as if to comfort it. Head still bowed, she stood resolutely until the mourners behind her shuffled away.

No one offered condolences or even a supportive

squeeze of her arm. She understood, and forgave them their awkwardness, considering the circumstances.

"Is there anything I can do for you, Miss O'Malley?" the minister murmured quietly. "I'm not of your faith, but with Father Gallagher away in Tucson, I 'spect I'd do in a pinch."

She smiled wanly. "Solitude's all I'm needing right now, Preacher—thank you." With a solemn nod, he turned and strode toward his buggy.

Four men lowered the caskets by ropes into the trenches prepared to receive them, then reached for shovels speared blade first into the mounded dirt. The hollow sound of clods thudding against the coffins' pine lids echoed in Megan's heart.

She hugged herself tighter and tried to close her ears to death's thunder. There was no denying it, and no hope of ever forgetting its mournful toll. Her veil fluttered as a sob escaped her lips.

Shoulders sagging, she whispered, "Good-bye," and turned to walk away. When she paused at the cemetery's gate, a torrent of bittersweet memories washed through her mind.

Could it be only sixteen years have passed since I left Ireland, dreaming of the gold I'd prize from the earth? Oh, I've scratched, and dug, and reaped that bounty, too—time and time again.

She looked back at the two rocky promontories. And I'd give back every ounce of it to change one yesterday, and to give *them* a tomorrow.

# Chapter Two

"Oh, Frances, have you ever seen a thing so lovely as that?" Megan asked, pointing to the S.S. *Wardlow* anchored near the mouth of Cobh Bay.

To her fourteen-year-old eyes, the pine masts towering above the deck stood like sentries guarding the castle door. Only three of the brigantine's eleven sails were rigged, but that was enough for Megan to imagine a crew of eye-patched pirates at the helm.

How graceful the *Wardlow* will be when she's fully decked in her canvas finery, Megan thought. I reckon that ship'll glide through the ocean's swells as easy as a birch leaf on the Bride River.

Filling her lungs with the sea's briny mist, she broke into an Irish ditty her father sang whenever a chore demanded more brawn than brain.

"Ah, it's a pretty bairn you are, and strong as oxen, but you can't carry a tune in a pail," her older sister teased.

Megan gave Frances a mock scowl, then, using a satchel for a seat, gandered at the seaport she'd never seen before and would probably never see again.

The city of Cobh spilled down one hill and half-climbed another. Like its citizens, it was lean and poor, yet neat and freshly whitewashed as if a mask of gentility could disguise its circumstances.

Most doorways propped up a shabby dandy or two. Dressed in tattered breeches and dusty tailcoats, rapturously puffing on a shared Liverpool cigar, the vagrants' cheeks and chins looked sore in need of a dabble of spit and a good scrub.

"Mackerel, fresh caught yesterday!" "Apples!" "Dress goods, cheap!" screeched the raggedy crones who peddled their wares along the quay. Megan was tempted to meander among the stalls but didn't think the sellers would take kindly to a browser.

"Glory be, aren't they ever goin' to take us aboard?" she sighed.

"Lass, if a two hours wait on shore frets you so mightily, how'll you ever stand the two months voyage to America?"

"That's different—it's an adventure to behold, Frances! Now tell me true, did I grouse, even once, the twenty miles we walked from Rathcormac?"

"It's true. We've come a hard road the last few days—in more ways than that, and you've been a trooper, I'd say."

Hearing a twinge of melancholy in her sister's voice, Megan turned and looked up at her angular profile. At twenty-two, Frances had a bony build no sharetender's larder could soften, and dull brindle hair plaited and wound into a tight crown.

Unlike Megan, Frances hadn't inherited their father Mikaleen's Moorish coloring or their mother Selma's lush figure. But even the fairest beauties stood a slim chance of boasting wedding bands on their ring fingers.

Twenty years after the potatoes first rotted in the fields, there was still little work for the sons of Ireland, and no money at all for its daughters' dowries.

"I reckon, if not for Squire Bernard's doing right by us, there wouldn't be an adventure to behold, would there," Megan stated, more than asked. "Grand it was, his giving us enough for Da's stock and the house goods to pay our passage."

"Hmmph. Depends on how you measure it. Da and Mama labored in his paddocks and fields until they dropped. I'm a'thinkin' it's *their* backs we're goin' on, not the squire's generosity."

Megan stared out over the bay's lapping waves, her belly clenching as it did whenever her parents were mentioned.

She'd never heard coppers jingle in Mikaleen's pockets. And Selma took as mindful care of her two dresses as a queen's handmaiden would. There'd been scarcely enough food in their cottage to beckon a mouse, but there'd always been love abounding.

"Look sharp, girl," Frances said. "You've gotten your wish. The ship's taking on passengers."

Megan squealed as clutches of people gathered around a

sailor standing at the end of the pier. After a cursory examination of each passenger's ticket, he gruffly shoved the holder aside and beckoned impatiently to the next.

The emigrants' eyes gleamed with more white than iris as they shuffled forward. For all their bright hopes and earlier excitement, they now seemed as confused and frightened as a flock of sheep in a thunderstorm.

A crewman beckoned Frances toward a rickety rowboat. She regarded it warily, then accepted the sailor's hand and stepped onto the floorboards. Megan's more exuberant, unassisted boarding brought glaring reproofs from both her sister and the crewman.

As they neared the *Wardlow*'s hull, a man seated in front of Megan grumbled loudly about the ship's patched planking and weary appearance.

"Have no concern that this tub'll take us to America, me friends," he sneered. "Aye, from the look of her, I'd say she landed Columbus there, so *surely* she knows the way."

While Frances stifled a giggle behind her hand, Megan bit back a sharp retort. She'd seen the same blemishes and bang-ups and preferred to think of them as the scars of sea battles sought and survived.

Once on deck, Megan's footfalls immediately took to the brig's rhythmic sway, but Frances kept tottering like a newborn calf.

"I'm not likin' this heave and ho," she groaned. "It's turnin' my bones to butter."

Megan slipped a steadying arm around her sister's waist and crooned, "Take no notice of the rockin'. Relax and move with it and you'll find your feet soon enough."

"Leave me then, while I'm learnin' the steps to this jig."

As Megan's lips parted in protest, Frances ordered, "Off with you, if you please."

Reluctantly she obeyed.

At twenty paces wide by forty long, the *Wardlow* measured smaller than she'd have guessed. Stepping around coils of thick hempen rope and piled bundles, she made her way to the prow. At its apex, she stared in rapt fascination at the carved, curvaceous figurehead. In silhouette, the vigilant enchantress looked hauntingly lifelike.

"That there's Lorelei," a raspy voice declared from behind her. "She was a beauty 'til time and the sea stole her looks."

Noting the fancy insignia on his cap, Megan smiled and asked, "Then why don't you get a new one, Captain . . ."

"Jorgenson. Nehemiah Jorgenson. Nah, Lorelei belongs to the ship and it to her. Besides, a man don't set a lady adrift just 'cause she's faded a mite."

"Is she named for your wife?"

"No, Sprout. The Atlantic is my wife and the Pacific, my mistress. If I'm not in the arms of one or t'other, I get to feelin' like a cat shut up in a cupboard."

Megan nodded solemnly. "I don't think I'm the marryin' kind either, Captain Jorgenson. Leastways, not 'til I've made my fortune."

He started to laugh, then squelched it when he saw her sober expression. "Well now, I like a gal that knows her mind. But don't be boltin' any doors 'til you're sure what's on t'other side."

The captain shifted his weight and glanced upward at a crewman scaling an enormous rope net as nimbly as a spider in its web.

"I must take my leave, Sprout. There's work to be done to ready the ship for her journey. You'd be wise to claim berth space below. We've got more aboard than we should, and this late in the year, the crossing won't be patty-cakes."

"I'll do that, Captain," she said, then smiling broadly added, "and so's you'll know the next time we meet, my name is Megan O'Malley."

With a grin that would have shown teeth if he'd had any, Jorgenson tipped his cap brim and said, "Pleased to make your acquaintance . . . Sprout," then sauntered away.

Megan found the main hatch and climbed down a ladder into the *Wardlow*'s belly. With every rung, the stench of urine and vomit grew stronger. In the anemic light cast by kerosene lanterns, women scrambled to arrange straw mattresses and stow their families' possessions inside pens built of splintery scrap lumber.

"The unmarrieds are quartered over there," droned a sailor, pointing toward rows of one- and two-person bunks strung longships between stanchions. "Women to star-board—men to port. See that you keep to your side of the canvas. The captain don't cotton to sleepwalkers."

All the romantic ideas of sailing the high seas that Megan carried in her heart vanished like smoke in a strong wind. She knew that when Frances saw, smelled, and heard the hellish condition of the hold, she'd have them back in a rowboat and heading toward shore in a finger snap.

"We're about to set sail," she whispered when Megan rejoined her at the railing. "Let's stay on deck until our beloved Ireland disappears in the mist."

Megan hesitated, then stammered, "When you see our quarters, you mayn't want to leave a'tall. Hurry, come with me before the anchor is raised—"

Frances laid a comforting hand over her sister's smaller one. "There's nothing left for us in Ireland but memories, lass. I hear tell that America is a 'hoping' place. And a body *needs* hope that tomorrow will be better than yesterday."

A lump swelled in Megan's throat. Please God, give Frances the home she longs for. That's not so much to ask, now is it?

By the time Cobh disappeared from the horizon, the *Wardlow*'s pitch was as gentle as a cradle's. Megan escorted Frances to the hatch and followed her down the ladder. At least a hundred passengers were jammed cheek-to-jowl below ships.

Frances grimaced, but gamely followed Megan to a pair of empty berths. The pungent odor of chlorate of lime and carbolic acid testified to some semblance of disinfection, but no chemical on earth could dispel the human reeks.

Plopping a cloth satchel filled with all she owned in the world on a hammock, Frances chucked Megan under the chin and said, "Don't you be broodin', little one. It's not like it's lace tablecloths and sterling candlesticks I'm accustomed to."

By that night, though, the color had drained from Frances's face and her bravado with it. With limbs trembling and a cold sweat beading her brow, she stretched out on her narrow berth and burrowed beneath a threadbare blanket. The rough-planked hull would not creak beneath her weight until weeks later.

"How's our girl doin'?" asked Missus McBee, the ship's robust Mother Confessor who'd taken the O'Malleys under her ample wing.

Megan was bathing Frances's forehead with a rag dipped in seawater, as she had done countless times since they sailed from Cobh. "Alas, she was rallyin'—sat up awhile a few days ago—but the storms put her down again."

"It's a saint ye are for staying with her, Megan, and you hardly more than a child."

"She's my sister, Missus McBee. And I'm nigh full-grown."

"Takes yer credits when they're given, says I. Whenever the others go topside for a storytellin' or a jig, you stay fast to this pesthole with its squallin' babes, sick folks, and stinks. Why, it's a wonder you ain't caught ship fever or the rotten throat yerself!"

"It's good you've been to us, watching over Frances when I did take to the deck."

"Pshaw," Missus McBee snorted. "I've birthed nine children and buried five and their father. If there's anythin' I'm good for it's seein' to the sick and diggin' taties. And I'm here to tell ye, I favor the first one over the last."

In a more hushed voice, she snickered, "Didja hear what the crew did to Liz D'Arcy?"

Megan merely shook her head, knowing full well nothing short of sudden death would prevent Missus McBee from jabbering on.

"As surely ye know, that hussy's lifted her skirts to every buck in buttoned breeches since we left the homeland. Ain't bathed a lick since then, neither. Well, Cap'n Jorgenson got wind of what Liz was a'doin', and how she was a'smellin', and ordered her taken topside and drenched her with a fire hose."

Missus McBee's mountainous bosom jiggled with her laughter. " 'Twas a donnybrook what broke out then, I tell ye. That slut was a'spittin' curses that was makin' the sailors blush a'fore they locked her up for the duration."

Megan couldn't keep herself from chuckling at the mental image of the blowsy Jezebel's "bath."

"Ah, well, I'd best be gettin' back to me boys. Too many days locked up down here's settin' them a'twitchin' and trouble's sure to follow. You fetch me if ye need me, hear?"

After Missus McBee trundled off, Frances moaned, "To think I promised Mama that I'd take care of you, Megan. And here I am, too weak to lift my head."

"Don't be vexin' yourself with such thoughts," Megan soothed. "If it was me who took seasick, you'd be doin' the nursing. Hush now—take a sip of your tea and try another bite of this hardtack."

When Frances drifted off to sleep again, Megan slipped away quietly to stand near a patch of feeble light cast by the open hatch. For three days, storms kept the *Wardlow* lurching violently from stem to stern. A particularly savage wrench would send passengers, their possessions, and brimming slop jars crashing against the opposite side of the ship like marbles on a slant board.

Megan understood why the *Wardlow*'s owners had taken on more passengers than it could accommodate: the sea had already claimed eleven too frail to withstand the voyage. At least a dozen more might never see America's shores. She prayed that her sister would not be one of them.

A pair of cuffed trousers and hobnail boots rattled down the ladder. Megan was delighted to see they belonged to her new friend, Second Mate Rolf Tabor.

"This old tub can tumble, can't she?" he said. "Haven't seen squalls hang on like this since we carried goods from the West Indies to London."

"Frances is so ill, Rolf. How much longer do you think it'll last?"

"The captain was sure we'd hit calmer waters by midday, but the sky's black and rolly as far as the eye can see."

The ship's bow plummeted into a wave. Rolf lost his balance and his body pressed against Megan's tightly. She felt his hot breath on her cheek.

"Pardon *me*, ma'am. That one caught me off guard," he apologized, although it seemed to take an uncommonly long time for him to regain his footing.

He cleared his throat, then asked, "Uh, didn't that tea I gave you help your sister none?"

"Aye, she says it's delicious, and to be sure and thank you for her."

"I figgered as much since Captain Jorgenson sets such store by it," he said with a grin. "He'll never miss that bit I pinched from his larder."

"Oh, Rolf! You shouldn't have done that. I thought it came from the ship's rations."

"You seen anyone else havin' a spot of Oolong with their supper? He's got plenty on board, and there's plenty more where it come from."

"All the same, you'll not be stealing from Captain Jorgenson—or anyone else, for that matter," Megan said sternly.

"Ach, don't you be harpin' about it. I didn't come down for no preachin'—I came to ask if you wanted to go up top with me for a while. It ain't rainin', and the fresh air will bring the roses to your cheeks."

"You've been a grand fellow for lettin' me go on deck more than my share, but I don't think I should leave Frances."

"Is she sleepin'?"

"Yes, but—"

"Then let's go! It stinks to Billy Thunder down here and I've had all I want of it."

Mindful of her skirts, Megan took to the ladder behind Rolf. The minute her head peeped above the hatch, the brisk sea air washed over her like a spring shower.

Standing by the rail was too risky, so she leaned her back against a mast and wrapped her arms loosely behind her.

" 'Tis a thoughtful lad you are Rolf, and I'm glad you brought me here. Oh, if only Frances were strong enough, a few minutes on deck would do her a world of good."

"As soon as she's able, I'll help you get her topside, sweetheart."

Megan was taken aback by the endearment and the sudden dark dullness of his eyes. "Umm, yes . . . well, maybe before the week's out—"

"A'carse, it'll take more than a 'thank you, Rolf' for that kind of nursemaidin'," he drawled, his voice deepening to a growl.

"What do you mean?"

"Fair's fair, my darlin'. I've given you lots of privileges the others ain't gettin'." He edged uncomfortably close to her. "A spoonful of honey instead of molasses for your bread. First turn at the washtubs so you needn't rinse your delicates in other folks' dirty leavings. High time I took a few in return."

Before Megan could say a word or move, he crushed his mouth against hers. His tongue slid across her clenched teeth. He pawed at her breast and muffled grunts, like an animal's, sounded in his throat. The more Megan struggled, the harder Rolf ground his body into hers.

"Ever touched a man's prime? Not bloodly likely, I'd reckon."

Seizing her hand, he angled his body slightly and stroked her palm up and down the length of his erection. He moaned with surprise and pleasure when she sought and fondled his testicles. Distracted by desire, his lips explored the tender valley beneath her ear while, with her other hand, Megan groped at his waist until her fingers closed around the hilt of his knife.

Easing it from the sheath dangling from his belt, she warned softly but distinctly, "If you value the manhood you were born with, I'd not be a'pesterin' me further."

He threw back his head and chortled wickedly. "And what'll you do if I've a mind to? Fall into a swoon?"

Holding the curving stiletto where he could see its blade, she answered evenly, "My father raised the best Berkshire pork in Ireland. Havin' no sons, he taught me to cut the boars. Da bragged that I could slit one before he could say 'Jack Robinson.' "

Squaring her shoulders like a streetfighter, she squeezed the keepsakes in her hand. "Want to wager I still can?"

"Are you threatenin' me, Megan?"

"No, me boyo, it's a promise I'm makin' ya."

From the way his eyes darted, Megan knew he was considering wresting the knife from her grasp. Tightening her grip on its whalebone handle, she met his steely gaze without blinking.

Rolf stepped back, freeing himself in the process. "A few days with nothin' but air in your gut'll tamp the fire in ya. Then we'll see who's wantin' to bargain."

He shoved her roughly. Megan bolted for the hatch. En route, she sent his knife skittering amidships. It clattered across the planking and disappeared beneath an enormous jumble of crates.

Frances was awake when Megan reached her bunk. "Goodness, lass, aren't you wide-eyed and puffing like a spent fox," she said, a frown cleaving the space between her eyebrows. "What's wrong? Are you takin' sick, too?"

Megan tried glossing over the incident but Frances would have none of it. When she recounted the assault, it was with all the venom she could muster.

"It's the captain you should be tellin' of this," Frances said grimly, "and that swabby should be flogged."

"If you'd seen Tabor's face, you'd know I'd seen to the matter well enough. He'll be keepin' his favors—and his hands—to himself."

Still, the next day, when Megan was sloshing some garments in a half barrel on deck and heard the approach of heavy footsteps, she hied up defensively.

"You're jumpy as a toad today, Sprout," Captain Jorgenson said. "I daresay, for good reason."

"Oh? And what might that be?"

Jorgenson grunted and pulled a scrap of notepaper from his jacket pocket. "According to your sister, one of my men took liberties with you yesterday. Rolf Tabor, she says. Is that true?"

Megan chafed her palms together slowly as if warming them. She was uncertain how she should answer and angry that Frances had seen fit to tattle to the captain.

"There was a speck of unpleasantness, to be sure. But there's no cause for Frances to be botherin' you. I took care of it myself."

Jorgenson's expression was that of a father reprimanding an errant child. "My dear Miss O'Malley, anything that happens on this ship is my responsibility. I've no doubt that you pinned Mister Tabor's ears back, but did you stop to think that the next girl he accosted might not have your grit?"

Megan bowed her head and stared at her shoe tips. "No, Captain," she said meekly, "I didn't."

"Can you understand that Tabor's behavior cannot be borne, but that I must be informed of it to take proper measures?"

"Yes, sir. I'm truly sorry, sir. I should've told you myself."

"Well you should have." He slipped a callused finger beneath her chin and raised her eyes to his. "You're a brave girl and a smart one, but you can't fight all life's battles by yourself. There's no shame in asking for help, Sprout."

"I'll not be forgettin' that, Captain Jorgenson."

"See here now, don't you go to blubberin'. Get them chores done and see to your sister. We're only a few days out of Boston and I want her to walk off this ship the same as she walked onto it."

"Yes, *sir!*"

# Chapter Three

Megan was brushing the night's snarls from her shoulder-length sable hair when excited shouts swept through the hold like a wildfire.

"The mate's sighted land!"

"Land ho!"

"Are you hearin' that, Frances? It's America they've spied!"

Her sister smiled and struggled to raise herself from the saggy trench in her canvas berth. Her eyelids fluttered, and although she set her jaw determinedly, a groan escaped her lips as she dangled her legs over the side.

Megan crossed her arms and demanded, "Look at you, now—weaker than a pup on a hind teat. Lie down and rest until we dock. I'll not mind carrying your satchel, but I can't carry you, too."

Frances snorted, and canted back against the taut canvas divider. "I'd say you're getting a mite big for your britches, missy. Standin' there, pitchin' a royal fit, why you're the spittin' image of Mama—temper and all."

"Well, if Mama were here, bless her memory, she'd have you flat on your back before you said, 'Boo!'"

"Well, she's *not*, and I'm going to have a gander at this city they call Boston."

Frances's enthusiasm belied her frailty. Nine weeks of meals coming back up within hours of eating them had melted away at least twenty pounds she couldn't afford to lose. Dehydration had sunken and purpled the hollows beneath her eyes and her skin was as dry and pale as parchment.

Though less affected, Megan's faded cotton dress did hang loosely at the bustline and waist. At too many meal-times, she'd seen grimy fingers probe for a platter's choice bits of salt meat and noticed dinner's broth lapping against the crusty scum left by the morning's porridge. Her appetite vanished; her stomach rumbled in vain.

She started to argue with Frances, then thought better of it. Actually, she was delighted that her sister felt strong enough to go topside. More than anything, she wanted to savor every second of their arrival in America.

Squatting on the spray-slick planks, Megan reached down into the hatch opening to help Frances scale the ladder's upper rungs, but her hand was brushed aside. Once on deck, Frances shuddered in the chill breeze, yet after wrapping herself in blankets and settling on an upturned crate, the sunshine and blue skies acted like a tonic. With gusto, she bit into the heel of bread spread with lard and molasses that Megan had given her.

"Mind now, don't you be swallowin' that whole," Missus McBee cautioned. "Yer belly'll loop-de-doo all over again, then where'll ye be?"

"The sea's a tad choppy, but I'm feelin' better," Frances mumbled, her mouth crooking up in a syrupy grin.

"Will you look there," Megan said with a chuckle, gesturing toward the stern. "Alaster Candless is a'fiddlin' like the devil's nippin' at his tailcoat, and Darby Cunningham's cuttin' a jig fit for a schoolboy."

"They're from a village in Kerry," Missus McBee informed. "Crazy as loons the both of them, but ain't it the loveliest music they're makin'? Don't matter that nary a one of us has more to our names than we're wearin'. It's a grand day to be alive."

"So it is, ma'am," Frances chimed in heartily. "So it is."

With her sails snapping like gunshots, the *Wardlow* whisked through the coastal approaches and into Boston Harbor. As she glided by all classes of vessels, from steamers and sailing ships to dainty sloops, the weary wraiths on her deck fell into an awestruck silence. Clutched to many a bosom were drawstring bags of Irish earth to scatter on American soil, symbolizing the marriage of the old country to the new.

Beyond the harbor's choppy waters, churches' snow-white spires spiked the city's skyline. Tall stacks, like sooty pump-organ pipes, belched streams of gray smoke. December's chill had stripped the trees of foliage, but their number promised enough green to satisfy a country girl, come spring.

"If it isn't just like the fairyland Da told us about in stories when we were little," Megan whispered in her sister's ear. "Could there be as many red brick buildings as that in all of Ireland?"

When the ship anchored at the pier, the passengers were in such a hubbub to leave, they all but trampled each other. The cries of bawling children separated from their parents mixed with the scuffling of a hundred feet.

It didn't take Megan long to gather their sparse belongings and return to the deck. By the time she did, the way was clearer and those waiting were less rambunctious.

Megan was poised to disembark when from the corner of her eye she caught a glimpse of a familiar cap. Leaving Frances at the rail, she hurried toward Captain Jorgenson, who was standing near the aft mast.

"I was hopin' for a word with you, Sprout. It ain't often an old seadog like me meets up with such a fine young lady. You've got a lot to learn, but you're already wise beyond your years. You'll go far, I suspect, and'll leave your mark along the way."

Shyly, she stretched on her tiptoes and kissed his bewhiskered cheek. "Thank you, Captain Jorgenson, for bringing us here safely—for everything. I'm a'promisin', truly, I'll not ever forget you."

Scampering back to Frances, Megan heard him say softly, "Nor I you, Miss Megan O'Malley."

The brigantine was a smallish ship, and rode low in the water. Since the pier was built for larger crafts, the *Wardlow*'s wobbly gangplank belayed at an upward slant.

With Frances leaning against her and two satchel handles gripped in one fist, Megan's calves ached from the strain before she gained the pier. Then, practically the instant they stepped onto it, she stumbled, and stumbled again, nearly falling to her knees and taking her sister down with her.

"Goodness, lass! You're staggerin' like Aberdeen Gill when he stayed overlong at the Ball and Musket."

"Sorry—I almost gave us both a smart tumble. After so long aboard ship, my legs forgot how to walk on dry land."

A sharp blow at her back sent her reeling. Rolf Tabor's hands were manacled behind him and a crewman had one arm clenched tightly, but the prisoner had enough leverage to jab Megan squarely between her shoulder blades with his elbow.

"You've cost me plenty. Someday, I'll come collectin'," he snarled before his captor yanked him away.

A shiver of fear ricked down her backbone. How could I have mistaken someone so evil for a friend? she thought. Quickly she shut her eyes and crossed herself.

Assuring Frances that she wasn't injured, they headed for the squat, dingy building they'd seen fellow passengers enter. Inside, the air was stifling; fetid with the odor of damp wool and unwashed bodies. Sweat meandered between Megan's breasts and spread beneath her arms.

A prim woman with spectacles perched on her nose sat at a puncheon table interrogating the couple in front of Megan and Frances.

"Have you a certificate of matrimony?"

"Uh, no, ma'am," the man stuttered, "but our joinin' was wrote in the book at the parish house in Derry."

"I suppose I must take your word for that. Tell me, what *are* those nasty sores on your faces? Syphilis?"

"Lordy, no! That ship was crawlin' with all manner of stingin', bitin' things. Jiminy, we ain't got the *pox*!"

"I'll *thank* you not to raise your voice," the woman shot back testily. "For your information, an immigrant ship docked last week whose passengers were carrying cholera. You're fortunate the sanitary commission only ordered a spot check of incoming ships and not a quarantine."

"I'm not meanin' to be rude, ma'am," he mumbled, twisting his cap in his hands. "It's just that we're a mite tired from the crossin', and Shela here, bein' with child and all—"

"Step over there to Doctor Grigsby," the woman commanded. "If he says you're sound, you can be on your way."

"But—"

"It's that or reboard the ship! *You* decide."

The young mother's shoulders quaked with her sobs as her husband led her toward a stooped, wild-haired gent wearing a stained, once-white coat. Hawking loudly, the doctor spat a brown stream in the general direction of a cuspidor.

"Names, ages, place of origin," the woman barked without taking her eyes off the form in front of her.

"Megan and Frances O'Malley. Fourteen and twenty-two. Rathcormac, County Cork, Ireland," Megan answered. "Uh, beggin' your pardon ... that's R-A-T-H-C-O-R-M-A-C."

The woman's scrawling halted in midloop. Her head jerked up like a puppet's. "How *well* you have memorized the spelling."

"Oh, I can read, ma'am, and write, too, though not as fine and dainty as you do."

"Hmmph. I've yet to see a paddy that could do either. In fact, I thought schooling was against the law in your country."

"Yes'm, it was. A priest taught our mother when she was a lass, and she taught our da, and Frances, and me."

"I see. And did she also teach you impudence? Let's get on with it, shall we? Since you're such scholarly sorts, what *are* your occupations?"

Megan counted to ten before saying, "We're not indentured. We'll be gettin' positions soon as we're settled."

Peering over the rim of her glasses, the woman gave Megan a once-over. Frances received more careful scrutiny. "That one's in a bad way," she remarked, stabbing the tip of her pen toward Frances. "We've enough of your kind in this city already without taking in the sickly."

Megan stiffened, but a warning jab from her sister gave her pause. With utmost respect, she said, "Frances suffered the seasickness, and it weakened her. She'll be rarin' in a day or two—I'll see to that."

"Boston can't risk a cholera epidemic. You're detained until Doctor Grigsby examines her."

Megan stood stock-still, anger welling hotly within her. From across the room she could see the doctor's dirt-rimmed fingernails, and there was certainly no gentleness in the way he was "examining" Shela.

"If the captain swears my sister doesn't have cholera, will you let us pass?"

"I might. Then again, I might not."

Whirling around, Megan spotted Andrew McBee's coppery curls near the end of the line. "Andy! Scat back to the ship and get Captain Jorgenson. Tell him Megan O'Malley's a'needin' his help."

With an approving nod from his mother, the boy dashed from the building. Megan and Frances sidled out of the

way so those behind them could take their turn before
the inquisitor.

At least a half hour passed before Andy and Captain
Jorgenson burst through the door. "What is it, Sprout?"
the latter asked, breathing hard from the galloping pace his
escort had set.

"That *woman* thinks Frances has cholera—says she's got
to see the doctor before we can pass."

"Sounds no more'n a tempest in a teapot to me," he
replied. "Frances isn't choleric, so let the sawbones take a
look at her and be done with it."

"Captain, do you see that man over there in the corner?
Now, tell me true—would you be lettin' him lay as much
as a finger on *your* sister?"

Jorgenson scratched his ear thoughtfully as he regarded
the scruffy physician. "Ummm. Now that you mention it,
can't say I would, Sprout. Can't say I'd let that rummy
yank a calf out'n Ol' Bossy."

Frances postured herself as soldierly as she could. "The
woman might take your word if you'd vouch for me, sir."

"All right. I'll do what I can, Miss O'Malley."

Megan only caught fragments of his appeal, but enough
to know Jorgenson was having to fight for his quarter.
Waiting passengers edged forward, shamelessly eavesdropping. The outcome could either speed their passage or
delay it interminably.

When the captain turned and graced them with a twinkle-
eyed grin, both sisters released whooshing sighs of relief.

"Get crackin' before that witch changes her mind," he
advised. "She's a razor-tongued harridan, and I don't believe I can best her twice."

"Thank you again, Captain Jorgenson," Megan said. Not
knowing what else to do, she proffered her hand for a
grateful shake.

Rather than clasp it, he brought it to his lips and kissed
her palm like a sovereign's courtier. "Be well, Sprout, and
be happy." Then, with a tip of his cap, he strode away
without a backward glance.

It took a goodly stretch of the legs to reach the city
proper. Megan sputtered every step of the way until Frances warned, "That's *quite* enough, lass. If Father Brennan
could hear you there'd be a sermon and a month of Hail
Marys for you."

"But it's a puzzlement. Those we've met so far are either God's angels or Satan's own."

Frances tucked her hand in the crook of her sister's arm. "Count your blessings for the first and skip way 'round the others. Remember, we've come from a village where no one's a stranger. Why, ask anyone in Rathcormac what color your grandfathers' eyes were and they'd tell you. It's careful we must be, here."

"Yes, I suppose . . ."

Concentrating so hard on her troubles, Megan had paid scarce attention to the city noise. Soon she was aware of the pounding clop of horseshoes on the cobbled street. Nearby factories throbbed, rumbled, and roared. Sidewalk drummers yammered like magpies: "Rags an' ol' clothes!" or "Eee-ice here, eee-ice man comin'!"

Reeling from the sounds thundering at her from every side, Megan's heart thumped faster in her chest. She could see that Frances was talking, but couldn't understand the words—it was as if her sister were speaking a foreign language.

During the voyage, night terrors of the ship becoming lost at sea had left her sweat-chilled and sleepless. But feeling adrift on solid ground was infinitely more frightening.

She couldn't tell east from west. Mortared, mountainous buildings loomed above her leaving only a narrow slice of sky visible. People scurried along the sidewalk like ants spewing from a stirred hill.

A clutch of women aimed half-lidded, reproachful glares at her and made snide remarks to their companions. Until then, Megan had felt almost regal wearing her mother's handloomed cloak with its starburst brooch pinned at her neck. Now, beside such Yankee elegance, *she* was the shabby dandy lurking in the shadows.

She jumped when a gangly scarecrow of a man skipped over the curb and hailed, "Top o' the day to ye, ladies." Doffing his rumpled, kelly-green hat unleashed a thatch of greasy, black hair. "I'm from the Immigrants Association—Jackson Walsh is me name. And you lovelies would be . . . ?"

"The Immigrants Association?" Frances repeated suspiciously.

"Ayep. Whether it's a friendly welcome ashore or assistance you're needin', I'm your man, Miss . . . ?"

"I beg your pardon, Mister Walsh, but we're quite—" Frances began.

"Saints preserve us, you're the answer to a prayer," Megan gushed, ignoring her sister's warning headshake. "We've just got off the ship and scarcely know up from down."

Walsh favored her with a smile so broad his freckles danced. "That's part and parcel of bein' a greenhorn, lassie. You'll learn. Meantimes, I suspect there's a roof over your heads and jobs what needs tendin' to."

At Megan's eager nod, he stooped to pick up their baggage, prattling, "A friend o' mine runs a lodgin' house up yonder on Kingston Street. Kindly follow me, and I'll take you there, then we'll see another bloke I know—"

"Mister Walsh," Frances interrupted, clipping the words like scissor blades. "Set aside our belongin's and be off with you."

"Ye daren't be hasty, miss. There's scalawags about— shoulder hitters they's called. Them squints'll pry the gold out'n your teeth afore you takes your last breath."

Megan wagged her head between her stern-faced sister and the eager Samaritan, but Frances showed no sign of relenting.

"Father Brennan is coming for us any minute," she declared. "If it's smart you are, I'd be gone before he gets here."

Muttering in disgust, Walsh flung their satchels on the herringbone bricks and stomped away.

"Frances, you lied as bold as brass! Father Brennan is an ocean away in Cobh!"

"Don't take such notice of it. That scoundrel was a pot callin' the kettle black if ever there was one. Up to his jug ears in blarney, I'd say."

Planting her hands firmly on her hips, Megan parried, "Maybe true, maybe not, except we're still without bed nor broomstick, and you're fadin' as white as my shift."

From behind came a wildly waving Missus McBee, shouting like a farmer's wife shooing geese from the garden. She hugged them both tightly and cooed, "Ah, me lost lambs. I'd despaired of ever findin' ye again."

"Is something wrong, Missus McBee?" Megan asked.

"Not a'tall, lass, everything's righter'n rain. I been a'lookin' for ye 'cause I've a room to let if ye'll have it.

Shoulda told ye on the ship, but I got all addlepated when we landed."

Megan and Frances glanced at each other in amazement as their friend babbled on, "Me nephew Kevin—that's me sister Sophie's boy—put money down on rooms when he knew me and the bairns was comin'. I'm told there's a garret—prob'ly a wee one at that—but ye're tiny gals and welcome to it if ye can pay a smidge toward the rent."

"Done!" Megan blurted. Guiltily she peered over her shoulder at Frances. She was relieved to see her smiling assent.

The three women linked arms, trailing a quartet of young McBees in their wake. Despite her girth and continual banter, their benefactress stepped lively. Megan recited each street name aloud as they passed: Utica, Lincoln, Albany . . . and was practically jerked out of her shoes when Missus McBee veered sharply left onto Hudson.

"Six doors to the greengrocer's and we're there," she singsonged, jouncing Frances along like a rag doll.

Missus McBee paused at a narrow doorway. A steep stairway rose from it and disappeared into the gloom. The odor of boiled cabbage, rotting garbage, and spilled slops melded and billowed down upon them like a rank fog. She obviously paid it no mind.

Each riser bowed and squalled irritably as the processional made its way to the second floor. From the depths of her cleavage, Missus McBee fished out a skeleton key dangling from a twine necklace. It turned in the lock, but the new tenant had to butt the door with her shoulder to open it.

The unmistakable skitter of rats accompanied their entrance to a murky room hardly twelve feet square. In the mean light leaking through a pair of streaked windows, Megan noted a smaller, rectangular room on her right, a corner with wall cupboards and a tin sink to her left, and a slapdash ladder leading to an opening in the ceiling.

"A good brush and bucket scrubbin' and this place'll be fit for Queen Victoria her own self," Missus McBee chirped, while her sons fanned out to explore their new home. "Ease Frances onto that davenport, then fetch me the lamp there by the sink, lass."

Rasping a lucifer across her shoe sole, the older woman lit the lantern and handed it back to Megan. "Now, scurry up and see if that loft suits ye. If it does, it's yers fer the takin'."

Megan stood a fraction over five feet tall, but when she reached the attic's plank floor, her head cleared cobwebs from the rafters. The space was dusty, coop-sized, and freezing, but the pair of iron bedsteads with rolled, varmint-chewed mattresses standing forlornly against the far wall looked awfully inviting.

Someday, she thought, it's a fine lady I'll be, with a bed-chamber rigged up in gold and white, tapestry portieres draping the doors and windows, and satin and lace pillows for my head. There'll be a maid to bring my morning tea and another to draw my bath.

God willin', someday will come. For now, this'll do for a shabby Irish greenhorn.

Megan's knees ached from rocking on them for hours, seesawing a coarse, bristled brush over the flat's filthy hard-wood floors. Her fingers were puffy and stiff from wringing gallons of cold, murky water from the rags she'd used to scrub walls and woodwork.

"It don't have to look clean," Missus McBee chided when Megan complained that her labors hardly showed. "Just so's we know *'tis* clean."

Frances did her share of the homemaking by sewing snip-pets of fabric Sean McBee had ferreted from trash heaps into colorful patchwork curtains. As best she could, she also repaired the rents in their mattresses and bed linens.

With their first Saturday night in America came the rea-son their chores had been done at such a frantic pace.

"Come in, come in!" Missus McBee cried gleefully as neighbor after neighbor arrived to welcome the newcomers. "Bless this 'umble mew with yer company."

Like most housewarmings, those attending brought gifts: a teapot with the merest chip in its spout, plates of cookies or loaves of gold-crusted bread, tatted doilies, and hemmed flour-sack towels.

"This is for you and your sister," said Leander Kerrigan, the owner of the grocery downstairs. The shiny, red tin box Megan took and turned in her hands was still sticky from a fresh coat of lacquer.

"Like these 'kitchen rackets' we old-timers have for you greenhorns, my gift is also an American tradition," he explained. "It's a penny bank, and whatever coins you can spare must be saved in it. At first, they'll rattle around and not seem worth the sacrifice, but careful scrimping will soon give it weight."

"Thank you, Mister Kerrigan. Heavy it will be, and soon, have no doubt of it."

Kerrigan smiled paternally. "You showed courage in coming here, yet this life is no easier than the one you left. Never forget that pennies become dollars—and it's dollars you must have to escape this hellhole the newspapers call 'Shantytown' "

"Hellhole! How dare you call it that? So it's poor we are and scrappers we must be to put food in our mouths. Find me a place with better people in it than these here tonight and I'll take my leave at sunup!"

"Aye, I'll not argue that," he said, then sighed with resignation. "But if we're to survive, we must mean more to this country than cheap labor. I've heard it said that there's only one thing more rare than a four-leaf clover in Dublin."

"Oh, and what might that be?"

"A gray-haired Irishman in Boston," he answered solemnly.

# Chapter Four

Megan swallowed hard before easing open the Hotel Drake's massive oak and brass door. Soft light from three crystal chandeliers gave the lobby the effect of having been carved from a single block of white marble.

A copse of lush ferns and schefflera, wing chairs upholstered in leather or plush velvet, and seascapes framed in gilt added a homey touch, but failed to warm the atmosphere of the sumptuous ice palace.

The desk clerk's waistcoat sported enough fringed epaulets, brass buttons, and scrolled piping for a European monarch. His gray hair, parted precisely at center, gleamed with Makassar oil.

"May I help you?" he inquired with practiced haughtiness.

"I've come to apply for a position."

"Well, if it isn't another Bridget fresh from the Emerald Isle," he sneered. "Go 'round to the back and make it snappy. Don't *ever* use the street entrance again, you hear?"

Megan raised her chin high and wheeled to retrace her steps through the cavernous foyer. Oh, how she wanted to slap her palm smartly on the door's facing as she took her leave. But she didn't.

The hotel, which laid claim to an entire block, was constructed of dove-gray granite, softened by Palladian windows and ironworked balconies. In a city where buildings of more than three stories were uncommon, the Drake's five floors were as imposing as they were architecturally embellished.

Despite its swanky facade, the alley behind it was as slimy and foul-smelling as any other.

Gusty winds barreling in from the sea sliced through

Megan's woolen cloak like knife blades and slick cobbles punished her feet with every step.

Decent jobs were scarcer than diamonds in a coal mine, especially for seekers with Celtic surnames and a brogue to match. Three months of searching had worn Megan's shoe soles to paper thinness.

Had she been male, she could have snatched up a shovel and joined her countrymen pitching sludge into Boston harbor. That municipal project had been implemented to solve two ever-worsening problems: waste disposal and overcrowding. Once the shoreline was sufficiently backfilled, the land it created would be used for expansion.

Thousands of paddies were earning a paltry fifty cents to a dollar for a day's toil. The women were even less fortunate: noisy, firetrap garment factories were their best chance for employment. Hour by hour, their lungs filled with airborne lint while they operated dangerous machines until they were bleary-eyed with fatigue.

Every day, dozens of hungry hopefuls stood against a far wall like vultures, waiting to replace any line worker who became ill or was injured. Megan was once among those desperate scavengers. When she realized she was eagerly awaiting one gaunt-faced seamstress's collapse, Megan ran from the building in shame and never returned.

Now, zigzagging around the alley's putrid puddles, she told a cat that was hunched atop an ash bin, "Damned if I'll sell myself or take work away from another to earn my bread, but no peacocky Tory that totes baggage for a livin's gonna best me, either!"

An iron, strap-hinged door promised relief from the bitter weather. Megan hopped over its high threshold without a thought to where it might lead.

A shadowy hallway stretched before her, empty, save for crates and barrels with excelsior whiskers sprouting from their rims. She followed the sound of voices drifting in the distance.

"Christ, Phil. You had no problem hiring a French chef to strawboss the kitchen, an English concierge straight from Windsor Castle, and a staff of two hundred that's so competent, I may even get an hour off now and then. But here I am, two days away from this mausoleum's opening ceremonies and you're telling me you can't find a lousy elevator operator?"

"Not as long as you insist on one with experience, no. I daresay, the ink probably isn't dry on Otis's patent for passenger cars, Bryant. There aren't a half-dozen operators in the whole blasted country."

Megan wiped a wicked grin off her face before rapping sharply on the partially open door. "Pardon me, gentlemen, but I couldn't help overhearin' your conversation."

She paused momentarily before uttering the biggest lie she'd ever told in her life: "If it's an elevator operator you're a'wantin' so sorely, you needn't look any further."

The portly, middle-aged man seated behind a desk—general manager Bryant Deatheridge, according to a brass plate—graced Megan with a bemused expression.

"Young lady, if you're an elevator jockey, *I'm* Paul Revere."

"Let's not be hasty, Bryant," Phil cautioned as he nuzzled the wall with his back. The action, his slanted green eyes, and tall, lean build were distinctly feral.

He gave Megan a languid look-see, much like a butcher assessing a slab of prime beef. "After all, some New York hotels did hire women after the men were sent south for cannon fodder."

"The war's been over for four years," Bryant scoffed. "Look at her—this kid would have still been in pinafores, playing jacks back then."

Megan felt a blush rising upward from her neck. "I can speak for myself, Mister Deatheridge, if you'll listen."

"Oh? Well, by all means . . ."

"Like your friend said, I worked for a hotel in New York City before my sister and I came here," she blurted, fully expecting lightning to strike her dead in midsentence. "It moved goods, not people, but with a wee bit of practice, I'm promisin', your guests will think they're heaven bound on a feather bed."

Noting the man's obvious skepticism, she added, "All I'm askin' is to prove myself. If I don't, it won't cost you a penny's wages."

Deatheridge and his personnel director eyed each other as if discussing her proposition by mental telepathy.

"What's your name, miss?" Phil asked.

"Megan O'Malley."

He brought out his pocket watch with a dramatic flourish. "All right, it's ten o'clock. We'll give you until noon to acquaint yourself with the machinery. At that hour, Mister Deatheridge and I will be your first passengers. If your performance fails to meet our standards, rest assured, you'll be back on the sidewalk by 12:05."

"Fair 'nough, sir." Her smile was as binding as a handshake. "Now, if you'd kindly show me the way? Time's a'wastin'!"

Their route took them past a leather-and-walnut-appointed sitting area. An intricately patterned Persian carpet spanned the space; its jeweled colors enriched by the subtle glow of brass reading lamps. Even the flames licking at logs stacked in the fireplace were unnaturally well behaved.

A filigreed glass wall enclosed a dining room. Tables laid with starched pastel linens, silver-banded china, and sterling flatware waited graciously for their users. Crystal stemware, resting bowl end down, encircled each table's floral centerpiece like well-scrubbed children around a Maypole.

I've got as much business here as a billy goat in Squire Bernard's stables, Megan thought. I wonder if rich folks worry as much about losing their money as I do about never having any. Seems to me that putting on such airs might be harder work than sweeping streets.

As the director led her past the lobby desk, Megan winked at the clerk. His jaw dropped in astonishment, then shut with a peeved snap.

Phil's arm draped Megan's shoulders like a favorite uncle during her one-minute introduction to the contraption's mechanism. Before he bid her farewell, he smirked and pointedly tapped his watch pocket with a manicured fingernail.

Megan caressed the car's satiny mahogany walls, their polished oxblood color intensified by dark burls. Oval murals of fox hunters galloping through a misty glen were inset in the bowed ceiling panels. Tasseled tapestry cushions padded the benches wrapping around three of the walls. She shut the car's scissor-hinged gate, hoping her touch wouldn't tarnish the brass.

"Quit gawkin' like a goose," she muttered. "Just because you've never even *seen* an elevator before, you'd best get crackin' and divine how to fly this pretty cage."

Straddling two ropes that disappeared through slots in the ceiling and floor, she glanced over her shoulder to be certain no one was watching, then spit on her palms and rubbed them together. With the cables grasped in a two-handed choke hold, she pulled with all her might.

The elevator didn't so much as wiggle.

A firm tug on one rope set off a metallic rasp from somewhere above the car, but no movement.

Megan clamped her tongue between her lips and jerked hard on the other cable. The car lurched upward, then halted so suddenly she almost lost her balance.

"Why, this thing's no different than pealing the tower bells at St. Anthony's in Rathcormac."

Mindful of her skirts, she bent slightly at the waist to prevent their snagging. So positioned, she slipped her palms down the cable with each hand-over-hand turn. Her view of the lobby's marble floor soon gave way to a common brick wall. Increasing her rhythm, she passed what she guessed were the alcoves to the upper floors in the same manner.

She was so proud of herself, she almost forgot to slow down when the light from the fifth floor's archway fell away like a window shade lowering.

Megan reversed the elevator's direction, trying her best to meet each threshold evenly with the car's.

"Twelve casts on the rope between floors going up; ten times between on the downside," she chanted as she bobbed the conveyance repeatedly along its perpendicular path.

Smooth landings and departures proved difficult to master, however. The lobby level was a particularly stubborn nemesis. No matter how she counted or how gently she feathered the ropes, the car either jolted to a stop or refused to lay cheek-to-jowl with its threshold.

Megan dug her knuckles into her hips and glared at the infernal cables that defied every trick she'd tried. She whirled around, gasping, when Mister Deatheridge said from behind her, "It's noon, Miss O'Malley. Are you ready to take on passengers?"

"Why, uh . . . yes, sir."

Peering around the car, he asked, "Where is Mister Yates?"

"Who?"

"Philbeck Yates, my personnel director—who obviously

didn't bother introducing himself. I haven't seen him since the two of you left my office together."

"I don't—"

"Forgive my tardiness, Bryant," Phil apologized as he stepped into the car. Grinning slyly, he hoisted a brimming glass of red wine. "It is my habit to partake of a spot of claret before lunch, Miss O'Malley. Bear in mind that I intend to drink it. I do not intend to wear it."

Her insides fluttered. She turned to grip the taut cables. Cringing when the car wobbled as it lifted, she reminded herself that even if she failed to pass Yates's "test," at least she'd tried.

Neither man said a word to her or each other. Megan sensed them watching her every move. Tapping her toes to the beat of her silent cadence, the starts and stops smoothed somewhat, but were far short of the "heavenly ride" she'd bragged about earlier.

Pausing at the second floor as if taking on additional riders, Megan dared herself to coax the car to a rest at the lobby as gently as an oak leaf meets meadow grass. She sucked in a deep breath and held it.

"Brav-o!" Yates exclaimed when the rig settled gracefully. "I'd doff my hat, if I were wearing one."

"I'll ease the bumps with a speck more practicin'—"

"Bah! Not a drop of wine flowed anywhere except down my gullet. Why, I'm so delighted I could kiss you—"

"But you *won't*," Deatheridge cut in. Nodding toward the open gate, he continued, "Come with me to my office, Miss O'Malley. We have some things to discuss."

When Yates's free hand reached for Megan's elbow, Deatheridge said tersely, "Philbeck, I'll join you for lunch in the Versailles Room after she and I finish our talk."

"Hold on now, *Mister* Deatheridge," Yates sputtered. "Who's in charge of the hiring and firing at this fine establishment? You? Or me?"

Deatheridge regarded him coldly. "For the moment, *I* am."

Megan trailed obediently behind the waddling manager. Only after he fetched her a chair from an adjacent office did she murmur a quiet "Thank you." Clearly, it was Philbeck Yates's tipsiness that had angered him, but oddly, Megan felt partially to blame.

Deatheridge seated himself behind the desk and steepled

his fingertips. He fixed his gaze upon Megan so directly, her nervousness returned with a rush.

"You have *never* operated an elevator before," he stated.

Suddenly intent upon picking lint flecks from her skirt, she admitted, "No, sir, I haven't."

"Oh, I'll grant, you did an admirable job of learning the ropes, so to speak, and in little more than two hours, at that. But can you give me one good reason why I would want a liar in my employ?"

Megan's head snapped up; her eyes meeting his without wavering. "I doubt you'd understand why I fibbed to you. Probably wouldn't believe my reasons either, and I can't say as I'd blame you."

"Try me."

She cleared her throat and sat up board straight. "I dreamed of coming to America so long . . . it never crossed my mind that America might not be wantin' *me*. Seems that 'Irish' is a nasty word to most folks. The minute I open my mouth askin' for work, doors slam in my face. So, I lied to you. I wanted a chance to show there's a brain in this head and strength in my bones, that's all. That's all I've been wantin' since I got here."

Deatheridge rocked forward and anchored his elbows on the desk blotter. "Bigotry is vile, Miss O'Malley, in whatever form. Assuming the worst of me, without cause, is as much a type of bigotry as the assumption that all Irish are drunken louts."

She wiped her sweaty hands on her skirt before countering, "That's a fine, fair way of thinkin', Mister Deatheridge. But I suspect that sittin' on that side of the desk makes it a mite easier for you to judge me, too."

Rising to shrug on her coat, she added, "I thank you kindly for your time, sir, and it's a good day I'll bid—"

"Stop flapping your arms like a demented crow and sit down. Do you want this job or don't you?"

"Do you mean you're offerin' it?"

"Don't answer a question with a question, Miss O'Malley."

With a triumphant grin she assured, "Aye, Mister Deatheridge. I very *much* want the position."

"Well, you're not very damned good at it, but you're all I've got. I don't care what you have to do—from taking your meals in that car to sleeping in it—come Friday, you'd better run that machine as if you'd been born in it. Horatio Bonneventure Drake himself will be among the dignitaries we'll host this weekend. He suffers neither fools nor incompetents gladly."

"If I have to wear the ropes to ribbons, I'll do you proud."

"Surely that won't be necessary," Deatheridge replied sardonically. "Here—take my card to Lemuel Holtzenstein's tailor shop. He'll outfit you in a proper uniform, which consists of a jacket and trousers. I pray you're not scandalized—wearing a dress is too dangerous. Your hem could easily tangle in the cables."

"A lady isn't made by the cut of her clothes, sir."

Deatheridge allowed himself a half-smile, then a scowl tightened his features. "That reminds me: I'd advise you to keep your wits about you around Philbeck Yates. Sober, he believes he's God's gift to the fairer gender. After imbibing, he believes they're God's gifts to *him*."

Relaxing on a bench in the public gardens, Megan reveled in late winter's tease of springlike temperatures. She imagined the dormant beds abloom with a palette of flowers, and wooden boats, crafted and painted to mimic the live swans that paddled behind them, rippling over the lake's glassy blue waters.

She was jolted from her daydreams when she saw Frances approaching.

"Megan? Is that truly you?"

"Hmmpf," Megan snorted. "I reckon since you're workin' for swells like the Sidemores, all us commoners start lookin' alike."

"Oh, not everyone, lass—just ones dressed up like an organ grinder's monkey."

Megan cast a rueful glance at her uniform. At first sight, she'd been less than fond of it, although Lemuel Holtzenstein had taken tucks and tapered it to fit curves the original design hadn't anticipated.

Cut from soft navy wool, the trousers had narrow, red satin stripes running down each side seam, which matched the curliqued piping on the cropped coat's facings, mandarin collar, and cuffs.

She was shod in a pair of glossy brogans that were far

from fashionable, but did keep her feet from rebelling at the twelve-to fourteen-hour shifts she worked.

But it was the duck-billed, pillbox cap mashed down over a chignon of her own creation that never failed to attract comments—few of them complimentary.

"If I thought Mister Deatheridge wouldn't take it out of my hide, I'd be lettin' a horse stomp this silly cap and be done with it."

"Pay it no mind, lass. I was just surprised to see my sister duded up like a brother. Why, you'd be beautiful wearin' nothing but a tatie bag and carpet slippers."

Before Megan could comment further, Frances added, "I can scarcely believe we haven't seen each other since before Christmas."

"I thought when the Sidemores hired you for a nanny that you were to have Sunday afternoons off."

"That was the agreement—but the lovely Beatrice and her beloved Randolph are in such *demand* these days, allowin' me a few hours away from their 'precious darlin's' has *simply* been out of the *question.*"

Megan laughed at her sister's imitation of Beatrice Sidemore's gushy Southern drawl. Frances had already implied that the reason five-year-old Cyril and seven-year-old Randolph Jr. were such hellions was because their parents were more concerned with raising their social standing than with raising their children.

"If it wasn't for Charles, I'd have surely quit by now—like the eleven before me," Frances grumbled. "He's said more than once that those boys'll grow up to be priests or highwaymen, and there's not much either of us can do to assure one over the other."

"Who's Charles? The butler?"

"Gracious sakes, no. Charles Brandywine is Cyril and Randolph's tutor. Such a cultured, elegant man ... yet, hard as he tries to educate those boys, I fear he might as well be reading Longfellow to a pair of stumps."

Megan hesitated, then teased, "Listen to you, now. Aren't you just speakin' like a regular toff these days. And I do believe you're smitten with this Brandywine fellow."

Her face radiant with happiness, she answered quietly, "And he with me."

"Truly? Has he asked you to marry him?"

"No-o-o-o. We haven't really stepped out together yet—

my being so tied down to my job and all. But what he whispers in my ear when we're alone is sheer poetry—love sonnets, they are. Oh, Megan, he's going to ask me soon, I can just *feel* it."

"I couldn't be happier for you." Megan clasped her sister's bone-ridged hands tightly. For the first time she could remember, they were as warm as her own.

"That's enough about me, lass. Catch me up on your goin's-on."

Megan settled back on the bench and sighed. "Lo, the hotel's grand opening was a sight to behold. I'd finally taught that contraption do my biddin', and it's a lucky thing, too. You've never *seen* the like! Ladies wearin' one gown for the welcome address and tea in the lobby, changin' to another for the banquet, and still another for the ball. And jewels? Why, if I'd looked too sharp at all the tiaras and necklaces and earbobs, they'd have blinded me, sure."

Frances shook her head and clucked, "Tiny as you are, I swear I don't know how you hoist carloads of people up and down all day."

"Counterweights do most of the work. The cables control the speed and where and when to stop. It's the long hours that's wearin' on me. I'm trainin' a helper, a burly monster of a lad named, of all things, Clair Poteet, so we can spell each other. Problem is, Clair could likely heft a carload and tote it clear to Concord on his back, but his big paws can't gentle the cables worth a hoot."

Megan then described how crowded Missus McBee's flat had become now that she'd taken on a family of four as tenants.

"I'd have been sleepin' in a doorway if you hadn't lent me board money until I found a position. But I wonder now, why are you still payin' a share since you're livin' with the Sidemores?"

"Because I know Missus McBee needs it. Doing catch-as-catch-can piecework won't feed a family."

"Aye, even that isn't enough to keep the wolf from the door. None of her boys are goin' to school anymore. Sean's still rag-pickin' for Neil Cashman. Michael's a hod carrier when the weather lets him. Gilead's pockets are always a'jingle—his ma doesn't know how, and's afraid of askin'. Even wee Andrew hawks newspapers down at the docks."

"Times are hard, lass, it's true," Frances said with a sigh. "Praise God, neither of us has cause for complaint. The Sidemores are a trial, but the wages are a far-sight better than I'd get at a factory. And you *do* earn a decent day's pay and tips for wearin' that monkey suit."

Megan drew herself up haughtily. "My dear sister, I hear tell, none other than Mister Horatio Bonneventure Drake himself designed this uniform, and I'll warrant that Himself wouldn't take kindly to *your* calling *mine* a 'monkey suit.' "

"Ah, well, it's a thousand pardons I'll ask of ye, and please extend my humblest apologies to Mister Whatcha-macallit Drake."

"That I'll do, and you can tell Mister Brandywine that he *certainly* picked the right sister to fall in love with."

"Really, now? And why is that, if I might ask?"

Megan's eyes sparkled as she said, "The way I figure it, any man who married me, after all the 'I dos' were done, would have the devil's own time decidin' who'd wear the pants in the family."

The late-afternoon sun had surrendered to evening's frost by the time Megan started up the stairs to her flat. As usual, she was greeted by a gust of steamy cooking odors and the hubbub of too many people jammed in too small a space.

"Ah, me lass, tell me quick how our Frances is," Missus McBee cooed. "Lord above, how I've missed that girl."

Knowing the landlady wouldn't be satisfied with a brief account, Megan relayed every detail, saving news of Frances's budding romance until last.

"Mark me words, it's a blushing bride we'll be havin' a'fore long," Missus McBee declared.

When she and Ada Sullivan, matriarch of the other tenant family, began reminiscing about their own courtships, Megan crossed the room to where a battered trunk lay beside the sofa—her bed since the Sullivans moved into the garret.

The trunk lid's leather hinges groaned as it raised and Megan reminded herself to borrow some neat's-foot oil from Mister Kerrigan. Burrowing a hand beneath the clothing and keepsakes inside, she froze when she discovered that the penny bank was not in the corner where she'd left it.

With both hands tumbling through her carefully hand-washed and ironed garments, she found it lying on its side in a near corner of the trunk.

Prying it open, she sighed with relief at the happy clatter of coins. She folded the money Frances had given her around the thickening wad of banknotes.

How could you be so careless with Frances's dowry? she chastised herself. Only, when I checked it last, I could swear I wrapped the bank in a handkerchief and tucked it in a back corner of the trunk.

She studied the tin as if clues to the mystery were stamped on its sides, then methodically swaddled it in her mother's Sunday shawl. Nesting it upright and precisely in the trunk's far left corner, she folded two nightgowns on top of the precious bundle.

"I'll not be forgettin' to bury our treasure properly again," she vowed as she reclosed the trunk.

# Chapter Five

"That's *my* soldier, Cy."

"Is not, Junior. It's mine!"

"Give it to me—*now*!"

Frances and Randolph Sidemore, both racing grim-faced for the playroom, collided in the third floor's hallway.

"Miss O'Malley, I demand you put a stop to that infernal racket *immediately*!" he bellowed.

At six feet two, with pomaded, dung-colored hair and carefully trimmed walrus mustaches, the Man of the House obviously thought himself an imposing figure.

At first sight, Frances had thought him a pompous ass. She'd had no reason to alter that original impression.

"Outshoutin' your sons only worsens their behavior," she argued, hastily tacking on a "sir."

"Do not use that imperious tone with *me*, woman. This is *my* house and I will comport myself in it as I *damned well please*."

"Forgive me, Mister Sidemore," she said, trying not to choke on the words, "but expectin' Junior and Cyrus to share everything causes most of their disagreements. Neither boy feels he has a toy or book to call his very own."

"Poppycock. You and Beatrice spoil them at every turn. It is left to *me* to make men of them, and I will not *tolerate* your interference."

"You're right, sir. They'll have to learn the ways of the adult world soon enough," Frances baited. Sidemore jutted his chin triumphantly, and she pounced. "Except, mightn't it be better to let them be little boys awhile, first?"

He shot her a venomous look before clambering downstairs. His sons weren't acknowledged at all.

The two raven-haired, sky-eyed children sat motionless just inside the playroom's doorway. Frances's heart ached when Junior, seeing a fat teardrop meander down his brother's cheek, took the younger boy's hand and squeezed it gently.

"Men like us don't cry, Cyril. If we show Nanny how good we can be, maybe she'll tell Father, and then maybe he'll come visit us later."

As if cued to add a note of cheerfulness, the sun broke out of the clouds and beamed through the playroom's wall of windows. Books and gimcracks posed in the enameled cabinets lent a kaleidoscope of color to the predominately white room. Yet, they were arranged as precisely as heirloom glassware—effectively a see-but-don't-touch display.

Frances settled into a cushioned, spindle-backed rocker. "Climb up on my lap, boys, and I'll tell you a story."

With a listener snuggled in each arm, she spun a tale of gallant knights and fiercesome jousts until the buzzer sounded, signaling that Cook was ready to serve the younger Sidemores' breakfast.

They scatted from the room with more glee than hunger. The coast was clear; they knew their immaculately groomed father, resplendent in one of his custom-tailored, silk suits, had left for the day and likely half the night. Their mother's constant fussing about wrinkled clothing, breaches in etiquette, and ungentlemanly behavior wouldn't start until well after Beatrice awakened at half past eleven.

Frances hurried to her own room to put the finishing touches on her toilette. Charles Brandywine was due soon. She must be presentable.

"You are a daffodil among roses," he'd said during one of their stolen moments. "When their beauty fades, yours, though less flamboyant, will have only begun to blossom."

For the hundredth time, his poetic words waltzed through her mind and she thrilled at them all over again. Yesterday, he'd pulled her close and kissed her. The memory left her as breathless now as the soft touch of his lips had then.

"Charles is falling in love with me," she assured the mirror. But it reflected the same unremarkable gray eyes, set in a horsey face, framed by a coronet of meager braids.

"So I'm not a great beauty. Charles doesn't want an ornament on his arm—he wants a loyal helpmate. He wants *me*."

She pinched her cheekbones to add splotches of color to her pallid complexion. Licking the tip of a pinkie finger, she traced the arch of her brows. After smoothing the storytelling's wrinkles from her skirt, she swayed from side to side in front of the mirror as if dancing with a ghost, before nodding her approval.

"Cyril and Junior were quite tame today, Frances," Charles remarked when the morning's tutelage was done. "Your influence is benefiting them greatly."

"Why thank you, but I'm a'thinkin' Mister Sidemore would argue."

He sniffed disdainfully. "How many times must I tell you? 'I believe' is grammatically correct. 'I'm a'thinkin' is an abomination."

"Oh, I—I'm sorry—"

"In any vernacular, Randolph Senior is nothing but a cad in Savile Row raiments and Beatrice is no better. That simpering belle's talents were bought and paid for the same as a street corner harlot's."

"Charles!"

His brow furrowed with a glance at his pocket watch. "I'll agree, it's rather treasonous of me to slap the Sidemores with one hand while extending the other for my fee."

He snapped its case closed and returned it to its pocket, making sure the chain dangled just so. "But I grow impatient with the moneyed and their self-centered attitudes."

Frances twirled an errant lock of hair around her finger. "Perhaps you'd be happier teachin' in a school somewhere away from the city. Many are the times I've yearned for sweet clover fields and rollin' hills like those we had in Ireland."

"Shall I carry you off to the lone prairie where we can live in a soddy happily every after?"

He fogged the chip diamond solitaire he brandished on his right ring finger, polished it on his sleeve like an apple, then extended both arms, palm side up.

"I ask you, are these the hands of a country schoolmaster? Fit for stoking a wood stove and drawing water from a well? For smiting a half-grown farm boy's backside with a hickory switch because he can't recite his ABCs?"

Ill at ease, she fumbled nervously with her cameo locket. "Ignorance doesn't just grow in the country, like corn. I've noticed that it does quite well in the city, too."

"How profound, Frances. Boston is no utopia, but I would shrivel and die so far removed from civilization. A pioneer, I am not. I am a scholar and aficionado of the arts—I must have music and the theater for my very survival."

Looking up from under her eyelashes coyly, she hinted, "I've never been to a play or heard professional musicians."

The statement hung in the air while the tutor busied himself shuffling papers and sliding them into a briefcase. His blue eyes, enlarged and flattened like a fish's by thick spectacles, avoided hers.

"I daresay that oversight is easily remedied. There *are* matinee performances, both professional and amateur. I suggest you attend one."

Frances turned toward the playroom's windows, loath to let him see the disappointed tears stinging her eyelids. "Yes, Charles, I'll do that. I'll ask my sister to go with me."

He took her completely off guard when he spun her around into a crushing embrace. Tracing the vein beside her jaw with his lips, he whispered, "And with two such lovely ladies present . . . the performers will find it taxing . . . to keep the attention of the gentlemen . . . in the audience."

She shuddered, and was light-headed from the heat raging through her body. Encircling his neck with her arms, she kissed him—not like a woman who had received her first only yesterday, but with a passion she hadn't known she possessed.

"Oh, Charles, I lo—"

"Shhh. There's a spy in our midst," he cautioned and nodded toward the door. The height of the shock of dark hair peeping from its frame easily identified the intruder.

"Cyril, please go back to your room and finish your nap," Frances said.

"I not sleepy."

"Then get into your bed and lie there until I tell you to get up."

"Don't want to."

"I didn't ask if you wanted to. You've been such an angel today, please do as I say."

"No!"

With a weary sigh, she asked, "Must I fetch the paddle and *make* you mind?"

Moving fully into the threshold, Cyril stamped his foot. "You better *not* or I'll tell Father you and Mister Brandywine was *kissin'*."

# Chapter Six

Knees drawn up to her chin, Megan sat hunched on the lumpy sofa, staring out the window at the sheets of water cascading from the roof. Its incessant slapping sound, combined with the little Sullivan girls' high-pitched whines and Michael and Gilead McBee bickering in the next room, set the hairs to prickling on her neck.

"Grand weather for ducks, ain't it, dearie?" Missus McBee hollered from the kitchen alcove. Megan groaned inwardly. At times, her landlady's abundant cheerfulness was as irritating as a boil.

April was half over and the sun had yet to make an appearance. She'd taken to carrying her shoes and uniform to work and changing when she arrived, but lawsy, she was tired of slogging through puddles and getting drenched by passing carriages whenever she strayed too close to the curb.

Home was hardly a respite. With four adults and six children quarantined by the weather, tempers and tantrums flared like sparks to gunpowder.

"Goin' to work so early?" Missus McBee asked when Megan snatched up her bundle of clothing.

"I've got the fidgets something fierce, ma'am. I can't bear being cooped up here any longer—no offense."

"Aye, none taken. Gloomy skies do make for pining souls, lass."

Stroking Megan's hair with a gentle hand, she clucked, "Change is unsettlin' even when it's to the good, ye know. It's a fine new road you're a'travelin', but that don't mean ye won't get a pebble in yer shoe now and again."

"It's impatient I get, ma'am. Sometimes it seems the only difference between this place and Ireland is the scenery."

Missus McBee pecked Megan on the cheek, then twirled her around and swatted her behind. "So, if'n ye ain't satisfied with what ye got, get out there and find what it is ye want. Sittin' and wishin' won't sell the cow."

Megan's lips parted in a broad smile. She winked over her shoulder at the older woman before tugging the door shut behind her.

With plenty of time for the two-mile walk to the hotel, when Shantytown gave way to the tonier district, she slowed to a dawdle. Here, rows of humped canvas awnings sheltered her from the downpour.

Shop windows were festooned with cobwebby lace and polished chintz. Displays of imported teas, cakes and candies of all kinds, linens, hats, and the latest gowns made Megan hanker for a fairy godmother. Deciding what she'd ask for if suddenly granted three wishes distracted her from her squishy shoes.

Those fantasies evaporated when the desk clerk shoved a slip of paper toward her as she passed on her way to the elevator.

"Hey, Bridget—got a message for you from Mister Yates."

Reaching for the note, Megan regarded him just as she would a clump of fresh horse apples in the street. She sidled away from the desk so the clerk couldn't snoop over her shoulder, then abruptly about-faced and struck off for the personnel manager's office.

In the two months since her hiring, Yates had flirted with her several times, but to no avail. Lately, if not ignoring her completely, he carped that her uniform buttons needed a buffing or that her cap was crooked.

According to the hotel grapevine, the arrogant Lothario was now in hot pursuit of an impossibly buxom French chambermaid. Megan and the other female employees sincerely hoped he'd suffocate in her arms.

After knocking and receiving a curt "Come in," Megan asked, "You wanted to see me, Mister Yates?"

His features were stony and sinister like a gambler holding a pair of treys, bluffing for a fat pot. Without prelude he intoned, "There will be a change in scheduling, beginning next week. Poteet will operate the elevator Thursdays through Mondays. You'll work Tuesdays, Wednesdays, and late shifts as needed."

Megan's pulse pounded in her temples. "May I ask *why*?" she said through gritted teeth.

"Poteet has a wife and two children to support."

"Well, I'm pretty partial to three squares a day myself. And I was hired first."

"That is of no consequence to me."

"But I trained *him,* and he still can't run the car as well as I do."

"He'll learn," the director sneered. "You of all people should recognize the importance of practice, Miss O'Malley."

She balled her fingers so tightly her knuckles bleached a bloodless white. "I can't live on two days wages—ones when tips are slim at that. Why are you doin' this?"

An ill-concealed smirk showed how much he was enjoying her distress. "There have been complaints. Guests say they don't feel safe with you—that you're too young and dainty to be fully in control of the car."

"That's nothin' more than a flock of hens peckin' and you damn well know it!"

"Calm yourself, Miss O'Malley. It seems I must remind you that the Drake is in business to provide its guests comfort, for which they pay handsomely—not to demonstrate Elisha G. Otis's mechanical genius."

Bending his head to riffle through a ledger, Yates reached for the pen resting in its onyx inkwell. "There's nothing further to discuss. You may go."

The leaded glass rattled in its frame when Megan yanked the door open and rushed out as if her trousers were on fire. You blackhearted bastard, she seethed. Wait 'til Bryant Deatheridge hears about this.

Shoe leather slapped against the floor like rifle shots as she marched down the hall to the general manager's office. When only a few yards away, she slackened her speed, then stopped.

What good'll it do to tattle to him? she asked herself. Even if Mister Deatheridge takes my side, sure as the sun rises in the mornin', Yates'll be so riled, he'll find a way to fire me outright.

Shoulders sagging, she backtracked what seemed like miles to the lobby. Clair Poteet stood beside the elevator waiting for her, as friendly as an oversize, blond pup.

"There you are," he said, "I was afraid you were sick or something." His brow wrinkled in a concerned frown. "Uh, matter-of-factly, you lookin' kinda peaked, Miss Megan."

"I've never been sick a day in my life," she said brusquely. "It's your family that needs your tendin' to—not me."

Clair hesitated as if hoping her harshness was a joke. "I, uh, 'spect you're right. I'll bid you good day then."

Ambling away, he glanced at her once again, shook his head in confusion, and disappeared behind one of the lobby's marble columns.

Megan felt a twinge of guilt for her shabby behavior. It's a fool you are for treating your enemies kindlier than your friends. After all, it isn't Clair's fault that you'll barely meet the rent on Yates's new schedule.

Although its operators were not allowed to sit on the car's benches, Megan slouched on a corner cushion. The melancholy engulfing her was too heavy to bear.

She was lost in stormy thought when two soldiers dressed in full military regalia moved smartly to either side of the gate. In a few seconds, a ruggedly handsome, middle-aged gentleman entered the car. A plume of smoke snaked upward from the fat cigar he held behind his back.

Megan stood and inquired flatly, "What floor, please?"

"Can you raise this contraption with us three brutes aboard?" the smoker asked with a chuckle.

"Easy as drawin' water from a well, sir."

"Then take us to the top, if you please."

She pulled on a cable, expecting him to take a seat. Instead, he leaned toward her and squinted at the nameplate pinned to her jacket. "Megan, eh? Pretty name. My daughter Nellie's about your age."

Unsure how or if to respond, she merely nodded.

He studied her closely, but seemed such a decent sort she didn't feel threatened by his attentions. After taking a deep draw on his cigar, he canted his head back and spewed a stream of smoke at the ceiling.

"Most times, my daughter's a delight, but when the cat's got her tongue, I know she's packing a passel of worry and a hair-triggered temper. A wise man watches his p's and q's when a magpie becomes a mouse."

Something in his voice eased her slumping spirits. Her lips curled into an impish grin. "I'm a'thinkin' there's a bit o' the blarney in you, Mister . . . ?"

"Grant. Ulysses Simpson Grant. Quite a handle for an old horse soldier, wouldn't you say?"

Megan's jaw went slack and her hands skittered down the cable. The car groaned to a wobbling halt.

"Jesus, Mary, and Joseph—" she wheezed. "You're the President of the United States."

"Duly sworn on the good book five weeks ago. Can't say I've gotten accustomed to it myself, yet."

"You haven't?"

"Politics is a strange business, Megan. I was sadly mistaken when I thought General Joe Johnston was the slyest fox I'd ever do battle with. I swear, ol' fightin' Joe couldn't hold a candle to some of those jacklegs in Congress."

She laughed as she cast downward on the cable again. On the surface, there was nothing terribly special about him. He was of average height, with a sparrow-shouldered build. His hair and beard were in need of barbering. But his charm was completely natural, and he wore an aura of benevolent power as comfortably as other men wore a waistcoat.

"I hear a lilt of Ireland when you speak," he said. "It's none of my business, but do you mind telling me why you came here?"

"Sad to say, my homeland is as beautiful as it is damned, President Grant. Frances, my sister, called America a hoping place. I thought it was too when I got here. Lately, I've been wonderin' if my dreams of a better life are truly that: just wispy dreams."

The soldiers whisked from the car the moment the fifth-floor landing was reached. Grant tarried, stroking his beard with a lazy forefinger.

"Young lady, I don't think you belong in this city—or any other, for that matter. You didn't ask for advice but I'm going to give you some like I would my own daughter: Go West where your kind of sand is appreciated and respected. It's a renegade land; wild, free, and not easily tamed. It needs women like you."

Megan noticed the admiring glances of several young men as she strolled toward the Lyceum Theater. And she did feel quite ravishing in her powder-blue lawn dress with yellow embroidery on the cuffs, collar, and facing.

Sean McBee had given her the garment a week earlier, saying he'd found it in a tote sack near the tenement's red-light district. Megan had been too delighted by the gift to question him further.

A soapy scrub and careful mending restored it to like-new condition. Two stiffly starched petticoats gave a fashionably belled shape to its full skirt.

Her landlady had fussed at her to carry a parasol to shade her skin from the harsh afternoon sun, but Megan wanted to feel its warmth, and let the breeze brush her hair off her shoulders.

The Lyceum Theater was as plain and square as a giant packing case—a design better suited to educational pursuits than entertainment. Five skimpy, double-sashed windows, two on the ground floor and three across the second story, weren't decorative enough to relieve its expanse of ugly, pumpkin-colored clay bricks.

Frances beckoned impatiently from beneath the Lyceum's narrow portico. The severe tailoring of her brown cotton nanny's uniform straightened what few curves her sister possessed. Adding to the matronly affect, loops of black braid coiled across the bosom and hem.

"Hurry, Megan. The first act's about to begin!"

From their seats in the upper tier, the repertory company's actors looked as tiny as leprechauns, but the sisters were soon enthralled by Hamlet's indecision whether to avenge his father's murder. The plot's simmering intrigue had them cheering for the capricious prince one moment and booing at him the next.

When the curtain fell after the final encore, Megan's palms were stinging from her enthusiastic applause. She and Frances made their way toward the exit trading excited "Did you sees?" and "Wasn't it wonderful whens?"

Blinking in the bright sunlight, Megan shaded her eyes. Frances was staring into the distance, her complexion as white as the playbill crumpled in her hand. Megan followed her gaze.

She'd met Charles Brandywine a few weeks earlier when he accompanied her sister during one of their Sunday visits in the Gardens. To Megan's disgust, he'd paid no more attention to Frances than he had the bench they were seated on. But he certainly wasn't ignoring the statuesque redhead whose hand was tucked possessively in the crook of his arm.

"Let's go, Frances."

"Not before I say 'hallo' to Charles."

"Don't be torturin' yourself. He's a bounder—let him have his fancy woman. You're much too good for him."

Frances shook her head and marched stiffly toward the cooing couple.

"Why, Charles, what a lovely surprise," she gushed. "I thought the play was simply marvelous, didn't you?"

The tutor grunted, then answered snidely, "Oh, to be *sure*. I enjoy nothing more than listening to a pudgy has-been mangle Shakespeare's brilliant dialogue."

"Who is this woman, Charles?" the redhead asked petulantly.

"Pardon my rudeness, darling. This is Frances O'Malley, the Sidemores' nanny, and the young lady lurking in her wake is her sister, Megan. The Misses O'Malley, allow me to introduce my fiancée, Miss Letitia Burnette—of the Philadelphia Burnettes."

When she stiffened, Frances's shoulder blades jutted sharply against the thin cotton of her dress. "Please accept our congratulations, Charles, Miss Burnette. I can't imagine two people who are more deservin' of one another."

With that, she turned and moved quickly through the milling crowd. By the time Megan caught up with her, tears were streaming down Frances's face, yet she refused to stop walking or even slow down.

"I don't care to hear what a scoundrel you think Charles is," she warned. "I love him, and I always will. Insults will do nothin' to change that."

Megan wrapped her arm around Frances's waist; the only comforting gesture her sister would allow. Not another word was spoken until they reached the corner where they usually parted company.

"I'll stay at the Sidemores tonight, but I'll leave there for good before Charles arrives in the morning," Frances stated in a world-weary, lifeless tone. "With no job and likely no references, Providence will have to point the way from there."

Megan looked her straight in the eye. "I'm a'thinkin' it already has. Remember me tellin' you what President Grant said? I do believe it's time we took his advice. Don't you?"

# Chapter Seven

Frances arrived at the Hudson Street flat with parcels beneath her arms and a rigid expression. Missus McBee shooed Megan away, relieved the elder O'Malley of her burdens, then took Frances's hands in her own.

"I'm sorry for yer heartache," she said gently, "but it pleases me so to have ye home again. I've missed ye, dearie."

"Megan and I are like alley cats, Missus McBee. We may wander, but whenever we take a lickin', we scat straight to your door for comfort."

"You'll always have a home here, no matter how far ye stray or how long ye be gone. Remember that."

Megan bear-hugged her sister, then led her to the table. Two uneven lengths of lace had been crisscrossed to make runners. In the center, a cracked shaving mug held a perky bouquet of jonquils.

The aroma drifting from the teapot was heavenly. Megan poured each of them a cup of the strong amber brew.

"I hear yer goin' West . . . . " the landlady prompted.

"Well, I suppose it's as good a place as any to make a fresh start," Frances replied. "Boston's too crowded—her people too quick to hate." She took a sip of tea, then added, "Funny, isn't it? They seem to have forgotten that their kin were once poor immigrants eager for a better life, too."

"Now, ye can't judge everyone by the actions of a few," Missus McBee chided. "Paradise ain't to be found in this life, child. Gettin' by is the best ye can hope for on hard ground."

Megan blurted, "Didn't you ever have dreams?"

The spindly chair supporting Missus McBee's bulk squawked in time to her hearty laughter. "Mercy me, if I had a greenback for every clover leaf I've pinched, we'd be takin' our tea in a mansion house." More soberly, she continued, "With a family to feed and fields to tend, it's only sleepin' dreams ye have—not the wakin' kind."

"But mine are one and the same," Megan argued. "Clair has this book called *A Comprehensive Guide to the Western Goldfields*. I read it on the sly when there weren't any guests needin' my services. Oh, if I could only prospect half the gold Alexander Van Dusen did—that's the author—*I'd* be in *bloomin'* clover!"

"What are we to do with her, Missus McBee? First she sashays around in a man's britches, and now she dreams of bein' a miner. I'll swan, I think my sister should have been born a brother."

"Saints preserve us, don't wish that on her, Frances. Why, I'd trade all four of my whelps for either of you girls, straight up!"

Megan pushed away from the table and sauntered to her trunk. She pawed through the garments inside, then held the glossy red penny bank up like a loving cup.

"Posh on you both. Let's see just how rich we O'Malleys already are."

The tin's lid was loosened carefully. With a flourish, Megan tipped the bank, expecting a merry cascade of notes and coins to stream from its mouth.

A dirty cobble thunked onto the oak tabletop. For several seconds, the echo of its landing was the only sound in the room.

Megan looked hard at Frances. She knew they shared the same thought. This was no prank. Someone had stolen their hard-saved money. And that someone could only be Gilead McBee.

"Shake that box, Megan," his mother cried. "Mebbe the paper's catchin' the coins inside."

After she performed the useless gesture, the older woman laid her head on her arms and sobbed. "I knew that boy was up to no good. I stropped 'im—prayed for 'im. Couldn't stop 'im. Been gone three days. He ain't a'comin' back."

Megan's stomach pitched violently. She hadn't counted it lately, but knew they had stashed away at least a hundred dollars.

With her hours cut, and slim chance of Frances finding another couple who'd pay as handsomely as the Sidemores, they'd be stuck in Boston for at least another year. Much as her heart told her to, she couldn't bring herself to offer solace to Missus McBee.

An hour later, the landlady had retired to the davenport with a cool cloth draped over her brow, pleading a sick headache. Megan and Frances sat hunched over the table, staring into their empty teacups as if the dregs really could foretell their futures.

"I have an errand to do," Frances whispered, although her words seemed forged in steel.

"Errand? What kind of an errand?"

"That's not important. Just watch over Missus McBee while I'm gone. Right now, I wouldn't trade places with her for *all* the gold your Mister Van Dusen mined."

# Chapter Eight

Blisters swelled on Frances's heels and the balls of her feet. Until this morning, most of her walking had been done on carpets spanning the Sidemore home's third-floor nursery. Such coddling was now extracting a painful price.

Trying for some measure of comfort, she shifted her weight awkwardly to the outsides of her shoes. In the distance a church bell tolled twice.

I've got less than an hour before Charles and the boys return from their visit to the library, she thought. Hurrying her pace, she abandoned the ducklike gait and winced when the insoles again chafed her tender skin. She refused to consider that those plans might have changed since she tendered her resignation that morning.

The Sidemores' stately home, constructed of ruddy bricks with granite facings around the doors and windows, seemed more imposing than ever as Frances scurried along the clipped privet hedge bounding the property line. Before her nerve abandoned her entirely, she swung open the door to the servants' entrance as if she still had a right to use it.

Other than a lid clapping atop a steaming cauldron in the adjacent kitchen, the house was as quiet as a moonlit graveyard.

She crept up the back stairs, skipping treads she knew would squawk with her weight. A sharp ear and a quick surveillance told her the third floor was deserted.

"Father's so silly," Cy had told her one afternoon amid a fit of giggles. "That big ol' clock's not a mailbox!"

Frances had no idea what the boy was babbling about until Cy reached inside the hallway's towering grandfather clock's hollow base and pulled out a thick envelope. "See? The pos'man won't never look here for Father's letter."

Just as she'd guessed when she'd returned the packet to its hiding place, ripping open a corner of the envelope revealed a stack of crisp currency. Her hands shook as she gripped the parcel tightly. It held more than enough to pay their fares west—more than enough to send her to prison if her plan failed.

She crammed the envelope into her reticule, then slipped a folded sheet of stationery into the niche where it had lain. On it was a signed promissory note assuring the Sidemores she'd repay the "loan" with interest as soon as possible.

Gooseflesh scuttled up her arms, but Frances felt feverish as she tiptoed to the ground floor. With every footfall along the crackling gravel drive, she expected to hear cries of "Stop, thief!" shouted from the rooftop.

Limping the five miles home, she repeated a silent litany: I'll pay back every penny if I have to scrub floors for the rest of my life to do it.

Megan blinked in disbelief when Frances entered the elevator like titled royalty. "Why, this isn't a machine," she gasped. "It's a work of art."

"Oh, Frances, you didn't come through the street entrance did you?" Megan groaned, fearing that any second they'd both be unemployed.

"After the way you were treated? I should say *not*. I slipped in the back door and waited behind one of those big bushes in the lobby until the clerk turned his back."

Megan shook her head and grinned at her sister's uncustomary behavior. "But why? I can't imagine you're that curious about what I do all day."

Rather than answer, Frances waved two ticket books under her sister's nose. Her eyes waggled back and forth with the motion until she squealed, "Train tickets! You've got train tickets?"

"For heaven's sake, *hush* before someone thinks there's a murder bein' done."

"Where did you get the money?" Megan inquired suspiciously. "And don't tell me the fairies left it under your pillow."

Frances cocked her head. "As a matter of fact, it's none of your business where it came from. A nameless benefactor is as close as I'll come to tellin'."

Her sister's expression remained as innocent as a newborn lamb's, but Megan detected a flicker of guile in those smoky eyes.

"Oh, is it, now?" she replied. "There's never been secrets between us—"

"I'm leaving for San Francisco tomorrow morning. Are you coming with me or aren't you?"

"Of course, but—"

"Then quit shilly-shallyin'. Get out of that silly suit and tell Mister Yates to find himself another monkey to wear it. We've got a train to catch."

The sprawling passenger depot was as bustling as a bee-hive. Men in tailored suits and ladies dressed in lace and ruffled finery scurried alongside others wearing buckskin, linsey-woolsey, and calico.

"This basket weighs as much as Missus McBee," Megan groaned as they made their way along the crowded wooden platform. "Are you sure she didn't stow away inside?"

Frances was having her own struggles with three plump satchels, a lap robe, and her reticule. "Shame on you, Megan. She must have hocked her soul to Mister Kerrigan's mercantile to give us those victuals."

"I'm not begrudgin' her generosity. It's her way of making up for Gilead stealing our money. But glory be, she didn't have to buy enough to feed everyone on the whole damned train, did she?"

A piercing whistle and crackling hiss of steam escaping an adjacent locomotive startled Megan so badly she almost dropped the basket. While it was a cloudless, balmy June day, the human clamor mixed with roaring machinery belching great gusts of smoke reminded her of the hell Father Brennan warned about during many a childhood Sunday.

"I'd say you're getting mighty free with the swear words," Frances reprimanded. "I don't like it a bit, and Mama'd have your hide for it."

Megan shifted the basket to her other hand and shot back, "Well now, Miss Bossy Britches, just who do you think I *learned* them from?"

Frances's lips parted, then set in a thin line. Not until they neared a partially empty Boston & Albany coach did she mutter, "I should have helped myself to Cy's paddle when I had the chance."

They propped their belongings against one of the station's awning posts to check their tickets before boarding.

"Goodness, we're cross as two boars tussling over the same sow," Frances said with a conciliatory smile.

"Aye, too much rush and not enough rest. I'm promisin', I'll try not to say da— I mean, swear so much. Only sometimes, it fits what I'm feelin' so *well*."

"You're the bonniest lass County Cork ever bore," Frances said, laughing. "I wouldn't change you for the world; I'm only tryin' to hone the raw edges a mite."

With the tension between them eased, Megan set her sights on the locomotive nearest the boarding dock. Its moniker, "The Titan," was scrolled in gilt below the engineer's cab window. Buffed brass fittings sparkled in the sun. Its red spoked wheels, cowcatcher, sandbox, and headlamp's casing lent jaunty contrast to a jet-black, cylindrical snout and fluted stack.

Frances was comparing the times printed on their tickets to the signboard's departure listings when Megan felt a gentle tap on her shoulder.

"Them tickets can be tricky. Are you needing some assistance, ladies?"

Megan's eyes ranged upward until they met a soft brown pair belonging to a uniformed constable. He ducked his hat bill in a friendly salute.

"No, I think we—"

Megan turned to see why Frances had stopped talking in midsentence. Her sister was standing stiff as a statue with her mouth agape. Megan laid a hand on her trembling forearm. "Frances, what's the matter?"

Probably fearing she was about to swoon, the officer lunged toward Frances. She shied against the post, terror contorting her face. "No, please! I'll give it all—"

The constable and Megan froze in place, trading perplexed glances, neither sure what to do next.

Recovering some measure of composure, Frances stammered, "Uh, forgive me, the both of you. I'm fine now. Truly I am. My breakfast isn't agreeing with me, that's all."

Megan's eyebrows arched and she folded her arms in front of her. "That's the fastest case of the vapors I ever saw. You were fitter'n a fiddle a minute ago."

"Naw, it's nervous flusters," the officer diagnosed. "The

wife suffers 'em regular. Here, let me tote them bags aboard for you before the last call."

When Frances protested, he insisted, "It's no trouble, ma'am. I'm glad to do it."

Sweat was glistening on his forehead by the time he'd crammed their belongings in the stingy space beneath the coach's upholstered bench. " 'Twas like putting six gallons of water in a five-gallon bucket, but they should pass the conductor's notice."

Megan smiled gratefully. "Thank you so kindly—"

"Yes. Thank you," Frances echoed in a dismissive tone.

He looked at Megan and spread his arms as if to say, "There's just no pleasing some women," then tipped his hat and lumbered down the aisle.

"What has come over you, Frances O'Malley?" Megan hissed when he was out of earshot. "That man showed us nothin' but friendliness and you treated him like a cutpurse."

"I told you, I was woozy—"

"Woozy, my Aunt Agnes! You looked like you'd seen a spook, and it had nary a thing to do with this mornin's porridge and bacon!"

Frances gazed out the window for several minutes. Finally, in a hushed voice she said, "Policemen frighten me, Megan. Don't you remember the ones that came with Squire Bernard to see we didn't take so much as a candle stub that wasn't ours from the cottage? Surly gaffers they were. It pleasured them to watch us jig to their tune."

Megan didn't respond. They kept to an uneasy silence, unbroken even when the conductor punched their tickets and wished them a pleasant journey.

The locomotive bucked, and a thundering whoosh of steam smothered their car in dense vapor. The coach lurched, dragged, then feinted backward as if unwilling to follow its leader. With a neck-wrenching jerk, it snailed forward along the rails, gaining speed with each whuff-chug of the engine's powerful pistons.

Megan's mind churned with unanswered questions. Frances hadn't lied exactly, but she knew her sister's explanation was more of an excuse than the reason for her apprehension.

Buildings and boulevards soon gave way to verdant fields dotted with livestock and whitewashed outbuildings. Megan breathed in the sweet scent of country air only to wrinkle her nose at the taint of acrid wood smoke streaming from the Titan's stack.

She'd been so intent upon solving the riddle of Frances's bizarre behavior that she'd paid scant attention as fellow passengers claimed their seats. To her surprise, the scenery inside the car was as diverse as the panorama rushing by outside.

Four rough-hewn characters slouched in the front seats, baiting each other with profane remarks. Their beards were drizzled with tobacco juice and they wore hats fashioned from animal skins, complete with ringed tails dangling down the wearers' necks.

What a silly idea, Megan giggled to herself. They look like they've got tabby cats perched atop their heads.

Behind them, a jowly parson dozed beside a birdlike woman—presumably his wife. She was studiously reading the Scriptures while miles of God's pastoral handiwork whisked past the windows unnoticed.

Across the aisle, two women were talking in covert voices. Their hair was sculpted into elaborate curls and ringlets, and they wore enough rouge on their cheeks to appear contagious.

The taller one seated closer to Megan was lushly proportioned, with an olive complexion and handsome features. She looked younger than Frances, but like a peach's soft rind disguised a tough core, hurt and hardship ages from within and doesn't always leave visible traces.

She caught Megan staring at her and fairly purred, "Are you a rude little snippet, or are you merely stunned by my beauty?"

Megan laughed aloud. "Stunned, to be sure, ma'am."

"Undoubtedly the wiser reply. It salvages pride for the both of us."

The coach rocked as it bested a curve. The woman groaned when the bench's armrest gouged her ribs. "The rails are mixing my innards already and we're not halfway to Chicago. Is that your destination?"

"Only for changin' trains. My sister and I are going to San Francisco."

"We're bound for the City by the Bay ourselves. Wayfaring husbands awaiting you, I suppose?"

"No, neither of us is married."

"Well, you could be no sooner than your heels hit the platform, my dear. There's a hundred hes for every she in California. A pretty thing like you will start fistfights all over town."

"If there's a ruckus raised, it'll be for Frances's hand," Megan said with a chuckle. "It's a job and a fortune I'm seekin', not a husband."

One slender eyebrow arched as the woman appraised Megan from stem to stern. "And what kind of work are you suited to? I might be able to help."

Megan sat up eagerly. "Oh, I can learn most anything, the better it pays, the faster I learn, too."

In the wake of a porter bearing a water can came a young news-butcher peddling his wares. "Pay-pers, cay-a-ndee, cee-gars," he called in a practiced singsong pitch. The racket awakened Frances and she peered around as if unsure of where she was or how she got there.

Megan licked her lips at the thought of a peppermint stick or a chocolate drop—only Frances literally held the purse strings in a tightfisted grip. She knew better than to ask for a few pennies' worth of sheer pleasure.

Grudgingly, she lifted the basket, balanced it across her knees, and drew two tongue sandwiches and apples from their stores, offering one of each to her sister. Others doled out paper-wrapped morsels to their kith and kin, but most of the passengers answered the conductor's instruction to follow him to the dining car.

Having a meal on wheels was an innovation a few railroad owners were testing. The agent who'd stamped their tickets had extolled the virtues of the new service. In glowing terms he described what a pleasant diversion it was to dine restaurant style while traveling—that the waiters were duty-bound to keep passengers' coffee cups brimming—no extra charge.

"Seventy-five cents for little more than a boxed lunch ought to buy a bathtub full of coffee," Frances had remarked.

While the sisters chatted between bites of their own victuals, Frances clearly showed no intention of discussing the morning's incident any further. Instead, Megan palavered about how men were as plentiful in San Francisco as grapes on a vine and just as ripe for plucking.

"Seems to me," she said, as much to herself as Frances,

"that a town with that many men and not many women must be starved for a homecooked meal."

"They say the way to a man's heart is through his stomach," Frances quipped.

"Oh, but I can surely feed a gang of 'em, and delight when their silver dances in my restaurant's cash box."

"And what, may I ask, do you know about running a restaurant?"

"About as much as I did about runnin' an elevator."

A swish of petticoats brushing against taffeta preceded the return of Megan's across-the-way neighbors. After settling herself, the woman on the aisle flicked open a fan and waved it lazily to stir a private breeze.

"If you don't mind me troublin' you, ma'am," Megan started, "could you tell me if San Francisco is in need of a good restaurant? Nothin' fancy, just hearty food at a reasonable price."

She smiled coquettishly and answered, "Believe me, any service a man doesn't have that he'll pay a woman to get means money in her pocket."

Megan mulled over the woman's words—and what they likely implied. Boston's Shantytown had been home to hundreds of prostitutes; most of them coarse, bawdy cows who'd jiggle their breasts at any man sober enough to see them. But this immaculately groomed, sloe-eyed beauty spoke and comported herself like a lady.

"By the way, the name's Kate Elder," she said, breaking the spell of Megan's pondering. "Some call me 'Big-Nose Kate'—for obvious reasons."

Megan stammered an introduction of Frances and herself, then fell silent again. Maybe she was getting so sleepy she couldn't think straight, but she felt a sort of kinship toward Kate regardless of the way her living was earned.

"Me and Della have a house on Kearny near Washington," she added. "If ever's the time you need anything, ring the bell and ask for me. I'll do what I can."

"It's a generous woman you are, Miss Elder."

"What goes 'round, comes 'round, gal. It doesn't matter a whit who starts the circle spinning."

Megan nodded as she scrunched down in the seat, her weariness succumbing to the train's gentle sway. She drifted off dreaming of tableware clattering against tin plates, apron pockets heavy with coins, and a glittering city sloping gracefully toward a brilliant blue bay.

# Chapter Nine

Megan unpinned her hair and waggled her head side to side. The strands lightly flicked her skin like a horse's tail shooing flies. Leaning comfortably back on her hands, she surveyed the scene below.

The three railcars, resembling oversize pine coffins with windows where the pallbearers' grips would be, hunkered on a siding. Eventually, they'd be coupled with a passing train for the final leg of the journey to San Francisco. For two days, their passengers had waited, lolling on blankets or stretched out in the pillowy, cool grass.

Peals of laughter drifted up from the birch grove. Megan was astounded to see Frances, sitting cozily in the shade with Oran Dannelly and giggling like a schoolgirl. She also suspected that a convenient fold of Frances's dress hid the couple's clasped hands.

The sisters first noticed the burly young man soon after the train ground to a halt near Bisuka, Idaho. A herd of buffalo, blissfully ignorant of the Central Pacific's eminent domain, was lumbering across the tracks behind the lead bull.

The animal's massive, fleecy head and shoulders tapered to narrow, smooth-coated haunches. One horn was broken off at midcurve and his flanks bore numerous battle scars.

As the bull and his drove spread out across the prairie to graze, a troupe of dapper Dans, resplendent in jacquard vests and bowlers, leapt from a coach car. Quickly bringing rifles to their shoulders, they fired on the milling animals.

Fifty yards away, a cow's forelegs crumpled beneath her and she pitched forward. She collapsed on her side, grunting and twitching. A gust of powdery dirt swirled up around her. Its clearing revealed a bewildered, bawling calf nuzzling at her udder.

"Bull's-eye, Gaston!" one of the shooters exclaimed, clapping the marksman on the shoulder.

A lean, dark-haired fellow stepped in front of the crowd of spectators and proclaimed, "Ah yes, and it's proud you should be. To peg a bullet square a'twixt the eyes of a dumb animal—and a mother at that—is gallantry at its *finest*."

From his expression, the rifleman couldn't decide for a moment whether he was being complimented or insulted.

"Hey, Gaston, you aren't going to take that kind of guff off a Mick are you?" another of his cronies sneered.

"Beg pardon, gents. The name's Oran Dannelly, not 'Mick.' And it's not a ruckus I'm wantin', but a hungry man can't abide watchin' a ton of prime meat get left to spoil just for sport of it."

The crowd murmured in agreement. Gaston's hands gripped the rifle barrel. In a flash, he jerked up the Winchester and lunged. With a sickening splat, its brass-plated butt split a fine gash in Oran's cheek.

"Open your mouth again and you'll be talking to the bore end, *Mick*," he snarled, then swung around and stalked away.

Before fists started flying, the conductor's boarding call sent the emigrants rushing toward their accommodations behind the livestock cars, and the express passengers to their sumptuous compartments at the fore.

Now, from her hilltop vantage point, Megan could still see the ugly, purple-red welt that marred Oran's face from below his eye to his jawbone.

Her curiosity won out over a lazy bask in the sun. Megan stood, ruffled her skirt, and strolled down the hill to find out why her prim sister was hee-hawing like a mule.

Nearing, she heard Oran say, ". . . so the lady replied, 'I already have a dog that growls, a parrot that swears, a fireplace that smokes, and a cat that stays out all night. So why the devil would I want to get married?' "

Megan chuckled as she knelt down beside her sister. "The jester's holdin' court again, I see."

"Aye, the last time I got serious, my pretty face paid for the privilege," he replied. "But it's mendin', and so are my ways."

"Well, I thought what you did was quite brave."

Oran worked his jaw and touched the wound gently.

"Maybe so, but Franny's kisses lay gentler on my cheek than that rifle butt did."

"For heaven's sake," Frances muttered. "Can't you bellow a mite louder? There may be some that didn't hear you say I'm a hussy!"

A huge grin spread across his handsome features. He winked slyly at Megan. "I reckon I've grievously besmirched your reputation, Franny darlin'. There's nothing for me to do but make an honest woman of ya."

Though the sisters didn't much resemble each other, their looks of stunned surprise were identical.

Megan was the first to recover her voice, and she fairly growled a warning. "Mister Dannelly, that remark had a sore lack of humor to it."

Oran looked down at Frances's slim fingers intertwined with his rough, scarred ones. His piercing blue eyes caught and held Megan's. "I'm not on bended knee. There's nary a thing in my pockets save lint. But seein' as how you're her only kin, if she'll have me, I'm askin' for your sister's hand."

"Gracious, we haven't known each other a week," Frances gasped.

He cradled her chin in his palm. "I know all I need to. You're the kindest, most givin' woman I've ever met. I figure if it takes the rest of our lives to get acquainted proper, so be it."

When he leaned to kiss her, kinsmen who'd been huddling behind the tree trunks like highwaymen whooped and applauded their approval.

The engagement party that immediately commenced lacked the traditional platters of food and bottomless tankards of ale, but high spirits and well wishes for the future were in abundance. Even the sullen Rhinelanders, the last group to stroll over and investigate the commotion, offered their sincere congratulations.

Later, under a silver-dollar moon, the men who had them gathered blankets to once again sleep out under the stars. Rumors of snakes thicker than a lumberjack's thigh and wolf packs prowling amid the chaparral nagged at their minds, but piling down in a thicket was infinitely more restful than sprawling higgledy-piggledy between the cars' benches and in the aisle.

With her stocking feet crossed at the ankles and braced

between two window frames, Megan lay on a bench pondering the afternoon's events and trying to make sense of them.

"Frances? Are you asleep?" she whispered to the still form on the adjacent bench.

"Ummm, no."

"Are you too weary to talk a little while?"

"Is there something botherin' you, lass?"

Megan wriggled onto her side and propped her head with her hand. "Not botherin', exactly ... it's, well, it's about you and Oran."

"Don't you like him?"

"Oh, I think he's a grand sort, only, if'n you don't mind me sayin', he's—different."

"How so?"

"Remember back in Rathcormac when you'd set your cap for that brooding poet, Devon Cahill? I thought he was a twit, but if I'd have said as much, you'd have boxed my ears. Then you got all swoony over Charles Brandywine—"

"I'm a simple woman, Megan. I was hugely flattered that such sophisticated men seemed attracted to me."

"Sophisticated, my foot. Snooty prigs, the both of them. Much as I hated for you to be hurt, I've thanked heaven a thousand times that we saw Charles and Miss La-Di-Da at the Lyceum that day."

"So have I, but if Devon and Charles did nothing else, they taught me the difference between infatuation and love."

"Then you truly do *love* Oran? Neither of you declared it this afternoon."

For several minutes, only the snuffs and snorts of fitful sleepers resounded in the darkness. When Frances spoke, her voice trembled with emotion. "From the moment I met Oran, after that brute attacked him so viciously, I've felt peaceful in his company. You're right, he is different. With him, I can be exactly what I am, and it's enough."

"But doesn't it worry you that you don't really know him?"

"That's where you're wrong, lass. We've talked more than some folks do in a lifetime. Unlike Devon and Charles, Oran listens, he makes me laugh, and he never laughs *at* me."

It was Megan's turn to fall silent. Is that what love is,

she asked herself. A comfort? What about passion, throbbing hearts, and the fiery kisses described in sonnets and books? And what of those mysterious "relations" between men and women?

Like any farmer's daughter, she knew about procreation, but with people it was different. Much more complicated. She'd never admit it to a living soul, but when Rolf Tabor fondled her, she'd been revolted—as much by his lechery as by a fluttering sensation in her loins.

She daren't ask Frances about such stirrings. *That* was a subject her sister simply would not discuss. In fact, the only time Megan had tried, Frances was shocked by her "shameful" questions and chastised her severely.

Sighing wistfully, she murmured, "Then if it's Oran you've chosen for your husband, it's pleased I'll be to have him for my brother."

# Chapter Ten

"Look, Frances. The whole city is a garden," Megan exclaimed. She twisted back to give her sister a better view through the railcar's open window.

Stately live oaks, tilted slightly inland by trade winds, sheltered splashes of vivid geraniums, verbenas, roses, and dozens of blooming stalks and shrubs Megan couldn't name.

From cottage to mansion-size, private homes were landscaped with luxuriant tropical plantings and flowers. Their expansive lawns allowed plenty of room for string-straight vegetable rows and orchards.

"What a bonny place we're settlin' in to raise a family," Frances said.

"Uh, sorry, my girl, but that there's Oakland," Oran informed. "San Francisco's on t'other side of the bay."

His beloved admitted later that had she known the last three and a half miles of their journey involved bouncing along in a ferry, being blasted by gale-force winds, and drenched by sea spray, she'd have dug in her heels and refused to leave Oakland.

Hugging against the ferry's cabin and squinting to protect her eyes from the stinging spray, Megan felt very small and vulnerable—much as she had when the train chugged for days across the Great Plains. That sense of vastness was as wondrous as it was frightening.

No sooner had the trio gathered their soggy belongings and stepped onto dry land than they were swarmed by eager hackmen and hotel-runners. A closer inspection of Oran's grimy neck and the sisters' cheap, unstylish clothing sent the dock rats in search of more prosperous fares.

Their view of the city tunneled up Market Street. Buildings stair-stepped like a pack team rambling nose to tail up an incline. Parallel, partially visible avenues slanted upward as well.

"Saints have mercy," Megan puffed after several minutes tramp up Market's steep grade. " 'City by the Bay,' indeed. 'City Made for Billy Goats,' I'd say."

"But just think of the fortune you'd earn runnin' an elevator up and down these sidewalks," Oran quipped.

Turning to give him her thoughts on that notion, Megan's voice caught in her throat. At this height, the masts of the hundreds of sailing ships at anchor in the mouth of the bay looked like a graceful, floating forest. A gossamer fog bank divided the crystal blue sky from the deeper blue waves rushing elegantly to shore. No wonder San Francisco's residents took her hilly terrain in stride. The panorama from their summits was nothing less than magnificent.

From time to time, Oran asked passersby where inexpensive lodgings could be found. "Full up" was the response they received at every hotel and boardinghouse they tried. Trudging onward, they were thoroughly exhausted when they turned south to continue their search along Fifth Street.

"There's a sign offering rooms to let," Frances exclaimed, pointing toward a sooty, clapboard structure.

Three-storied, with a severely gambreled roof, the parched, forlorn-looking structure was wedged midblock between its betters like a mongrel amid a litter of purebred hounds.

"Why, if you sneezed out the window, your neighbor'd catch cold," Megan observed, chuckling.

"Aye, but I'll risk it for a basin of hot water and a clean, soft bed," Oran countered. Nudging Frances, he added, "That's all I want . . . for now, anyway."

Frances bowed her head demurely, but not before Megan saw her blush to the roots of her hair.

The puddled street slurped rudely at their every step. Megan grimaced as the cold ooze crept through the stitching of her shoes.

Oran yanked the boardinghouse's bell cord twice before a frumpy slattern stuck her head out the door and rasped, "Whaddya want?"

He frowned over his shoulder at Frances before answering, "Rooms, if you have any."

"Only got one, unless old man Thackeray's dead in his bed."

"Uh, well, we need two—one for the ladies and one for myself."

"That's right gentlemanly of you, but I cain't make my house any bigger than it is. Got one room, Bub, and probably won't have it by nightfall. Take it or take your chances. It don't make me no never mind."

"Take it, Oran," Frances whispered, slipping some folded banknotes into his hand. "It can't be any worse than the train. As soon as we're rested, maybe we can find a nicer place."

Megan knew by the way he crumpled it in his fist that he hated using their money. She squeezed his arm reassuringly, but he averted his eyes. Thrusting several notes at the landlady, he said gruffly, "That should pay a few days board."

The woman snatched the bills, flattened them, and aligned their edges neatly. She licked her thumb, then riffled through them as quickly as a card sharp counting the night's take.

"Three days, to be exact. That's 'til Thursday noon. And if you can't pay up then, don't bother askin' for credit. You ain't gonna get it."

"Done," he agreed. "Now show us to our room, please, if it won't trouble you over much."

Introducing herself as Missus Braggonier, she led them down a creaky hardwood hall to the back of the house and cocked a thumb toward an open doorway. After tucking the cash into the crevasse formed by her commodious bosom, she sniffed disdainfully before making her way up the back stairs.

Megan's eyes goggled when she peered into the room. A full-sized iron bed was skirted in muslin and topped by a gorgeous wedding ring-patterned quilt. Beside it, an oil lamp rested atop a slickly beeswaxed, claw-footed table. The cat-cornered highboy was draped with extra bed linens and bath towels, and the seat of a dainty lady's chair held a leather-bound Bible with a red satin page marker clasped between the leaves.

She sniffed—and sniffed again. The room's delightful vanilla-and-cinnamon fragrance made her mouth water.

"Well, I'll be damned . . ." Oran grunted. "Kinda frilly for a fireman, but I reckoned we'd be findin' roaches big enough to wrestle."

Megan turned toward him abruptly. "You're truly a fireman?"

"Yup. A three-year veteran of New York City's Company Number Nine."

"Well, I'll be damned."

Frances cut in wryly, "While you two are busy 'be damnin'' your way to the devil's lair, do you mind if I make myself to home?"

Megan and Oran exchanged guilty looks, which eased quickly into grins. They watched Frances meander about smoothing invisible wrinkles from the bedcover, edging the lamp over a fraction, and peeking inside the bureau's empty drawers.

"Since you ladies have such a fine nest to feather, I'll be off to attend to some business," he announced.

Frances whirled around. "What business? We've only just got here! And from the look of you, a good soak, a shave, and a nap is what needs tendin' to the most."

"Lord above, I haven't given her my name yet and already she's harpin' like a fishwife."

"Oh, take it from me, she's a champ-een at makin' folks toe the mark," Megan teased.

Stamping her foot petulantly, Frances shot back, "Hush now, the both of you. I've had quite enough of this two against one."

Oran strode across the room and planted a kiss on her pouty lips. "Have it out with your sister then, darlin'. I'll be back by the by."

Hours later, seated at the lace-clothed dinner table, Megan was pushing fried potatoes around on her plate with her fork. Hungry as she was, she'd only been able to get a few bites of fish past the iron fist clutching at her insides.

At the head of the table, old man Thackeray had tamed his beard by tying his napkin bandanna style below his lower lip. Hardly on his deathbed, he gummed his meal with a healthy, smacking gusto.

Between mouthfuls, Desiree Van Damme, a voluptuous gypsy whose bangled wrists and earbobs jingled with every breath, warned of dire star signs and the catastrophes they were certain to cause.

Anchoring the opposite end, Miss Charity Jones chewed her food like a cud and sipped her tea with her pinkie extended. All the while she stared at the rosebud-decorated china as if expecting it to bloom before her eyes.

The chair beside a dour, jittery Frances was empty.

Missus Braggonier set a bowl heaped with corn bread beside the meat platter. "Where's your gentleman friend?" she asked Frances. "I cook one meal a day, and boarders don't get two chances at it."

"He's away . . . on business."

The landlady's laughter boomed like barrels rolling off a dray. "Oh, and there's lots of business being done down at Moriarity's and the Skull and Stein."

"Mister Dannelly does not imbibe, Missus Braggonier."

The landlady waggled her head and started back to the kitchen. Pausing at the threshold she said, with a knowing smirk, "I'll not hold you to that when he staggers in wailin' 'Danny Boy' at the top of his lungs."

It gave Frances scant pleasure that Oran proved the woman wrong. He did not burst into the boardinghouse that night, sloshing with ale.

Beside her on the bed, Megan looked on helplessly as Frances gazed up at the room's punched tin ceiling. The tears spilling from her eyes glistened in the early morning sunlight.

Oran had not come home at all.

# Chapter Eleven

A row of scarlet crescents marked Megan's palms. For three hours she'd wheedled and cajoled, trying to get Frances off her duff and out into the city's hurly-burly streets.

Amid the shouts of peddlers and clattering, bell-harnessed horse carriages, a gloriously rip-snorting city awaited their exploration.

Frances would have none of it; not as long as Oran's whereabouts remained a mystery.

With every tick of the hallway's fussy French timepiece, Megan's fractiousness increased. "Lawsy, I'm fidgety as a mouse with a cat at its tail."

"Please stop pestering me," Frances whined. "Can't you see I'm already worried sick about Oran?"

"Lord above, he's a grown man and he's actin' just like one," Megan parried, trying to keep the entire boarding-house from hearing. "I wouldn't give a fat hen for his whereabouts and I'll not sit a vigil 'til he returns."

"For all we know, he could be hurt or sick. What if he tried getting word to me and I was off gallivantin' with you?"

"Swear and be damned if I know how that poor soul's lived twenty-five years without your smotherin'."

Frances squinted and shot back defiantly, "I'm *not* smothering him. I love Oran—I'll gladly spend this day, and the rest God gives me, concerned about his welfare."

"Well, if you're duty-bound to stew about somethin', divine how we're to keep body and soul together when your reticule's flat."

"God will provide."

That calmly delivered phrase only enraged Megan further. She felt like a boiling teakettle with a corked spout. "Hah! It's Oran Dannelly you're a'prayin' will provide! But

*I* don't portend on hitchin' my wagon to anyone's horse 'til I own 'em both!"

A fresh trail of tears meandered down Frances's face. "Why are you being so horrid to me?"

The younger O'Malley sighed deeply several times to check her temper, then squatted down on her heels beside her sister's chair. "It's fine for you to want a man to take care of you, and to believe he always will. Most women do. Only I'm not most women."

Frances's chuckle was more patronizing than mirthful. "Lass, you're far too young to know how you feel about anything."

Megan scrambled to her feet and paced the small room. "That riles me to distraction. I'm supposed to be grown-up enough to hold your wants in high regard, then damned if you're not forever sayin' I'm too much a child to know my *own* mind."

"You're only fifteen—"

"Same age as Mama when she had you at her breast and livestock and fields to tend. It wasn't a child workin' shifts at the Drake, either."

Frances looked hard at her sister for a moment. Her eyes held a glimmer of respect. "No, I suppose it wasn't. It wasn't a child that cared for me during the crossin', either."

She realized the sentiment was a peace offering, but Megan couldn't curb her pent-up frustration. "Then understand this: I won't fret the day away waiting for Oran to rescue us. It's time I set my own wheels a'turnin'."

Frances rose from the chair and laced her arms tightly against her chest. "Are you implying that I've stopped you? Have you forgotten whose money brought you west?"

Swirling on her cloak like a toreador's cape, Megan countered slyly, "And whose money was it? Certainly not yours."

"As I've already told you, where it came from doesn't matter. Fact is, it's thanks to *me* that you're exactly where you wanted to be."

With a toss of her head, Megan replied, "I'll give you that. Only now that I am, I want to know how much is left of that bundle of greenbacks you've penny-pinched since we left Boston. Why, on the train, we never got more than one meal a day at an eatin' station."

"At the dear prices they charged? I'd say not!"

"Stop jiggin' 'round and tell me true—do we have enough to meet the rent come Thursday?"

Frances straightened her shoulders and brought her chin up regally. "I gave the last of it to Oran yesterday."

A hiss escaped Megan's lips. "Aye, and not a nickel you'd give me to warm my pocket, but—"

Ignoring the outburst, Frances continued, "There's nothing to worry your pretty head about. Oran is a fireman. He'll find work, easy. Then we'll put down on a nice place, big enough for the three of us."

Charging toward the door, Megan whirled and cried, "You didn't listen to a thing I said, did you? I'll not be tied to you or anyone else for my keep. Mama went to her grave lackin' two tuppence to lay on her eyes, but *I* won't!"

Slamming the bedroom door, and the entry's for good measure, she stamped along furiously for a half block before falling into a heap on a gritty stoop.

If Frances never speaks to you again, it'll be a day too soon, she wailed to herself. You're tired and scared and you're sick of being treated like a babe in arms. So what did you do? Tossed a proper tantrum and did your best to break your sister's heart.

Her sleeves were damp through to the skin before her tears were finally spent. Sniffling and blinking in the bright sunlight, she wiped her eyes with a corner of her cloak.

She sat up straight and anchored her elbows on her knees. Her conscience told her to rush back to Frances and apologize. But, although her words had been harsh and mean-spoken, she'd meant every one of them. To beg Frances's forgiveness would be the same as a retraction.

Listen to your heart and use your head, chimed a voice in the back of her mind. You know Frances will never abide your going off on your own. Make a clean break while you can.

Up the street, a driver reined in a horse-drawn pumper in front of Missus Braggonier's boardinghouse. Megan scrunched behind and peered around the corner of the handrail's banister. She saw Oran jump down from the back of the rig and wave at its driver.

" 'Preciate the ride, Worchinsky," he called. "See you at the firehouse come shift-change."

The driver nodded and flicked the horse's hindquarters

with his whip. The animal strained against its harness and set off at a plodding gait.

Like I tried to tell your betrothed, Megan observed, you didn't spend the night kickin' up your heels, now did you, Oran? Pride sent you out to find work and you wouldn't face Frances again 'til you got it.

A bushy set of muttonchop whiskers surrounding a chubby, florid face loomed into view. "Are you lost, miss? Or ill?"

"I'm just fine, sir, thank you for askin'. Only restin' a spell to get my bearings."

Megan brought herself up straight and bobbed her head smartly. "Matter-of-factly, I'm rock-certain where I'm bound for now."

"I see. Well, if you don't mind an old nosy Parker asking, where might that be?"

"Away, sir. I'm goin' away."

# Chapter Twelve

Like flotsam adrift on the sea, Megan drifted along San Francisco's crowded boardwalks. Eighteen months had passed since her last and tearful promenade. She hadn't known the city well enough then to judge how much or how little it had changed.

In her most recent letter, Frances had written: "Oran, baby Tommy, and I are moving to a house at 814 Davis Street at week's end. It's a lovely place, with twin bay windows overlooking the sea. It's larger, too—space we'll need when the new baby comes."

Megan smiled to herself. How surprised Frances will be when she opens the door and finds her wayfaring sister standing there. Oh, what a grand reunion that'll be!

She felt quite smart in her crisp navy bombazine suit. The jacket's single-button, cinched waist design was a becoming contrast to her high-collared, ruffled blouse. A straw chapeau with a fan of peacock feathers at its band finished off her stylish ensemble.

But Lord above, she thought, an Eskimo would swoon under these layers. And only a man could've invented the bustle. No female with a brain in her head would divine tacking a pillow under her dress so it waddled up and down on her behind with every step.

It was simply too muggy to by-guess and by-golly her way to the Dannelly home. Megan considered hailing a hack, then dismissed the notion as an unnecessary extravagance.

Hoping to find a patron who was familiar with the area, she entered the respectable-looking Saratoga Supper Club. Its interior's Havana-smoky haze made dust motes sparkle along the shafts of light angling through the windows. The dining room was empty, but a dapper, bow-tied gent with garters blousing his shirtsleeves was wiping down the bar as gently as a mother drying a fresh-bathed infant.

"What can I do for you, missy?" he asked, his voice booming in the quiet room. "Fresh outta sarsaparilla, and you're a tad short in the stirrups for anything stronger."

"I didn't come here for refreshment," she replied haughtily, "but I'm certainly old enough to imbibe if I'd a mind to."

"Not while ol' Quillan's doing the pouring, you're not," he declared, jabbing a thumb against his chest. "Your getup may say twenty-five, but the face under that bird's nest doesn't look an hour over eighteen. And that's too young for elbow-bending in my book."

Since he'd guessed her age a whole year older than she was, Megan silently forgave him for insulting her beautiful bonnet.

"Mister Quillan, if you want shed of me, I'll thank you to direct me to Davis Street. I've got business—"

"That does it." The crow's-feet at the corners of his eyes splayed when he grinned. "Who hired you for this leg pullin'? Haskell Polk? Zeke Carson?"

She squinted at the barkeep as if that could clarify what she'd heard. "What on earth are you talkin' about? I just got off the stage and I'm tryin' to find my sister's home."

Mindlessly circling the rag over the bar's mahogany surface, he tamped a chubby cigar with his other hand. Not taking his eyes off her, he brought the Havana to his lips and puffed until its stub glowed orange. "Honest Injun?"

With an exasperated "harrumph," Megan grabbed at her skirt and wheeled to leave.

"Hey, lady, don't go off all snarly. Why, Haskell and Zeke are forever bedeviling me. Between the fancy duds and saying you had 'business' in the godforsakenist part of Frisco, I figured you were in cahoots with them to josh me." His expression was as woebegone as a thirteen-hand horse hitched to a ten-ton wagon.

"Seems to me, you could use some practice at pickin' your friends."

"Could be. Except if your sister really does live on Davis, I'd say she's pretty poor at picking neighborhoods."

"Then you know where it is?"

"Yep. Down near the waterfront, and no place for a lady.

Hell, I wouldn't venture there without the cavalry at my back."

Megan paused thoughtfully, then slipped a tattered envelope from her reticule. Frowning, she reread that part of Frances's letter as much to herself as Quillan. "I knew I wasn't mistaken. It says right here, 814 Davis Street."

"Then it gives me no pleasure to tell you, your sister must've fallen on real hard times."

"Hard times is all she's ever known," Megan said wistfully. "I'm not meanin' to doubt your word, sir. I just don't understand. Her husband is a fireman and they have a year-old son—"

"A fireman, you say? For what company?"

"The Knickerbockers."

"Jaysus! That's the lick-splittenist crew of smoke warriors in town. Couple of weeks ago, they led a New Year's Day parade, in uniform, all spit and polished like royalty. Fact is, they're the closest thing Frisco has to crown princes. What's your brother-in-law's name?"

Megan had hiked her skirt and sidesaddled onto a bar stool while he extolled the Knickerbockers' virtues. Questions and concerns swirled in her head like sand devils, but she managed to stammer, "It's Oran. Oran Dannelly."

The bartender's brows met and he seesawed a forefinger against his jaw. "Hmmmm, I swear that name's familiar. One of my regulars? Nah ... can't put a face on the moniker."

While Quillan pondered, she marveled at the enormous, mirrored back bar behind him. She'd never seen so many shapes and sizes of glassware as those neatly marching two-by-two across its mahogany shelves.

Liquor in clear bottles and colored flasks wore labels with black or gilded medallions and scrolled lettering arched across their upper edges. Megan wrinkled her nose at the yeasty beer smell wafting from a row of tap handles jutting from beneath the bar.

She startled when he smacked it with his fist. "Got it. There was a story in the *Alta California* a few months back. Dannelly rescued a kid from a tenement fire. Not a scratch on the child, but he got burned bad. Said he came running out of the building with his clothes flaming like a torch, holding that little boy tight to his heart."

She felt the blood drain from her face. "I must find Frances. Please—tell me how to get there."

Quillan yanked at his apron cord. He whisked it from around his waist and tossed it on the bar. "I'll go you one better. I'll take you to her."

"Oh, it's a kindly man you are to offer, but what about your position? You'll be sacked in a finger snap if your boss finds out."

He hurriedly shucked into a waistcoat and jacket, then steered her toward the door. Extracting a key from his pocket, he latched it, rattling the knob to be sure the bolt was secure.

"Don't worry, my dear. I won't get fired," he assured her, then chuckled. "I can't afford to lose my most valuable employee."

"You're the owner? And you tend the bar, too?"

"Best way to get to know my customers—find out what they like and what they don't. Evenings, I serve up a steak folks can cut with a fork. So do a hundred other eatin' houses. It's the trimmings, like pouring the smoothest sipping whiskey and having a friend behind the bar to tell a joke to while they're sippin' it that keeps them coming back."

"That makes good sense," Megan agreed, stepping along smartly to keep up with his leggy strides. "Treat the customers like kinfolk and the cash box'll take care of itself."

A caravan of freight wagons rumbled down the street; their iron-rimmed tires and horses' hooves thundering on the woodblock-and-asphalt Nicholsen pavement. Megan had to shout to be heard.

"I cooked for a two-bit house in Virginia City the last year and a half. Different kind of customers, those. All they wanted was a bargain and a bellyful."

"Not many jobs harder on a body than that," he replied, a note of admiration in his tone. "Especially for a girl as young as you—no insult intended."

She grinned. "None taken. Oh, it wasn't so bad, really, Euphonimous Tripp, the owner, was a pucker-faced old coot, but he was mighty good to me. With me tendin' the stove, he'd head for the hills, prospectin' a week or two at a stretch."

She paused when her voice caught. "The coroner said

he'd been lyin' in his cabin for a week, stiffer than a fence post, by the time anyone went lookin' for him.''

Quillan's hazel eyes narrowed sympathetically. "Friends are hard to come by and harder to lose.''

"Aye, they are. Euphonimous was cantankerous, but he had a kind heart. You see, when I got to Virginia City, I wanted to open my own restaurant, only all the bankers I called on for a loan turned me down flat. No collateral.''

"That's the way of it. A man can't borrow a damned cent unless he can prove he doesn't need it.''

"Well, Euphonimous liked nothin' better than besting a 'duded-up Yankee moneychanger.' We struck a gentleman's agreement—he kept most of my wages in what he called an 'escrow.' Soon as there was enough to buy out his interest, he was to deed the place to me. That'd be my collateral, if I ever needed it. He even let me fix up a storeroom to live in.''

Quillan took her elbow and guided her around a corner. The buildings they now passed were as weather-beaten as driftwood. Orange peels, tins, and trash scuttled across the sidewalk like autumn leaves.

Megan's throat constricted and she coughed to clear it. Just like Boston's Shantytown, the indescribable, unforgettable stench of poverty would warn a blind man that he'd strayed beyond civilization.

"Something tells me your business deal went sour," Quillan prompted.

She knew he was trying to keep her mind occupied and off Frances's plight, yet he also sounded sincerely interested.

"The Grim Reaper was a silent partner we hadn't counted on. We didn't put anything on paper. Didn't think we needed to. I couldn't prove my escrow ever existed, let alone how much was in it.''

"Well, if that don't beat all. You mean, you worked that long and got nothing to show for it?''

"Not exactly. After Euphonimous passed, the new owner had a wife to do the cookin', so I was left high and dry. I cussed that old rascal and pitied myself a fair bit, too. Then, while she was cleaning out the rat's nest Euphonimous called a pantry, she found a cigar box with 'Megan' scratched on the lid. It was full of money—my lost wages.

She sent for me and handed it over without battin' an eyelash."

"Ah, well, a happy ending to the story at—"

With a grunt, Quillan flung out his arm and knocked her reeling into a mercantile's clapboard facade. As he skittered backward, a putrid stream from an upturned slop jar splattered the spot where they'd been walking only seconds before.

The barkeep looked up and shook his fist. "You mule-brained son of a bitch! I oughta drag you down here and mop the sidewalk with your backside."

Megan couldn't help laughing. Quillan was so furious, his eyes bugged like a bullfrog's and his face was beet-red.

He glanced over and beckoned her to his side. "That was awful rough talk with a lady present, and I apologize for it."

She slipped her hand into the crook of his arm. "These dainty ears have heard worse, and they haven't shriveled up and fallen off yet."

Pressing her fingers against his ribs, he chuckled good-naturedly. "You're a caution, Miss Megan. A rip-stavin', gen-you-ine caution."

Although they walked along companionably, she sensed his increasing tension. The sun never shone here. Filth ran in the gutters and swashed wide around the intersections. Gulls by the hundreds squalled and swooped down, scavenging for rotted scraps.

A shuffling vagrant with a grotesque empty socket where his left eye should be veered toward them. His pale, thin lips turned up in a sneer. "What 'ave we here? A pair of toffs out adventurin'? Or is you missionaries pledged to save our immortal souls?"

Quillan stared directly ahead. His pace stayed constant and he nudged Megan, signaling that she should do likewise. They breezed past the surly seaman as if he were invisible.

" 'Ey there, Fancy Dan. I ain't et for two days. Can ye spare a coupla bits like a Christian or do I takes my tithe off'n yer corpse?"

Megan stiffened. Icy fingers of fear traced her spine. She started to glance over her shoulder when Quillan whispered, "Don't. Just keep walking. He's ginned to his earlobes and couldn't whip a sick dog, but if we challenge him, there'll be a dozen more where he came from."

Taking a deep breath, she dipped her chin slightly to tell him she understood. She was queasy and feverish as if succumbing to ague. God help her, Frances *lived* in this grisly cesspool.

What remained of a brothel's hammered tin numerals told her they were within a block of her sister's home. Megan tugged at her hat brim. Looking up from beneath it, she could see where she was going while keeping her head discreetly bowed.

"That was eight-fourteen, right?" Quillan asked quietly.

Before she could answer, a swaggering lout with a Jezebel on each arm stepped out of a saloon in front of them. Quillan stopped midstride and Megan's neck snapped back painfully.

"Pardon us, folks," the sailor said jauntily. "We shoulda cleared the decks ... why, damned if it ain't Miss Megan O'Malley."

She met Rolf Tabor's cold black eyes. Her worst nightmare leered at her from not ten feet away. Megan felt as if her clothing were transparent—that he was ogling her naked flesh.

"You know this man?" Quillan asked incredulously.

"We're old chums, ain't we, Sprout?" Rolf taunted. "Ah, but she was a juicy piece back then. I'll bet she's seasoned into a prime cut, ain't she, Bub?"

An ominous rumble sounded from Quillan's craw. He eased Megan's hand from his arm and stepped away. "I can't abide your filthy mouth, mister."

"Quillan, please. Don't truck with—"

Tabor chuckled. "Quillan, eh? Fine name for a Nancy-boy. Whatcha plannin' to do, Bub? Wash my mouth out with soap?"

The doxies guffawed and one reached to chuck Quillan under the chin with the curving claw of her fingernail. "Learn 'im some manners, Nancy-boy. I'd give a night's earnin's to see ya try."

"You owe the lady an apology," Quillan stated menacingly.

"That's where yer wrong, mate. It's her that's beholden to me—to the tune of a crossing's wages and a ... uh, personal debt."

The barkeep slipped a hand into his trousers pocket. "I didn't ask for your memoirs, swabby." When he eased that fist behind his back, his bent knuckles were bridged by a strip of thick, raised brass.

"I ain't *askin'* for nothin' either. I figger a gent like you's got what's owed me in his poke. Hand it over, and me and Megan'll be square." Tabor scratched himself vulgarly and added, "I s'pect she'll trade it out with ya, later."

Muscles twitched along Quillan's jaw. He threw a powerful uppercut with his armored fist. The sailor ducked. Megan glimpsed the long-bladed dagger he'd drawn from its scabbard.

"Quillan! Watch out—he's got—"

Tabor raised up and drove the knife to its hilt in Quillan's belly. The barkeep doubled over. His knees wobbled as if boneless. With a gurgling groan, he collapsed against his assailant.

The killer yanked the dagger free and twisted away. Blood coated the blade like barn paint. When Quillan toppled forward, Tabor clubbed the base of his neck.

Megan's screams quickly brought a crowd of curious onlookers. They gawked, fascinated, but made no move to help Quillan or restrain Tabor. She clutched the sleeve of the man closest to her. "Get a policeman. Hurry."

"Aw, 'taint no use, lady. This be no-man's-land. Ain't no uniform gonna come within a mile."

Tabor chucked a toe of his boot under Quillan's body and rolled him over. He flipped the dying man's jacket open and snatched a leather wallet from the inside pocket.

"You won't get away with this," Megan blurted. "I'll report it to the police myself."

Tabor stood, glowering like a jackal. In two strides, he was so close, Megan smelled the cheap perfume his whores had marked him with. He traced a line across her throat with the tip of his knife. She knew a thready trail of Quillan's blood smutched her skin like a second smile.

"It ain't smart to threaten a man who ain't got nothin' to lose."

She shuddered violently. The blade nicked her just below the ear. Lazily, a drop of blood wobbled down her neck. Hate and defiance surrendered to self-preservation. She lowered her eyes submissively.

Tabor eased the dagger away and sheathed it. "Ah, that's

my girl,'' he crooned, then planted a slobbery kiss on her cheek.

It was all she could do to keep from spitting the bitter bile she tasted at his smirking face.

He turned, shoved through the circle of bystanders, and strolled casually up the street. Cackling like witches, the prostitutes sashayed off at his heels.

Megan dropped to her knees beside Quillan's still body. Tears poured down her face and splashed on the bloodstain spreading across his white shirt. Gently, she closed his sightless eyes, then laid her head on his chest and sobbed for the friend she knew only as "Quillan."

Scuffling feet and muttered reinactments of the murder told her that the onlookers were dispersing. The excitement was over.

A hand brushed her back and a raspy voice whispered in her ear, "Megan, darlin', let's go home."

She cringed. Tabor? No . . . but who? Easing cautiously onto her haunches, she looked up at the man leaning over her. Gasping in horror, she covered her mouth to keep from screaming.

Half of his face and neck were pearl-slick and shiny; the features melted like a wax figurine left overlong on a sunny windowsill. The other's perfection only intensified the gruesome contrast. One eye swaled cruelly at the corner, but there was no mistaking that bottomless sapphire color.

"I'll take you to Franny," Oran said, offering her his hand. "The undertaker's been sent for. I'll come back and stay with the body until he gets here."

Later, as she scooped water from a dented bucket and splashed it on her face, Megan pondered how different their family reunion had been from what she'd anticipated.

Rather than let out a whoop and hug Frances tightly, she'd greeted her woodenly. As Megan recovered from the initial shock of Quillan's death, others hit her like waves crashing over a ship's prow.

There was no furniture to speak of in the Dannellys' one-room, squalid flat. Flimsy crates held jar lids fitted with candle stubs. A straw pallet and dirty blanket served as the family's bed.

Sitting on an ottoman with clumps of horsehair spewing from its upholstery, she'd recoiled and tucked her legs under when a rat the size of a prairie dog swaggered across the floor.

Tommy, her carrot-haired nephew, giggled and toddled after the rodent as if it were a peek-a-boo playmate. The barefooted child often tripped over the hem of his hand-me-down undershirt, yet a smile was as much a part of his features as his father's brilliant blue eyes.

"When they brought Oran home to die," Frances recounted, "his face, arm, torso, and leg were black and plashy like broiled meat. He was screaming in agony."

Megan knew by her expression and hushed voice that describing that moment was the same as reliving it.

"Me and God were the only ones who believed he'd live. Many nights, I wondered if it would've been kinder to let him die—to give him relief from the pain.

"Our savin's—sparse as they were—went for ointments, gauze, and laudanum. The firemen's wives brought food baskets from time to time and the men passed the hat for collections, but it wasn't near enough. And I couldn't leave Oran alone so's I could find a position."

To Megan, her sister's matchstick thinness and hugely rounded abdomen looked almost obscene. Frances had said Oran was still too weak to work. They'd lived on handouts and scraps foraged from rubbish bins for nearly six months, and there'd be another mouth to feed very soon.

Why hadn't Frances told her of their plight? How had they fallen into such dire straits?

As if she'd read Megan's mind, Frances continued, "Oran was earnin' good wages. We didn't have much put by, though—we'd just moved into a pretty cottage near the Golden Gate—"

"With twin bay windows and a Pacific view?"

Her sister ignored the remark. "The doctor confirmed my suspicions that another baby was comin' the day Oran got hurt. Afterward, our landlady couldn't afford to let us stay when we didn't have the rent money. From there, we've gone from pillar to post."

Megan's insides churned. She couldn't remember ever being so angry. "Why'd you lie to me in your letters? I could've sent money—I'd have come and helped you."

Frances's weary eyes rimmed with tears. "Because the last person I'd admit failure to is you."

Silence lingered expectantly as Megan weighed those

words and measured her reply. Frances was ashamed of their circumstances, regardless of what brought them about. There was no reason to be. Megan believed the only shame attached to poverty was the acceptance of it. Those who struggled against its grip should be prideful of their ambition.

"Are you sorry you left Ireland?" she asked.

Her sister blinked in confusion. "Why, heavens no, not a'tall."

"Do you wish you'd never met Oran? Never married him?"

"Of course not! He's the most wonderful man I've ever known."

"And what of your children? Wouldn't things have been easier without Tommy and without the child you're carrying now?"

"Why are you asking me such awful questions? Children are God's greatest gifts. I couldn't be more blessed."

Megan stroked Frances's cheek. "Then how is it you've failed? The house with starched curtains and a garden out back will come again. I'll do everything I can to see you get them, if only you'll let me."

"Da and Mama must be spinnin' in their graves," she moaned. "Bad enough to take charity from strangers. I can't bear takin' it from my baby sister."

"Oh, Frances, won't you ever understand? I haven't been your baby sister for a long time. I'm a woman grown—one who loves you dearly and wants to give the same as you'd give me. That's not charity, damn it, that's *family*."

A flicker of a smile edged Frances's lips. As it spread, the pinched, haunted look vanished from her face. "It's wise you are, Megan. I've mothered you far too long."

She chuckled and asked coyly, "So, there's to be no more Miss Bossy Britches houndin' at my heels?"

"We-ll now, I'm not so sure about that. You've been known to give as good as you get . . . baby sister."

When Oran returned, they were hugging, laughing, and crying all at the same time. He scratched his head. "From wailin' to weepin' with joy in the span of an hour. Hell, I'll never understand how a woman's mind works."

Sobering immediately, Megan asked, "Quillan has . . . is he gone?"

Oran nodded. "The undertaker knew him. Said he'd make proper arrangements for the buryin'."

A heaviness in her chest made speaking impossible for a moment. "Well then, I have some arrangements to make myself. After I talk with the police—"

"Oh, Megan, no," Frances blurted. "Oran told me about Tabor's threats. That thug knows where to find you, and'll kill you for it, sure as the world."

"Franny's right. It'll do no good to put yourself at risk, anyhow. Them coppers don't care whose blood gets spilled on the waterfront as long as it's not their own."

Megan held up a hand to quiet them. "Spar 'til you're breathless if you've a mind to, but the police will be told. As for Tabor, I'm quittin' the city on tomorrow's stage. He'll not get the chance to harm a hair on my head."

"But you only just got here."

"I never planned on stayin' longer than a day. There's a cook's job awaitin' at a silver mine in Pioche, Nevada. When I'm not rustlin' victuals for the miners, I'll be swingin' the stout end of a pickax, prospectin'."

Oran and Frances traded glances, then stared at her as if she'd sprouted a second head.

Megan laughed aloud at their expressions as she anchored her hands on her hips. "One way or the other, I reckon this family's damn well due some good luck. And I'm promisin', you'll be the first to know when it comes to call."

# Chapter Thirteen

What dust she hadn't inhaled or swallowed left muddy trailings in every crease in Megan's face and neck. The sun's unrelenting glare and the stagecoach's cramped quarters made her feel like venison broiling on a spit.

Seated across from her, Lambert Jacobs, owner and publisher of the daily *Pioche Record,* vainly mopped his brow with a monogrammed handkerchief. Despite the heat, his charcoal broadcloth suit and vest were securely buttoned and his tie noosed around his neck as if he were on his way to Sunday services.

Megan regarded her wilted bombazine suit and vowed she'd burn it the moment they arrived at their destination. What had been a most enchanting ensemble but a few weeks ago now served as stifling penance for impulsive self-indulgence.

Slouched against the coach's other wall, flint-eyed Moses Keegan looked blessedly cool in riveted Levi's, his shirt collar gaped and sleeves rolled up, even though the fabric stuck to the twenty-year-old's chest like a second skin—as did the holster tucked between his thigh and the bowed wood.

Jacobs regarded Megan with a bemused expression. "Are you sure we're going to Pioche, or is it fiery perdition we're bound for?"

"Never heared of no Perdition in these parts," grumbled the exceedingly rotund, excessively perfumed tart wedged between the two men. "But sure as my name's Clarissa Crabtree, it's hotter'n *hell* in here."

Megan sighed deeply. "Aye, but if it's a spatula I'm to wield for my keep, I'd best get accustomed to it."

"Why a pretty piece like you wants to hire on for a pot rustler, I cain't say," Clarissa harrumphed. "I may be too fat for frolickin', but my girls keeps me wallowin' in velvet

and whorin's a damn sight easier on the back than wrestlin'
a twenty-egg skillet."

"*Miss* Crabtree, I'll thank you to comport yourself like
a lady," Felicity Blount cautioned. Clad in black from chin
to shoe tips, Megan thought her seatmate had the peckish
look of one who'd begun life colicky and never fully
recovered.

"Well, I ain't no lady, and I ain't no hippo-cryte about
it neither, like some folks I could mention."

"Forgive me for attributing qualities you so obviously
lack, but for all our sakes, a pretense of gentility would be
most welcome. Miss O'Malley's exposure to crudity will
come soon enough."

"Hah! High time she learned, the only difference 'twixt
a lady and a whore is that a whore's smart enough to palm
a man's money a'fore she—"

"That'll do, Clarissa," Moses growled. "This coop's too
sparse for a hen fight."

They rode in a tight-lipped silence for several minutes
before Missus Blount proclaimed, "It's my duty as a Christian to discourage you from hiring on as a mine camp cook,
Miss O'Malley. Those miners are scurrilous ruffians and a
woman who casts her lot among them is . . . well—I'll just
say it right out—is just asking to suffer unspeakable
depravities."

Jacobs chortled and brought his handkerchief to his face
as if damming a sneeze. But the twinkle in his eyes didn't
escape Megan's notice—or Felicity Blount's.

"My concerns strike you as humorous, Mister Jacobs? I
daresay you'd think differently if you'd fathered a daughter
and not a son."

"No, Missus Blount, I wouldn't. Ambition gains my respect regardless of which gender possesses it."

"Then I presume Miss Crabtree's vocation is an 'ambitious' one, by your definition," she retorted snidely.

"More to the point, madam, unlike you, I don't consider
anyone's life or lifestyle any of my business."

"Might I remind you that Blount's General Mercantile
is one of your newspaper's biggest advertisers? I'm sure my
Hiram will be most distressed to learn how liberally you
regard our community's lascivious element."

"What's 'lascivious' mean?" Clarissa whispered to
Moses.

"Couldn't say, but I don't reckon it's a compliment."

Jacobs directed a withering gaze at the shopkeeper's wife. "Dear lady, your beloved Hiram is quite aware which side of Main Street keeps your bread so richly buttered."

While she realized she'd be wise to sit quietly and watch Nevada Territory's parched barrens lurch past the window, Megan couldn't contain herself any longer.

Turning toward Missus Blount, she said evenly, "I appreciate your frettin' for me, but there's nothing more evil than an empty gullet and no means to fill it. These hands won't rest 'til I know that gnaw's been cured—permanent—in me and my kin."

"But there are other ways of earning money without risking your . . . reputation. I'm sure my husband can be persuaded to hire you to clerk at our store."

"At two dollars a day plus board?"

"Oh, my goodness! We couldn't afford that much, but—"

"Girl, you'd make twice that layin' on a feather bed if'n ya went to work for me," Clarissa chirped.

Jacobs cleared his throat to silence the debate. "I don't believe Miss O'Malley is in need of advice or of alternative employment opportunities. Might I suggest we curtail the discussion and traverse the last few miles in peace?"

Missus Blount was still sputtering and glaring at the publisher when the driver reined the stage to a halt in front of Pioche's clapboard Wells, Fargo office.

Preceding the women out the door, Jacobs offered a helping hand first to Clarissa, who stepped out and curtsied graciously, and then to Missus Blount. The latter grasped it between her forefinger and thumb as one would a shatted diaper. His gallantry was rewarded with a dismissive sniff before she stalked away.

Shaking his head, Jacobs reached up and steadied Megan's descent. "May I show you to the Sanders and Meredith office? It's a couple of miles from town and loath that I am to echo Felicity Blount's meddlesomeness, I don't advise you to travel there alone."

Megan chuckled. "My sister and I sailed the Atlantic and lived in parts of Boston and San Francisco that'd give Missus Blount a fatal dyspepsia. I think I can hash a short buggy ride."

Jacobs swiped the dust from his shoulders and blew off his bowler before tapping it in place. "The nearest law is over four hundred miles away," he informed in a fatherly tone. "To the best of my knowledge, none of those buried in Boot Hill have died of natural causes. Indulge an old man's offer of chaperonage, eh? It's been many a year since he's shared a buggy seat with such a delightful young woman."

"I notice you didn't extend the same courtesy to Miss Crabtree."

"I believe the inestimable Clarissa is quite capable of fending off unseemly advances without my assistance."

"Truth to tell," Megan whispered, "I don't reckon she's 'fended' very many of 'em."

The publisher belly-laughed and waggled a plump finger at her. "I like your sass, Miss O'Malley, if you don't mind my saying so."

"It's 'Megan' to my friends."

"Count me among them and call me 'Lambert,' if you please. Now informalities aside, may I assist you into my humble rig?"

As the couple drove companionably along Main Street, he pointed out landmarks and shared anecdotes like a tour guide.

"Pioche is a workingman's town, and like most places born of a rich hole in the ground, not the prettiest piece of real estate you'll ever see."

With most buildings constructed of wooden framing walled by taut-stretched canvas, they could, and literally did, spring up overnight. In a few sections, structures were aligned in traditional rows, but much of the city was plotted in a slap-bang style like seeds broadcast by a giant's hand.

"There's about seven thousand people living here now, give or take a few hundred," he explained. "And more than its share wear more aliases than horn buttons."

Along with its constantly tinkling piano music, ever-flowing whiskey, and crooked faro games, the part of town decent folks ignored was home to mothers' nightmares known as "Sweetmouth Annie," the bottle-blond twins "Venus and Apollo," and scores of other lace-and-feathered floozies.

Shootists who made reputations more on luck than good aim looked for trouble and usually found it. In the gambling halls and saloons, grifters easily separated the liquor-stupid from their pay envelopes and pokes.

As they gained the west end, nearing the scrubby rise known as Treasure Hill, Megan asked why the streets zigzagged and curved as if traced by a rattlesnake.

"Actually, they were laid out by horse sense," Lambert answered. "Instinctively, ore wagon teams follow ravines and secure the best footing whether there's a road beneath their hooves or not. Instead of holding the horses to narrow, man-made tracks just so they'd be ruler-straight, teamsters let the animals pick where to put them, then cut them plenty wide."

She was astounded to learn that less than a decade earlier, before a band of Paiutes traded a cache of silver bullion they called "panacre" for food and clothing, the area was nothing but a desolate valley ringed by nondescript foothills.

Despite the boomtown's eruption, the Central Pacific Railroad still came no closer than Palisade, almost three hundred miles north. Otherwise, between Pioche and Salt Lake City, Phoenix, or Los Angeles, there was, as their stage driver had quipped, but "a whole lotta nothin'."

The open carriage certainly gave more air than the coach had, but Megan still felt as if she were melting. *Missus Blount will be scandalized,* she thought, *but it's a man's britches and a linsey-woolsey shirt I'll be buyin' for work tomorrow.*

Lambert had hardly reined his mare to a halt when a lanky, bedeviled-looking man pushed out the Sanders and Meredith Mining Company's main shaft house's door.

"If you ain't Megan O'Malley, then lie to me and say you is," he bawled as mournfully as a hound.

"Well, I suppose it depends on who's askin' and why," she replied.

"Barlow P. Bainbridge is the name, but you can call me 'Barlow P.' and save wind. I'm the manager of this here glory hole, and I reckon I'm also a man sore in need of a woman."

"Now listen here—" Lambert started indignantly.

"Aw hell, Jacobs, don't get your braces in a swivet. I ain't defamin' this gal and you know it. Fact is, I got me sixty hungry pick-swingers a'comin' up the hoist in a couple of hours an' no grub to feed 'em with."

"Sanchez walk out on you?"

"Nope. Just weren't in no mood fer workin' I'd guess.

Gonna fire the bastard next time—sorry, ma'am—next time I sees him. Damned greaser—sorry, ma'am—ain't never been more dependable than a tetched mule."

"You're not expecting Miss O'Malley to tie on an apron this instant, are you?"

"Yup."

"That's absolutely absurd! Why—"

"Gentlemen, please, since I'm so much a part of this conversation, do either of you mind my joining it?" Megan inquired sweetly.

After giving them both a chance to tuck their chins in embarrassment, she continued, "Barlow P., I'd be delighted to rustle up a meal for your men ... at double wages for the inconvenience, of course."

"Oh, yes, ma'am. Double wages, sure thang. Thank ya, ma'am." He scrambled to help her from the carriage.

"And, Lambert, it's grateful I am for the lovely ride and the pleasure of your company. Perhaps we'll meet again soon."

Her escort looked past her toward the mine manager. "What time should Miss O'Malley be finished tonight, Barlow P.?"

" 'Long 'bout ten, I'd reckon."

Affixing her with a no-nonsense gaze, Lambert said sternly, "My son David will return at a quarter to the hour to fetch you to your hotel," then clucked the bay into motion.

The camp's kitchen was a tacked-on affair twice again the size of Euphonimous Tripp's Virginia City restaurant. Few mine operators fed their crews, but Jeb Sanders and Carter Meredith believed a well-nourished miner was more alert and made fewer mistakes.

The employees started and finished later than at other mines. They worked eleven-hour days and were paid for only ten plus meals, but none balked at the arrangement.

Though the kitchen's exterior was sided by patchworked scrap lumber no self-respecting carpenter would claim, its interior walls were whitewashed and the wood floor much cleaner than Megan expected. The rectangular space was regrettably short on breeze, but long on elbow room.

She regarded the twin stoves, a sink deep enough to bathe in, a ten-foot-long butcher-block worktable, and wide

oak food safes with punched-tin panels approvingly, then
set to the task at hand.

Just as she'd hoped, a peek into a cupboard beside a
washbasin yielded a man's soiled but serviceable trousers
and a nubby cotton shirt.

Listening carefully for the sound of approaching footsteps, she yanked the britches up under her skirt, then giggled when they slithered back down around her ankles the
minute she let go of the waistband. Bunching them tightly
at her midriff, she tottered over and rifled several drawers
before finding a ball of twine and cutting a length to use
as a belt.

Struggling out of her dress as quickly as she could, she
dove into the scratchy, open-necked shirt. It, too, was several sizes too large. She wrinkled her nose as the briny
scent of its owner filled her nostrils.

The voluminous fabric bunched around her hips when
she tucked it into her trousers, but she couldn't have cared
less about her clownish appearance. For the first time that
day, she didn't feel like a winter-pelted animal sweltering
before the spring shed.

A cauldron of pinto beans simmering on one stove
begged for a pinch of salt, and she answered it accordingly.
Then she climbed a four-legged stool and snatched two
smoked hams from their ceiling hooks. Finding roasters
large enough to accommodate them, she basted the meat
with brown sugar, butter, and water and slid them into the
ovens to warm and moisten.

After setting a huge crockery bowl on the worktable, she
scurried over and cranked a goodly measure of flour
through the sifter. *I don't know whether the men groaned
or grinned at what Sanchez put on their plates,* she mused,
*but my baking powder biscuits are lighter than an angel's
eyelashes. Sopped with sweet butter and honey, I warrant
they'll cut a sure path to these miners' hearts.*

Over the next two hours, Megan's calves began aching
from the paths she cut back and forth across the kitchen
and out to the woodpile. One stove burned down to ashes
before she notice, and keeping two kindling-eaters stoked
was a constant, hellishly hot chore.

Ferreting out the necessary utensils and supplies had
taken minutes she didn't have to spare. Too hastily jerking
the second ham from the oven sent the meat skittering

forward. Drops of steaming pan liquor peppered her forearms.

From the adjacent dining hall, she heard the men grumbling for their dinner. There was no time to waste on tears.

Like a madwoman she dashed from stove to pantry to sawbuck filling bowls and platters with beans, ham slices, bread and butter pickles, canned peaches, and a variety of condiments.

Later, listening through a crack in the door, she grinned when she heard gruff voices proclaim:

"Best grub we ever had."

"Look at them crazy Cornish Jacks fightin' over the biscuits!"

"Sanchez sure as hell ain't cookin' tonight. Wonder who is?"

"Dunno. Don't care, long as he don't take over ag'in."

The four miners whose turn it was to serve and clear the meal reported a steady stream of compliments, yet Megan was disgusted with herself for making the hungry men wait.

"Tell the boys there'll be a double batch of biscuits and a tinned fruit cobbler for dessert tomorrow night," she instructed her helpers, hoping the treats would make up for her tardiness. She'd have told them herself, but Barlow P. had made it clear that she was not to "get anywhar's near them gopher-brained rascals."

When Barlow P. came by well after supper, her arm was stinging like fire and her back aching from washing dishes bent over the high-sided sink. He stopped short, staring at her, then eased a hand beneath his battered felt hat and scratched his head.

"Coulda swore I hired me a gal this afternoon," he drawled.

Megan made a face at him as she rinsed the last of five dozen plates and stacked it on the drainboard. "You did. I just figured I was worth more to you alive than dead from the heat prostration."

"Never did seem sensical that women wear all them damned—sorry, ma'am—them petticoats and foofaraws and such. And Sanchez won't miss the getup, no how. Fool went and got a Arkansas toothpick stuck betwixt his ribs tonight."

"He's dead?"

"Colder'n a wagon tire. Got any fixin's left from supper?"

She hesitated shuddering slightly at the thought of wearing a dead man's clothing. "Uh . . . no, sorry. Not a speck. I'd be happy to—"

"Naw. Ain't that hungry anyway. You et your vittles a'fore you fed them vultures, I hope."

She wrinkled her nose, then chuckled. "Food's the last thing I wanted after smellin' it, stirrin' it, and scrapin' the leavings into a slop can."

Shifting his weight, he asked hesitantly, "You'll be here in the mornin' won't ya? 'Bout six? Men gets here 'round eight for breakfast."

"It'll be ready. And on time."

" 'Preciate yer helpin' me out, Miss Megan. Sorry I'm haffin' to work ya like a plow ox from the get-go."

With that, he shambled out again before she had a chance to respond.

It was nearing midnight before the last flour sack towel was draped over the table's edge to dry. She glanced toward the washbowl and considered freshening up and changing back into her own clothes, then decided the hotel clerk could go hang if he didn't like the look of her.

The flimsy door seemed as heavy as iron as she pushed it open and stepped out onto the hard ground.

Lambert Jacobs's buggy was silhouetted in the moonlight, his bay pawing the dust impatiently. A tall, broadshouldered young man stood beside it.

"Miss O'Malley? I'm David Jacobs. My father sent me to take you to the hotel."

Suddenly wishing she'd remembered Lambert's parting remark, Megan merely shrugged and smiled wanly as she looked up at his son.

He was at least a foot taller than she; his thick, black hair fell in waves to his shoulders, framing an angular face with prominent cheekbones. Even in the sparse light she could see that he was an exceptionally handsome man, but it was his quicksilver eyes that almost took her breath away.

She felt as if she were drowning in their depths—and would gladly stay submerged there for an eternity.

# Chapter Fourteen

Over the next several days, Megan dedicated herself to bringing order to her predecessor's chaos. On one shelf alone, a ruptured bag of salt slouched against jars of marmalade, a stoppered bottle of Perry Davis's Vegetable Pain Killer, various tinned stores, and half-smoked cigar butts.

"Sanchez must've been blindfolded when he put this stuff away," she grumbled, starting to clear away the mess. "Or blind drunk."

She felt a tap on her shoulder and spun around, slapping a hand over her pounding heart. "Jesus, Mary, and—Barlow P.! You scared me out of a year's growth."

He waggled the toothpick clenched between his teeth. "Hmmph. Figger you're done growin' anyhow. I got an errand in town. Wanta go with me?"

She glanced ruefully at the strewn floor and ransacked cabinets. "I do need some things from the mercantile . . . but I probably shouldn't . . ."

He took a step toward the door. "Suit yerself."

"Wait—can't you give me a minute to think?" she stalled, mentally listing the day's chores and the hour needed to complete them.

"Huh-*uhh*. A thinkin' woman's more dangerous than a Comanche war party."

"Is that so?" she sparred, wadding her canvas apron into a ball. "So, then, what's a thinkin' man?"

He edged away, his eyes fixed on the cloth. "I dunno."

The hurled apron flattened against his chest. "Neither do I. Never met one." Grinning hugely, she added, "Now fetch that spring wagon. We're goin' to town."

The moseying buckskin team lurched them over every rut and rock in the winding road. Gripping the wagon's splintered seat tightly, Megan studied the manager's profile.

He had the leather-grained, weathered look of a man

who'd spent more nights in bedrolls than on feather mattresses. At the corners of his eyes and above the bridge of
his nose, deep, tined creases said life had dealt him as many
humorous moments as heartaches.

"How old are you, Barlow P.?"

"Oh, 'bout twice older'n you."

"Where you from?"

He glanced at her quizzically. "Growed up on a farm in
Indiany. Larned right quick I weren't cut out to be no
sodbuster."

She tried picturing him at the business end of a plow and
almost giggled aloud. Without a doubt, Barlow P. was as
restless as a bottle fly. He couldn't light anywhere for
longer than a few minutes.

"Have you ever been married?"

"Je-hosophat, gal," he snorted. "You're nosier than a
sow rootin' slops this mornin'."

She simply arched an eyebrow and waited for an answer.

"No, I ain't never been married and don't aim to get
that way." Noting her purposefully impassive expression,
he recited irritably, "I got me a fourth-grade ed-jication,
served under Sherman durin' the war, was raised Pres-by-
terian, vote Re-publican, and wear size eleven boots. Anythin' else ya wanna know?"

"Uh-huh . . . ."

"Whut?"

Megan smiled prettily before inquiring, "Aren't you glad
you asked me to come with you today?"

# Chapter Fifteen

David caught a glimpse of Megan through the *Record*'s plate glass window just before a caravan of ore wagons blocked his view.

Tipped back in his father's swivel chair, boots crossed at the ankles, and heels anchored on the desk, he tapped his toes together impatiently.

God, what a thoroughbred she is, he sighed to himself. But stubborn as a crooked nail. "Thank you kindly, but I can find my way to the hotel," she'd insisted in a low, melodic brogue when he'd offered regular transportation the night they met.

And she wasn't merely playing hard to get either, he admitted ruefully.

Once the dust settled, the scenery outside was once again to his liking. David stared at Megan with the shamelessness of a man certain he wouldn't get caught.

She stood on the boardwalk in front of Blount's Mercantile, peering expectantly west toward Pritchard's Fast Freight Office. Long-limbed for such a petite woman, her stiff, new jeans were thickly cuff-rolled above her boot laces. That the pants pockets curved snugly over her derriere, and the center seam defined a cleavage no cowhand ever brandished, did not escape David's notice.

He let out a long whistle as his eyes roamed upward. Megan's tucked-in shirt billowed over her belt in the back, but draped provocatively over her high, full breasts. She stretched to skim a few stray hairs from her forehead, then tightened the kerchief cinching her sable mane.

To his eyes, she was more feminine by far than any woman he'd ever seen decked out in ruffles and lace. A stream of images flickered in his mind. He groaned at the effect she was having on him even from yards away.

Pushing back from the desk, he slipped a finger under

his collar to ease its choke hold, then rose and headed out to join her.

"Good morning, Megan," he said as he strode up beside her.

She tilted her head and smiled broadly. "Why, hullo, David. Have you some shopping to do, too?"

"No, as a matter of fact, I'm playing hooky. I'm supposed to be proofreading classified ads while Father is at the coroner's office compiling tomorrow's obituaries."

She grimaced. "Gruesome . . . and a mite frightenin', to boot."

"Pioche came by its shoot-'em-up reputation quite honestly, you know. That's why I offered hack service your first night at Sanders and Meredith."

Her eyes sparkled merrily. "Aye, Barlow P.'s told me stories that, like he says, would 'put ringlets in an Apache's hair.'" Jabbing the air between them with her index finger, she snickered, "And darned if he hasn't found cause to come to town every mornin' and night about the time my shift begins or ends, too."

David cocked his head and crossed his arms against his chest. "I'm certainly glad to hear you're not wandering the streets alone, only what's that old buzzard got that I don't have? Besides you sitting next to him in a spring wagon twice a day."

Her face reddened, and she glanced over her shoulder as if suddenly fearful for the safety of her packages stacked on a nearby bench.

"I . . . um, Barlow P. ought to be along any minute. He's fetchin' a shipment of bits that was due in today."

*She's as innocent as a newborn fawn,* he marveled. *I wonder how many hearts she's broken without ever knowing it. And damned if my own isn't thumping like a smitten schoolboy's.*

"Better finish what I came for then," he said more casually than he felt. "There's a dance at the Young Men's Social Club Saturday night. I'd be honored if you'd go with me."

Megan gasped as if he'd asked her to walk down a church aisle in her shimmy. "Oh, but I *couldn't*!"

"And why not? Don't tell me another fellow's beaten me to the punch."

"Not a'tall ... it's just that, uh, I don't know how to dance."

"Well, I do, and I'd like nothing better than teaching you."

Thoughtfully, she looked down at her outfit and frowned. "That's mighty kind of you, David ... except I don't have a proper dress to wear, either. I won't be shamin' you by goin' in my work clothes."

That quiet, honest confession made him long to wrap his arms around her and hold her close. Such a beautiful, spirited woman should have trunks full to bursting with gowns and finery—whatever her heart desired. And lucky would be the man afforded that privilege.

"Megan, I wouldn't be ashamed of you if you wore a flea-bitten horse blanket and a feather headdress. Please— go to the dance with me. I'll show you a good time, I promise."

Her head waggled a gentle "no" at the same time her dark doe eyes hinted "yes." After a few moments hesitation, she grinned at him mischievously. "All right. If you're willin' to risk it, then so am I."

After giving her the particulars, David walked briskly back toward the office before she had a chance to change her mind. Looking back to wave from the *Record*'s threshold, he was surprised to see her dash into Blount's with her arms full of wrapped packages.

# Chapter Sixteen

Megan slumped cross-legged on the kitchen's worktable, her back to the blessedly cool breeze drifting in the kitchen door.

"Damn and double damn," she hissed when the needle jabbed her already tender fingertip. She stuck it in her mouth for comfort and to keep blood droplets from smirching the yards of posy-printed calico heaped in her lap.

The screen door slapped shut. "Coffee on the stove?" Barlow P. asked as he made his way toward his dented tin cup dangling from a hook above the sink.

"Um-hmm," she confirmed, still tending her wound.

"Got any canned cow juice?"

Megan jerked her finger out and cracked, "Yeah, but I toted the last of it to the spring house this mornin'."

"What the hell'd ya do that fer?"

"Saints preserve us, Barlow P. Are you blind, or just helpless? The milk's there in the locker, right at the end of your nose, like it's always been."

While dribbling the lightener into his cup, he muttered, "A man tries to pass the time of day with a female and gets his head blowed off fer his trouble."

"What was that again?"

"Aw, nothin'."

Leaning his flat behind against the sink, he sniffed after the aroma of beef brisket roasting in the oven and grunted approvingly. Then, he squinted one eye and asked, "What's that mess of flowerdy stuff you're fussin' over? Ya ain't turnin' silly on me and makin' curtains for this ol' grub shack, are ya?"

She held up a length of the yard goods and said proudly, "I'm sewing me a dress for the dance Saturday night. It'll be pretty when I'm done, don't you think?"

"Hmmph. Steppin' out with that Jacobs boy, I reckon."

"David Jacobs is not a *boy,* and no, I'm not 'steppin' out' with him. We're just friends."

He took a slow, thoughtful sip of his coffee. His Adam's apple bounced when he swallowed. After tracing the edge of his brushy mustaches with his tongue, he grunted, "Sez who?"

"Says me, that's who. What's the matter with you, Barlow P.? You're twitching like a pouncy tomcat."

He glowered at her, then ambled to the stove for a refill. "Yup, that Jacobs feller's friendly all right. Ask any filly this side of Bullionville—she'll tell ya how friendly he is."

Megan laughed, shaking her head. "You sound more like my da every day—or Felicity Blount. I've got more folks fearin' for my virtue than Carter has oats."

In four strides he'd recrossed the room, then hitched one leg over the corner of the table and settled himself. A lazy, lopsided grin spread across his homely face. "If'n a man likened me to that vinegar-pussed harpy, I'd shoot 'im."

He fixed his gaze on the cup cradled in both hands. "Now listen up, gal. I ain't knowed ya long, but long enough that it'd vex me fierce to see ya get hurt. Seen too many hearts broke from sweet-talkin' in the moonlight and forgetfulness the next mornin'."

His bagged, doleful eyes met hers directly. "Don't want that happenin' to you, Megan." Squirming somewhat, he rasped a fingernail across his stubbled jaw. "Hell, a good cook's scarcer than hen's teeth 'round here. Damned if I wanta break in a new one anytime soon."

She smiled at him, thinking, Mister Bainbridge, if you aren't just like a cactus—prickly on the outside, and soft on the inside.

Digging through the crumpled fabric for the seam she was stitching, Megan said reassuringly, "Cupid can keep his arrows quivered far as I'm concerned, Barlow P."

"Cupid my sweet a— Aunt Gertrude. It ain't no buck-naked baby I'm worried about."

"Truth to tell, I'm a'thinkin' it's a guilty conscience naggin' you," she teased. "I'll bet you've caused a fair share of female heart trouble, too."

When he answered, his voice was harsh and cold. "Jes' once, gal. That was once too—"

The mine's steam whistle shrieked to life. Megan clapped her hands over her ears. Barlow P.'s face went slack, then

set like steel. He slammed his cup down on the table and
sprinted out the door.

No sooner than it reached full pitch, the piercing bleat
faded away. She sighed with relief. The short duration
probably meant a heat-sickened miner was being hoisted
up for a rest.

Other than at mealtimes and shift changes, that signal
harkened grimmer tidings. The longer it blew, the more
serious the trouble. It not only alerted miners in all the
Sanders and Meredith shafts to an emergency, its echoes,
heard clear to Pioche, were cries for help.

Comstock. Humboldt. Clear Creek. Barlow P.'s bloodcurdling accounts of prior tragedies resounded in Megan's
mind. She prayed she'd never feel the shudder of a tunnel
collapsing into a miner's graveyard—hear that banshee wail
for the men who were buried alive.

"Bless you, Frances," Megan sighed, twirling in front of
the pier glass. "You had to lash me to a hearth bench to
teach me needlework, but it's grateful I am to you now."

Her skin was creamy as froth in a milking pail against the
dress's crimson background sprinkled with tiny periwinkles.
Missus Blount was so delighted by Megan's sudden interest
in ladies' fashions, she'd donated one of her daughter's
dress patterns to the cause. That young Constance Blount
was built like a pickle barrel with legs was dismissed with
a remark that "minor" alterations might be needed.

Row upon row of tucks in the bodice and up the back
decoratively reduced it to a kid-glove fit. Rather than cut
the skirt smaller, Megan simply gathered the fabric more
tightly before stitching it to the pointed yoke. As a result,
the material not only belled gracefully over her hips, her
waist looked small enough for a man's hands to span.

Gazing in wonderment at the lovely woman she saw re-
flected in the mirror, Megan whispered, "I am pretty,
Mama . . . like you always said I'd be." She added wistfully,
"Almost as pretty as you were."

A knock jolted her out of her reverie. She took a deep,
calming breath and let it out slowly before opening the
door.

David cast an imposing shadow along the Baedeker Hotel's narrow, gas-lit hallway. His broad-shouldered, lean
physique was the kind for which claw-hammer coats, waist-

coats, and knife-creased trousers were made. The nap of the black felt Stetson he clasped against his chest showed scuffs from a recent brushing.

His eyes widened when he saw her, and his mouth dropped open. "Holy shit . . ."

She chuckled at his dumbfounded expression. "Well, and good evening to you, *too,* Mister Jacobs."

A ruddy flush spread upward from his collar like flame to dry tinder. "Oh, Lord, Megan, I'm truly sorry."

She waved a hand dismissively, then reached for her shawl. "I'll take it for a compliment and be done with it, if it's all the same to you."

Draping her wrap over her shoulders, she turned to lock the door. Gently, David lifted her hair from beneath the delicately crocheted folds. She shivered at the unexpected, tender intimacy. She laid a hand over the arm he offered and they started toward the stairway.

Willy Ray Mahoney, the night clerk, did a double take as they crossed the lobby.

" 'Izzat *you,* Miss O'Malley?" he boomed, his cigar's arc halting midway to his mouth. "Jay-sus, you look like a lady."

Megan rolled her eyes up at her escort. "I never realized a dress could drive so many men to profanity."

"Ah, but it's not the dress, my dear, lovely as it is," David fairly growled. "It's the beautiful woman who's wearing it. I expect every buck in the district will flutter around you like fireflies this evening."

She bowed her head demurely to hide a sly grin. I'll wager there'll be many a dewy maiden hoping for your attention, too, she thought. Never before had a man set her heart hammering in her chest. She felt as if she were floating on air, and that was as disconcerting as it was bewitching.

Sitting beside him in his father's rig, she took great gulps of the cool evening air to settle her nerves. In the distance, light beamed from a mullion-windowed mansion rising from a northern foothill.

The golden pools silhouetted a towering, colonnaded portico that spanned the width of the red brick facade. On the second story, four pairs of Palladian windows stared out over the town like shining sentinels. Several buggies lined the crescent driveway.

"Who lives in that grand house on the hill?" Megan asked, pointing toward it. "One of the mine owners?"

"No, that's the home of Missus Delia Terhune, the Widow Terhune, most folks call her. A wealthy Georgia belle who settled here practically the day F.L.A. Pioche founded our fair city."

"Why here?"

David shrugged. "No one knows. But she's been the queen bee from day one, that's for sure. I couldn't begin to estimate how much money she's donated to charity and for civic improvements. Unfortunately, what pies the Widow Terhune doesn't have her benevolent fingers in, Artemus Rath holds in his vile clutches."

"Him, I know about. Barlow P. says if there was any justice in this world, Rath'd be shot, stabbed, horse-whipped, and hanged twice for good measure."

"If it's trouble you're looking for, Artemus Rath's the man to see. If it's trouble you're *in,* the Widow Terhune may be your only salvation. They're the district's kingpins, each in their own way."

As they turned onto Cedar Street, the haunting melody of "Lorena" drifted from the Young Men's Social Club's open door. Megan had loved the soulful ballad the first time she'd heard it played during the Hotel Drake's Grand Ball. She hummed along quietly as David guided her toward the entrance.

Once inside, she was surprised to see that the fiddler coaxing out the last chords of the refrain was a woman. Her lace-trimmed snowy gown was suitable for a maiden bride, but the face peeping from beneath a calico, coal scuttle bonnet was withered like an apple head doll's. With her eyes closed in rapt concentration, her gnarled fingers plied the instrument's strings with a gossamer touch.

The guitar player leaned forward and laid his hand on the fiddler's shoulder. Instantly she stopped playing. The crowd burst into rousing applause. When she raised her head, Megan saw a jagged red scar running from earlobe to earlobe.

David leaned close. "We call her 'Miracle.' Indians attacked her wagon train, tortured, then murdered everyone in it and set the wagons on fire. They punctured her eardrums and slit her throat, but by some miracle, she survived—hence, her name. A prospecting party found her leaning against a boulder, playing her violin. The Widow Terhune took her in and nursed her back to health. Miracle may be a deaf-mute, but plays music fit for the angels."

"But how?"

He pointed at the guitarist. "Bob French signals what and when to play, and when to stop. Somehow, she learns new songs just by watching his fingers on the guitar and by feeling the strings' vibrations."

David clasped her arm and began a whirl of introductions. Dozens of new faces and names rushed past Megan like steam from a locomotive.

Next thing she knew, the band thrummed the opening chords of "Beautiful Dreamer." The covey of greeters parted as David led her to the edge of the dance floor.

"Time for your first lesson," he whispered, moving her around to face him. Laying her left hand on his shoulder, he laid his right against her waist and took her other hand in his.

Megan gazed up at him, feeling like a sleepwalker. With gentle pressure, David steered her to follow his steps. He murmured, in time with the music, "One, two; back, three, four; side, five, six; forward, seven, eight."

"I'm stiff as a jig dancin' doll," she groaned, bobbing her chin with the rhythm. "And treadin' your toes like a stone-bruised mule."

"Just relax, darlin'. Even in Pioche, smudging a man's boot tips isn't a hanging offense."

Smiling gratefully, she willed the tension from her muscles. Graceful or awkward, she was in the arms of the handsomest man at the party. Letting herself sway with the lilting music, she soon recognized the pattern their steps traced repeatedly.

"Why, it's a box we're makin' with our feet," she cried softly. "My heels come together at the corners, then cut to a side."

"Simple as that." His eyes glistened as he eased her a fraction closer to his chest. Deftly, he led her into the circle of other couples. They weaved and spun as if they'd danced together all their lives. For that magical moment, there was no one else in the room, save them.

At the end of the song, the musicians bowed their thanks for the applause and laid their instruments down carefully on the stage for a well-deserved break.

I2 Suzann Ledbetter

The men strode over to wet their whistles at the make-
shift bar while the women scuttled to the refreshment table.
Those Megan hadn't met graciously introduced themselves.

"Your dress is simply divine," Adelaide Jefferson
gushed.

"Thank you—"

Johnna Schmidt piped in, "Have you known David Jacobs long? How'd you meet him? Have you got kinfolk
in town?"

"Uh, no, I—"

"That man's right smitten with ya," proclaimed Velmira
Holtzenholter. "He's quite the catch, you know, and he
ain't taken his eyes off you for a second."

Like magpies roosting in a mulberry tree, their comments
and questions yammered at Megan from all sides. She tossed
her head to and fro trying to answer, or at least acknowledge
each speaker, but it proved impossible.

None seemed to notice when she slipped from the hen's
huddle. Lacing her fingers behind her back, she sauntered
the length of the hall to where the men held court around
the beer barrel

A burly lumberjack of a fellow asked, "Didja hear 'bout
ol' Cranston Farthing's assay? Three hunnert and fifty to
the ton, they say . . ."

Megan's ears pricked up.

"Whar'd he find it?" a baritone voice boomed from the
corner.

"South o' town, in that wash he's scrabbled in fer
months. And I coulda bought the sumbitch for a shot of
whiskey last time Farthing's gullet got parched," was the
reply. " 'Spect I'll take a mosey out that way in the
mornin'."

The lanky gent beside him drawled, "Hell, I ought just
get me missus and take her for a moonlight stroll *tonight*."

"Never figgered you for a Romeo, Preston," another
jeered. "S'pose it beats bustin' your ass in Meadow Valley's
number seven though, don't it?"

David spied Megan and held up his hand. "Gentlemen,
please. There's a lady present."

All eyes pivoted toward her. None appeared particularly
happy about the intrusion.

"Oh, don't mind me," she blurted. "I'm a prospector,
too, and such talk is gettin' my hands all itchy."

A moment of stunned silence was followed by uproarious laughter. The way they were acting, she expected to be patted on the head and sent back to the punch and cookies like a wayward child. She set her chin defiantly, daring anyone to try.

"Lady, you're too sparse to heft a pick, much less swing one," the gent sputtered between chortles.

"You don't say." She grinned slyly and crossed her arms at her chest. "I'll grant I'm short on husky, but I'm powerful long on stubborn. We'll see which pays off by the by."

At that, her audience traded sideward glances and slow nods. Some amused expressions gave way to beetle-browed thoughtfulness.

An unseen speaker challenged, "Well, does the grubstaker in petticoats know what color the bullion might be?"

"In these parts, it's likely blue," she shot back. "But it could be yellow, or brown. It depends."

"Shiny, too, ain't it."

"Not very. Once the air hits it, it'll tarnish like a spinster's tea set."

"Sounds like ya knows it when ya sees it, now don'tcha, little lady . . . ?" the big man inquired craftily.

"Not for certain, 'til it's assayed. And if I packed vials of nitric and hydrochloric acid to test it myself, why . . ." she paused, and winked prettily at her inquisitor, "I'd likely find Saint Peter a'fore I found the Mother Lode."

This time the men laughed with her, not at her. Megan knew she'd passed their silly test. She was so delighted at being welcomed into their conversation, she hardly noticed when the musicians began another set.

She startled when David whispered in her ear, "Shall we dance?"

"Oh, uh, yes . . . of course. Soon as Henry finishes tellin' me how he fared in the Comstock."

Later, one by one, indignant wives and lady friends towed their silver barons onto the dance floor. Megan was thirsty, but the refreshment table had been stripped of its cloth and shoved against a wall.

She peered around and saw David gliding gracefully with Amanda Meredith, the mine owner's frail-looking, quiet daughter.

Oh, I hope this song ends soon, she thought, tapping her foot impatiently. And that "Good Night, Ladies" is next. I can't wait to tell David I'm lightin' out with Henry Bryce and Duncan Cheever at dawn.

She rubbed her palms together and heaved a sigh of pure joy. Before the sun drops behind Treasure Hill again, she vowed silently, there'll be a claim staked with my name on it.

# Chapter Seventeen

The brazen glare crowning the hilltops sent kangaroo rats scurrying for their burrows. When the sun reached its apex, a silvery curtain of heat shimmers would remind parishioners of the morning's hellfire and brimstone sermons.

Several yards behind Megan, Henry Bryce's and Duncan Cheever's boots scraped over the hardscrabble terrain. Between their gear clanking against their backs and their huffed breathing, the men sounded like a pair of consumptive pack animals.

"Hey, gal!" Bryce hollered. "We ain't runnin' from no prairie fire."

Her only response was to swat a gnat so hard that a handprint scorched her forearm.

Damn you, David Jacobs, she cursed silently. I'd walk clear to Kansas if it'd get you out of my mind. How dare you expect me to simper and bat my lashes last night while there was business to be done.

He hadn't danced with her again until the last song of the evening. Vividly she remembered his expression as he led her onto the floor—that politely bored look a man gets when trapped into sipping tea with an aged maiden aunt.

Confused and angry, Megan lashed out during the ride back to the hotel, "If playin' patty-fingers is all you think I'm good for, you should've taken Amanda Meredith to the dance in the first place."

Hot tears sprang to her eyes as she heard the echo of his voice answering coldly, "At least the stars in Amanda's eyes shone for me—not inspired by visions of a blue-veined hunk of quartz."

She kicked a fist-sized rock over a clump of sagebrush. "Men are just tall boys with whiskers," she muttered. "Every damned one of 'em."

Glancing over her shoulder, she stopped short when she

saw Bryce and Cheever squatted on their haunches and glaring at her.

"For heaven's sake. We're miles from the diggings and you're already tuckerin' on me."

Cheever snapped a rag from his back pocket and wiped his brow. "I've seen buffalo stampede slower'n you. They's a darn sight more sociable whilst they done it, too."

Megan backtracked and knelt in the dust beside them. Snatching up pebbles, she flicked them at an invisible target. "You didn't put the burr under my saddle, but I've made you suffer for it since we left town. I'm truly sorry for that."

Bryce drawled, "Now don'tcha be gettin' all snivelly on us. A little exercise ain't never kilt nobody—"

"Leastwise, not yet," Duncan interrupted sarcastically. "But the last filly that loped like you did it on four legs and wore a bridle."

Megan thwacked her knee and laughed. Her dark mood drifted away like dandelion puffs in a breeze. Rising to her feet, she declared, "The racin's done, but it's high time we got movin' again. No use sittin' here burnin' daylight."

The trio cast a single, elongated shadow as they set out again heading due south. This close to town, stakes with fluttering claim notices sprouted from the ground like greasewood, but Henry Bryce knew of a riverbanked bluff that appeared promising.

"Last winter, I spied a party of greenhorns peckin' around there. Never laid claim to it, though. I reckon they expected the ore to tap them on the shoulder and say, 'Howdy do.'"

Cheever grunted. "Don't know where some folks get such foolish notions."

"From the newspapers, mostly," Megan said. "To read Virginia City's *Territorial Enterprise,* a body'd think nuggets were as easy to gather as eggs in a chicken house."

Cussing and discussing their various experiences with gold-fevered greenhorns, they'd put a fair piece of the district behind them before they realized it.

Henry nudged his slouch hat above his brows and squinted. "The river's a skip behind the clump of trees over yonder. That crag beyond's whar we're bound."

Gazing at the sloped, stubby elevation, Megan tried to imagine a hoard of bullion hiding behind its silty facade. A half-mile or more wide at its base, it jutted upward, then crooked at its crest like a Paiute's nose.

When they reached the grove of trees, Duncan snorted, "Christ, Henry. You call this a 'river'? Many's the mornin' I've let down more water'n that."

The trickle cutting the sides of a shallow gully could have been stepped across without straining a muscle. Oozing from a fissure in the earth, it meandered for a hundred yards or so before disappearing into a subterranean channel.

"This is Nevada Territory, bucko," Henry quipped. "Spit in the same spot long enough and folks'll swear it's a lake."

At the foot of the bluff, she parted company with her mentors as they'd agreed during the journey. The men had worked several claims together and were no more in favor of splitting a bonanza three ways than Megan was.

She scrutinized the length of the outcropping's pocked face. Silver rarely peeped out from Mother Nature's rocky skirt folds, but she hoped intuition would divine a lode-bearing pocket.

Roving around to its western flank, she gandered at a ledge about fifteen feet above her head. Along the way, chiseled gashes attested to previous prospecting, but the surface above the stony lip was unblemished.

"I s'pose that's as good a place to start as any," she speculated.

After clambering atop a boulder, she drove the pointed blade of her pickax into an nearby crack. Using its handle as a stair railing, she pulled herself up. Flattening herself like a fly against the rock, she repeated the process until she stepped onto the outcropping.

A diamondback rattler lay stretched in the sun. To her terrified eyes, it looked longer than a freight train. Megan caught and held the scream welling in her throat.

Its triangular head rose and reared back. Sinuously, its body formed a sinister coil. The tip of its tail twitched, rattles buzzing fair warning. The snake studied her for agonizingly slow seconds. Tears rimmed Megan's eyes, begging for the blink she dared not risk.

The ominous chirrups sputtered, then stopped. Lowering its head, the rattler languidly uncurled and slithered away.

"Mother of God," she wheezed, slumping bonelessly against the bluff. She shivered as icy sweat sprang from her pores. "Ah well, me lass, what creature did you expect to find guarding a treasure trove? A bloomin' turtledove?"

Realizing the gnaw in her midsection wasn't just from frayed nerves, she retrieved two cold biscuits from her pack. Alternating chewing and sipping water from a canteen, she pondered how a terrain so stark and rugged could be as soothing to the soul as the verdant landscape of her homeland.

Except there's no gold or silver in Ireland's hills, she thought, scrambling to her feet. Gently running her hand over the gritty wall, she traced a crow's-footed crack with her fingers.

"Wouldn't Henry and Duncan just split their britches laughin' at me, takin' this for a sign?" she chuckled to herself.

Spreading her legs like a prizefighter's, she chinked a gad into the center gap and started pounding it with a two-pound hammer.

Chips flew like snowflakes. Now and then, a chunk broke loose, threatening shins and toes before waddling off the ledge. When her left shoulder ached from the strain, she quickly switched hands.

Despite heavy cowhide gloves, puffy blisters soon rose on her palms and ruptured. The leather linings grew slick with a mixture of blood and grimy sweat.

At first, the hammer occasionally caught more of her thumb and forefinger than the crown of the gad. Bellowed "Damn it to hells!" reverberating across the barrens hardly lessened the throbbing, but did improve her aim.

By late afternoon, a V-shaped gash in the rock proved her diligence, but not a trace of mineral veining was evident. Megan squinted at the sun, reckoning it was nigh time to meet the men at the riverbank for the long trek back to town.

She winced as she tapped the wooden stake into the hole she'd excavated. On it, a wrinkled piece of foolscap declared:

*Upon this date, July 16, in the year of our Lord 1871, I, the undersigned, claim one claim, of three hundred feet, extending north and south from this notice, with all its dips, spurs, and angles, variations and sinuosities, together with fifty feet of ground on either side for working the same.*

*Megan O'Malley*

Furtively, she peered around before planting a kiss beneath her signature. "Come tomorrow, you'll be duly registered the Trinity Mine. There's silver, maybe even gold, lurking behind your ugly face, and I aim to have 'em."

She found Bryce and Cheever slumped in the stingy shade of a birch tree. Their sweat-drenched shirts clung to their stocky frames; their necks and arms were corded from exertion.

"Any luck?" Duncan asked, sounding as weary as she felt.

"Not yet, but I claimed my ground, and I'll work it 'til it pays."

They hadn't traveled far when Henry remarked quietly, "Uh, it prob'ly ain't my place to say so, but I think you're goin' at it kinda backward—"

"Ain't often I agree with ol' Bryce," Duncan broke in. "But, ma'am, a prospector don't file no claim 'til he's found color. Seems to me—unless you're fibbin' to us—that mostly you've got a pig in a poke with your name stuck to it."

"I won't argue—too much sense in what you say. But I reckon there's three ways of doin' anything: a right way, a wrong way, and my way. So far, my way's served me best."

Duncan scuffed a boot heel and shook his head. "God Almighty, you're a stubborn wench."

"I told you that last night."

What energy they had left was spent putting one foot in front of the other. The sky was deepening from azure to spangled navy when the pale corona of Pioche's gaslights became visible on the horizon.

Megan heard the cadence of a horse's hooves before she recognized the animal and the rig it pulled. The driver reined in abruptly, geeing the bay a half-turn.

"Consarn it, Jacobs," Henry howled. He yanked off his hat and waved it irritably. "I already et my fill of dust today."

"Sorry, I didn't see you until I'd almost run you down," David replied from within the buggy's cowl. More softly he added, "Good evening, Megan."

She nodded curtly in his general direction.

In the same motion, he stepped from the buggy and removed his hat. "May I offer you a ride back to town?"

"I'll walk."

David set his jaw firmly and extended his hand. "Do me the honor . . . please."

When Megan didn't budge an inch, Duncan muttered, "Listen, Irish, don't never walk when you can ride. In these parts, there's just too much country a'twixt here and yonder."

Her lips parted in protest, but clamped shut again. Without uttering a word, she strode to the buggy and threw her pack on the floorboard. She wedged herself as tightly against the cab's far side as her hips allowed.

The buggy lurched when David settled in beside her. He grasped the reins and clucked the mare into a trot. Megan stole a glance at him.

Looks as grim as a pallbearer, she thought smugly.

"About last night," he started. "I'm not proud of the way I acted—"

"Hmmph. Can't say I blame you."

David slapped back against the seat. "You are the most infuriating woman I've ever met. Goddamn it, can't you see I'm trying to *apologize*?"

The way his voice climbed an octave with the last sentence set her to giggling. The nostril-flaring, menacing glare he shot at her brought forth peals of laughter.

"I—I'm sorry. Not—makin' sport—of you. Honest—I'm not."

He snorted, and regarded her with a wry expression. "You're a hard woman to love, Miss Megan O'Malley."

Her head jerked toward him, laughter dying in her throat. His brows were drawn together in a frown; his gray eyes were velvet soft. Vulnerable.

When she was a little girl, she sometimes dreamed she had fallen off a cliff; was hurtling toward an unseen abyss. That same sensation of weightless anticipation surged through her. She was scarcely aware of the rig lurching to a halt.

David leaned toward her, and it seemed only natural to lay her cheek in the palm of his hand. His lips brushed hers, then sweetly lingered.

When they parted, he whispered huskily, "I've wanted to do that since the day I met you."

"David, I—"

"Don't say a word. Let your head tell your heart that this isn't real—that it's too soon—that it won't last. I know better, and someday, so will you."

# Chapter Eighteen

Megan leaned against the camp kitchen's sink peering past her windowed reflection into the inky darkness. Mindlessly scouring mucky stew pots, she pondered the events of the last six weeks.

After a worrisome silence, Frances had written that baby Ellen was crawling and learning quickly how to aggravate her big brother. Oran was earning a full day's pay, and the family's new flat was in a much nicer, safer sector of San Francisco—though Frances still yearned for a house with a yard for Tommy to play in. Every penny of the drafts Megan sent was being saved for that purpose.

"I hope you're tellin' me square this time, Frances," Megan said.

Suddenly David's face shimmered in her mind. Her heart fluttered at the image. I love that man, she admitted silently. There's no sense denying it.

She'd lost count of the dinners, dances, starlit buggy rides, and quiet conversations they'd shared—and the arguments over her weekly treks out to work the Trinity.

Whenever he said, "Come to church with Father and me next Sunday," she knew he meant, "Put me first; ahead of your ambitions."

Looking down at her soapy, callused hands, she said, "Not yet, David. I can't, just yet." She emptied the sink and replugged its drain. Grasping the bale on a bucket of boiling water, she hefted it off the stove, poured it into the basin, and pumped in several gushes of well water to cool it to bearably scalding.

Fistfuls of tableware clattered to the bottom to soak. She wearily regarded the towering heap of supper dishes. "Much as I love cooking for the miners, I'm beginning to hate this part of it."

Maybe Barlow P. could be persuaded to hire me a pearl-diver, she mused. To scrub up the evening meal's mess, at least.

Hearing footsteps approach, she assumed it was him dropping by for his evening cup of Arbuckle's. Instead, Carter Meredith rushed in, flustered and uncharacteristically disheveled. His oiled, mousy hair peaked at the crown like a rooster's cock and his red-rimmed eyes looked fire-branded into his pallid face.

He thrust an invoice at her. "What are you trying to do—bankrupt me? The charges for last month's supplies are outrageous. I demand an explanation."

Megan could only gawk at him, dumbfounded. For all the months she worked at the mine, she'd never seen her employer but from a distance. And this was hardly the slight, nattily dressed businessman Barlow P. had pointed out. The gent pacing the floor, ranting and spitting curses, was a raving lunatic.

"Mister Meredith, please," she said sternly, wiping her hands on her apron. "Such language belongs in the Stars and Garters Saloon—not in my kitchen."

Meredith stopped in his tracks as if he'd been gut-shot. With a sharp tug on its lapels, he righted his suit coat, then fussed with his shirt collar.

"Yes, well. I'll admit to overstepping the bounds of polite society. But I will not abide this kind of willful mismanagement."

Her eyes narrowed to slits. "Willful—what? Exactly what are you accusin' me of, sir?"

He pecked at the paper with his forefinger. "Look at this bill. The amount's nearly double what Sanchez spent on supplies, and it's a hundred dollars higher than even you incurred last month."

"There's twenty-five more men on the payroll this month than last. If you want me to shave portions, that I'll gladly do, but I can't feed two hundred for the same as a hundred and seventy-five."

"That's a fact, Carter," Barlow P. agreed from the doorway. "It ain't the cook's fault that them shafts is fillin' with water. That's what's got yer tail in a knot and ya damn well know it."

The mine owner whirled angrily. Barlow P. stood his ground, hands on his hips, as rigid as a corner post.

When Meredith's shoulders sagged, the manager

drawled, "Go home and get some shut-eye. I'll come to yer office, first light Monday. We'll finagle a way to pay for them new pumps."

Meredith rubbed his brow and nodded. He looked over his shoulder at Megan, too exhausted to say the words, but begging her pardon with his eyes. Despite his earlier bluster, he appeared to be on the verge of collapse.

"Rest well, Mister Meredith," she said softly. "I'll stretch the victuals as best I can. The men'll never know the difference."

With that, he crumpled the invoice in his fist and strode out the door.

Barlow P. stared after him. "He's a good feller, Megan. Don't judge him by that speck of devilment."

"I won't."

Hooking both thumbs on his braces, he added as if thinking aloud, "If'n Jeb Sanders—that worthless whey-belly— wasn't buckin' the tiger at every faro table in town, Carter wouldn't have to squeeze two bits outta every dime."

"How bad is the flooding?"

"Bad enough. One thing's for damned sure: Once the water starts flowin' in, it don't dry up. Only gets worse."

Megan recognized the lines etching his face and forehead as concern and frustrated helplessness. Hard as he tried to hide it, Barlow P. was a sensitive human barometer. The pressure of a friend's personal storms affected his well-being, too.

She resumed her chores, and he reached over her head for his cup. "It doesn't make sense, does it?" she asked pensively. "This territory's dry as a bleached bone on the topside, but down below, there's an ocean if you dig far enough."

"Yup. Got my knees wet eventually in every mine I ever worked. This one ain't the only one sinkin', neither. Speakin' of such, how's your dig a'comin'?"

She finished rinsing the bucket full of knives and forks under the pump spout before answering. "Well, I've burrowed a cave big enough to hide in if it rains."

Barlow P. grabbed a sack towel and began wiping down the plates. "No color yet, huh?"

"No. But it's there. I know it is."

"Four hands is twice better'n two ..." he hinted, waggling the cloth at her as she passed by.

She pulled a crockery bowl from the shelf beneath the worktable and dumped in the ingredients for Monday morning's biscuits. By draping the pans with a damp towel before reheating, they'd be as fluffy as fresh-baked.

"That's what David says, too. And it's grateful I am for the offers, but workin' that claim is something I have to do myself. Why can't either of you understand that?"

After refilling his cup, he moseyed over and hiked himself up on the end of the table. Megan diligently kneaded the gooey dough, occasionally blowing at a strand of hair tickling her forehead.

She knew by the silence that Barlow P. was cogitating something, and by experience that he wouldn't say what until he was darned good and ready.

Idly, he rubbed a hand up and down his skinny thigh. "So, are ya gonna marry that Jacobs boy?"

It rankled her when he called David a "boy," but rather than chastise him, she hedged, "He hasn't asked me."

The manager chewed on that for a moment, then wheedled, "Well, if'n he did, would ya?"

En route to the cupboard for the baking tins, she answered solemnly, "I don't know, Barlow P."

The tension in the room was as tangible as the wispy vapor meandering from the coffeepot's spout. That wasn't the answer you expected, now was it, she asked him silently. Please, just leave it be.

Megan felt him watching her bustle to the kitchen safe for lard, then lightly greasing the metal pans. Once the worktable was strewn with flour, she plopped the mound of dough in the middle. The heavy sawbuck wobbled with every stroke of the rolling pin.

From the corner of her eye, she saw him draw a finger through the edge of the powder. Grinning slyly, he edged sideways and took a swipe at her face.

"Lord above, woman. Can't you cut biscuits without gettin' flour on yer nose?"

She sneezed into the crook of her arm, then flicked the gobbets sticking to her fingertips back at him. He ducked, and hopped off the table.

"If you're not the most exasperatin' old buzzard on two legs." To herself, she added, and the best friend I've ever had.

\*     \*     \*

The next morning Megan was stooping to pick up the battered bowler Barlow P. had given her for luck when she noticed a folded slip of paper wedged under her hotel room's door.

"Meet me at Dan Light's Livery," it read, and was signed "David."

"When?" she asked aloud. "And why?" Flipping the paper over, she found no answers on the other side.

Completely perplexed, she struggled into her pack and hurried downstairs to the lobby. The foyer was deserted, but Willy Ray's hoggish snores resounded from a shadowy corner behind the desk.

She slapped its oak surface with the flat of her hand. The clerk's arms and legs flailed violently and he shot out of his chair like a cannonball.

"What the *hell*—? Oh, uh, mornin', Miss O'Malley." Stretching and scratching himself awake, he muttered, "Leastwise, I guess it's mornin'. Still dark as a well-digger's . . . uh, never mind."

Megan bit back a chuckle. "Open your eyes, Willy Ray. The sun's been up a half hour."

While he was blinking like a hoot owl, she inquired, "Did you put this note under my door?"

"Can't say I did, ma'am. Don't know nary a thing about it." Angling his head, he squinted at the paper. "I shore hope it ain't bad news . . ."

She whisked it away from his prying eyes and tucked it into her shirt pocket. "Go back to sawin' logs, then. I'm headed by the stables on my way out of town—in case anyone asks."

Clomping down the boardwalk, she swatted at the dust clouds boiling along the street. Rumbling columns of ore wagons didn't usually compete with church bells pealing their come-to-meeting calls.

While Sanders and Meredith was still observing the Sabbath, she realized that other operators must be working overtime to extract as much silver as possible before the flooding engulfed the shafts.

What'll I do if Mister Meredith starts opening his mines on Sunday? If I'm not at the diggings at least once every ten days, I'll forfeit my claim. Fretting and nibbling a thumbnail didn't lend any solutions.

"Oh, quit borrowin' trouble," she muttered. "You've got plenty enough as it is."

The musky aroma of hay, manure, and horseflesh greeted her before she entered the livery. A huge man mucking out a nearby stall hailed, "Be with you directly."

His shoulders were broad as an ox yoke and no neck was visible between his chin and collarbones. Dinner for two could have been laid on his chest with plenty of elbow room left over.

Brushing wisps of hay from his shirtsleeves, he inquired, "What can I do for you, miss?"

"Are you Dan Light?"

"Depends. You payin' cash for a mount or wantin' credit?"

"Neither," she answered, smiling. "I got a message from David Jacobs askin' me to meet him here. Have you seen him?"

"Ah, you must be Miss O'Malley. Jacobs ain't here, but there's someone else waitin' for you out back. Come with me."

Her curiosity spiked like a fever while she followed him down a narrow aisle running the length of the stable. On either side, boxy stalls fenced horses and mules of every color and description.

It wasn't until he sidled around the back door's facing that she saw a magnificent palomino gelding tethered to a stake.

Light unhitched the reins. "His name's Shiloh. He's a surefooted critter and don't shy easy. And don't worry for his size. Shiloh's trusty as a dobbin."

Megan gawked at the regal animal. He whickered and ducked his head as if pleased to make her acquaintance.

"Oh, yeah, I dang near forgot." Light shoved a hand into his jeans pocket and pulled out a wad of paper. "Jacobs said to give you this."

She smoothed the sweat-dampened sheet flat against her thigh. The ink had smudged, but was legible: "My dearest Megan, like Duncan told you, never walk when you can ride. I love you, David."

She let her eyes sweep the horse from muzzle to rump; so astonished, she was dizzy.

"He's all yours, ma'am. Rent and board's paid up for six months. I tried tellin' Jacobs you'd want a sidesaddle, you being a lady and all. I'll swap you even, and switch 'em in two shakes.''

It was several seconds before Megan could comprehend what the stable owner had said.

"No ... I mentioned once how sidesaddles are fine for parades and pastures, but not for gettin' from here to yonder. And he remembered."

Nodding sagely, Light handed her the reins.

Shiloh flicked his silky, cream-colored tail as Megan swung up on his back. While Light adjusted the stirrups, she leaned over the pommel and patted the animal's neck.

The horse needed no more direction than a gentle squeeze of her knees against the saddle's tooled leather fenders. Rocking easily with Shiloh's ambling gait, she turned and doffed her bowler at Dan Light.

Even held to a canter, the gelding's leggy strides ate up ground like a locomotive. The wind brushed Megan's cheeks, tousling the hair streaming down her back. She reveled in the sensation.

Reaching the stream, she let him lap up several mouthfuls of water before plodding across. She guided him to a sturdy clump of sagebrush near the mine and dismounted. Shiloh's snorts bespoke his attitude toward wearing the hobbles Megan found in the saddlebag.

"I still don't believe you're real," she murmured, watching the horse's ear pivot at the sound of her voice. "Maybe David understands me better than I thought he did."

Shiloh craned his neck and regarded her with doleful, black eyes. She scratched the white blaze on his forehead. "Oh, I know. Horse or human, you fellas always stick up for one another, don't you?"

Feeling as lighthearted as a child, she scrambled up to the Trinity's gaping oval mouth and retrieved her growing assortment of tools from its cavern. Now that a tunnel was taking shape, a pickax and shovel were needed most; the hammer and gad saved for stubborn outcroppings.

The ping of the pick's blade striking rock was sweet music to her ears. Thanks to David's generosity, I'm not as tired at the get-go as I have been, she mused. I'll wager I can chink out another three feet or better before sundown.

Regularly she stopped to shovel piles of sediment off the ledge while the dust settled inside the aperture. That same grit was plastered to her sweaty clothes, clung to her eyelashes, and filled her nose and lungs.

Late afternoon's unforgiving sun heated the tunnel like an oven. From time to time, Megan could have sworn she heard thunder rumbling in the distance. Peering out of the mine, she noticed that Shiloh, too, raised his head and sniffed at the air. But not even a feather of a cloud wandered by overhead.

Each shovel load she heaved over the precipice felt heavier and heavier. Leaning on its handle to catch her breath, she gazed wistfully at the gelding, tempted to quit and take a pleasurable lope back to town.

She heard a noise—like a rifle shot. Instinctively she dropped to a kneel.

The ledge beneath her boots trembled, then broke away from the bluff. Megan pitched forward in an uncontrollable, face first slide.

Jagged rocks tore at her clothing and skin. She choked on the dirt spilling into her mouth. Her chin and rib cage took a painful beating before she came to a sprawling stop on solid ground. She lay dazed for several minutes, afraid to move bones she was sure must be broken.

Finally, curling up and raising herself into a sitting position, she moaned aloud at the sight of her scraped hands and forearms. Gingerly touching her face, her fingertips came away traced with blood.

She glared at the rubbled heap behind her. Howling "Damn, damn, *damn,*" she beat her fists against her legs with each word. "A month and a half's work gone in an instant!"

The shadowy hole mocked her from its now inaccessible height. Beneath it, the wide gouge left by the ledge's collapse curved upward at its edges like a dead man's smile.

Megan blinked, and stared at the milky, crystalline mineral lining the formation, unwilling to trust her own eyes. She rose to her feet and staggered toward the bluff.

Amid the slag were scattered fragments of the dense substance. "Jesus, Mary, and Joseph," she wheezed, picking up an orange-sized chunk of the quartz.

Dull gunmetal-blue streaks laced its pearly surface like veins marbled an old woman's hands.

# Chapter Nineteen

Megan sat cross-legged in the middle of her bed, examined the hunks of quartz strewn about on the quilt. She'd chosen five—none larger than a teacup—for assay samples.

Holding one up to the light to study its cobwebbed facets, she glimpsed her reflection in the windowpane. She dropped the stone, then reached between the bars of the iron bedstead and lowered the shade.

When she'd returned to Pioche that evening, it had seemed as though everyone she passed knew that a chamois bag heavy with ore was hidden beneath her shirt. During the brisk walk from Light's Livery to the hotel, she feared each corner and dark doorway hid a highwayman waiting to snatch her precious bundle.

"Are you treasure or are you just pretty rocks?" she mused, rolling them around like a kitten batting a ball of yarn.

Muscle by muscle, her body began reminding her of the punishment it received that afternoon. Splashing in the stream had washed away most of the blood, but she was mottled by bruises and abrasions from forehead to ankles.

She eased onto the pillow, curling around the samples, not caring about muddying the covers with her mucky clothes. Her mind wandered back to that awestruck moment of discovery. Drowsiness crept over her like sunlight seeping through a break in the clouds.

A tap at the door caused her heavy eyelids to raise a fraction. But that white, porcelain knob looked so far away . . .

Insistent pounding rattled the door in its jamb. Megan pushed herself up with one arm and swung her socked feet to the floor. She shoved the quartz back into the bag and stashed it beneath the pillow.

Another battering and a muffled inquiry came from the

hall while she was plumping the goose feathers to disguise their secret hoard.

"This hotel had damned well better be on fire," she snarled as she tottered across the room.

Snapping the bolt back, she swung the door wide. At the sight of her, David's expression changed from irritation to shock.

"What happened? Are you all right?" He reached to embrace her, then hesitated, obviously afraid his comforting might hurt her.

She ducked her head like an errant child. "I, uh, took a little tumble off the ledge, that's all. No real harm done." But when David gently touched her scratched, swollen cheek, Megan winced and drew back.

His hand ambled down her arm until it reached her own. Turning it palm up, he kissed the scrapes and stone bruises. A delicious shiver tickled up her spine.

Just then, the Cantrells, who occupied the room next door, strolled down the hallway on their way to the stairs. Gwendolyn Cantrell's bemusement at the tender scene was evident. She was cooing like a pigeon as she passed out of sight.

David straightened up and glared at the woman's back. "Must I stand out here like a messenger boy?"

Megan glanced at the mussed bed linens—and the pillow-case. I'll not tell him about the silver until the assay proves me right, she decided. If it's a fool I am, it's better kept secret than found a fact.

"We'll leave the door open," David wheedled. "And I'll stay in that chair like a parson come to call. You can tie me to it, if you want to."

Megan chuckled at his pleading tone. "I s'pose I can trust you not to ravish me. I'd say I'm a far sight from fetchin', anyhow."

Taking that as an invitation, he strode inside, directly toward the spindle-back Windsor cat-cornered beside the washstand.

"You're bewitching even with a shiner blossoming around your eye," he assured, settling himself as promised.

"A what ...? Oh, Lord! Folks'll think I've been brawlin'."

He laughed at her howling dismay. "If they saw you ride

out, more likely they'll think Shiloh cut a fair dido and dragged you for a couple of counties."

She rolled her eyes heavenward. "Here I am, frettin' about my silly face and not a word of thanks I've given for your thoughtfulness. Shiloh was a wondrous surprise ... I felt like a fairy princess astride his—"

"How I wish I'd seen you galloping across the barrens. But I was afraid you'd give me no end of reasons why you couldn't accept my gift if I showed up at the livery."

Caressing his shoulder, she regarded him solemnly. "And I can't accept it, you know. Nor should I have ridden him today. I just couldn't help myself when Dan Light offered me the reins."

"Shiloh is yours, Megan," David argued. "Proprieties be damned. He's hired, not bought outright. You won't allow me to drive you to the mine and I can't abide you walking that distance alone."

She paused, letting her eyes express the love she felt for him. Her knees crackled like dry twigs when she knelt beside the chair.

"Aye, it's two peas in a pod we are. You won't step into your father's shoes, happy as it would make him if you would. You want a newspaper to call your own.

"But I've got to earn my own way, too. Just as you refuse your father's help, lovingly as it's offered, I must refuse yours."

His lips parted, then closed again. Tenderly he ran his fingers through her hair. With a sigh, he nodded his surrender. "Believe it or not, I do understand. I'll not interfere again. But I'm a man of many dreams, Megan, some meant to be shared. Have you only one?"

Her pulse quickened. It would be so easy to tell him of the many nights I've dreamed of becoming his wife, she thought. Tell him I will, just as soon as I've done the name "O'Malley" proud.

An impish grin spread across her face. "Oh, there's others, me lad," she said, in a singsong brogue. "It's Irish I am and full I be of taties, blarney, and dreams."

He laughed as he rose from the chair and pulled her up and into his arms. "That's not all you're full of, my darlin'."

"Da-vid ... you promised to behave your—"

"Proprieties, be damned." He kissed her hungrily, his

tongue seeking hers in passionate abandon. She pressed against him, molding to him as if made for that purpose.

When their lips parted, he held her close, swaying to and fro, clinging to each other.

"Do you love me, Megan?"

"You know I do."

"Tell me. Say the words."

She looked up into his eyes, her body trembling with emotion. "I love you, David. I will *always* love you."

When dressing the next morning, Megan's arms and legs were stiff as rusty pump handles. She frowned at the mirror. Her shadowed, puffy eye and the rosy polt on her chin would certainly attract Barlow P.'s attention and a passel of teasing.

"No use lettin' him get grumpy waitin' in the buckboard," she said, peeking out the window at the figure fidgeting below. "Give 'im his hoot and be done with it."

Impulsively she donned her lucky bowler. Its brim rested on the bridge of her nose, doing a passable job of veiling much of her face. She grabbed the lumpy chamois bag of samples and blew out the lamp.

Barlow P. turned his head at the thud of her boots on the boardwalk.

"Mornin'," she crowed, then gritted her teeth and vaulted onto the seat.

He pushed his Stetson upward, studying her so intently that his grizzled eyebrows angled like a barn owl's. "Hmmmm. Ain't never heard of no bears 'round here."

Megan ducked her chin, muttering, "Best giddap to the mine. I've got work to do."

The buckskins strained at the harness. Barlow P. swung them into the street and gave them their lead. "Musta been a grizzly ya tangled with," he opined casually. "Or mebbe one of them painthers."

"Have your sport, you ol' grissel-heel. If I'd broken my fool neck, it'd be you fryin' flapjacks for the boys today."

"So, what'd ya do? Ya look like ya romanced the wrong end of a plow ox."

She punched him soundly on the shoulder. "By God, I'm a lady, Mister Bainbridge, and I'll thank you to remember it."

He clucked at the team, trying unsuccessfully to hide an ornery grin. "Beg pardon, ma'am. I plumb forgot myself."

The spring wagon's wheels caught in a swale worn deep by heavy traffic. On impact, the wagon juddered from tongue to rear axle. Megan's tender rib cage twisted like a corn stalk in a thunderstorm. She bit her lip, but couldn't stifle an agonized gasp.

A pair of anxious blue eyes traced over her. Barlow P. reached and anchored a finger under her chin, turning her face to his. A sigh heaved his chest and he shook his head slowly.

"I'm takin' you back to the hotel. Then I'm sendin' for Doc Pfeiffer."

Megan sat straight up in the seat. "The hell you are."

"The hell I ain't."

She laid her hand on his arm. "Please, I don't need your motherin'. I need your help."

Drawing the bag from behind her back, she worked its strings open while inching across the board bench until her shoulder touched his. "If this is what I think it is, there's no better cure for what ails me . . ."

Barlow P. squinted at the opening. "That come from the Trinity?"

"Sure did. When the ledge gave way—with me standin' on it—the rift it left in the rock fairly glows with quartz." She held a sample where he could see it clearly.

His eyes waggled from the chunk of mineral to Megan and back again. "Could be mica. Could be galena and heavier in lead than silver. Always been partial to gold myself. A man don't hafta guess what he's got, only to find out he ain't got nuthin'."

"True enough, but if it tests out high, this paddy's in clover!"

"Mebbe. Only it might not show up worth a plug nickel. Could be a gash vein that pinches out after a few feet."

The hallelujahs Megan expected weren't going to happen. Her mouth puckered at one edge, showing her disappointment at a fellow prospector's lukewarm reaction. Above all, she'd thought Barlow P. would be excited by her find and eager to learn its worth.

"Gotta swot over them ledgers with Carter this mornin' . . . but there's a load of shorin' timbers needin' hauled a'fore midday . . ."

Her heart skipped a beat. "From Sherwood's Lumber Yard?"

"Yup. Best I can recollect, it ain't but a nip 'n tuck over to the assay office."

She craned her neck, waiting breathlessly for the invitation to come along. Barlow P. stared straight ahead, his face as inscrutable as a cigar store Indian's.

After several moments silence, she blurted, "For heaven's sake! Can I go with you when you come back to town? Please?"

Stroking his stubbled jaw like a banker cogitating a borrower's collateral, he drawled, "Aw, I reckon," then nudged her with his elbow. "Now plant yer hindquarters over there where they belong. Them pick-swingers'll think yer sweet on me or sumthin'."

She chuckled wickedly as her fingertips burrowed through the ore sack. "Why, I purely *am* sweet on you, Barlow P.," she simpered. Tucking an acorn-sized fragment into his vest's watch pocket, she added, "And here's a share of the Trinity's mother lode to prove my undying affection."

"Consarn it, woman. Hush up, scoot over, and leave me the hell alone."

The spring wagon topped the hill and lurched into the yard. Near the lean-to, a miners' contingent milled around expectantly. Their stance and dour expressions bespoke anger and wariness, like gunmen forced to defend reputations they hadn't earned.

Barlow P. jumped down from the seat. "Quite a welcomin' party. You boys extra peckish this mornin'?"

Several men chuckled nervously. One crossed his arms over his chest and rocked on his heels as if spoiling for a fight.

"I hear our wages is gettin' cut, Bainbridge. That true?" Though his words sounded threatening, his twitching walrus mustache almost set Megan to giggling.

Without taking his eyes off the man, Barlow P. pulled out his pocketknife and sliced off a twist of Rough & Ready. Wallowing the plug around in his mouth, he glanced at her and jerked his head toward the kitchen.

He's smellin' trouble and wants me out of harm's way, Megan thought. She lowered her eyes obediently and strode through the assembly toward the door. Once inside

*Suzann Ledbetter*

the building, she jammed the ore sack and her derby in a cupboard and hastened to the open window.

"Cain't say fer sure, one way or t'other, Reuben," Barlow P. replied evenly.

"Can't? Or won't?" he snapped back. Harrying mutters echoed from the crowd.

Barlow P. hooked his thumbs in his braces. He eyed the ringleader, each of his cronies, and back again. "Ya'lls mighty tetchy. Ain't gonna make a lick's difference what I say. If'n you men is swear-and-be-damned itchin' fer a strike, then get yer skinny asses off Sanders and Meredith property right now."

Megan saw many sidelong looks exchanged, but Reuben didn't move a muscle. "Didn't say nothin' about no strike. But we ain't ridin' no cages 'til we know what it pays."

He jabbed a finger at Barlow P. "And get this straight: If Meredith thinks he's gonna sweeten his take with our blood and sweat, he's got another think comin'."

The air fairly crackled with tension. By nature, miners weren't a violent lot, but Megan knew that fear could explode as quickly as blasting powder. None but the greenest butty had to be told a salary decrease forbode a failing mine operation. She was as sympathetic to the men's plight as she was concerned for Barlow P.'s safety.

The manager slapped Reuben's hand aside. His rumbling voice held more menace than a shout. "Mister, don't never point nothin' at me that don't have a barrel and a loaded breechblock."

Reuben blanched; his ruddy whiskers seeming to stand away from his skin. He dropped his arms to his sides.

Barlow P. spit a brown stream toward the wagon. "Ya'll can trust me and Carter to do the best we can by ya, or fetch yer gear from the change house and skedaddle." With that, he turned on one heel and sauntered in the direction of the mine office.

Megan smiled with relief and no small measure of pride. Barlow P. didn't give an inch, but he didn't back Reuben into a corner, either.

Before she had the lumps beaten out of a bowl of flapjack batter, the yard outside was deserted. Yet the day wore on as inauspiciously as it began.

Doublejackers in shaft number two got edgy when rats started skittering around their feet, a superstitious omen of an imminent collapse. The miners hollered for the buckets to take them above ground, but the newly hired banksman refused. Although no cave-in commenced, when the doublejackers came up at shift change, they beat the banksman bloody.

Just before noon, the kitchen pump stopped spewing forth any water. Megan worked the handle like a handshake. There was no pressure in the line. The shovel stiff Barlow P. sent to fix it found the break easily enough, but digging up the pipe and repairing it would take the rest of the day.

"I spent my childhood ferrying water from the Bride River to the cottage," she muttered as she trudged from the well house with a slopping bucket in each hand. "And I disremembered how much I hated that chore until now."

At half past two, Barlow P. loped in. "I'm headin' for Pioche. Tear that apron off and let's *git*."

On the way, he didn't tender any information about his meeting with Carter Meredith. His brooding scowl told Megan it was best not to ask.

A few doors from the assay office, a waiting buggy and a stream of jaywalking pedestrians blocked their progress. While Barlow P. was hollering curses at all concerned, Megan announced, "I'll get off here. And I'll hurry as fast as I can."

The office's fresh coat of whitewash appeared both inviting and prosperous. An oval signboard chained to the overhang's rafters read: ZADOCK BEMENT & SON, INDEPENDENT ASSAYERS & MINERAL PURVEYORS.

Tinkling brass bells announced her entrance. As she approached the counter, a jowly gent with kinky gray hair and muttonchops emerged from a back room. Dingy moons of perspiration darkened the underarms of his boiled shirt. Its sleeves were rucked above frayed garters.

His brow furrowed when he saw Megan. "How may I help you, madam?" he asked in the wearied tone of one accustomed to frequent requests for charitable contributions.

"I have some ore samples I want assayed," she replied, and dumped out the contents of the bag.

Behind his spectacles, his eyes widened in surprise. "Oh, well, it isn't often that a pretty young lady is in need of my services. Let me see here."

Bement examined one chunk with a magnifying glass, rotating the quartz slowly in front of the thick convex lens. "Heavy adulteration," he intoned as much to himself as his customer. "Copper ... flecks of gold ... veining appears to be chloride of silver.

"Can't be positive without an acid test, but it appears promising. Where'd you find these, miss? Or were they given to you by a ... gentleman friend?"

Megan ignored his questions and his leer. "How long will the test take, Mister Bement?" she asked coldly.

He brayed like a mule and tapped her wrist with his fingertips. "That's not very friendly. Call me 'Zadock'—"

"There are other assayers in Pioche, Mister Bement." She scooped up the nearest sample and dropped it into the bag.

"Wait now, don't be so hasty. Business is business, eh?" He cleared his throat and held out a beefy palm to receive the poke. "Come back Thursday morning. I'll have the certified report ready for you then."

"Thursday! That's three whole days from now."

"The best are always the busiest," Bement retorted haughtily. "And these fragments must be pulverized before testing—a task I usually don't perform, but will as a favor to you."

He waggled his fingers impatiently. Against her better judgment, Megan plopped her treasure into his hand.

# Chapter Twenty

The Regulator's hands pegged at ten twenty-three. Snorting in disgust, Megan whacked the chicken's sternum with a cleaver like a woodsman splits firewood.

"Only four minutes later'n the last time I looked," she grumbled, flopping another carcass onto the slimy block. "I thought Tuesday and Wednesday passed like terrapins in a peat bog. God Almighty, icicles melt faster'n that clock's tickin' today."

She shot the timepiece a hateful glare as if that would set the hands spinning like windmill paddles.

"Miss Megan?" a voice whispered through the window. "You in there, Miss Megan?"

"There's a door to this kitchen. Use it," she answered irritably.

Kansas Hughes slunk inside just far enough so the screen door wouldn't spank him when it shut. Wringing his felt skullcap in both hands, the young muckman locked his eyes on one of the floorboard's nail heads.

If that bashful pup had a tail it'd be tucked square between his legs, she mused. Aloud she said, "There's shortcakes coolin' over there. I s'pose I wouldn't miss a corner, if you're hungry."

"No thankee, ma'am." His tongue darted over his lips and he squirmed uncomfortably. "I, uh, kin see yer right busy, but I was sent to fetch ya."

"Fetch me where?"

For all his earlier shyness, the explanation flowed like rainwater from a downspout. "It's like this, ma'am. Sell Trenoweth's been pitchin' his cookies since daybreak. The boys was coverin' for 'im thinkin' he'd get better directly, only he ain't't, and Sell's skeered spitless that K-Dub Frayley'll catch wind of it and fire 'im for slackin'. There's bad blood betwixt 'em, and K-Dub'll send Sell skedaddlin' in a wink, so me and the boys was hopin' you'd smuggle down and take a look at Sell and see if'n—"

"Whoa there, Kansas," she broke in, chuckling heartily. She untied the blood-splattered apron and slipped her head out of the neck strap. "That's reasons enough, lad. Lead the way." Megan snatched her canvas medicine bag from its hook beside the door and hung the apron in its place.

Shortly after she'd hired on, an apprentice tar baby had crushed his fingers between a spool and the cable he was lubricating. After Megan soaked his hand in tepid water laced with Epsom salt and massaged it with elderberry salve, the miner went back to work singing praises to her miraculous healing abilities. She'd been called on to remedy minor injuries and illnesses ever since.

"Damn slackers crack their heads upside the shaft walls so's they can come visit Mother Megan," Barlow P. grumbled occasionally. But he paid for her supply of herbs, elixirs, and nostrums out of his own pocket.

"There's no shingle at my door, but I'm a'thinkin' I do more doctorin' than cookin' these days," she teased as she marched beside Kansas. "I'll swan, you boys are forever gettin' banged up."

His peach-fuzzy cheeks plumped into a huge grin. "Yep, we's a buncha flubdrubbers awright. Good thang we got us an angel of mercy close by, that's fer sher."

They passed the carpentry, blacksmith, and machinist shops' wings that extended from the enormous building housing the shaft head and hoisting works.

Kansas had to shout to be heard over the clanking engines inside. "Frayley's snuck off ta the cribs by now, but he won't be gone long . . ."

"Whorin' on company time, eh?" Megan retorted.

K. W. Frayley was a bastard by birth and by disposition. She'd have no qualms about informing Barlow P. of his skirt-chasing.

Fear washed over the young man's face. "Jesus, if K-Dub finds out I let that fly, I'll catch a bullet in the back, dead-bang."

"He won't," she assured. "That's a promise I'm givin'."

Upon entering the cavernous structure, her eyes were drawn to the mouth of the main shaft. Steam clouds rolled from the aperture like vapor from the bowels of hell. With its polished hardwood floors, lofty forty-five-foot ceilings, and thunderous hoisting engines, the room was an odd cross between a factory and a cathedral.

Kansas took Megan's arm and guided her into one of the cages. She didn't need his reminder to keep her elbows, feet, and head inside the iron-framed, open cubicle. At the speed they descended, framing timbers could lop off an arm faster than a buzzsaw's blade.

Light flashed and died with each level they passed. The suffocating, humid air was like breathing through a pillow. This ungodly hole in the ground scares me spitless, she said silently, but damned if I'll admit it.

The cage stopped at the fifteen-hundred-foot level. Because of the intense heat, men working the drift wore little more than breechcloths or cut-off long underwear bottoms. Their taut-muscled skin glistened like wet marble in the flickering candle- and lamplight.

Megan's nostrils filled with the musky, dank odor peculiar to caverns and the briny tang of drenching sweat. With her head bowed, practically walking on Kansas's heels, she chanted under her breath, "Hail Mary, full of grace ..." trying hard not to steal admiring glances at those gleaming subterranean gladiators.

Rivulets of hot water trickled from crevices in the walls and slickened the pocked floor. On tiptoes, she picked her way around puddles and the ribbons of narrow gauge track laid for ore carts. She flinched with the constant, ringing blows of sledgehammers on drillheads.

Kansas veered into a narrower crosscut tunnel, hugging its wall for another ten yards. There, Sell Trenoweth slumped against a shoring timber; his ashen face partially hidden by a grimy, brimmed hat. Bile seared Megan's throat at the sight of three rats nuzzling the pelt of vomit-flecked hair on Sell's chest.

"Ah, my beautay," he wheezed. "A stinkin' Jack, be I ... me guts strewed all abowt."

She dampened a rag in the runoff leaking down the wall's craggy surface. Gently she cleansed the putrid lather from the Cornishman's face and neck. His skin felt cool and clammy, but he was panting like a thirsty animal.

"Sell, you must go topland," Megan said sternly. "It's heat stroke you're sufferin'. You know the signs as well as I do."

"Now 'taint," he argued. " 'Twas 'at dom Hoe Joe whiskey I guzzled down te the tavern." He turned his head and retched. "Ach, 'twas pizen I tell ye ... pure pizen."

She looked up at Kansas. "Get a couple of the boys and a wheelbarrow." The mucker nodded, then trotted off toward the main shaft.

Returning her attention to the stricken miner, she stated, "K-Dub Frayley isn't going to sack you, I don't have time to bury you. You're goin' home to rest, and I don't mean maybe."

The Cornishman smiled wanly. "Bless ye, my beautay."

When Kansas and his helpers returned, Megan supervised as Sell was lifted into the wheelbarrow and rolled to a waiting cage.

Upon reaching the hoisting room, the mucker went back down to shovel the ore heaps that had accumulated in his absence. Two other volunteers interlaced their fingers to make a litter. They struck off down the hill with Sell wobbling in their arms like a tipsy potentate.

Megan scurried toward the cook shack, then spun around on one heel when Barlow P. bellowed, "There ya is. By God, I've been lookin' all over hell's half acre for ya!"

He towered over her, glowering. "Ya been down in that shaft, ain't ya?"

"Sell Trenoweth was sicker than a dog on green grass," she countered defiantly. "The heat got to him."

"How many times have I told you not to get anywheres near that goddamn mine?" he roared. "Patchin' up them butties in the kitchen is one thing, but a woman ain't got no business traipsin' through them tunnels with a buncha half-nekkid men."

Megan simply stood with her head cocked to one side while the storm blew itself out—even Barlow P. couldn't cuss and stomp forever. He was still sputtering when she said softly, "Sell wouldn't come to me. Do you know why?"

"Hell no, but I'm likely to."

"He was afraid if K-Dub Frayley found out he was ailin', he'd be out of a job. Now, do you know why your shaft boss didn't catch me comin' or goin'?"

Barlow P. grunted. " 'Cause yer sneakier than a goddamn greased polecat."

Smiling coyly as if she'd been complimented, she replied, "Because K-Dub has a chippy in town he's servicin' every mornin' on Sanders and Meredith's nickel."

He gazed over her head at Pioche's rooftops checker-boarding the valley below. "Hmmmph. I thought that sumbitch was disappearin' purty regular. Oughta be kinda fun catchin' him with his co—, er, uh, his drawers swimmin' round his ankles."

Megan glanced over her shoulder at the lean-to. "Want a cup of coffee? There's lunch to fix and a ton of chicken to fry for supper."

"Later, mebbe. Got more work to do than a one-armed smithy."

She nodded and took a few steps before turning to ask, "Are you still peeved at me?"

He squinted, but not enough to hide the twinkle in his eyes. "Yup. May be spring a'fore I simmer down."

"Guess I shouldn't ask a favor, then."

"You can ask. Probably won't get it, but you can ask."

Megan looked skyward and sighed. "Can I borrow a saddle and one of the buckskins this afternoon? I've got to go to the assay office."

"Ain't got no saddle, and them horses ain't ridin' stock, gal. They'll jar your gizzard up betwixt yer ears."

"Please?"

He swiped the air with a paw-sized hand. "Aw, hell, I don't mind bein' yer stablehand. I'll jes' flop a blanket on one o' them dilseys, stick a bridle in her teeth, and you can ride 'er like a squaw fer all I care."

Pausing to set one hand on his hip, he pointed a skinny finger at her and warned, "But I'll tell ya what, that fried chicken had by God better be the best this feller's ever put his lips to, ya hear?"

Megan grimaced as she swung her right leg over the mare's neck and slid off onto the street. Wrapping the reins around the hitching post, she looked the buckskin square in the eyes and said, "Girl, you've got a backbone like a split rail fence."

The assay office was again empty when Megan entered, but no one responded to the door chimes. She rapped her knuckles on the counter and called toward the back room, "Mister Bement?"

Zadock's younger, stouter replica answered the summons. Judging by his expression, he was annoyed by the interruption.

"Yes? I am Hyam Bement," he sniffed, giving her dusty clothes a disdainful glimpse. "And who might you be?"

"The name's Megan O'Malley. I'm here to collect my assay certificate."

"You must be mistaken, miss. I have no certificate registered in that name."

She gripped the counter's edge to curb her temper. "I left my samples with your father on Monday. I'd appreciate it if you checked your records again."

Bement reached beneath the counter, drew out a square, lidded box, and slammed it down in front of her. He riffled through several buff-colored slips of stiff parchment, then dropped the stack into the file and reclosed its lid.

"There is no certificate in the name of O'Malley."

Megan fought down the panic rising in her chest. In a trembling voice, she said, "I want to speak with your father. Now."

The younger Bement fairly chortled. "Then I suggest you take yourself to the cemetery, Miss O'Malley. We buried the old boy yesterday morning."

She felt the blood drain from her face. Confusion swirled in her mind, but she knew arguing further was a waste of breath. She turned and scuffed out the door.

"Well, pardon me," huffed the portly woman Megan collided with on the boardwalk. Then, peering more closely, she inquired, "Are you ill, miss?"

As suddenly as it descended, the muzziness in Megan's mind evaporated. After apologizing for her clumsiness and thanking the woman for her concern, she whipped the reins loose, pulled the mare alongside an empty wagon, and used its footboard as a mounting platform.

All I've lost is a few days time, Megan reasoned. Soon as the evening chores are done, I'm heading for the Trinity for another batch of samples.

She stroked the horse's mane. Like Barlow P. says, there's more'n one way to skin a cat besides stickin' it in a boot jack and pullin' its tail.

Squirming on the blanket trying to seat herself with some measure of comfort, she heard David hail her from across the street. He waved, then zigzagged through convoys of passing rigs and horsemen to reach her side.

"What are you doing in town in the middle of the afternoon, darlin'?"

"Oh, I had an errand to do."

"That's quite a steed you've got under you," he teased. "A paragon of equine loveliness, no doubt—and blanket-broke, too."

Megan stuck her tongue out at him. "She got me here, and'll get me home."

"I surely hope so. The gorgeous Irish lass astride her back is attending a minstrel show with her sweetheart tonight."

Mary, Jesus, and Joseph, she exclaimed to herself. I completely forgot. When David asked me, I thought we'd have a bonanza to celebrate. I can't go now.

"Megan?" he said, squeezing her knee gently. "You're looking a bit peaked all of a sudden."

"Uh, I . . . " she stammered and rubbed her temple. "It's just a little headache ..." Swallowing hard, she turned away. The concern in David's eyes made her feel like six kinds of traitor. But, first things first. When she explained later, he'd understand.

"Damn it, you're working too hard, darlin'. And that spill you took shook you up more than you'll admit."

"I'm fine, truly."

"I say you're not, and you're not going to sashay all over town tonight, either." He raised a hand to stem further discussion. "Don't bother arguing. I'm driving you to the hotel after your shift and tucking you in for the night."

"But—"

"No buts about it. Now get this glue pot movin' and I'll see you this evening." Before slapping the buckskin's rump, he added softly, "I love you, Megan. Very much."

With a heart as heavy as a grindstone, she averted her eyes and geed the mare toward Treasure Hill.

Later, as the sun splashed a bank of buttermilk clouds with faint rosy rays, Megan cursed herself for the supper menu she'd divined. Cauldrons rimmed with gravy and mashed potato leavings and a stack of greasy iron skillets littered the floor; the sink's drainboard wasn't large enough to hold them all.

"I must get the washin' up done before David gets here," she grumbled, scouring gummy plates like a madwoman. She was rinsing the last of the pots when Barlow P. stomped into the kitchen.

"*G-od-d-damn,* what a day this's been. And the sumbitch

ain't over yet." He leaned against the sawbuck and rubbed
his eyes. His shoulders sagged well beyond his customary
slouch.

With a heaving sigh, he hitched up his britches and said,
"Jes' came by to tell ya I cain't jitney ya back to town
tonight. Got a burnt-up hoist engine in number one. Without it, I can't get men up nor down, can't heave out the
ore, and the water's gushin' in like sixty."

"Don't waste another minute frettin' about me. David's
comin' for me before long anyhow."

I won't be here, she continued to herself, but I'll leave
a note so neither of you need worry.

He grinned wearily. "Shit—wish that pump'd fix that
easy. Gotta get back after it." Striding across the room to
give her shoulders a squeeze, he said, "See ya in the mornin', gal," then turned to leave.

"Good night, Barlow P."

He was almost out the door when he snapped his fingers
and pulled up short. "Hell's bells, I dang near forgot.
How'd them rocks assay out?"

Megan hesitated, then shook her head. "The report
wasn't ready yet."

His eyebrows peaked in surprise. "Yer takin' that purty
calmlike, considerin' you been jumpy as a June bug all
week."

"Pitchin' a hissy won't get the assay done any faster."

"Hmmph. Never stopped ya before, though," he drawled,
regarding her quizzically. "Ain't ya powerful curious?"

"Of course I am," she retorted, stopping herself before
she divulged more than she intended.

"Well, I prob'ly oughta let Bement tell ya . . ."

"Tell me what?"

He grinned like a pup with its first bone. "I dribbled a
smidge of acid on that chunk ya gave me. It's silver, gal.
Cain't say how high it'll grade, but it's the gen-you-wine
article."

With that, he wheeled and sauntered from the kitchen.

"Mary, Mother of us all, it's truly silver," she breathed.
"I've got to get to the Trinity for those new samples."

She glared at the crusty frying pans. On impulse she
scooped them up and stashed them in the tin-lined larder.
Following a hasty tidying up, she sauntered out to the yard
as if taking a rest between chores.

Voices drifted down from adjacent buildings. A mangy dog, which had claimed the mine property as his home, snuffed for scraps near the overflowing ash cans.

Thanks to a feeble quarter moon, the area lying between the lean-to and the stable was cast in deep shadow. She held her breath and sprinted across the rocky ground.

Unwilling to risk lighting the lantern she'd brought, she bridled the snorting, skittish horse by feel. Megan flinched at the sensation of warm slobber oozing down her wrist. Grimacing, she wiped it on the blanket, then smoothed the cover over the animal's back and led it outside.

Light spilling from the kitchen window jolted her memory. Damn, she thought, I forgot to leave that note for Barlow P. and David. The mare's white patches glowed like phosphorous in the moonlight. Oh, well, I can't risk it now.

Megan yanked the reins and broke into a dogtrot until she was well down the hill. A boulder as big as a wagon tire gave her a needed leg-up onto the buckskin's back. Cantering wide around Pioche's perimeter, she gritted her teeth and heeled the mare into a gallop.

For a dray horse, the animal possessed a smoother gait than Megan expected. Because she'd traveled the route so many times, she knew the location of every ravine and wash and guided her mount accordingly.

The buckskin was no Shiloh, and the blanket provided scant comfort, but the familiar craggy hump loomed into view, seemingly, in record time.

After draping the reins around an outcropping, Megan scraped a lucifer against her boot sole and held the flame to the lantern's wick. In the cloaking darkness, its globe burned as brightly as a lighthouse beacon. She blinked and looked around, realizing the pool of light was visible for miles.

"Holler if you see any spooks," she hissed to the buckskin, and giggled nervously. Her pulse raced as she loped to the rubble heap left by the slide.

"Well, that's odd," she muttered. "I could swear I reset my claim stake over there on the far side of that slag heap."

The notice leaned whomperjawed against the bluff. She got down on one knee in front of it and held the lantern higher.

"No!" Her scream echoed across the barrens. "The Trinity is *mine*!"

She jerked the stake out of the rock and hurled it against the bluff. It clattered to a halt; the paper's inscription faceup and all too visible: "Upon this date, September 13 . . ."

Through spilling tears, Megan's eyes skipped to the signature line. In fluid, formal script it read: "Moses Keegan."

# Chapter Twenty-one

Barlow P.'s eyes jerked open when the cabin door exploded inward. Before it slammed against the adjacent wall, he'd rolled off the far edge of the bunk and hit the floor belly-first.

"What the hell's goin'—"

A voice roared from the threshold, "Where's Megan?"

The mine manager raised up on his hands and knees and looked over the edge of the mattress. "Shit fire ... That you, Jacobs?"

A match snicked and flared. The flame arced upward. Its flickering, orange glow etched macabre shadows into David's angular, scowling face. He turned and lit the peg lamp bracketed nearby.

Barlow P. gained his feet, watching warily as the intruder scanned the meagerly furnished room. David's eyes lingered on the bunk's jumbled bed linens.

"I suppose I should be delighted to find you sleeping alone," he stated coldly.

Barlow P.'s solid roundhouse sent the editor staggering backward. Backbone met doorjamb with a sickening thud. He grunted as the air rushed from his lungs. David's head snapped up; hands clenched into fists.

"Best make it a good 'un, ya ghost-eyed bastard," the older man taunted. "Ya won't git another 'un."

David stared hard at Barlow P., then looked down. He stooped over, reaching to snag his Stetson from the floor. "My temper gets the best of me sometimes," he muttered.

Barlow P. scratched through his union suit at an imaginary itch. "Temper didn't bust my goddamned door, Jacobs. That was pure damfoolishness."

"May-be," he parried, rubbing the welt rising on his cheekbone. "But there's no question that Megan's quite fond of you."

Fury set Barlow P.'s temples throbbing. He edged close enough to count the hairs bridging the other man's nose. "Yer same as callin' her a whore, boy."

David stepped back, his jaw jutting defensively. "I didn't mean . . . All right. I was crazy jealous when I couldn't find her. The cook shack's deserted, she's not at the hotel—"

"So ya figgered she was warmin' my sheets, eh? You sorry sumbitch. I oughta kill ya just fer thinkin' it."

A guttural grunt seemed to expel any fight left in the newspaperman. "Yeah, you probably should." Currying his mustaches thoughtfully, he asked, as much to himself as his rival, "But if she isn't here, then where in God's name could she be?"

Planting his hands on his hips, Barlow P. glared at him. "I reckon, nigh on a thousand places." To himself, he quipped, and if ya had a brain under all that hair, ya'd *know* where she's gone off to.

Adopting a more fatherly tone, Barlow P. said, "Frettin' gets wimmen addlepated sometimes—even sandy ones like Megan. And she's been skittish as a colt ever since she found them rocks last Sunday."

"Rocks? What rocks?"

"Je-hosophat, man! That poke fulla ore-bearin' quartz she hauled outta the Trinity."

David just stood there wearing a dumbfounded expression.

"Listen careful now, Jacobs. Unless I miss my guess, that little gal's got a king's ransom in silver. Betcha that's why the assayer's not done with the report. Her claim's so rich, he ain't believin' his own tests."

David cocked his head. "She found the ore on Sunday? You're sure? When was it assayed?"

"Took the samples in Monday. Scampered to town this afternoon for the results, only they ain't ready yet."

The editor studied his hat brim for a long moment. Then, with a shaky hand, he placed it on his head and tapped it in place. He turned toward the door, then paused and looked back at Barlow P.

"Megan didn't tell me. I was with her Sunday night and again this afternoon. She never said a word." He squared his shoulders and walked out of the cabin.

The jangle of his buggy's harness faded into the night before Barlow P. had wrestled into his clothes. "Damned if I don't feel kinda sorry for that boy," he mumbled, gripping his boot by the mule ears to tug it on. "That gal's got a heap of fence-mendin' to do."

Finding the buckskin missing from the stable confirmed his suspicions. After bridling its mate, he hurdled onto its bare back.

"I ain't rid Injun style in twenty year," he warned his mount as they clopped down the hill. "Don'tcha git loco on me or I'll skin ya alive and eat ya fer breakfast."

He wasn't far from Pioche when he caught sight of another rider in the distance. He slowed the mare to a walk. Swaying with the animal's rocking chair gait, Barlow P. curled his palm over the handle of his Army Colt. He squinted, trying to identify the indistinct form.

When the other horse started angling eastward, he assumed its rider had seen him and was cautiously avoiding a meeting.

"Trottin' over there'll likely get me kilt a'fore I can say 'Howdy,' " he opined, reining in to a halt. He cupped his hands around his mouth and hollered, "Yo, Megan? It's Barlow P." His bellowed query cut the stillness like a panther's growl.

The rider pulled up. Barlow P. again sought the hardware strapped to his hip. When the other horse commenced a moseyed haw in his direction, the short hairs rose on his neck.

Muscles rippled in the buckskin's meaty shoulders. It whickered and pawed the ground. An answering whinny sent a low whistle of relief through Barlow P.'s lips. He wiped his sweaty brow with his shirtsleeve. "Goddamn it, Megan. Why didn't ya give a hail back there?"

Her head bobbed as limply as a rag doll's. She was slumped like a dozing night herder and appeared frightfully small—almost shrunken. Barlow P. couldn't understand why he hadn't realized it was her sooner.

She drew up alongside and turned toward him. Pale ribbons trailed down her face where tears had washed away the dust. He'd seen that glassy, defeated look before. At Antietam, he'd cajoled and comforted many a boy soldier who knew he'd lost his last battle.

Barlow P.'s boot soles clapped against the hard-baked barrens. He raised his arms and swung Megan off the buckskin's back. She clung to him, sobs wracking her body.

"There now, baby gal," he crooned, holding her tightly against his chest. "Nothin's so bad that we cain't fix it."

Her voice was muffled by his shirt, but there was no mistaking the hatred in it. "He stole my claim . . . took the Trinity away from me."

The manager ducked his chin trying to catch a glimpse of her face. "Who's 'he'?"

"M-Moses Keegan. There's a fresh notice where mine used to be. His name's scrawled on it. He's not even a prospector. I knew when we met on the stagecoach that he's a short-trigger man."

Like a scrapper gaining his second wind, Barlow P. could feel a surge of feistiness race through her. That's my gal, he cheered silently. Soppin' my shirt ain't yer style, Megan O'Malley. Get butt-kickin', noose-knottin' mad.

"Keegan, eh?" he retorted aloud. "He ain't no lone wolf, neither. He's one of Artemus Rath's pistol-whippers."

Barlow P. paused to cogitate those implications. "That crew's slicker'n snakes in a lard bucket, but we ain't barefoot. Reckon you'd best tell me what the hell's been goin' on, and I mean everything."

When Megan stepped back, a wan smile softened her face and a spirited glint sparkled in her eyes. She laced her fingers through his rough ones and held his hand firmly.

"Half of nothin' is nothin', and that may be all the Trinity's worth. But whatever happens, from now on out, we're partners. If we get that mine back, it's split shares, right down the line."

"Ain't no call fer—"

She tossed her head and chuckled. "Like you tell me about six times a day, shut your mouth and open your ears." A recount of both visits to Bement's, why she'd hightailed it to the mine, and her discovery of Keegan's notice followed.

Barlow P. propped an elbow on his horse's rump. He stroked his chin thoughtfully; he considered their options.

"Old Zadock shoulda given ya a receipt for them samples. Sounds like the sight of a pretty woman sent his brains slidin' south. To compound the foolishness, the knothead turns up deader'n a can of corned beef."

"You don't think he did it on purpose?"

"What? Banked his own fire?"

Megan groaned in exasperation. "Good Lord, no. I mean, maybe he didn't just 'forget' that receipt."

"Nah. Folks find out fast when an assayer gets greedy." To himself he added, Zadock was a straight arrow, but I ain't so sure about that boy of his. Gonna poke around and see what kinda dirt shakes loose.

A jaw-cracking yawn preceded Megan's weary sigh. "I'm so tired, none of this makes any sense. Without an assay provin' high grade ore, why'd Keegan bother to jump my claim?"

"Wouldn't of. But a stick in the ground with a piece of paper tacked on it don't mean much anyhow. Yer claim's registered with the district recorder. File a complaint against ol' Keegan and the miner's court'll fix his wagon. Seems to me, Rath's gittin' sloppy with his flimflams. Or figgers nobody'd dare call his bluff."

"Uh-huh. And that was his second mistake."

Barlow P. grinned, waggling his head like a wet dog. He, too, was wearing down from the long day. "How 'bout you leg up behind me and we'll start for town. Cain't unscramble them eggs 'til mornin' no how, and the sun'll be up soon enough."

While he was mounting his buckskin, Megan turned its twin around, then handed him the reins. She felt as light as a child when he pulled her up behind him.

Before long, her head joggled on his shoulder. Her quiet, even breathing told him she'd fallen asleep.

The *tink-a-tink-a-tink* of a saloon's piano reached his ears. Behind every pair of batwings a bar rail hitched up scores of boots and the air reeked of cheap cigars, slopped beer, and rotgut whiskey. Mostly, the hell-raisers stayed to their end of Pioche, and sloshed off to bed about the time the good shepherds departed theirs.

Barlow P. tried to keep his eyes peeled for bounders roving the streets, but the sensation of Megan's soft breasts pressing into his back fuddled his concentration.

He felt guilty; ashamed of his arousal . . . and, God help him, more like a man than he had in years. He squirmed, trying to relieve his distress but at the same time trying not to remedy its cause.

Light glinted off an upraised bottle as the familiar figure grasping it took a pull at the contents. The man's other arm hugged an awning post like a lover. He stared out, wide-eyed, then blinked as if that could cure a bad case of double vision.

Barlow P. took grim satisfaction in tipping his hat as they passed by. Jacobs, if ya thought my fist packed a wallop, jes' wait 'til them Kentucky corn squeezin's git their licks in.

"Daybreak's comin' in a few hours, boy," he said softly. "Megan's dead-tuckered. I'm bunkin' her at the cabin so's she can sleep long as she can. Any objections?"

He took the newspaperman's groaning heave for a "no." With his lips curving into a sly grin, Barlow P. sneered, "Never could abide a man what cain't hold his likker."

When they arrived at the cabin, he had the devil's own time dismounting without unseating his groggy passenger. Megan virtually tumbled off the horse and into his arms.

He carried her inside and laid her on the bunk. She mewed like a kitten as he pulled the blanket up to her chin, then curled up on her side.

After stabling the horses, Barlow P. fashioned a pallet across the cabin's threshold and stretched out, fully dressed. His last thought was how beautiful Megan looked with her hair fanning across his pillow.

# Chapter Twenty-two

Late the next afternoon, Megan burst into the district recorder's office like Sherman's march to the sea. If Barlow
P. hadn't "loaned" her a few of his men to help with the
chores, she'd never have made it to the office before it
closed.

Harlan Ivers's eyes frogged behind his pince-nez when
she demanded, "Fetch me the claim ledger. Please."

"Yes, ma'am!"

He slid the thick, leather-bound book down the counter
toward her and edged away as if she might hurl it back at
him. The book's string stitching creaked when she spread
it open and started flipping through its ruled pages.

Her finger traced down a column of claim numbers,
slowed, then stopped when she found her own. On the line
adjacent, where she'd proudly signed her name only six
weeks earlier, "Moses Keegan" glared boldly from the
page.

White-hot rage coursed through Megan's body. She
pointed at the hated signature. "This record's been al-
tered, mister."

Sweat beaded on Ivers's balding pate. Mopping it with
his handkerchief, he stammered, "N-no, ma'am. That's simply not possible. I double-check every entry and that ledger's locked up in the safe at night."

"And I'll wager you don't remember me affixin' my
name in it last July, now do you? Don't recall tellin' me I
was the first woman who'd staked one since you took
office."

He studied her for a moment, then averted his eyes. "No,
ma'am, I don't. I've never seen you before in my life."

There was nothing else to say. From what Barlow P. had
told her, with no proof that she'd ever darkened Bement's
door and now her name obliterated from the public record

as the claim holder, the Trinity belonged to Moses Keegan—or more accurately Artemus Rath.

Megan ambled from the office and on down the boardwalk. Her mind was as blank as a wiped slate. She couldn't
believe her dream had vanished as quickly as a desert
mirage.

Plopping on a bench, she absently watched the ladies and
gents stroll by. Their cheerful banter tolled in her ears like
cold-hearted insults.

A flash of brilliant white caught her eye. Miracle's fitted
blouse and voluminous skirt were as spotless as a snowbank. She swung a split-oak market basket heaped with
fresh vegetables as effortlessly as a reticule.

The fiddler cocked her head toward Megan. Recognition
sparked in her eyes, yet her inscrutable, masklike expression remained.

"Evening," Megan said morosely.

Miracle hesitated, then returned the greeting with a curt
nod. Rather than move on, she stopped and scrutinized
Megan intently.

"Is there something wrong, Miracle? Why are you staring
at me like that?"

The woman raised a trembling finger to her throat, traced
the jagged scar, and pointed at Megan's heart. Twice, she
repeated the strange gesture. Not until Miracle sat down
beside Megan and tenderly patted her hand did Megan decipher what Miracle was trying to communicate.

Yanking a mercantile receipt and stubby pencil from her
pocket, Megan wrote, "Are you askin' if I'm troubled?"

Miracle nodded solemnly.

Next, she scrawled, "How did you know?"

The fiddler forked two fingers and laid them beneath
her eyes.

Megan sat motionless for a moment, amazed by the
woman's powers of perception. Then, at the bottom of the
sheet, she wrote, "Bless you for caring, but don't fret for
me. Hearts break, but they keep on beating."

At that, Miracle shook her head emphatically. She
jumped up and grabbed Megan by the arm. "Where are
we going," she gasped, practically running to keep pace
with the taller woman's stride. Miracle's only response was
to grip her hostage more tightly.

As they stormed through town, Megan's curiosity overcame her initial fright. How awful it must be to not be able to speak or hear, she thought. She stole a surreptitious peek at the welted wound slashing beneath the woman's ear and shuddered.

Her legs were wobbling before she realized where Miracle was taking her. In the twilight, the classic lines of Delia Terhune's antebellum manse rose like a phoenix from the hardscrabble earth.

On its portico, a liveried footman was assisting a lady from a cobalt-blue landau replete with gilded scrollwork. A formally attired gent with his hands clasped behind his back waited nearby.

Miracle veered toward the side of the house. Megan closed her eyes and breathed in the delicate scent of lilacs banking the brick wall. She was rousted from her reverie when her guide halted at the rear stoop.

"I can't go in there, Miracle. The Widow Terhune has guests."

Whether the fiddler understood or not, she all but shoved Megan through the door, then pulled her along a narrow hallway. They whisked through a library with towering walnut bookshelves and plush crimson velvet furnishings. Miracle threw open the double doors to what Megan guessed was the back parlor.

The older woman scurried over to a camel-backed rosewood settee. She beckoned to Megan, gesturing for her to sit down. The second she complied, Miracle nodded and left the room, closing the doors behind her.

Megan tapped her fingertips together while gandering around the lavishly decorated room. From every wall, a veritable army of framed daguerreotypes frowned disapprovingly at her. She crinkled her nose at the thought of attending family reunions with those hawkish men and grim, martyred women.

The room was good-sized, but its imposing Victorian furnishings, tawny velveteen draperies, and cluttered bric-a-brac made it seem stuffy and cramped.

Several times Megan awakened with a start, unaware she'd dozed off. She had no idea how many hours she'd waited when Miracle again appeared at an adjacent pair of doors and summoned her with a crooked finger.

The mansion's pink-and-gray-mottled Italian marble foyer was as big as a ballroom. A serpentine stairway leading to the second floor certainly provided the lady of the house a grand avenue for dramatic entrances. Megan gaped at the monstrous chandelier suspended from a painted ceiling depicting plump, naked cherubs frolicking among fluffy clouds.

A leather heel stamped against the polished stone. Standing like a sentinel, Miracle was signing an unquestionable "Come here!"

Laying a hand against Megan's back, she hastened her into a cherry-paneled, softly lit study. Brown, thronelike leather chairs and a matching davenport were arranged in a crescent in front of the fireplace.

To Megan's left, an octagonal game table and castored chairs nestled in front of an expansive bay window. Considering the parlor and foyer's lavish excesses, the study appeared almost barren, cozily conservative, and oddly masculine.

A desk the size of a buckboard's bed dwarfed the woman seated behind it. Enormous sloe eyes, the same color as the lilacs blooming outside, were framed by a sorrel chignon braided with strands of opalesque pearls. When she stood, her lavender satin gown clung to an enviable hourglass figure. The low-cut, chemisette bodice revealed the kind of cleavage men dreamed of.

"I'm Missus Delia Terhune," she drawled, folding her bejeweled, manicured hands in front of her. "Welcome to my home."

Megan affected a shallow curtsy and introduced herself.

"O'Malley, you say? That name seems familiar. Do you have people in Atlanta?"

"Not hardly, ma'am . . ." She giggled nervously. "My sister and I came from Ireland just three years ago."

"Oh, I see. And what brought you here?"

Megan hesitated, then answered in a rush, "I staked a claim south of town that showed color. In fact, I'm sure there's silver there 'cause a yellow-bellied—"

The Widow Terhune's laughter rang like wind chimes in the wind. "Mercy me, I meant, what brought you and your sister to America? I want to hear every smidgen of your adventure. Please join me for tea, and some of Cook's delightful little cakes."

"That's very kind of you, but this isn't really a social call."

"My dear Miss O'Malley, Southern hospitality allows for no other kind." She smiled, adding, "I realize you've come to me for help—Miracle would not have tucked you under her wing otherwise. But let's get acquainted first, shall we?"

Ensconced in one of the fireplace chairs, Megan watched Miracle pour the steaming beverage from a filigreed silver pot. Missus Terhune waved to catch the server's attention, then said, "Thank you, Miracle."

The deaf-mute tottered off to a corner chair. She tugged a needleworked sampler from the canvas bag lying beside it.

"I've tried stopping her, but Miracle simply waits on me hand and foot," the widow commented wistfully. "I often wonder what thoughts churn inside that silenced mind."

She selected a chocolate petit four, holding it aloft with her pinkie bent like a scorpion's tail. "But if she wasn't deaf, the poor thing'd probably be bored by my ramblings anyway. Oh, well, enough of that—I'm dying to hear all about you."

As simply as she could, Megan described the ocean voyage, Boston, and the relocation to San Francisco.

"Did your sister come with you to Pioche?"

Relieving her parched mouth with a sip of tea, Megan shook her head. "No, Frances married a man she met on the train—Oran Dannelly."

She was taken aback when the widow's eyes squinted, instantly returning to a look of rapt fascination. Perhaps she doesn't approve of such whirlwind romances, Megan mused. "They had a rough row to hoe for a while. Oran's a fireman and he was burned somethin' awful last year. But everything's fine now, and they have a darlin' little boy and a baby girl."

"Ummmm, how lovely . . ."

For all her earlier enthusiasm, Megan interpreted the widow's bland expression as polite indifference.

"It's getting late, Missus Terhune, and I don't want to wear out my welcome. I am sore in need of your help and would be forever beholden if you can give it."

"Of course. I'll do whatever I can."

Megan eased forward in her chair and launched into her tale, keeping her voice calm and businesslike. When she related the nightmare of finding Moses Keegan's claim notice and implicated Artemus Rath in the theft, the widow's lips flattened into a thin line.

"Those are serious accusations you're making," she remarked sternly.

"It's worse than that, ma'am. I visited the district recorder's office this afternoon. Keegan's name has replaced mine in the record book."

The Widow Terhune sat silent for several minutes. Her tone was sympathetic, yet dismissive when she said, "I'm sorry, Miss O'Malley, but I don't believe there's anything I can do. Artemus Rath is a loathsome thug, but quite adept at manipulating the law to suit his vile purposes. You're not the first he's cheated out of a fortune. Sadly, I doubt you'll be the last."

"But, Missus Terhune, you're not without influence—*powerful* influence from what I've been told. If Rath knew you were on my side—"

The study's pocket doors slid open and rumbled into their hollows. A deep, slurry baritone called out, "Delia, my pet, we've a splendiferous victory to celebrate. Champagne for everyone!"

Megan craned her neck around the side of the chair to see who was making such a ruckus. Recognition turned her blood to ice.

Artemus Rath stood in the threshold with his arms outstretched, a foil-crowned bottle in each hand. Behind him, Hyam Bement was grinning like a fat-faced schoolboy.

# Chapter Twenty-three

With a handsome head of steel-gray hair, olive skin, and patrician features, Artemus Rath fairly oozed gentility and decorum. He reminded Megan of a sea siren—bewitching, attractive, and deadly.

She leapt from the chair. "Isn't this the man you called loathsome thug? Why, you're in *league* with that shyster."

The Widow Terhune's lips turned up in a bemused, feline smile. An evil chuckle rumbled in her throat. "No, Miss O'Malley. Mister Rath, as you so charmingly put it, is in league with me."

Megan stood stock-still, too stunned to reply.

"Who is this woman, Delia?" Rath inquired as he strolled toward her. "Another one of your foundlings?"

"Shut up, Artemus. You've done quite enough damage for one evening," she snarled, rising to her feet. "How dare you burst in here unannounced."

The attorney traced a finger across his crony's voluptuous bosom. "But I so often do, Delia dar—"

The widow slapped his arm away. "Get out. Both of you. And don't come back until you're summoned."

Bement stammered, "A thousand pardons, ma'am."

"I said, get *out!*"

The two men spun on their heels to leave. Megan glanced at the oblivious Miracle, then started to follow the men.

"Not you, my dear," Delia purred. "We have business to discuss."

"The *hell* we do. 'Twas a fine run of schemin' you've had, but it's over. I'll see to that."

The woman's eyelids fluttered beguilingly. "Oh, really. And who do you think will believe a cheeky guttersnipe like you?"

"David Jacobs, for one. I'm sure plenty of folks who've

jigged to your tune and suffered your connivin' will shout
to the skies—and the marshal—once the truth comes out."

Delia's face hardened like granite. "Silly fool." Her crin-
olined skirt swished as she glided over to the desk. She
thrashed through a pile of papers in one of its drawers.

With a grunt of satisfaction, she extracted an ivory linen
envelope and waved it lazily at Megan. "There will be no
disclosures made, darling girl. None whatsoever. I daresay,
this letter guarantees it."

The widow's tone held no bluff—only cool confidence.
But what could a letter . . .

"I've known more about you than you realized from the
moment you mentioned your sister's name, Miss O'Malley.
Among other things, I'm a sponge. I absorb countless
pieces of information. It's amazing how many of them become valuable later on."

Megan snorted in exasperation. "Stop toying with me."

Azure sparks flew from Delia's diamond rings as she
drew her fingers provocatively along the edge of the envelope. "Very well. I know all about you and Frances stealing
money for your fares to San Francisco. Two hundred dollars, I believe? Of course, with interest, I'd say the debt is
nearer five hundred by now."

"I've never stolen a nickel in my life! We—" Suddenly,
she remembered the empty penny bank, Frances presenting
her with train tickets and never explaining where the
money had come from.

"Ah, judging by your expression, your sister acted alone.
All the better."

Delia fanned her fingers on the desk and leaned forward.
"Breathe a word of what transpired this evening or make
any further accusations regarding your claim's, shall we say,
change in ownership, and Frances will be arrested and
clapped in irons."

She smiled humorlessly, adding, "What a shame it would
be for those sweet children to grow up without a mother."

Megan could scarcely breathe. She hunched over, hugging her midsection as if she'd been mule-kicked. Slowly
she turned pleading eyes toward Miracle. She thought she
saw a tear trickle down the deaf-mute's wizened cheek.
Miracle blinked and looked down to pull a thread through
the canvas.

"All right," she said to Delia. "You win. But how did you know . . . about the money, I mean?"

The Widow Terhune laughed heartily as if a joke had just been told. "It's so deliciously ironic, darling. Your beloved Frances stole it from her employers, the esteemed Clarence and Beatrice Sidemore of Boston."

Megan gawked at her, perplexed. "But—?"

"Had you ever met her, I'm sure you'd have noticed a resemblance," the woman gloated. "You see, Beatrice Sidemore is *my* sister."

Megan wasn't alone when she started the walk back to town. Anger, heartache, betrayal, and despair accompanied her, jabbing at her like circled schoolboys playing soldier with stick bayonets.

I won't brand Frances a thief, she thought. I'll never believe she didn't intend to repay that money. But why didn't she tell me? The debt is as much mine as hers.

Guilt clawed at her insides. A shrill voice inside her head asked, so why didn't you make her tell you? You could have, but you chose not to.

She clasped her hands behind her back. There were no tears left to shed, no revenge to plot. She felt numb, resigned to play the hand fate had dealt her.

What's done is done, she adjudged. No going back—no fixing it. Learn from it, and put it to rest.

Oddly, a glimmer of hope sparked within her. "The Trinity's gone, but that's not the only pocket of silver in this territory. And I'm just as strong and twice smarter'n I was a few weeks ago. I'll find me another rich claim, and rub Delia Terhune's slutty face in the tailin's."

Gazing at the ratchety hills where Sanders and Meredith's hoisting works was outlined against the night sky, she decided, "I'll move out of the hotel. Sleep on a cot in the kitchen. That'll thicken my pay envelope. Won't be long before the Sidemores'll get back every cent they're owed."

Gunshots and cries of *"Viva la Mehico"* and *"Diez y seis de Septiembre"* erupted several hundred yards before the barrens gave way to Main Street's rutted length. A series of horrific explosions rent the air.

The earth bucked under Megan's feet. She was hurled backward, arms pinwheeling helplessly. Landing flat on her back, she cried out when sharp rocks stabbed into her skin.

Churning, mushroom-shaped fireballs surged skyward from Pioche's business district. It looked as if the end of the world had come.

She squatted on her heels, then stood up. Staggering like a drunkard, she cradled her pounding head in both hands. Even with her ears covered, she could hear women and children screaming, men shouting for water and help.

Dizziness set the scene spinning. Megan groaned, dropped to her knees, and vomited.

More reports sounded like cannons firing. Flames capered across rooftops. Smoke billowed upward, blotting out the stars.

She wiped her mouth with her kerchief, then tied it across her nose. Limping, and still nauseous, she clenched her jaw and plodded toward the inferno.

From the Panacre Saloon to the Western Union office, a bucket brigade was trying valiantly to douse the roaring wall of fire rapidly consuming every building between. A second crew was forming to soak the tinder-dry structures in the flames' probable path.

Windows exploded. Deadly shrapnel spewed in all directions. Megan thought she heard a steam whistle wail, but the crackling, thunderous blaze surrounding her grew louder, swallowing all sound except its own.

Merchants scrambled frantically, heaving merchandise into the street. Horses whinnied in terror, some still harnessed to buggies and wagons; others trailing reins and rearing on their hind legs.

Smoke stung Megan's eyes and seared her throat. Weaving through the crowd of burnished-bronze faces, she pulled up short. Where Blount's Mercantile had stood—and at least a half-dozen other adjacent businesses—only a yawning, smoldering crater remained.

Flames swept across the roof of the Bank of Pioche's shake shingles and licked at the eaves of Chudomelka's Bakery. Time and again, a woman ducked a pail in a trough and flung water at the fire. Ropy strands of hair had escaped their plait and straggled down her neck. Two little towheads in homespun nightshirts were partially hidden in the folds of her flimsy cotton gown.

Megan jerked her kerchief under her chin. "Let me spell you so you can see to your children," she shouted, reaching for the bucket's bale.

The woman swiped her face with her sleeve. "Bless you, ma'am, but if you truly want to help, take my young'uns up to the church house. If it's still standin', the boys'll be safe there."

She cast rueful eyes at the smoke streaming through cracks in the bakery's clapboards. "My shop's done for, but I ain't up to leavin' it yet."

Megan beckoned to the taller, freckle-faced boy. His stance and expression were so rigid, he seemed like an adult in miniature. She told him her name, then said, "Your mama's asked me to take your little brother to the church house. Except I haven't lived here very long and I don't know where it is. Do you?"

He hesitated a moment, then answered solemnly, "Yes, ma'am."

"Will you lead us there?"

At his mother's nod, he took his younger brother by the wrist. "Follow me, ma'am."

He headed west where most of the damage was confined to buildings collapsed by the concussion. He's a smart one, Megan thought. Taking the long way around is safer than battling through the frenzy.

Aloud, she asked her charges to introduce themselves.

Her guide jerked a thumb toward his sibling. "Me and Ma call him 'Skeeter' 'cause he's a baby, but his right name's Jonah. Ma says he'll grow into it, 'ventually."

She chuckled and started to ruffle his hair. Don't, she admonished silently. The little man'll take it for an insult. "And what might your name be?"

He regarded her gravely. "It's Dillon, and you'd best not laugh or you can find the dad-blamed church all by yourself."

"Laugh? Why, I wouldn't dream of it, Dillon. That's a grand Celtic name. It means faithful and true, and that you are, lad."

He scuffled up dust clouds with his bare feet, then raised his sunken, soot-streaked face to hers. "I ain't no lad, Miss Megan. Since Pa died, Ma says I'm the man of the family."

His voice was too world-weary for a child of six or seven. Like meat at every meal and store-bought clothes, youthful abandon was a luxury poor folks couldn't afford.

Megan remembered all too well when her own childhood had ended. She'd been watching the last of her father's barrows being loaded into Squire Bernard's wagon.

"I'll expect you off my land in a fortnight," the land-lord stated.

Mikaleen O'Malley argued quietly, "My father was born in that cottage, Squire, and my grandfather before him."

Bernard stabbed the loamy earth with his cane. "And so it's charity you're beggin', is it? Aye, and if you were half the man your father or grandfather were, you'd die before you'd take it."

Late that night, a gunshot awakened Megan and Frances. Their mother shushed them and told them to go back to sleep. The next morning they were told their father was dead. That he'd been in the shed cleaning his fowling piece and hadn't known it was loaded.

Dillon's prideful announcement ended Megan's wool-gathering. "There's the church house, ma'am. Told ya I could find it."

"Aye, and I never doubted it, son."

The Prince of Peace Lutheran Church gleamed with fresh whitewash. Hardly larger than a cottage, its facade boasted a gorgeous stained glass window portraying Jesus nailed to the cross that probably cost its congregation more than the building itself.

Open double doors offered safe haven to anyone in need. As Megan and the boys crossed the threshold, she saw that it was being used as a hospital as well. Many pews held blanket-draped victims of the holocaust. Groans and non-sensical mutterings echoed off the cantilevered ceiling.

A grandmotherly sort waddled up to them. "Why, Skee-ter and Dillon Chudomelka! You boys look plumb peckish. Scat over there to Missus Abernathy and she'll scratch you up something to eat."

The towheads didn't need any more encouragement. They skipped off hand in hand toward a young woman frantically emptying baskets of donated food onto a table. Beside her, two little girls were slicing bread and spreading it with butter.

People streamed through every door. Some cried in pain, their hair singed away and flesh red-black from burns. Others lugged blankets, buckets of milk and water, cookies, bread; whatever they could bring to help the hurt and homeless.

"Elizabeth . . . ?" the matron whispered to Megan.

"The boys' mother? No, she's trying to save her business. I fear it's likely in ashes by now."

"The Lord says forgive those who trespass against us," the woman intoned, "but it'll be a true test of faith to forgive the ones responsible for this."

"You know what caused the explosion?"

"Heathens, it was. A band of Mexicans. They were hurrahing the town and broke into Blount's for more whiskey. Set off a whole shipment of gunpowder."

A heavy sigh rushed through Megan's lips. "I wondered. A hole's all that's left of that entire block."

"Oh, it's a sad day, but we're doing our best to care for the livin'. Time enough later to grieve for the dead."

Missus Abernathy called out, "Matilda? Could you come here for a moment, please?"

She turned and nodded, then told Megan, "I must go. Please help yourself to some food."

"Thank you, ma'am, but I'm goin' back to check on Missus Chudomelka and make sure she's all right."

"Tell her not to worry. I'll watch over her boys like they're my own."

Megan stepped back out into the acrid, smoky air. Fire had already cut a wide swath through the business district and was rampaging through residential neighborhoods. In wagons and on foot, scores of citizens were evacuating their homes, hauling or carrying what possessions they could grab.

She broke into a dogtrot, retracing the path she and the boys had taken to the church. She'd just angled onto Main Street when someone grabbed her from behind and spun her around.

"Lambert!" she gasped, her heart hammering in her chest. "You scared me out of my wits."

David's father stared at her, his face pale and gaunt. "I'm so relieved that you're safe. My son and I were afraid you'd been trapped inside the hotel. Baedeker's is gone, you know."

*And everything I owned in the world with it,* she wailed inwardly. Reaching to squeeze his bare, sweaty forearm, she drew her hand back the moment her fingertips touched his skin. "You're cold as ice, Lambert."

"So many dead and dying," he rambled as if in a trance. "Friends caught in the blast . . . immolated in seconds. I saw a man screaming . . . running . . . his clothing ablaze like a human bonfire."

Megan's stomach lurched. "How awful."

He covered his face with his hands. "The *Record*'s gone
. . . seems so petty to mourn it amid such suffering."

He's in shock, Megan realized. Poor dear man. If only I
could do something.

"I'm surprised you're not at the mine," he continued.
"They say three, maybe four shafts caved in after the
explosion."

"What? I thought I heard a steam whistle earlier—" She
grabbed him at the shirtsleeves and shook him. "Lambert,
please listen to me. I promised I'd check on Missus Chudomelka. I took her boys to the church a while ago, but I
must get up to the mine. Can you see that she's all right
for me?"

A hint of color flushed his face. "Elizabeth? Yes . . . certainly. Of course, I will."

Megan raised to tiptoes and kissed his cheek, then started
running west, hell-bent-for-leather.

Her lungs ached; she fought for every breath by the time
she reached Sanders and Meredith property. It was eerily
still; not even the coyotes were yipping at the moon.

The kitchen window framed a meager patch of light. She
rushed through the door. Barlow P. was slumped over the
worktable, his head cradled in his arms.

Megan shook his shoulder gently. When he raised up,
she hardly recognized him. Bleary, bloodshot eyes glowered
from a face that had aged a decade overnight.

"I thought you was dead, too, baby gal."

She smelled whiskey on his breath. Dearest friend, she
said silently, I wouldn't blame you if you've swallowed a
gallon of it.

Aloud, she asserted, "Thank God the mines were down
for the night."

His laughter was hollow, thunderous. It chilled her to the
bone. "Shoulda been. Carter came to the shaft head 'bout
quittin' time. Asked for volunteers to work late."

Her voice caught in her throat. "Were many of our boys
hurt?" she rasped, already knowing the answer.

"Dozens of 'em. Buried alive. Water busted in. Cain't
even dig the poor sumbitches out to bury 'em."

He rared back and sent a bottle crashing against the wall.
"I'll go to my grave hearin' 'em scream."

# Chapter Twenty-four

From her vantage point near the cook's shack, Megan surveyed the valley below. Black wisps of smoke striped the sunrise's golden hue like the tigers depicted on faro chips.

Though the fire was out, Pioche smoldered, reeking of wet ashes. Beyond the gutted commercial district, a vast, dark blot spread in all directions like ink spilled on parchment.

Two thousand people had lost their homes and businesses. The death toll rose steadily as charred remains were pulled from the wreckage. A few hours earlier, Carter Meredith had added another hash mark to that tally.

She'd been pouring coffee into Barlow P. when Carter stumbled into the kitchen. A long-barreled revolver dangled from his thumb and forefinger.

"I shot Jeb Sanders," the mine owner said matter-of-factly. "An eye for an eye."

Barlow P. lurched across the room. He yanked the weapon from Carter's hand. "Goddamn it, ain't enough men died here tonight to suit ya?"

Carter stared vacantly as if he hadn't heard. "I couldn't understand why it was the newer shafts that caved. They should have been stronger. The scaffolding was closer together ..."

"Wondered about that myself," his manager prompted.

"A while ago, Jeb came staggering into my office. Drunk, crying like a baby. Said he'd cut a deal with a fellow at the lumberyard. Billed us for top-grade shoring timbers and substituted cullers. They split the difference in price."

"Oh, dear God ..." Megan whispered. "Jeb Sanders same as murdered those miners."

Barlow P. put his arm around Carter's shoulders and wheeled him toward the door. "Damned if ya'll wear a noose fer killin' 'im. Come on. We're gonna bury the bastard where the buzzards won't even find 'im."

When he returned from the gruesome task, Barlow P. sat Megan down in a chair. "Gal, there ain't no use lily-whitin' things fer ya. This mine's busted. Gonna be that way fer months. Mebbe forever."

Megan folded her hands in her lap. "I s'pose there's no need for a cook any longer, is there?"

"Nope. Not much call for a manager, neither."

That blunt, honest appraisal still echoed in her mind as she turned and walked back to the kitchen. A flour sack lay crumpled on the worktable. What few possessions she'd kept at the mine were stuffed inside. Slipping a hand within the confines, she felt around for the letter she'd written to David.

The folded sheets rustled beneath her fingers. I'll mail it from the goldfields at Denver . . . or maybe Coeur d'Alene, Megan thought. Batting back tears, she willed herself not to cry.

I came to Pioche dreaming of a fortune and I'm slinking away like the thief Delia Terhune—and my heart—know me to be. That shame rests squarely on my shoulders. It doesn't matter that Frances took the money. I knew it was ill-gotten—knew it *must* have belonged to the Sidemores. Where else could it have come from? But I wanted away from Boston too badly to admit any of that, even to myself.

Until that debt is paid, I'm not fit to wipe David Jacobs's boots, let alone become his wife.

The screen door slapped shut. Hastily she wiped her eyes. Expecting Barlow P., she was taken aback when she saw Miracle's ghostly form in the doorway.

The fiddler eased a long ivory envelope from her skirt pocket and held it out. Megan hesitated, then took it, knowing what it contained.

"So you did hear what happened last night, didn't you?"

Miracle shook her head and placed a finger against her lips. She opened and closed her mouth several times before Megan understood.

"You watch the way folks' mouths move and figure out what they're *saying*? I'll wager the Widow Terhune doesn't know you can do that."

Miracle's eyes widened in fear. She wagged her head violently.

"No, please, don't fret. Your secret's safe with me, just as you hold mine. I know how beholden you must feel to Missus Terhune for giving you a home. All I can say is, thank you."

The woman reached out and tapped the envelope. Megan squinted at two lines of jagged handwriting: "God be with you," it read, and was signed "Octavia Merriwether."

"Octavia Merriwether," she repeated, letting each syllable roll off her tongue. "What a beautiful name."

The fiddler's lips curved into an innocent, childlike smile. She pecked Megan on the cheek, then scampered out the door.

Megan hastened to the stove and pulled out a box of wooden matches. Striking one on the griddle, she held the envelope over the flame.

"Even without this you can carry out your threat, Delia *darlin'*. But you'll never wave it under my nose again."

She watched the paper scorch and curl until her fingers no longer had a corner to pinch. Opening the firebox, she tossed the scrap on the glowing embers.

Barlow P. sauntered in, sniffing like a bloodhound. "Whole dad-blamed district reeks a' smoke. A man cain't find any air fit fer breathin'."

"Barlow P. . . ." Megan started. "I, uh . . . I guess this is good-bye."

"What the hell ya talkin' about, gal?"

"I've got to move on—find another position. There's nothin' left for me in Pioche."

He pushed his hat back and scratched his head. "No, I reckon there ain't, 'ceptin' that Jacobs boy."

She bowed her head. "No, not even that."

"Yer sure?"

With a lump hardening in her throat, she could only nod. He seemed to know she was about to break down, and waited patiently for her composure to return. Presently he asked, "Where ya aimin' to go, gal?"

Megan swallowed, then raised her chin determinedly. "I don't know, exactly. I s'pose I'll know the right place when I get there."

Barlow P. looked away and gazed out the window. He shifted his weight from foot to foot. "Think ya'd mind havin' company?"

"I can take care of myself."

"Didn't say ya couldn't."

Megan chuckled softly. "You're not gonna boss me around all the time?"

"Didn't say that, neither."

An expectant hush fell over the room. She pushed away from the stove and strode over to the worktable. Throwing the flour sack over her shoulder, she wheeled around and said, "Then let's get goin', you old coot. We're burnin' daylight."

# PART TWO

# Chapter Twenty-five

"Pardon the intrusion, ma'am," said the uniformed gent towering above the restaurant table. "Are you, perchance, Miss Megan O'Malley?"

"She sure ain't Jesus-Loves-Me Armbrewster, the onliest other white gal in these parts," Barlow P. shot back.

After gracing her partner with a withering look, Megan replied cooly, "Yes ... ?"

The officer's ruddy features softened when he smiled. "It isn't often one makes the acquaintance of a living legend."

She lifted her chin slightly; her black eyes boldly challenging his blue pair. "Nor is it often that a lady converses with a man whose name is unknown to her."

He bent at the waist, sweeping his hat to rest over his heart. "My humblest apologies, Miss O'Malley. I'm Captain Stephen Joscelyn, Fort Wrangel's commanding officer."

Megan acknowledged his apology with a demure nod, then introduced the glowering Barlow P. Indicating the empty chair between them, she asked, "Would you care to join us, for coffee, Captain Joscelyn?"

"I'd be delighted." As he settled himself on the rickety ladderback, Barlow P. scatted sideward a fraction. Megan risked a glance in his direction and chuckled silently at her old friend's murderous expression.

The officer folded his arms on the table and leaned forward. He was as clean-shaven as an Indian, unlike most north country males whose whiskers lent protection from frostbite.

"I'm staring at you quite rudely, I know," he admitted. "That such a lovely lady has earned a reputation as British Columbia's premier prospector is nigh beyond belief."

"Barlow P. and I've wrested our fair share of gold. So have many others."

"But the hardships you've endured! I daresay, most women contentedly stay to their parlors."

"I'm not most women, Captain. There's no parlor on earth that compares with glaciers gleaming blind-white in the sun. Or a river, swelled to roaring with snowmelt, raging through a scant canyon."

She paused when a wave of homesickness for the wilderness she'd loved at first sight rose within her like a fever. That panning the Cassiar District's frigid streams had finally yielded enough gold to pay the Sidemores—and a courier to deliver it to their doorstep—was secondary. British Columbia had long since become as dear to her as Ireland.

"Uh-huh," Barlow P. scoffed. "And nothin' by damn compares to sloggin' snow higher'n a man's . . . er, belt, and feelin' ever' breath freeze solid on yer beard."

"And grinnin' like a fat pup when 'color' shows at the diggin's. I'll swear, if you didn't have somethin' to grouse about, your mouth'd clamp shut, permanent."

"Hmmph."

Megan's attention returned to her guest. "Tell me, Captain, why did the Army reestablish its outpost here in Alaska? No insult intended, but I just can't imagine what you and your men *do* all day."

Joscelyn laughed heartily. "Why, we stand at alert, ready to quell Indian uprisings, Miss O'Malley."

Barlow P. snorted. "Them Tlingits is tamer'n terriers."

"They can be, Mister Bainbridge, but don't doubt their potential for savagery. They were, and still could be, fearsome warriors."

"Warriors, hell. Most of 'ems sloshed fulla hootch daybreak to dusk. And from what I hear, that missionary woman's puttin' the fear of God in them what ain't."

"Missus Armbrewster has gathered many a convert under her wing, except Chief Shustaks isn't one of them." To Megan he added, "The chief is quite a character. When Elvira Armbrewster warned him that his immortal soul was in danger, he told her he didn't care if he went to the hellfires because his people were already there."

A waiter pushed brusquely between them to refill their coffee cups. A puddle of the scalding black brew slopped over onto the oilcloth table cover. To her disgust, the man hiked a corner of his grimy apron and swiped at the spill. When he shuffled away, Megan said, "If Chophouse

Charley's is the best restaurant in town, mine's sure to make a fortune from day one."

"Is that why you're in Wrangel? You're opening an eating house?" Joscelyn inquired. "I understood you usually waited out the winter in Victoria."

"That's what we done since we come here," Barlow P. interjected. "What I figgered we'd do this time, too, only there ain't no de-mocracy in partnerin' with *her*. Man don't even get no vote."

"You're hardly lashed to my petticoats, Barlow P."

"Mebbe not, but I shoulda tethered yer bustle to a fence post five years ago, back in Pioche."

"That's in Nevada, isn't it?" the captain asked. "Rumor had it that you came from Arizona Territory."

Megan swallowed a sip of her coffee and chuckled. "I'll grant, we took the long way 'round to get here. We drifted through Prescott, Leadville, Boise City, Coeur d'Alene—lots of places in-between—but only stopped to take on grub and fill our canteens."

"Not enough, uh, 'color' there?"

She shook her head. "Too many have-gots runnin' things already. I learned the hard way, that leaves sparse room for the have-nots to prosper."

Joscelyn slumped back in his chair. A deep sigh whistled from between his lips. "You're nothing if not ambitious, Miss O'Malley. To rock a sluice half a year and spend the remainder running a restaurant? I grow weary just listening."

"It's ambition borne of a light poke, Captain. Barlow P. and I threw in with a big party last July and moved our camp above Eight Mile Creek. By the time we got a fair-sized bunkhouse shingled, snow was fallin' fast. Not much prospectin' done this season, and there's provisions to buy for next."

Joscelyn's sandy brows dipped and met above the bridge of his nose. He raised a hand to worry his chin thoughtfully. "Does your camp have a name?"

"Why, certainly. Camps get monikered before the first pan's washed." Realizing his expression suddenly resembled a pallbearer's, she added soberly, "Ours is the North Nevada. Most of the boys hail from there. Why do you ask?"

She glanced at Barlow P. He sat as still as caribou sighting a wolf pack on the horizon.

"Reluctant as I am to be the bearer of such tidings, a native packer, a Stick tribesman, brought word yesterday of a scurvy outbreak at the North Nevada. It seems your partners are in a bad way."

Megan's greasy dinner churned in her belly. Dying of scurvy was so slow, so agonizing, no man would wish it on his worst enemy.

"Ya did send supplies to help 'em," Barlow P. intoned.

"No, I didn't."

"Good God, Captain!" Megan cried, leaping from her chair. "And you've sat here for an hour, jabberin' like a magpie, as if you hadn't a care in the world?"

The room fell silent. Every eye probed the officer's back. He waggled his head side to side, a flush creeping above his collar. "Please, Miss O'Malley. You're making a spectacle of yourself."

Stiffly, she resettled in her chair. "Spectacle be damned, Captain Joscelyn. I demand that a rescue party be dispatched at dawn."

"Hear me out, please," he implored. "There's nothing I'd rather do than give that order, but your camp is in the Cassiar District, in *British Columbia*. That's beyond my jurisdiction."

"But—"

"Hush, gal. Let the feller speak his peace."

"I've sent word to the nearest Northwest Mounted Police outpost. Chief Shustaks's nephew, the messenger I hired, knows this country like his own skin. If anyone can get through, Shakheesh can."

Despite her anger and fear, Megan felt a twinge of sympathy for the man. He'd done all he could—likely more than most would in his position—knowing full well, as she did, that the prospectors would be dead before the Mounties ever reached them.

"I'm sorry I shouted at you, Captain Joscelyn," she said before her voice failed her.

"Believe me, Miss O'Malley, I'd lead a contingent myself if the decision were mine to make." With that, he rose awkwardly from the table and reached to shake Barlow P.'s hand. Wordlessly, he turned Megan's and kissed the knuckled ridge gallantly. "I regret the evening must end this way, yet I'll never regret its beginning," he murmured, then took his leave.

The partners sat in stony silence for several minutes. Back and forth, Megan's thumb traced the painted, maroon band around the mug's thick rim.

A scrape of chair legs against planking broke her trance. She raised her eyes just as Barlow P. tossed several coins on the table. Bundling up in her hooded, marmot fur-lined turka, she followed him outside like an obedient child.

Across the narrow inlet, the wolf totem looming above Fort Wrangel's parade ground brought to mind its commanding officer. Megan wondered if he was thrashing in his bunk, haunted by faceless wraiths crying for help.

Scurvy was caused by a diet lacking in fresh fruits or potatoes. Regardless of what or how much other food was eaten, a victim's body gradually deteriorated from the inside out. She shuddered at how her comrades must be suffering.

"Ya cold, gal?" Barlow P. asked, his voice muffled by the scarf wound around his mouth. "We ain't far from the boardin'house."

"I'm goin' back, Barlow P."

"Back where? To Chophouse Charley's?"

Great clouds of vapor burst from her lips when she sighed. "Back to the North Nevada."

He wrapped his arm around her waist, hugging her to him as closely as their heavy outer garments allowed. "I feel like a cannonball's gutted me, too, Megan. Them's good men up yonder."

"They're our friends, Barlow P."

"That's a fact. And here's another 'un: The Cassiar ain't seen weather like this fer as long as anyone can remember. Storms up in them mountains is droppin' snow six, seven feet at a whack."

Megan jutted her jaw stubbornly. "We've shoed through deep snow more times than I can count. The trail will be frozen slick—easier to neck the supply sheds."

"Ya cain't make every story come out the way ya want it, jes' 'cause ya want it to. Life ain't writ like that. Yer a scrapper—finest woman I ever knowed. But there's some things even you can't do."

Amber light from the boardinghouse's six-paned win-

dows checkerboarded the splintery walkway. She paused
outside the door and faced her companion.

"You're right, Barlow P. There are things even I can't
do. And headin' north come spring thaw to bury our friends
is one of them. I'm goin' back."

# Chapter Twenty-six

Megan's insides burned as if she'd eaten campfire faggots for breakfast. Boardinghouse owner Rupert Cleveland's notoriously vile coffee had coated her tongue with bitter, grainy leavings.

The night's fitful dozing left her shoulder muscles aching; she was as groggy as a bear wakened too soon from hibernation. Irritably, she shifted the rolled bundle of blankets clutched to her chest. "Feels like it's flour sacks I'm luggin'."

Her heart skipped a beat when she glimpsed a familiar-looking, crumple-crowned Stetson bobbing above other pedestrians' heads. Then, the stiff black hair falling like a mane beneath the brim identified its wearer as a Tlingit brave.

I wonder what Barlow P.'s doing, she mused. As if he were clomping along beside her, she heard him bellow in response, "Lookin' all over tar-damn-nation for you, that's what!"

Chuckling softly at the thought, she wiped the grin off her face when the tattered prospector walking just ahead of her cast a curious glance in her direction.

Smoke streamed from the pitched roof of Chief Shustaks's house, located on an inlet point opposite the town. Nearing the crude footbridge connecting the key to the mainland, Megan sucked in great drafts of frigid air to bolster her courage.

Shustaks was said to be cantankerous and not particularly fond of "Boston men," the natives' nickname for whites. Thanks to Elvira Armbrewster tenaciously shepherding the natives to Christ, Megan assumed the chief was even less partial to white women.

The happy shrieks of children kicking a lopsided ball made from an animal bladder greeted her. The smallest, a

copper-complected, doe-eyed beauty, regarded Megan with
a puzzled frown, then scampered through an oval hole cut
in the door to Chief Shustaks' barn-sized home.

Almost instantly the child emerged, followed by a powerfully built man, of nearly six feet in height. Sun and wind
had tanned his flattened features to a polished pecan hue.

"I've brought a small gift—uh, potlatch," Megan stammered, patting the blankets with a mittened hand. "May I
parley with you a moment, Chief?" Silently she prayed,
Please God, let this be the chief or I've committed a griev-
ous insult.

Searing black eyes scrutinized her and her offering. "You
God woman?" he fairly snarled.

"No, Chief Shustaks. I've never even met Missus
Armbrewster."

Without relaxing his scowl one iota, he gestured a
brusque welcome to enter his home.

The cedar-planked, windowless structure consisted of a
single room large enough to accommodate a governor's in-
augural ball. Carved, painted totems supported the roof,
with sleeping platforms banking the walls. Sturdy, hand-
hewn benches surrounded a centered, wagon-sized fire pit
dug out of the earth. A movable wind shield partially covered the flue hole in the ceiling above the pit.

Megan knew it was customary for a tribe's individual
clans, or totems, to live together in one house. Judging by
the number of men, women, and children milling about,
Shustaks's kin numbered a hundred or more.

The chief settled on one of the benches like a grumpy
Buddha. Inwardly bemoaning her ignorance of tribal etiquette, Megan knelt near his moccasined feet. Like a newborn colt testing its legs, she nudged the blankets toward
him.

Shustaks accepted them matter-of-factly. "You want
trade? Bring hootznahoo. We trade."

She resisted the smile tugging at her lips. "Sorry. No
liquor." Pointing at the woolen bundle, she added, "That's
a gift, a trade for your time."

The chief grunted angrily and waved over a young tribesman. In halting English, the brave introduced himself as
Toyatte and said he would act as interpreter.

As simply as possible, Megan told him she had come to
Shustaks to hire a guide capable of leading a rescue party

north to the Eight Mile Creek area. "My partner and I know the trail, but could lose it easily in the snow. Can you help us?"

During Toyatte's explanation, the chief gestured wildly and shoved the blankets off his lap. Perplexed by his actions, Megan was finally made to understand that he feared the prospectors were suffering from smallpox.

"Oh, no, Toyatte. Tell him it's scurvy—the bloody mouth."

Several exchanges commenced before the chief seemed convinced. Megan certainly understood his reluctance: years earlier, a smallpox epidemic had decimated the Tlingits and other northern tribes.

"Shustaks say Dekkenaw will go with you, but you must pay many blankets. Three hundred blankets."

"There aren't that many blankets in all the Yukon. Will the chief take dollars?"

While Shustaks waggled his head stubbornly, Toyatte bartered, "No dollars. He want Boston Man hootch. As many kegs as fingers on one hand."

She sat back on her haunches. Thoughts buzzed in her mind like bottle-flies. Although there were likely enough stills hidden in the village to blind-stagger every Tlingit living there, supplying them with liquor was against the law. But without a guide to lead them over trails rendered unrecognizable by snowfall, their odds of making it to The North Nevada dropped from slim to none.

"Tell him it's a deal. I'll expect Dekkenaw at Cleveland's tomorrow at dawn." Scrambling to her feet, she was midway across the room when she whirled and said, "Toyatte? The guide speaks English, doesn't he?"

The interpreter replied solemnly. "He speak fine English, like me. Missus Armbrewster teach us."

She nodded and turned toward the door. Before she reached it, a scowling Toyatte loomed beside her. "Trade will make Missus Armbrewster very angry. Make God very angry. Whiskey the devil's brew."

Bristling defensively, Megan almost snapped a curt reply, then thought better of it. Truth to tell, she admitted silently, under any other circumstances, *I'd side with Elvira Armbrewster myself.*

"Are all these people your family, Toyatte?"

He nodded.

"Would sparin' their lives be worth five kegs of whiskey?"

The brave's brow furrowed in contemplation, then his eyes widened and softened compassionately. His response was hardly louder than a whisper. "Yes, milady. It would."

William King Lear sat with his back to the door, hunched over a writing desk when Megan entered his mercantile. "Be with you directly . . . soon as I finish this ciphering," he assured cheerfully.

While waiting, she gandered at the array of merchandise packed higgledy-piggledy from floor to rafters. Steel-fanged bear traps dangled above enormous sacks of beans, flour, and sugar. Snowshoes leaned against open crates of wizened oranges and glossy-skinned apples. Atop a pyramid of milk sealed in airtights perched a floppy rag doll wearing a calico pinafore and smudgy white apron.

"Stars above, Miss O'Malley," Lear said from behind her. "I should be horsewhipped for ignoring you." The sparkle in the wiry shopkeeper's hazel eyes belied his wattled neck and liver-spotted hands.

"Don't vex yourself, Mister Lear," Megan said, chuckling. "Your company's always worth waiting for."

"Bless you, my dear. Now, sit there by the stove and tell me all that's happened since I saw you last. I'm too old to have adventures, but not too old to hanker for their telling."

Megan described last spring's stingy take along the Tahltan River, their move to the Second North Fork, and subsequent partnership with the Nevadans at Eight Mile Creek. "We're all afraid the color's lightenin', but figured a hundred hands works ever so much more ground than four."

"Ah, but the divvies stretch thin with so many pokes to fill."

She finger-combed her hair off her forehead. "We'll either boom or bust together next season. That's the way of this romantic business of minin'."

"What is it, Megan? What's troubling you?"

She drew up her knees and tethered her boot heels on the stool rung. Emotion constricted her chest like a shroud. She told him of the miners' plight and her intention to sled life-saving supplies to the camp.

Lear nearly hopped off his own stool for wont to argue.

Megan wouldn't allow a word in edgewise. With a tone as even as she could muster, she related the terms of the trade with Chief Shustaks.

"It sickens me to think of myself as a bootlegger, William. I'm no better than the greedy Hudson's Bay Company traders that plied the Indians with rum thirty years ago."

The storekeeper smiled ruefully. "Shall I refuse to sell you the whiskey to salve your conscience? Rest assured, with astonishing regularity, the Tlingits will drink themselves stupid whether the liquor comes from you or is fermented from molasses, yeast, berries, and anything else they find lying around to toss in the cooker."

"Oh, I know . . ."

"Megan, I'd be ashamed of you if this situation didn't weigh as heavily on your heart as the suffering of your friends. But Shustaks has you cornered. You can either accept his trade come-what-may or pray like sixty for an early thaw."

"I could take to the trail without a guide."

"That'd be a gentler death than scurvy, but just as preventable, and senseless."

She chuckled with more sorrow than mirth. "You make a fine devil's advocate."

"You can tell me to go to him, whenever you please."

"I really don't have much choice, do I?"

He shook his head solemnly. "Not really. Not one you can live with. Of course, if I were truly a friend, I'd give you a hundred reasons why the entire idea is madness, but I already know your answer to fools who say, 'You can't do that, Megan.' "

"You wanna bet!"

"Precisely. And if you were a racehorse with a broken leg, I'd put my last dollar on your nose to win. Since you're not, I'll merely donate the supplies you'll need to bring the roses back to those boys' cheeks."

Her jaw dropped like a stone. The mercantile owner was renowned for grubstaking down-on-their-luck miners. Poor families who found cartons of food on their stoops looked toward the wharf with grateful eyes. But this was too much.

"I can't let you do that, William," she stated softly. "I'll grant, my poke's too thin to pay for everything. I planned to ask for credit to cover the rest until the diggin's washed a profit, if you'd risk it."

Lear drew himself up to his full five feet two and clamped hands to hips as narrow as a boy's. "Pay for what you can. Let me give what you can't. Those fellows are my friends, too, you know."

"You're an angel of mercy, William King Lear," Megan declared.

"Tell that to Cayuse Jim and Osbert Macy. I cleaned their pockets like a Chinese laundry playing poker last night."

They spent the next hour composing a supply list, with seven hundred and fifty pounds of potatoes at its top. As both a scurvy preventative and an antidote, prospectors said that common vegetable was "as precious as grain in the sacks of Israel's sons in Egypt."

Megan frowned as notations marched down one side of a ledger sheet and started another. She knew the outlay was over a thousand dollars—not including their guide's liquid wages. Near as she could tell, since Lear refused to enter any prices, his share would exceed her own.

"Nine times nine ... Carry two ..." His mathematical mumblings were punctuated by furious pencil scratchings. "Provisions plus your gear is right at a short ton. Four hundred gut-bustin' pounds to a sled—it'll take five of 'em to do the job."

"Too bad we can't use dog teams."

"That'd be easier on your back, but the food they'd need would double the weight; they're more expensive to hire than men and too difficult to control on high country trails."

Megan worried her lower lip with her teeth. Barlow P. will go, she mused. He doesn't know it yet and he'll pitch a ruckus like a loco mule, but he'll throw in. And Dekkenaw, the guide, but finding two more volunteers'll be like whistling in the wind.

As if reading her mind, Lear said, "I'll wrestle another man out of Shustaks when I deliver his Forty Rod. And an hombre, name of Buckskin Pete Vladislov, owes me a favor. He's a trapper and a mouthy son of a gun, but he knows the region."

Before she could respond, the door burst open. "Woe unto him that giveth his neighbour drink!" a shrill voice recited.

Megan and Lear whirled around so quickly, they conked heads in the process.

Waving her cane above her head like a sword, the woman proclaimed, "The Lord shall return thy wickedness upon thine own head!"

"Good heavens, Elvira. Preach if you must, but have the good sense to shut the door first," the storekeeper said drolly.

The exceptionally well-fed matron looked blank for a moment, then complied with a slam that rattled several tobacco tins off their shelf. Waggling the hickory rod at Megan, she seethed, "How dare you tempt my flock with intoxicants. I'll see you in hell before I'll allow it."

"Oh, will you now? I suppose that means you'll be beat-in' me to the devil's lair."

A noise like a rooting boar sounded in Lear's throat. He rubbed a hand over his mouth, turned, and bent over the counter. Muffled chortles sounded in the quiet room.

Missus Armbrewster's malevolent glare wavered from Megan to the storekeeper's back. Missing her own toes by a whisker's width, she planted her cane with a sharp thud.

"Isaac Dennis, the Collector of Customs, will be most interested in your trade with Chief Shustaks. You aren't the first I've insisted he arrest."

"May I ask how my business became any of yours so quickly?"

"Toyatte came to me, terribly upset, and told me of your trafficking in strong spirits."

"I don't believe you."

"Well, it's the truth. I saw you sashaying across the foot-bridge, pretty as you please. Toyatte came later to cut stove wood and I demanded to know why you'd gone to the village. He was most distressed—"

"Toyatte understood why the deal was ... struck." Megan squinted at the stout cane. A dark suspicion flashed in her mind. "How many times did you strike *him* to get the answer you wanted?"

"He wouldn't—" Her expression changed from fury to cunning. "My dear Miss O'Malley, I fear deeply for your immortal soul. Repent your sins and accept Jesus as your savior before it's too late."

Megan answered coldly. "The blessed Virgin guides me, Missus Armbrewster."

"A *papist,* eh? More of a heathen than an ignorant savage."

Lear spun on one heel. His chin was scant inches above the missionary's colossal bosom when he warned, "You'll not insult this lady or her faith in my presence. Is that clear? She's got more Christian charity in her soul than you'll ever have, Elvira. Sure, you quote Scriptures with the best of 'em, but you don't have the slightest idea what they mean."

The matron huffed and waddled quickly to the door. "From this moment on, the mission's goods will come from Folsom's."

"Get *out,* Elvira. And I'll be sure to warn Folsom of your impending patronage—the poor bastard."

As the door suffered another jamb-rattling bang, he growled, "Her kind's enough to give God a bad name."

"She's barrelin' straight to the Customs' office," Megan predicted.

"No doubt of that, but don't worry. It's legal to sell liquor in some instances. If need be, I can bamboozle Isaac Dennis with that statute until you're well on your way."

He paused thoughtfully. "You figuring to head out in the morning?"

"Dekkenaw's meetin' me at the boardinghouse at dawn."

"Best set the clock back a few hours. I'll pass the word and have the sleds loaded by midnight. You'll be across the border into British Columbia before Mister Dennis yanks up his galluses."

# Chapter Twenty-seven

From its gaping mouth, the Stikine River curved sleek and gray like a monstrous eel until distance tapered its breadth. For the inexperienced cheechako, its platinum iridescence, banked by pillowy snowbanks, was as alluring, and deadly, as nightshade.

Mother Nature'll surely bare her cruel streak before this journey ends, Megan mused, but there's few folks hardier than a Mick with a cause.

She snickered at Barlow P.'s heavily clothed form, topped by the inveterate Stetson. He'd never told her what his middle initial stood for, but it certainly wasn't "Patience." He was as twitchy as a shootist's trigger finger.

If he'd had his way, she'd still be sleeping soundly at Cleveland's. Yesterday, when she'd bumped into him after leaving the mercantile, she steeled herself for a world-class cussin'. After explaining where she'd been, why, and that the rescue was proceeding as planned, his sheepish expression left her bumfuzzled. Come to find out, while she was skulking around finalizing her plans, he'd already talked to Lear about supplies and hiring packers, and sworn the shopkeeper to secrecy.

Megan knew he'd intended to set out without her, both to ensure her safety and so she could use those months earning a grubstake for the camp. But he'd wisely scotched that idea without a mention.

Her snowshoes made fwupping sounds as she marched in place to stay warm. Farther north, the crust would freeze like hardpan, but here, without "rug beaters" lashed to her boots, walking in fluffy, deep snow would be like kneading bread dough with her feet.

"Are you sure William's message said to meet him and the others here?"

Barlow P. sullied a snowbank with a brown stream of

tobacco. Stray droplets clung on his grizzled beard and froze. "Canoe with an Injun paddlin' was waitin' fer us at the wharf, weren't it?"

"Yes, but we'd decided earlier to meet at the boarding-house. I wonder what changed?"

"His mind, I reckon. Settin' out from the river saves 'bout ten miles' walk. Ain't no nosy Parkers watchin' us go, neither."

Shadowy figures gliding through the gloom caught Megan's eye. Seconds later, Lear's high-pitched "Land ho! Make for shore!" cut the still air like a lance.

The hull of an *eyakn otlan,* a vintage war canoe carved from a single cedar log and large enough to carry sixty paddlers, scraped to a halt not far from where Megan stood.

In the feeble moonlight, the carved bear's head at its prow looked so ferociously lifelike, she had to resist an impulse to step back.

Lear hopped from the craft with an exuberance that defied his fifty years and the lateness of the hour. Megan knew he'd had little, if any, time for sleep, but he started unloading freight like a man half his age.

Dekkenaw, nicknamed Mike, Buckskin Pete Vladislov, and Scutdoo were formally introduced. The latter's enigmatic expression—a trademark of his Tlingit ancestry—was apparent though he was hardly more than a boy. Fourteen at most, Megan guessed.

The canoers and the two native packers had camping gear lashed to one sled in short order. They secured provisions for the trek on another, and divided supplies for the North Nevada between the remaining three.

Megan folded her muffler and wound it around her neck to pad it against the sled's leather harness. Lear gripped Barlow P.'s hand and forearm, then turned toward her.

"Godspeed, my dear," he said in a husky voice. "And thank you."

"For what, William? Without you, this mission would be impossible."

"Ah, perhaps you're too young to understand, but you've allowed me a taste of this glorious adventure you're embarking on. Stealing away at the stroke of midnight, the bit of shystering I'm scheming for Isaac Dennis—it fires the blood in my veins."

She wrapped her arms around him. "Aye, and we'll have such yarns to swap when I get back. Save me a spot near the stove. I'll be there to claim it before you bank it for the summer."

"I'll hold you to that, Megan."

Mike, the lead packer, pulled his arms through the sled's single trace and positioned it across the back of his neck and under his armpits. Straining forward, he grunted when the runners jerked free from the snow. Head bowed slightly and arms pumping, he began breaking a trail for the others. Barlow P. followed.

Between the ungainly snowshoes and settling her sled's trace too high on her neck, when it was her turn to join the procession, Megan staggered as awkwardly as a slue-footed colt.

"Mother of God," she muttered, leaning back to slacken the strap. "If you aren't bumblin' around like a tenderfoot fresh off the boat."

"The trace is too high, Megan," Pete called at her back. "Let it ride just beside your collarbones."

Waving acknowledgment, she answered under her breath, "I know what I'm doin'. It's just been a while." With her weight shifted to the balls of her feet, the sled commenced skating behind her like a cumbersome shadow.

Once in line, she mimicked Barlow P.'s gliding shuffle and side-to-side sway. The smoother her movements, the less the trace tugged.

Visibility was as clear as window glass smeared with bear grease. A gauzy haze enveloped the landscape, robbing it of its true colors. Snow dervishes, whipped by gusting winds, pecked at her eyes and threatened to obscure Barlow P.'s dark form.

I mustn't lose sight of the old coot for long, she warned herself. Even with Pete behind me, if I stray too far from the trail, I might never find my way back.

Even through layers of woolen shirts and a bulky mackintosh, the seesawing motion of the sled's trace began chafing her skin. That burning sensation brought memories of '72; their first winter in the Cassiar.

Like *cheechakos* are wont to do, they hadn't listened to veterans' advice to head south to civilization before September snows blanketed the Ho-Tai-Lute Mountains. Once miles of white treachery lay between them and Victoria,

British Columbia, the very idea of dogging their gear on sleds via straps seemed ludicrous.

Instead, they tried hitching the traces across their chests. Not only did that method cause the drays to jerk rather than glide, Barlow P. ended up with a cracked rib to show for their ingenuity. Lowering the straps to span their waists resulted in a duck-walking posture that set off agonizing back spasms.

Pulling a heavy-laden sled by the shoulders and neck was far from comfortable, but as the argonauts before them had learned, it was the only way.

Time had no meaning in a region where mountains and glaciers had probed the sky for a millennium. Like a brainless machine, Megan planted one snowshoe, then the other along the Stikine's riverbank trail. When she peered up to check Barlow P.'s position, a humorless, quiet laugh burbled in her throat. *Lass, if you had a dollar for every hour you've spent watching that man's backside, you'd be fixed for life.*

When the sun reached its apex, aching thighs had long since taken her mind off the trace's discomfort. Snowshoes sank calf-deep with each step; she practically touched knee to chin to release them from the powdery bog.

Short rest breaks to gobble deer jerky and half-frozen oranges only made starting up again more painful. But none of the men complained, despite the strain pinching their faces.

The flatter river bottom terrain steadily inclined. Mountain peaks dressed in gray cloud-collars promised torturous climbs and treacherous descents. At any moment, they could shed their thick, white blankets, sending an avalanche pouring down their slopes like a roaring waterfall.

Sitka pines, blue spruce, and cedars tiering up their slopes would not divert the snowy stampede; they'd splinter and fall as easily as thrashed wheat.

"Best get onward, Megan O'Malley," she groaned softly. "The goin's only gonna get harder."

Mike called a halt at a broad clearing where the Katete River spilled into the Stikine. "We camp here," he announced. Judging by the striped shadows cast by the fir trees to her left, Megan estimated that fifteen hours had passed since she said farewell to William Lear.

The guide and Scutdoo trudged up the hillside to cut logs for a fire hearth. Megan plopped down on her sled to catch her breath.

"Where are we, Barlow P.? Alaska or British Columbia?"

The older man was pivoting his head and working his shoulders to ease the kinks from his muscles. "Can't rightly say fer sure. Map shows a black line betwixt 'em, but I ain't seen one yet. Mebbe the snow's covered it up."

Cold nipped Megan's tongue when she stuck it out at him. "Funny, Mister Bainbridge. Very funny."

Bending to loosen the straps binding his sled's cargo, he snorted, "Think so, eh? Well, you ain't Cle-o-patra astride no barge, missy. Get off yer duff and start wrasslin' us up some grub."

Before Megan could summon up a sufficiently rude reply, Pete warned, "That's no way to speak to a lady, mister. She necked her share today. Let her rest." The boulder he pitched off the precipice cracked like a rifle shot when it hit the ice-crusted river below.

Barlow P. rared up; his bloodshot eyes narrowing to slits. "I don't recall askin' yer opinion, Vladislov."

"Oh, stop growlin' like a couple of cur dogs, the both of you," Megan chided. To Pete, she added, "Me and him's squabbled for years. If he ever sweet-talked me, I swear I'd fall to a swoon."

The burly trapper shook his head and launched another rock toward the river. "Women. Doesn't matter what a man says, he's wrong every time."

"Amen to that, brother," Barlow P. drawled.

Camp-making chores were completed as if the rescuers had mushed together for years. Mike and Scutdoo stacked up a grated box from green timber, then built a fire atop it. Without the crude hearth, the fire would sink rapidly into a hole created by the melting snow.

Megan poured the first pail of slushy river water Pete hauled up from the river into a sizable speckled granite coffeepot. When steam curled out its spout, she saved a pint to make johnnycake, then tossed in a quarter pound of grounds.

The second bucket was bound for the tatie pot, and a third set aside to rinse bacon grease from the frying pan.

The aroma of hot coffee, corn bread, and sizzling fatback did much to speed the men's tent-pitching efforts.

"Lay lots of fir boughs in my tent, boys," Megan instructed. "You're doublin' up and I'm by my lonesome and the warmer the cook, the better your vittles'll be."

"Yes, ma'am," Mike replied, sniffing the air appreciately. Even Scutdoo seemed to understand that food was the topic of conversation.

Each tent required that five poles be driven into the snow at a slant to hold up the fly—a sixteen-foot square of cotton twill. Thanks to the sheltering trees and dearth of wind, brisket-sized rocks would anchor the corners.

Megan looked longingly at the thick green mat Scutdoo was tamping in her tent. Soon as my belly's full, she vowed, I'll lay down like an old sow in a warm wallow.

Nightfall draped its somber cloak over the landscape. The campfire threw a welcome amber circle of light and heat around the weary diners sitting cross-legged on blanket-draped boughs.

Megan thought the merry music of grunts, smacking lips, and spoons scraping greedily against tin plates was higher praise than spoken compliments.

With a groan, Barlow P. canted back against a supply sled. "If'n I eat another bite I'll—"

Scutdoo's upraised hand silenced the older man. Alert as a spaniel pointing a quail, the boy raised up on his haunches and stared into the darkness. Setting his plate aside, he murmured "Bos-ton" to Mike, then disappeared like a wraith into the trees.

Megan's head whirled around at the double clicks of rifle rounds being chambered. Mike wisely skedaddled behind the sled. Pete and Barlow P. eased to their feet.

Flames burnished the brass plate on the trapper's long-barreled Henry. Barlow P. had often told her his Union Army-issue Spencer's "load on Sunday, shoot all week" reputation was only slightly exaggerated. Its owner's lips barely moved when he growled, "Megan, get back there with Mike. *Now.*"

Just as she moved to comply, a voice boomed out, "Captain Stephen Joscelyn requests permission to enter the camp."

"Dumb sumbitch," Barlow P. snarled, lowering his rifle.

"I oughta shoot 'im fer upsettin' my di-gestion." Louder, he barked, "Permission denied. Go back whar ya come from."

Megan's heart pounded in her ears. Clearly, Elvira Armbrewster had made good her threat. Clenching her mittened hands into fists, she hollered, "Pay him no mind, Captain. The fire's hot and so's the coffee."

Four soldiers accompanying the officer stayed to the shadows. None seemed aware of the Tlingit boy crouched a few feet behind them. Joscelyn exchanged greetings with Megan's companions while she scrubbed her tin cup with snow and refilled it.

"Thank you, kindly, Miss O'Malley," he said, holding it in both hands. His head snapped back at the sting of boiling liquid flowing over blue lips.

"I don't reckon you and yer men're here to join up with us."

"No, unfortunately my jurisdictional boundaries haven't changed."

"Uh-huh. Well, best I can figure, this tea party's takin' place on the British Columbia side of the border."

Joscelyn looked over his shoulder and nodded. "I suspect you're right, Mister Bainbridge."

"Seems like a helluva hike fer a cup of coffee then, don't it?"

The captain's eyes crinkled at the corners. "This is a farsight better than Chophouse Charley serves, but I wouldn't have slogged twenty miles for it. I'm here to escort Miss O'Malley back to Wrangel."

Barlow P. brought the rifle back up to business level. "Megan stays right where she's at, Joscelyn. Like I said, yer on the wrong side of the line to be makin' any arrests."

Pete sidled next to her protectively and winked. "Prettiest desperado I've ever seen," he whispered.

The captain glanced from Barlow P. to Megan to Pete. "Heavenly days, I'm not here to arrest anyone! One of my men—Sergeant McCroskey—has ten days leave coming and is mustering out in a week, anyway. Because this trek is far too hazardous even for a woman of Miss O'Malley's fortitude, I've given him permission to take her place."

"Oh, have you now," Megan roared. "And *who* the hell are *you* to be givin' *anyone* permission to replace *me*?"

"But, Miss O'Malley—"

"Tell me this, Captain Joscelyn, how far has your man necked a sled?"

"I don't believe he has."

"Can he field-dress a caribou?"

"I'm sure he could learn, but—"

"How 'bout nursin'' men with sores oozin' pus all over their bodies, legs swollen like they're fit to bust, and blood tricklin' from their gums?"

In a calmer voice, she added, "There's nobody on this earth that can't be replaced, and it's grateful I am that your sergeant volunteered to help. But there's more needed on this 'trek' than strong backs, Captain Joscelyn."

"You have quite a temper, ma'am—a proper forge for a steel will. The former leaves me smarting from the scorch, but the latter garners my admiration." There was no mistaking the respect in his eyes as they caught and held hers.

"What the hell does that mean?" Barlow P. retorted.

Joscelyn chuckled. "That I appreciate your hospitality, and wish you good luck and a smooth journey."

"You're welcome to share our fire for the night," Megan offered.

The captain hesitated, then asked, "No hard feelings?"

"None a'tall. I'll warrant, my fuse can be kinda short, but the explosion doesn't last long."

She turned toward her tent, then paused. "Since you're in our jurisdiction, there is one rule of this camp you ought to know about."

"Oh? And what's that?"

"First man up makes the coffee," Barlow P. answered. "And takes a cup to her tent."

"Well, I'll consider that incentive for an early reveille, Mister Bainbridge."

"Hmmmph. Figgered you would."

# Chapter Twenty-eight

An ice bridge, formed months earlier when the water level was higher and the current slowed by dropping temperatures, cantilevered the nameless river's deep gorge.

"I ain't trudged up and down a thousand goddamn mountains fer two months jes' to kill myself crossin' that," Barlow P. declared.

Squinting through snowflakes as fat as goose down, Megan regarded the glistening arch with similar skepticism. It looked as fragile as a spun-sugar arbor on a wedding cake.

If that thing collapses, she thought grimly, the sled'll either break your neck on the way down, crush you when you land, or sink you like a stone.

"The river's not that wide, and frozen solid enough to hold our weight," Pete speculated. "How about us roping down to it and sending Scutdoo to monkey up the bluff on the other side? He could help haul the rest of us up, and then the sleds."

"Them rocks is slicker'n marble," Barlow P. shot back. "Scutdoo's nimble as a jackrabbit, but he can't climb straight up with nary a foothold."

The trapper surveyed the adjacent scarp. "Yeah, I suppose you're right. But we've followed this ridge for days. The bluffs are as steep here as back yonder."

"How about upriver, Mike?" Megan asked.

The Tlingit guide peered through the snowy curtain, then shook his head. "Maybe a better place. Maybe not. Maybe too far. We must go east to your camp, not north."

Barlow P. toed at the snow with his boot. "I told ya we shoulda followed the Stikine to the Grand Canyon—"

"No, sir," Mike cut in stubbornly. "Wall rocks big as mountains there. Too dark to see good, even with sun. And no trail now. Only shelf ice high over the water. If the shelf falls, the man falls, too—and dies."

"Uh-huh. Don't appear to be a helluva lot different here," Barlow P. argued.

A glacier's thunderous crack echoed in the distance. Megan startled at the rumble and sidled away from the ledge. Mike had told her, the Tlingits believed when The Old Woman Underneath grew fidgety, earthquakes rattled the ground and glaciers yawned like sleepy monsters.

Too bad the old crone can't twitch up some heat while she's at it, Megan said silently.

Lowering her scarf, she blew into her hands trying to melt ice droplets from her eyelashes. Her fingers and toes had stiffened like wooden pegs weeks ago. They stung mightily, but never truly thawed even when held near a fire.

The men were still debating what route to take. With their backs turned and their arms hugged to their chests, they looked like a roost of giant snowy owls. The crown of Barlow P.'s Stetson, anchored by a wrapped woolen scarf covering his entire head, bulged comically above his ears.

Scutdoo separated from the group and trotted toward the bridge.

"What'd you do?" Megan shouted. "Draw straws and give the boy the short one?" The words were hardly out before Scutdoo was waving from the far side of the ravine. On the return trip, he stopped midway to jump several times to test the bridge's strength.

"Jesus, Mary, and Joseph," she whispered, afraid to watch and unable to tear her eyes away.

When he returned, Scutdoo reported to Mike in their native tongue. "He says the ice did not shake or crack. But he is small and the sleds are heavy. He will cross again with a sled now."

"Why can't he scamper over with a rope tied to the sled, then just pull it across?" Megan asked.

"Can't guide it good enough on a long lead, gal," Barlow P. answered. "Them sleds has got vitals on 'em. Can't risk losin' one."

Scutdoo paused at the edge to adjust the trace around his neck, then eased the dray onto the span. Careful to keep the runners centered on the slender arch, each step was placed cautiously, but with rhythmic smoothness.

Vapor burst from four pairs of cheering lips when the sled humped to a halt on the far rim.

"All right, Megan, yer next," Barlow P. commanded.

"Why me?"

"We're doin' this by weight, and you ain't much heftier than that boy."

She looked hard at him for a long moment. "That means you're last then, doesn't it?"

"Yup."

As she passed by him, she said, "I expect to see you on the other side."

"One way or t'other, gal. One way or t'other."

Hard as she tried, she couldn't control the trembling that wracked her body. Her boots felt as heavy as anvils. Scutdoo, who was waving encouragement, seemed miles away.

She swallowed hard, clenched her teeth, and glided onto the bridge. Her own pulse pounding in her ears blotted out any sounds made by her passage. Snowflakes pestered her eyes like gnats. She squinted, concentrating with all her might on the grainy surface in front of her.

"Two, three, four . . ." At "nineteen" she stumbled onto solid ground. But for the rest of her life, those intervening minutes would remain as blank as a dead man's eyes.

In rapid succession, Mike traversed the span, then Pete.

"How's it holding up?" she asked the trapper.

He shrugged and crossed his arms over his chest.

She held her breath as Barlow P. scraped onto the span. The sled runners caught at the edge. His body lurched backward, arms flailing for balance.

With his chest heaving, he paused in place. Megan gnawed on the seam of her leather mitten to keep from screaming.

Barlow P. leaned forward against the trace. The sled runners rasped free. Step after slow, cautious step he inched closer. He was halfway across when ice particles began raining down from beneath the arch. The bridge groaned as if in pain.

His head jerked up. He glanced over his shoulder toward the sound. Like shattering glass, shards broke away from the far abutment. Jamming one heel after the other into the ice, he bowed his back, trying to run.

Pete tore his mittens off with his teeth. Swinging a looped rope over his head, he shouted, "Tuck up *tight*! Now!"

The rope wobbled over Barlow P.'s head, then fell and cinched his arms near the elbows. The bridge snapped like dry pine branches, and collapsed. Barlow P. dropped from sight. Megan heard the sled slam into the rock wall.

Mike and Scutdoo leapt to help Pete with the rope. Megan grabbed its free end and coiled it around a towering fir. "Pete—take this—you can sheave him up!"

The men grabbed for the line and hied back, hand over hand. Pete winced as the rough hemp scorched his bare palms.

Barlow P.'s lolling head crowned the ledge.

"You got him!" she cried. "Just a little more! Pull—hard!"

Barlow P.'s midsection jerked up and over.

Pete hollered, "Hold 'im! I gotta cut that sled loose!" Jerking his knife free of its sheath, he skidded on his knees beside the taut leather straps. Seconds later, a thud reverberated from the river below.

A crimson stain spread over the snow beneath Barlow P.'s head. As gently as she could, Megan unwrapped his scarf. "Boys, roll him toward you—easy. Far enough."

Tenderly, she parted his matted hair and probed his skull with her fingertips. She found a depression the size of her fist, soft with oozing blood—but nothing else.

"All right, lay him back, now."

She unbuttoned his mackinaw and the shirts beneath, the musk of wool and old sweat assailed her nostrils. His skin felt warm to the touch, but a swollen lump on his collarbone and two over his ribs promised broken bones.

"How bad is he?" Pete asked softly.

"Bad enough that we'll be campin' here a few days. I'd say he's lucky to be alive, but he's not a young man—"

"I ain't Methuselah neither, gal," Barlow P. wheezed. Fumbling with his mackinaw buttons, he added, "Bad enough ya took liberties. Now yer lettin' me freeze to death." With that, his arms fell listlessly to his sides.

"Get those tents staked and the fire a'goin'," she ordered. "And hand me over a couple of blankets before he *does* freeze."

Looking down into Barlow P.'s drowsy blue eyes, she whispered, "Don't talk and don't move. For the first time in a whole lotta years, this gal's gonna be takin' care of *you*."

When Megan wriggled backward from the tent the next morning, Pete was already up, hunkered near the fire. She hesitated, then shuffled over to squat beside him.

"How's Barlow P.?" he asked curtly, peering into the flames.

"Better, I think. Sleepin' sound."

He cocked his head toward her and back to the fire. "Reckon you should know."

The silence between them stretched as taut as telegraph wire. Megan studied his profile, then at the bark on the box-hearth. "You don't approve of me stayin' with him last night."

"No, ma'am, I don't."

"A lady doesn't sleep with a man she's not married to, eh?"

"Not where I come from, she doesn't."

She scooped up a clump of snow and tamped it between her mittens. Like flour from a sifter, the dry flakes rejoined their kin between her feet.

"Well, where I come from, a friend is a treasure to be cherished and guarded from harm. True ones, like Barlow P., are scarcer than diamonds and all the more precious."

Pete turned toward her again. This time, his eyes held puzzlement, not scorn. "I've never known a woman quite like you before. I'd like to know you better."

Megan fluttered a hand to her breast and gasped, "Hussy that I am? Why, glory be, your sainted mother would spin in her grave at the thought of it."

His laugh rumbled like wagon tires on a cobbled street. "My sainted mother, a displaced Russian princess, has had five husbands thus far, and raises goats on a farm in Peoria, Illinois."

In a more serious tone, he continued, "I'm a jealous man, perhaps, but not a judgmental one. If you'll have me, I'd be honored to be counted among your friends."

Megan smiled and she gained her feet. "That's what someone is, Pete, not what another makes of him."

# Chapter Twenty-nine

"Ow, damn ya," Barlow P. bellowed. "Yer 'bout as gentle as a grizzly bear."

Megan smiled sweetly and went right on binding his shoulder and chest with strips ripped from a blanket.

I'm trying to hurry, you old coot, she thought to herself. I'll wager you're nigh chilblained by now.

"Ain't like I'll be pullin' nothin' besides my own ass, anyhow. Sled's busted to smithereens. Feel like I've been chewed up and spit out. Lost a week, besides."

"It's blessings you ought to be countin'," she argued. "I could be lashin' your skinny carcass to a tree branch to keep animals from gnawin' your bones. And Scutdoo shinnied down to the river and saved most of the goods that tore free."

Not getting the argument she expected, she continued, "We haven't lost a week, either—just five days. Mike says it's barren ground, flatlands, most of the way from here. The nights'll just be shorter makin' up the difference."

Barlow P.'s Adam's apple bobbed as he gazed up at the pewter sky. "Wind's pickin' up. Don't like the looks of them clouds nary a bit."

"Nor do I," Pete agreed, speaking over Megan's shoulder. "Soon as you're trussed up proper, we'd better make tracks."

"Last thing ya need's a cripple draggin' ya down."

"That's right, Barlow P. Glad we don't have one to fret over."

Megan felt her old partner's back straighten and his chest puff out a bit. Thanks, Pete, she said silently, hearing his boots crunch away. That's exactly what Barlow P. needed to hear most.

With his left arm bound against his chest to immobilize his collarbone, she had to help him struggle into his mackinaw. When she reached to fasten it, he grunted, "I can cinch my own saddle, gal. Get yerself ready to mush."

They started east in the same order as before. Barlow P. stumbled occasionally over choppy snow riffles the native men left in their wake, but when he recovered, his pace didn't slacken.

Must be only having one arm free for balance that's makin' him clumsy, Megan decided. Still, she watched for signs of dizziness or blood seeping through the flour sack bandage she'd fashioned for his head.

The farther they trudged, the flatter and more stark the surroundings became. Trees scattered across the undulating expanse like pins impaled in a vast, white cushion. That fifteen or twenty feet of snow lay between their exposed branches and their roots seemed almost unbelievable.

The party's passage startled a herd of caribou. The animals dashed away with their necks bowed low, their hand-like antlers clutching at the sky.

By late afternoon, with no hills to deny its fury, the wind pummeled Megan like a howling, invisible bully. She blinked constantly to keep her eyeballs from drying and freezing. Teary droplets crusted the lids; icy rivulets streaked back from the corners.

The scarf protecting her face froze into an armored mask that thickened with each moist breath. She saw rather than felt her mittened hands rub her cheeks.

Misery turned to wretchedness when snow began swirling from all directions. Megan tucked her chin hoping the angle would deflect the blinding rampage.

Cold stung the inside of her nose like swarming bees. She peeled back the stiff scarf and pulled tufts of marmot fur from her mittens to stuff in her nostrils.

As the hours passed, one foot followed the other from habit, not conscious thought. Fresh, wind-whipped snow covered Barlow P.'s tracks as fast as he made them.

Fear gripped Megan's heart. God help me, she cried silently. I can't see—can't breathe. I feel like I'm drowning on dry land.

Blind panic drove her into Barlow P.'s back like a battering ram. Seconds later, Pete collided with her sled. One runner jabbed her calf. She dropped to her knees.

Unseen hands gripped the back of her parka and yanked

her upright. "Hurt?" Pete yelled over the wind's roar as the rest of the men gathered around.

She lied with a halting headshake.

"Can't go on," Mike shouted. "No sun. No trail."

"Pull your sleds back to these," Pete ordered. "We're diggin' in." His hazel eyes flicked to Megan. "Get flys. Blankets if you can. Stay here 'til I come for you."

The supply sled's frozen knots cruelly taunted her numb fingers. "Damn—you—bastards," she bellowed in frustration, beating them with her fists.

She knelt in the snow, her nose an inch from the entwined lashing at its center. Setting her jaw determinedly, she pushed and picked at the knot until it worked free.

Megan yanked the flys from under the straps securing them front and back. Barlow P. loomed beside her, bundling blankets to his chest.

"That'll do," he shouted, clutching her arm like a vise.

She lurched beside him, her snowshoes tangling with his at every step. When they reached the burrow the men had dug into the snow, Scutdoo grabbed the canvas from her arms. With one shoved in place covering its floor, he gestured, indicating the party should crawl inside.

Like puppies at the teat, the five would-be rescuers huddled together under blankets and the remaining flys. There was no room for a fire, even if they had wood to build one. Mike struck match after match before a feeble flame blossomed from the candle he'd staked in the snow floor.

In such a small, confined space, its heat could make the difference between life and death. But Megan knew if it went out during the night and their combined body heat failed to keep them warm, the den would become their tomb.

Nestled between Pete and Barlow P., she heard the older man's labored breathing over the wind howling outside. Raising her lips to his ear, she whispered, "Are you all right?"

"Aw, hell, gal, I'm just *dandy*," he growled sarcastically. "Ain't been *this* dandy since Antietam."

She awoke with a start. For a moment she thought she was back aboard the *Wardlow*. The air was thick with the stench from sour, snoring mouths, smoke, and unwashed skin.

The weight of Pete's arm crushed her ribs and his leg entrapped hers like a snare. She opened her eyes to the snow cave's ceiling hovering inches above her face.

I've heard tales of folks accidentally bein' buried alive, she mused wryly. If this is how it feels, no wonder some people put breathin' tubes in the dearly departeds' coffins.

She almost jumped out of her skin when Pete mumbled, "Good morning . . ."

"Mornin'? How can you tell?"

"I feel like I've slept twelve hours, at least. All things considered, it's the best I've had since I left Wrangel."

"No wonder," she shot back. "You sprawled all over me like a mattress."

He graciously removed the offending limbs, chuckling wickedly. "I believe it'd be wise not to comment upon what a lovely mattress it was—"

"Then don't," Barlow P. barked from Megan's other side. "Give a shove to them Injuns and let's get the hell outta here."

They used their boot soles to butt the air hole wide enough to tunnel through. Megan raised to a sitting position and crooked her arm over her brow to shield her eyes from the dazzling sunlight.

The blizzard's aftermath had painted the landscape with only two colors: blinding white and bright sapphire.

She gained her feet, stumbling around weakly in knee-deep snow. Stiff muscles and joints creaked and groaned like rusty hinges.

"Where's the sleds—the food?" she asked. The surrounding, snowy surface was a sea of rolling drifts.

" 'Round here somewheres," Barlow P. answered. "Get them flys and blankets. The rest of us'll fan out and start trampin'."

The searchers kick-stepped in a tight zigzag using their snowshoes' front lacings like scoops. Within a few yards, Pete crouched and started pawing snow between his legs, dog style. "Hey, over here."

Once the drays were dug out, the party descended on their contents like starving raptors. Each sled carried a portion of their provisions, but every scrap of food was stone-frozen. Without a fire to thaw it, the stores were worthless.

Back at the river camp, Megan had purposely wrapped a small parcel of jerky in blankets and stowed it at the bottom of Pete's sled in case of just such an emergency. Shucking back the paper covering, she grabbed at the strips of meat.

They shattered to frozen crumbs. She squinted at the remains in disbelief.

Barlow P. squatted beside her, his eyes locked on the paltry mound. He took off one of his mittens and licked a chapped, shaking finger. Gently touching its tip to the crumbs, he slowly brought it to his outstretched tongue.

Tears rimmed Megan's eyes. It was the most pitiful sight she'd ever witnessed.

One by one, the other men circled around. Not a word was spoken as five bare fingers tamped at the meager sustenance.

# Chapter Thirty

Five miles today—only five miles, Megan thought as she stirred the simmering pot of cornmeal mush. Pete had spent an hour pick-axing a hole in an icy creek just to get one half-pail of cooking water.

The campfire's lazy flames licked up from scrubwood gathered and saved bit by bit over that distance. She hoped the gruel cooked through before the gnarled boughs fell to ashes. Then the party'd move on. Fire was critical to survival and the barrens fostered precious little wood to build one.

Looking toward the men, she squinted against the sun's blinding glare. Funny how it seems colder when the sky's a clear, blue dome, she mused. Her four comrades were stamping and pounding their arms to keep warm while they talked to pass the time. With vapor streaming from their lips with every breath, they looked like a parley of scruffy dragons.

She reached for the stack of tin plates. "Come and get it, such as it is." The invitation was hardly made before a line formed beside her.

As she ladled a measure into Mike's plate, a drizzle of mush splatted his mitten. "I'm shakin' bad as a fat crow on a thin branch. Hope that didn't burn you."

His soft black eyes crinkled at the corners. "If I could feel the hot sting, I would welcome it, Miss Megan." Seated in a half circle near the dying embers, the rescuers fell to their meal. Megan scooped a spoonful and delivered it to her mouth. The gritty corn crunched between her teeth like sand, but she closed her eyes and savored the sensation of warm food sliding down her gullet.

"Ain't Delmonico's, gal," Barlow P. grunted between slurps. "But it'll damn well do." He winked at her, then glanced to his right. "Mike, ya'd best tell that boy to quit gobblin' so fast. His gut's too parched for shovelin' it in."

Megan felt a flush rise up her neck. She casually eased her plate from beneath her chin to her lap. A daintier spoonful was en route to its target when Pete hissed, "Don't move; don't even blink."

As her back, snow crunched in an irregular cadence. Then, the wet *whuffs* of an animal sniffing the air. Scarcely breathing, she was mesmerized by a huge, prong-headed shadow spreading like spilled oil a few feet in front of her.

"Bull moose," Pete whispered. "Acts like he's sick."

"Got yer rifle with ya?" Barlow P. murmured.

"On the sled. Yours?"

"Same."

"Shit . . ."

Megan thought her heart would stop when a bulbous nose nuzzled at her back. If it rears back and trumpets, she thought, I'll be dead before he's done.

The moose stood still for several minutes. Megan was about to scream from the torment when the choking odor of fresh manure fouled the air. Once he'd relieved himself, the animal turned and slogged away.

She craned her neck slowly at the departing intruder. The moose was half again as tall as she was. Its knock-kneed, spindly legs seemed incapable of carrying such an elongated, bulky body.

"Guess he told *you* what he thought o' yer cookin'," Barlow P. snickered.

As they were breaking camp, Scutdoo mixed ashes with the melted snow around the fire. Each of them swiped the dark goo beneath their eyes to help relieve sunblindness. The raccoonlike mask Barlow P. smeared on set Megan laughing so hard, her ribs hurt.

With their bellies full and the snow crusted like glass, the travelers fairly glided across the tundra. Time already lost wouldn't be made up, but, God willing, the North Nevadans should be sipping potato gruel within a week.

Scattered like milestones, then section posts, majestic firs stood as dignified as spinsters draped in green, Sunday-best skirts. Grudgingly the barrens were surrendering to an encroaching army of trees.

Rather than wrestle the sled over the frozen Toonya River's jagged banks, the men decided to portage them across. Taking advantage of their preoccupation, Megan quietly told Barlow P. that she was going to "take a stroll."

She scrambled up the far bank, then veered diagonally away from the cursing laborers. A copse of trees so massive they must have been saplings when Jesus drove the money-changers from the temple offered suitable privacy.

Then, while hurriedly hitching up, tucking in, and refastening numerous layers of clothing, Megan spied a ramshackle cabin about twenty yards downstream. Her vision was so hazy, she couldn't tell whether smoke drifted from its chimney or not.

"Hey, Megan," Barlow P. hollered. "Ya through doin' the moose yet?"

"Ornery old coot," she muttered as she stomped toward them. "One of these days, I'm gonna string you up by your bootlaces and put *me* outta my misery."

The men were still snickering like schoolboys when she rejoined them. "First law of the wilderness," she intoned, "is don't truck with the cook. You never know what she'll start usin' for seasonin'."

"Aw, Megan, we was jes' havin' sport with ya," Barlow P. drawled without a trace of remorse. "Where's yer sense of humor?"

She patted her toes inside her boot. Glory be, she thought, girls grow up to be women; boys just get taller and louder.

"In case you're interested, I found a cabin over yonder—can't tell if anyone's in it."

"Let's pay a call and find out," Pete said.

As they approached, Megan adjudged that bears could have built a better shelter. It had no windows, but gaps in its cedar plank siding would let in more air than a body could stand. The doorway looked as if it were cut to fit the door, instead of vice versa, and the entire structure leaned like a weary codger on his cane.

"Hallo the house," Barlow P. shouted. After a short pause he remarked, "Don't appear nobody's home. Would be right pleasant restin' up and havin' supper with a roof over our heads, don'tcha think?"

Leaving Mike and Scutdoo to gather wood and bring in the provisions, Megan, Pete, and Barlow P. used their snowshoes to scoop drifts away from the door. When they crossed the threshold, Pete muttered, "Can't see a damned thing. I'm blind as a kitten in a womb."

Like a swarm of fireflies, tiny yellow lights danced in Megan's eyes. She shuffled forward, hoping to find a bench to sit on until her vision cleared. She grunted when her head butted a bunk built into the far corner. Bending down, she found its lower companion and settled herself on its edge.

In the meantime the men were making their own discoveries. "Hearth seems purty sound—pile a' wood here, too," Barlow P. informed.

A muffled "Oof" came from across the room followed by Pete's announcement that he'd "found a table."

Weariness seeped into Megan's bones. Thoughts of resting a little while on an honest-to-God bed was as alluring as a suitor's embrace. Removing her scarf and mittens, she sighed and stretched out along the bunk's sideboard.

As she wriggled toward the center, her back shoved against something sharply angled and hard. If that's the wall, this is the skimpiest bunk I've ever seen, she grumbled to herself. Propped on one elbow, she reached under her chin to pat at the obstruction.

It took a moment for her to realize her hand was tracing the contours of a frozen, bearded face.

"Jesus, Mary, and Joseph," she cried, jumping straight up from the bed. Her head cracked sharply against the upper berth's rail. She stumbled and would have fallen if Pete hadn't caught her.

"What is it, Megan?"

The feel of the corpse's cold, stony skin seemed burned into her palm. She shuddered violently. "Dead man . . . in the bunk." Repeatedly she wiped her hand on her trouser leg.

A match flared near the fireplace. Barlow P.'s head cocked sideward as he steered the feeble flame toward a lantern's wick.

Pete guided Megan toward the table and leaned her against it. "We need that light over here. I think Megan's found the owner."

Barlow P. hung the lantern's bale on a nail driven into the wall. Kneeling beside the bunk, he craned his neck close to the cadaver's face.

"Goddamned if it ain't Finley James. And the angels

didn't carry 'im off whilst he was sleepin', neither. There's a hole the size of my thumb plugged square in his temple."

"Finley . . . ?" she gasped, raising her eyes. "What's he—?" She swallowed hard. "Dear God in heaven, there's another one, up above."

Barlow P. stood and peered over the rail. "Least Finley ain't alone. Appears Elmer Thorley's keepin' 'im company."

"You know these men?" Pete asked.

"They's partners in the North Nevada. Or were. Guess they went independent and got a bullet fer it. Sumbitches is shot up purty good."

Pete and Barlow P. whirled at the crash of firewood tumbling onto the cabin's planks. "Scutdoo will build fire. Miss Megan, what do you need from the sleds?"

"I ain't eatin' in no graveyard," Barlow P. snorted. "Saddle up, Mike. We're movin' on."

The guide seemed rooted to the floor, completely perplexed by Barlow P.'s curt command.

"There's a couple of prospectors sleeping off eternity over here," Pete explained. "Figure it's best not to disturb them."

"But we can't just leave them there," Megan argued. "Come spring, animals'll . . ." Thoughts of what would happen to the men's remains made her blood run cold.

"Well, we cain't bury 'em. Lashin' 'em up in a tree won't save 'em from the wolves, neither."

"Then we'll just have to take them with us," she snapped stubbornly.

Pete laid his hands on her shoulders. "I understand how you feel, but we can't do that, either. It'd add too much weight, and we've got all we can neck right now."

Megan bowed her head and murmured, "They're my friends, Pete. Their souls are with God, but I can't leave their bodies for the animals to tear apart." Looking up into his eyes, she added, "I just can't."

Barlow P.'s voice was as somber as a hanging judge's. "Then we'll burn the place. 'Bout all we can do, gal."

The trapper shook his head. "Others could come along, needing this cabin awful bad before winter blows out. There's been times when the only thing standin' between me and my Maker was an abandoned shack."

His words hung like a fog in the silent room.

Finally, Barlow P. snorted. "Damn it, I can't let the critters have 'em, either." He stomped across the cabin, ordering, "Mike, tell the boy to yank them sleds down the trail a'piece. Megan and Pete, get yer behinds outside. This tinderbox's gonna go up like prairie grass once I set a match to it."

Huddled with Pete and the native men, Megan said a quiet requiem, then crossed herself. Glass tinkled when Barlow P. hurled the lantern against the hearth. Through the open door, she saw flames licking up from the floor from the spreading oil.

The pyre raged into an inferno. Thick black smoke furled into the darkening sky; the dry cedar crackled and filled the air with its distinctive, sweet scent.

"It is good, we do this," Mike said softly. "It is the way of my people. The bodies will not be cold on their way to the Spirit Land. It is good."

Megan nodded, and walked over to her sled. Slipping the trace over her head, she said, "Right or wrong, we've done all we can for Finley and Elmer, God rest 'em. There's others needin' us where they came from. Let's go."

# Chapter Thirty-one

Reassuring fingers of smoke drifted from above the east bank of Eight Mile Creek a good half mile before the North Nevada's log headquarters came into view.

Near as I can figure, Megan calculated mentally, we've been seventy-seven days on the trail so . . . this must be the fifth, no, sixth of March.

Lord only knows where we were come Christmas. She chuckled softly. I wonder if dear William set off his annual crate of Chinese firecrackers to start '77 off with a bang.

Her grin widened at the image of Elvira Armbrewster being rousted from a sound sleep by the racket.

She sobered as they approached the forty-foot-long structure nestled in a windbreaking stand of trees. With toothy icicles dangling from its eaves, a white blanketed roof, and snow driven in the cracks of its rough-hewn walls, it looked like a giant gingerbread house.

Along the frozen creek bed, skeletal frameworks of a half-dozen flumes and Long Toms sat idle; their riffles awaiting the next opportunity to catch gold flakes sluicing through with the silt.

"The men'll be up to their knees in muck and cussin' a blue streak before long," she vowed under her breath. Wriggling free of the sled's trace and her snowshoes, she high-stepped her way to the building.

Mindful of the nail points protruding like porcupine quills from the door to deter hungry bears, Barlow P. whomped the facing with a chunk of kindling.

"Holster yer widdermakers, boys. It's Barlow P. 'n Megan."

He nudged it open with a log. Tongues of white vapor slithered over the threshold at the same time a sickening stench blasted out.

Bile rose in Megan's throat. The reek of death, human

waste, and putrid, rotting flesh slapped her senses like a physical blow. Repulsion battled with compassion for the men prostrated on their bunks and huddled in pallets on the floor.

"Izzat truly you, Megan?"

For a moment, she didn't recognize the speaker. His eyes were dark marbles sunk in an ashen, bone-ridged face. Rivulets of blood drizzled over his brushy blond mustaches and down to his beard, joining dried streaks of previous hemorrhages.

She clenched her hands into fists to fight her squeamishness, then quipped, "Me it is, Jerusha. Poor lad, a'hopin' you were shed of me 'til the river broke up, didn't you, now."

His feeble smile changed instantly to a grimace. "How in—"

"Quiet yourself and rest," she said as she shrugged out of her trail gear. "We'll swap lies after I get some decent food down your craw."

Hooking her turka, mittens, and scarves on the rack of caribou antlers beside the door, she ordered: "Mike, get a fire goin' outside, and I'll need a tripod lashed together to hold a cauldron. Tell Scutdoo to bring in the provisions.

"Pete, you scour out that laundry tub best you can, then help the boy chunk all the taties it'll hold. Barlow P., you—"

"Can damn well figger out what needs doin' without no bossy female a'tellin' me." He hastened toward the nearest tier of bunks. Obviously, he'd assigned himself the grisly task of separating the dead from the suffering.

Stiff socks, grimy shirts, and woolen underwear dangled from twine crisscrossing from corner to corner. Megan's heart ached at the thought of these frail skeletons bent over a washboard trying to scrub the filth from their clothing.

Sidling between a blanket-wrapped form and the wall to unhitch the clothesline, she knelt down and eased the cover back to check the man's condition. She wrinkled her nose at a gust of rancid breath, then gasped.

Kansas Hughes's once-boyish face was covered with pussy lesions. He slept, breathing raggedly, unaware or not caring that he'd fouled himself and the pallet beneath him.

She remembered the day he'd shuffled into her kitchen at the Sanders and Meredith mine asking her to help a friend who'd been stricken with heat sickness. Wringing his hat in his hands, he'd looked like a little boy caught snitching apples from a neighbor's orchard.

Now, with lips curled over toothless gums and bloody drool seeping from the corners, he had the mein of one who'd seen the wolf and was but a whisper away from his Creator.

"Don't you dare shrivel up and die on me, Kansas," she murmured. "I'll do everything I can to get you well, but you've gotta fight, too."

Barlow P. carried ten corpses out to join eighteen others awaiting burial in an equipment shed behind the bunkhouse.

Pete stoked the mud and rock "stove" in the center of the room, then balanced buckets of river water on the flat stone that served as its top. Megan stirred in handfuls of spearmint leaves to concoct a "tea" to soothe the sores.

Years earlier, during their roam through southern Nevada, she and Barlow P. made acquaintance with Wu-Nav-ai, a Paiute medicine woman. Megan was so fascinated by the Indian's curative powers, Wu-Nav-ai taught her many of the tribe's ancient herbal remedies.

Those potions'll surely be tested before this siege is over, Megan thought.

Once the cauldron, brimming with potatoes, was set on its rack to boil and a good supply of wood was chopped and stacked, Mike and Scutdoo packed a few provisions in knapsacks and left for Wrangel.

"Them Tlingits is scairt spitless that the boys've got the smallpox," Barlow P. grumbled. "Tried to talk 'em into restin' up a night a'fore takin' to the trail. Might as well've been sayin' 'nice kitty' to a bobcat."

Turning to Pete, he added, "Surprised you didn't light out with 'em. You didn't sign on fer no nursemaidin' duties, neither."

"I was on the receiving end once. I figure it's high time I evened the score."

Megan winced as her assistants stripped the living of their tattered, defiled clothing. Scurvy cruelly swelled a sufferer's bones and joints and hardened every muscle like granite. Even the slightest movement was gut-wrenching agony. Pete and Barlow P. tried to be gentle, but moans and shrieks rebounded through the huge room.

She set a bowlful of warm, fragrant water beside Nicodemus Callista's bunk and perched on its side rail. The wizened prospector had drawn his knees up to hide his nakedness, yet his watery eyes pleaded for comfort. Suppurating sores covered nearly every inch of his emaciated body.

"Back in Ireland I had five brothers and a sickly da," she lied in a matter-of-fact tone. "And I'm promisin', there ain't a thing under those hands I haven't seen before." As she wrung water from a rag, she crooned, "Stretch out whilst I bathe you squeaky, then I'll rub on some meadowsage salve. You're gonna be good as new in no time a'tall."

# Chapter Thirty-two

Barlow P. pursed his lips to sip a taste of the bubbling stew from the ladle. Chunks of potatoes, carrots, and the rabbit Pete shot that morning bobbed in a rich amber broth.

That's purty good, he adjudged silently, then snorted. By God, Megan ain't the only gut-robber in this outfit. One plate o' this, and Pete may start makin' cow eyes at *me*.

The trapper was snoring like a bull moose on the corner pallet Barlow P. vacated a few hours earlier. For three days, the pair kept the fires fed inside and out, strung clothes-lined walls with the boiled blankets and clothing Megan had washed, cut up pound after pound of potatoes for the cauldron, and pleaded with her to rest.

She'd bathed each of the thirty-odd survivors at least twice. When not doctoring their skin ulcers with salve, she was cradling their heads for drinks of spearmint tea and spooning mushy gruel between their cracked lips. Barlow P. marveled at her stamina and compassion.

Every man she ministered to felt as if he were the only one she cared about and had to care for. Most called her "Angel" now, with reverence shining in their eyes. To Barlow P.'s mind, it wasn't a coincidence that no bodies had been carried to the shed since she'd arrived.

He gave his stew a final stir, then poked his head around the hanging blankets until he found her squatting on her heels feeding Kansas Hughes. Beneath her lashes, puffy dark circles stood out like soot against her pale, drawn skin. Her hand trembled when she held the spoon to Kansas's mouth.

Barlow P. knew that, other than during these continual bedside nursings, Megan hadn't sat down for over thirty-six hours. Whenever he'd insisted she rest, she'd countered, "Soon as I finish scrubbin' this tub of britches," or "I've got to steep another bucket of tea," or "Can't just yet . . . Jake's due for some nourishment."

She patted Kansas's cheek and slowly rose to her feet. Her eyelids fluttered, and she faltered a step before regaining her balance.

"All right, that's it," Barlow P. drawled. "Yer gonna cover yer back with yer belly and that's all there is to it."

She smiled wanly. "Got to—"

"Ya don't 'got to' do a goddamn thing for a while. Them boys is perkin' up like parched ponies at a spring, but you're plumb tuckered out." He clapped a hand to her clammy forehead. "Gettin' the fever from it, too."

"I am a tad weary," she admitted with a sigh. "Soon as I wring out those blankets I've got soakin', I'll lay down, I promise."

Barlow P. took the bowl from her hands and set it on the table, then wrapped his arm around her shoulders. Without a word, he steered her to a section of unoccupied bunks.

She moaned as she stretched out on a clean blanket. Before he unfolded another to tuck under her chin, she was fast asleep.

Squatting on the side rail, he gently brushed tendrils of sweaty hair from her face. "Baby gal, I've loved ya since the first time I saw ya, sittin' all pert and pretty in Lambert Jacobs's buggy.

"Guess I ain't never gonna have the starch to tell ya so's ya can hear it. 'Fraid you'd think I was an old fool. But long as I'm breathin', ain't nothin' or nobody gonna hurt ya. I'll see to that."

# Chapter Thirty-three

In the midst of their early morning conversation, Megan felt a warm glow spread over her. Jerusha Howell had lost several teeth and a good measure of burliness, but his gregariousness hadn't been ravaged by disease.

The bunkhouse was quiet but for the snores and grunts of its residents. A flickering candle stub centered the table; its amber light softening the planes of Jerusha's ruggedly handsome face.

"Hard to believe this lot was rappin' on Saint Peter's gates a month ago, isn't it?" he murmured, then took a gulp from his cup.

"Jaysus, that's whangy. I know it's part of the cure, but what *is* this stuff? Boiled buffalo grass?"

"It's spearmint tea—good for what ails you."

"Must be. Anything that is always tastes like boiled buffalo grass."

"Jerusha, the truth of it is, I don't understand how you boys got in such straits. When Barlow P. and I set out for Wrangel last August, the pantry was chock-full."

He tilted back against the wall and fixed his eyes on the rafters. "An early blizzard came roarin' down the canyon about ten days later. A couple of cat-eyed jaspers, name of Erikson and Romney, blew in with it. We was snowbound with 'em for a day or three. They jawed every minute about this strike they'd panned outta the Toonya, west of here."

Megan's ears perked up. "If they'd washed a bonanza, why'd they leave it?"

"My question exactly. Erikson said they was fed up with the hard livin' and hellacious weather. All they wanted was to sell their claim and hightail it back to the States."

"Well, that doesn't even make good sense—"

"It did to Finley James and Elmer Thorley. Lord, them two like to pestered the rest of us blind to buy up that claim. Thorley kept yammerin', 'Ain't no use muckin' a dry hole here, when there's sure color over yonder.' "

Jerusha's stump seat thunked to the floor. He anchored his elbows on the table. "Finley and Elmer got the greedies real bad. Didn't have any money. Gold either, for that matter. None of us did. Shoulda suspected somethin' when they started wheedlin' to trade Erikson and Romney out in goods."

"You mean Elmer and Finley swapped the camp's supplies for a bar diggin's they'd never even *seen*?"

"I hope to shout, they did. Bastards cleaned the storehouse out by the back door one night. The jaspers lit out one direction with our grub, whilst Finley and Elmer tore off for the Toonya."

Megan thought back to the riverside cabin and the bodies she'd insisted upon giving Christian last rites. If there's any punishment paid in the hereafter, those two're surely roasting in hell. The irony of their cremation might have been humorous had twenty-eight good men not been stacked up like cord wood in the shed.

"I think I'd have posse-ed up and gone after the food, and the ones that traded it."

"We did, when we figgered out what'd happened," Jerusha replied. "The mornin' we found all four of 'em gone, we were so glad to be rid of 'em, we whooped and hollered like sixty.

"Had plenty of grub stacked there in the corner. Didn't know that was all we had until it started runnin' low. Can you imagine us openin' the door to the storeroom and findin' it empty as a leaky bucket?"

"No, I can't."

The North Nevadans were seasoned prospectors. Each would have known instantly that an empty larder, no money to buy more, and a bad winter closing in was nothing less than a death sentence.

"Jake and a half-dozen others went after Erikson and Romney," Jerusha said. "But they didn't know which way them scoundrels headed. Snow'd covered their tracks. Never found a trace of 'em. Me and a couple others tracked Elmer and Finley to a cabin—"

"I know. We found them on the way here."

"Miner's justice, it was, Megan," Jerusha replied defensively. "Pure and simple. If I got any regrets, it's that we shoulda left them to starve real slow like we damned near did."

She shook her head, almost unable to believe gold fever could induce two jovial, decent men to sacrifice their partners' lives so heartlessly.

"Thank God you got word to Captain Joscelyn at the fort." She shuddered at what she and Barlow P. would have found if they hadn't.

"That was Kansas's doin'. We scraped together what dust we had between us, and he set off for the tradin' post at Telegraph Creek. Poor fella had to decide whether to give it to an Indian messenger and hope he didn't circle back to spend it on hootch, or to buy what supplies he could with it ..."

She turned to look at the young man's form curled comfortably beneath a blanket. No wonder he'd been one of the sickest; it was a fifty-mile hike to the post. The temptation to use the money to fill his own growling belly must have been enormous.

"Storekeep up and gave Kansas all the food he could carry. Said there'd be more if we'd send a sled for it. Then storm after storm socked us. We just got too weak to go after it, and I reckon the trail got too treacherous for the keep to send it to us. How your party made it through, I'll never know."

In a way, Megan mused silently, that journey seems like it happened a long time ago and to someone else—as if I were told the story, instead of living it.

"Damn-fool stubbornness, a passel of luck, and a good guide's what got us here. I reckon God smiled on us, too, but there were a few times I feared He'd gone off to shepherd His other lambs."

Cracking joints and yawns of drowsy men stirring in their beds were sounding by the time Megan finished telling Jerusha the details of their adventure.

"I guess Captain Joscelyn wasn't far wrong when he called it 'my mad trip,' eh?"

Splaying her fingers on the table's planking, she rose and stretched the kinks from her back. "No rest for the wicked, or the cook. Bet you're hankerin' for some breakfast yourself."

"Soon as my legs'll do my biddin', I'll rustle you up the best stack of flapjacks you ever tasted," Jerusha promised.

"The best, you say—as in better than *mine*?"

She was hanging the oil lamp from its hook when Pete whispered, "What's for breakfast?" in her ear.

"Thun-der-ation, man! Who gave you leave to sneak behind and scare me outta my wits every time the sun comes up?"

"It's hardly my fault that you're jumpy as a hooked trout."

Ladies don't say out loud what I'm a'thinkin', she warned herself. Lord, if he isn't saint and devil combined. Tender as a woman with the sickly, then harries me at every turn.

Strange, too, how he looked so different than she'd imagined all those weeks when virtually all save his eyes were covered by scarves. Expecting the Slavic features his surname impled, she was surprised to find he resembled an auburn-headed George Armstrong Custer.

"From what I've read," she muttered under her breath, "you're as cocksure as the Seventh Cavalry's commander was, too."

"What was that?"

"I said if you want to make yourself useful, stoke up the fire."

Sitting back on his haunches, he grinned up at her while he poked at the embers. "That's not what you said, but it's probably better I don't know what aspersions you cast on my character."

" 'Aspersions'? Glory be, that's a two-dollar word if I ever heard one."

"My mother would be pleased to hear you say that. Much of my boyhood was spent memorizing a dictionary."

"Why on earth . . . ?"

Pete brushed his hands together to dust the ashes from them. "Ma said just because we were white trash didn't mean we had to talk like it."

"I think that's an awful thing to say to a child." She moved to the table to mix a batch of flapjack batter.

"Not really. Ma simply never saw a need to wrap stones in pretty paper. Being fooled into thinking life is easy, then finding out it's not, is hard to take."

He settled himself on the stump Jerusha had occupied earlier. "I get the feeling you weren't spared many cobbles along the way, either."

"She damn-sure wasn't," Barlow P. agreed, stepping out of the shadows.

Pete slapped his palm on the tabletop. "Why in God's name can't I talk to this woman without you butting right into the middle of it?"

Barlow P. grunted and scratched his belly. "I dunno. Why can't ya?"

Megan stole a glimpse at the trapper from beneath her lashes. She had to bite her lip to keep from laughing at Pete's livid expression.

"What *is* it with you two? You're not father and daughter, or husband and wife, but you guard her like a priest does a nun. And you"—he pointed a finger at Megan—"don't mind his meddling a bit, do you?"

With that, he stomped off. Seconds later the door banged shut behind him.

Barlow P. sucked his teeth noisily a few times. "Well, Sister Megan," he drawled. "When's them biscuits gonna be done?"

That afternoon, since most of her charges had recovered enough to play cards or write letters that couldn't be mailed for several more weeks, Megan decided to start tidying up the bunkhouse.

The men's illness had contributed greatly to the squalor, but in her absence, it was obvious that routine housekeeping chores had hardly been a priority.

She'd planned to enlist Pete's and Barlow P.'s help, but both had disappeared outside after lunch and hadn't returned.

"Haven't heard any gunshots," she muttered, "I s'pose they're walkin' and talkin' out their squabbles. That, or they read my mind and skedaddled."

Once clean linens and laundry were folded and stacked, she turned her attention to the trash littering the floor. Sweeping would undoubtedly cause choking clouds of dust, so she used the broom's head to wrest an ungodly accumulation from beneath the bunks.

Good-natured jibes rang out from all directions.

"Ain't that just like a woman? 'Bout the time a place gets nice 'n comfortable, out come the mop buckets 'n beeswax."

"Hey, Angel, how 'bout hangin' some o' them fancy porteers 'crost the door? That'd be right classy, don'tcha think?"

"Whoever said a man's home's his castle musta been a gol-durned bachelor."

Stuffing the heap into empty bean sacks, Megan waggled her head and chuckled. How grand it was to hear them tease and poke fun at her, just like old times. She grieved for the voices she'd never hear again, but even that couldn't dampen her high spirits.

"It's a rat's nest under there," Kansas warned when she edged the broom under his bunk. A tumble of wadded stationery, orange peels, dirt, and cigar stubs proved his honesty—and slovenliness.

"There's somethin' . . . heavy. Can't quite . . . get it."

"Prob'ly my papers. Don't trouble yourself. I'm savin' 'em for boot linin's."

"Newspapers? How'd you latch on to them way up here?"

"Remember Sell Trenoweth? The miner you sent home with heat stroke?"

"Ah, yes, my handsome. A lovely man, he is."

Kansas grinned at her lilting impersonation of the Cornishman's manner of speaking. "When I told Sell I was headin' Canada-way after the mine closed, he was just sure I'd die from the lonesomes. He can't read nor write, so he sends me the *Pioche Record* to keep me company. Calls 'em my 'letters from home.' "

"What a kindly thing to do."

"Yeah. 'Course mail delivery's pretty sparse. I get 'em in big batches, come spring and fall."

"Would you mind if I borrowed a few? I'd love to read what's been goin' on there since Barlow P. and I left town."

"Sure. Help yourself."

Like a child reaching into a cookie jar, she knelt down and grabbed as many copies as her hand could hold. Crossing her legs Indian style, she allowed herself a glance at each edition's front page while stacking them into a neat pile to pore over later.

She froze when she read a banner headline that fairly screamed in bold, black type: EDITOR WEDS MINING MAGNATE'S DAUGHTER.

Beneath it was a smudgy, crude lithograph of David Jacobs standing proudly beside his new bride, Amanda Meredith.

# Chapter Thirty-four

"Will you accompany me a ways upriver . . . ?" Pete's eyes met Megan's; a mixture of affection, gambled pride, and challenge in their depths. ". . . and without 'Bald Eagle' Bainbridge on our heels?"

The sadness weighting her heart was unexpected and discomfiting. She could only nod.

Farewells and godspeeds had already been exchanged with the North Nevadans milling around the bunkhouse. Barlow P. had gripped Pete's hand and upper arm and said gruffly, "I'm beholden to ya for savin' my hide, amigo."

"And been a burr in your blanket ever since, I'm afraid. Take care, Barlow P. I'm going to miss you." He laid a hand at the small of Megan's back, guiding her outside to where his gear was stowed.

She laced her fingers behind her as they strolled toward Eight Mile Creek's softening bank. the steady *tick-tick* sound of snow melting off the tree branches promised that Old Man Winter was easing his frigid grasp.

"Pelts may be scarce around Great Bear Lake this season, but that'll make them more dear." Pete cocked his head toward the sluices. "I suppose you're eager to reap your own rewards."

"No, Barlow P. and I have decided to move on, too. The gold's playin' out, and so are we."

"What will you do?"

She sighed, already anticipating the wrench of leaving the Cassiar, her second home. "Spend a few days in Wrangel, sayin' my good-byes and such. Then, I've got a sister in San Francisco and a passel of nieces and nephews I haven't seen in years. I'll settle there awhile—earn a grub-stake with an eating house or somethin'. Frisco's fallen on hard times, but if strikes are bein' made anywhere out West, I'll hear about 'em there."

"Beyond that?"

She stepped lightly over a patch of slushy bog. "God willin', Barlow P. and I plan to meet up later in Virginia City and go where the wind takes us."

"He'll not be accompanying you to San Francisco?"

"He's got family in Indiana to remind he's alive. Besides, he says he wouldn't set foot in California if the rest of the country broke off from its border. But it'll sure be strange not to have him tormentin' me every—"

He pulled her into his arms and held her tight against his chest. Soft lips grazed hers, then claimed them with tender passion.

Maybe it was a primal stirring borne of the fresh, loamy scent of the land's rebirth and the crackle of the river shedding its icy winter coat. Maybe it was just the finality of the occasion. Whatever the reason, she wound her arms around Pete's neck and gave him as good as she got.

When their lips parted, he murmured, "Come with me, Megan. I've got a cabin up where the Northern Lights sizzle across the sky in all their glory. It's the wildest, most beautiful country you've ever seen. We can roam every inch of it . . . together."

For one breathless, dizzying moment, she was tempted. She remembered the powerful ache; the longing that burned within her the morning she'd awakened huddled against him in the snow cave.

Caught between dream and reality, she'd wanted him, and had pressed her body against his before she realized what she was doing.

Once again, physical cravings threatened to deceive her heart. *God help me if sometimes I want so much to be made love to,* she cried silently. *To know those wondrous secrets a whole woman knows, and that I can only imagine. But I don't love Pete. To use him in that way would shame us both.*

"I can't . . . I—"

His arms fell to his sides and he stepped back. "You want to. I felt you trembling. I'll be gentleman enough not to ask again, or ask why."

An avalanche of emotions tumbled inside her. It would have been easier to keep her head bowed and not respond. Instead, she raised her chin and said, "You're a fine man, Pete. I'm proud to have you as a friend."

"Friend, eh?" He chuckled, but it held little mirth. "A distinction few have been graced by. It could be more, we both know that, but thank you, Megan. Perhaps we'll meet up again someday."

"I'd like that. Truly I would."

She watched as he walked away, hitching his knapsack's straps into the natural slopes of his broad shoulders. Then he paused and turned back to her. "What is it you're searching for?"

"I thought I knew, once. Now, I'm not sure."

"When you find it, promise me you'll grab it in both hands and not let go, no matter what. Don't live your life looking back, Megan, and regretting what might have been."

# Chapter Thirty-five

Just as she had every afternoon for the last five days, Megan gazed out the Virginia Belle's gingham-curtained window.

"You're getting to be a regular," the waitress said as she approached the booth. She topped off the coffee cup, but Megan didn't take her eyes off the people milling along the boardwalk outside.

"Stage from Salt Lake ought to be getting here about now. Hope your feller's on it this time."

"How could you possibly know . . . .?"

The twig-slender woman seemed quite pleased to have finally captured her attention. "It's simple, honey. You've drifted in every day this week about three o'clock. The Salt Lake run gets in around three-thirty."

A wry, split-toothed grin slashed her horsey face. "And who else would a fine-lookin' lady like you wait for so long, besides a gentleman friend, or . . ." An eyelid closed slowly, like a window shade lowering, then hurtled open again. She turned on one heel and sashayed back to the kitchen.

Megan was chuckling to herself when she caught sight of a Stetson that appeared to have been broken in during a cattle stampede. Her jaw dropped when its wearer cat-cornered across the street.

His immaculate, black clawhammer coat, necktie, and trousers sharply contrasted with a white boiled shirt and maroon waistcoat. Judging by their sheen, Megan could almost feel the leather custom-mades pinch his feet with every step.

The Virginia Belle's batwings parted like the Red Sea, whumping rhythmically after he passed through. With a grin as wide as a boy astride his first pony, Barlow P. doffed his hat and drawled, "G-a-w-d-damn, if ya ain't a sight fer sore eyes."

She scrambled from the booth with her arms raised to hug him. Hat and satchel hit the floor. He yanked her off her feet and swung her around.

"The last four years have felt like my right arm was cut off. Lord, how I've missed you, you old coot."

He set her down, took both her hands, and stepped back. "Still an ol' maid, I see. And still the purtiest gal west of the Big Muddy."

"Well, and isn't it a grand toff *you* are. Come, sit down and tell me—"

The waitress appeared, wielding another cup and saucer and the coffeepot. "You can start with what took you so long to get here, mister. This poor girl's been pinin' for you nigh on a week."

Barlow P. glared at her. "Ya wanna pull up a chair or can ya hear all right from 'crost the room?"

She opened her mouth to speak, then with a haughty sniff whirled and stomped away.

"The riggin's may have changed," Megan said, chuckling, "but the old leopard's spots haven't."

"Hmmmph. I'm damn well sheddin' this funeral suit first chance I get. Ain't natural fer a man to wear a noose 'round his neck 'lest there's a tree branch on t'other end."

She reached and patted his hand. "I'm listenin'."

"Aw, not much worth tellin', gal. Roland, the runt o' the litter, took over the farm back in '75. Rest of the clan's scattered like corn cobs in a tornado.

"Figgered Rollie could use my help. That kept my gullet full, but my pockets stayed flat, so I got me a job down to the feed lot." He snorted. "Didn't take long to recollect how much I hated shovelin' cow shit and why I left that flapjack prairie to start with."

Megan propped her chin in her palm. "Frisco was about the same for me. Oran and Frances's five children are darlin' bairns, truly. But they're kinda like fancy necklaces drippin' with diamonds—best admired from a distance.

"And the city'd grown so much! Buildings sprawl as far as the eye can see. Folks with their faces pinched real scowly are forever scurryin' like ants on a stirred hill."

"Yup. Good, bad, or in-betwixt, we're two of a kind, gal. Them that's happy bein' born, livin', and dyin' on the same patch of ground is flummoxed by us that jes' can't take root. But I ain't built that way, and there's no sense fightin' it.''

Megan nodded, her eyes tracing every pore of his weathered face. He must be over fifty years old, she mused silently. Yet his eyes still sparkle like sapphires in sunlight. She thought back to Pete's parting remark when he left the North Nevada. *I wonder what Barlow P.'s searching for? I reckon he wouldn't tell me, if he knew.*

"Frances surely tried to civilize me—settle me down. When I wasn't slingin' hash at the Maison Doree or ridin' herd over the children to give their mama a moment's peace, I was sittin' in the parlor with whatever stray buck Oran drug home to sweep me off my feet."

"Elizabeth, that's Rollie's wife, did a fair share of matchmakin' herself," Barlow P. muttered. "I bet I got cow-eyed by every widder and spinster in three counties." He shuddered, then added, "Married folk jes' can't get through their rock heads that there's a difference between bein' alone and bein' lonely."

Megan laughed at his doleful expression and sat back in the booth. "Oh, I got the lonesomes plenty of times—for you, mostly. And for places a body can breathe without suckin' in city stinks along with it."

"Ya missed me, eh?" A wide grin plumped his clean-shaven cheeks. They flushed as pink as rose petals. "And yer jes' itchin' to tell me where the air's more to yer likin', ain't ya?"

"I've gone one better than that, partner. You showed up just in time. We've got tickets for tomorrow's noon stage."

"Tar-damn-nation, woman! I ain't never gonna get no say so in nothin', am I?"

"Nope."

He shook his head and sighed resignedly. "So which way's them leprechauns in yer brain a'pointin' us this time?"

"Southeasterly, my friend. Right toward a rip-snortin', hell-bent-for-leather silver camp in Arizona Territory called 'Tombstone.' "

"I feel four inches shorter and older'n dirt," Megan muttered.

Their Tombstone–Tucson Express coach was equipped with leather strap through-braces instead of springs. She'd already opined several times that the line's owner should have supplied passengers with spurs, if not prize money, for surviving the seventeen-hour ordeal.

"Ya shore know how to pick 'em, gal. I told ya ten years ago that alkali dust don't make a meal, cactus don't give much shade, and sun hot enough to skin the hide off'n a gila monster jes' don't appeal to me none."

Palmer Shapiro, the paunchy, older gent juddering in the other seat, cleared his throat. "It is a beastly ride, I'll not argue, but the air should cool when we descend to Goose Flats."

"How far is that from Tombstone?"

"Dear lady, that *is* Tombstone, er, the name of the flat-lands surrounding it, anyway."

As he stroked his meticulously barbered goatee, sunlight sparked off his gaudy diamond pinkie ring. "May I be bold enough to ask why you and your father are traveling to that infamous community?"

Barlow P. grunted. "Father, my a—"

"Why, to make money, of course."

Shapiro's eyes flicked over her. "Have you . . . a trade?"

"Several, actually," Megan answered dryly, noting the implication in his pause. "I'm a prospector, Mister Shapiro, and a businesswoman." Cocking her head toward Barlow P., she continued, "The only thing I know of that he can't do is hire on for a wet nurse."

The inquisitor's kettle belly convulsed in time with his laughter. "My outlook is quite jaded, I realize. I have been too long among scoundrels, which is why I am selling my concerns and returning to the Seaboard as soon as possible."

"And what concerns might those be?"

"The Russ House restaurant and, in the manner of calling a spade a spade, a saloon called the 'One-Eyed Jack.' "

Barlow P.'s voice rumbled in his throat, "I know what yer cogitatin', gal. The eatin' house might be worth lookin' in to, but ya ain't gonna strawboss a goddamned saloon."

Looking past him out the window, she caught sight of Tombstone rising chock-a-block from the hardscrabble, mesquite-spiked terrain. Clapboard buildings, frame-and-canvas structures, and crouching adobes nestled together in riotous disharmony. Megan could almost feel the vibrance charging the air like ozone from a lightning strike.

She grinned at him wickedly. "Oh, it's a raffish hooligan of a town, and I can't wait to be slap-bang in the center of it."

Her button-busting exuberance was contagious. Barlow P. couldn't contain the smile dancing at the corners of his mouth. Megan took his expression as encouragement.

"We decided in Virginia City that we're too old to live on pan leavin's and hope, remember? Two businesses a'goin' means double profits, so we'll have money enough to go chasin' after glitter dust in half the time."

She paused for an argument that didn't come. "While I'm fillin' bellies, all you've gotta do is keep your own gullet dry and wet your fellow man's."

Shapiro sat straighter in the seat. "Are you sincerely interested? Or simply trifling with your, er . . ."

"Best friend in all the world," Megan finished for him. "Yes, I'm interested—dependin' on the price."

The merchant fumbled in the pocket of his coat on the seat beside him and extracted a card. "Call on me at your earliest convenience." He leaned forward, handing the slip to her. "Perhaps—"

With a crack of reins and the driver's "giddap!" the coach lurched forward at a full gallop. Storefronts, signs, and strolling citizens blurred together in flashing glimpses until the six-horse team dug in their hooves in front of the Cosmopolitan Hotel.

Megan pitched forward, bounced off Shapiro, and landed, laughing as merrily as a child, in a heap on the floor. "Whee, that was grand. Let's do it again."

Dust boiled through the open windows. Barlow P. swatted at the grit, growling, "Megan O'Malley, yer crazier than a heifer in a patch o' loco weed."

She was still giggling when they entered the Cosmopolitan's lavish lobby. She was not when Barlow P. grasped her arm and led her outside again.

"When that sumbitch lisped out the room rate, I thought he was tryin' to sell me the place."

A cowhand, full-dressed in leather chaps, powdery alkali, and with manure chocked on his boot heels barreled out of Hafford's Saloon next door.

"Hey, mister. Where's a man find a clean bed and a meal in this town without gettin' slab-sided?"

The slack-faced Samaritan brought up a finger and

pointed, more or less, northwest. "Fly's—that's a roomin' house—is 'bout a block that a way on Fremont Street."

Barlow P. nodded his thanks. He held Megan's arm tighter as they turned the corner onto Fourth. The people they passed were no less than a human menagerie: gents and ladies decked out midweek in their Sunday best; pig-tailed, dome-capped Chinese; dudes in creased, catalogue getups; beggars; pompadoured whores; dapper card sharps with their hats tilted a fraction; and pasty-skinned, muck-splattered miners.

The air was alive with traces of lavender water, witch hazel, sweat, dung, grilling meat, and cigar smoke. Bang-key piano renditions of "Oh, Dem Golden Slippers" and "Beautiful Dreamer" competed with disembodied voices bellowing, "Promenade to the bar" and "Free roll."

Megan grinned and squeezed Barlow P.'s hand against her ribs. For the first time since leaving the Cassiar, she felt she was where she belonged.

# Chapter Thirty-six

Megan picked at whiskers of batting that had worked through the quilt's octagonal patches. Barlow P. had told her to stay in her room until he returned from "sizin'" up the town." But it was nearing noon and morning's chill was a long-vanquished memory. Gazing out the window at Tombstone going about its business made her feel like a rheumatic child remanded to bedrest.

Impulsively she leapt up, whisked across the compact chamber and out the door.

Expecting the dining room to be empty, she stopped short in its threshold at the sight of a rangy, but quite handsome man seated at the table. He'd shoved his mostly uneaten breakfast aside to deal a hand of patience.

He was losing, but Megan sensed by the set of his blunt chin that defeat wasn't so calmly accepted when the game involved cash and other players. Bemused gray eyes leisurely assessed her charms while long, narrow fingers curried a pair of luxuriant handlebars.

"That nine of clubs'll play," she noted wryly.

He glanced at the upturned Linen Eagles and back at her. "Dear lady, how have I traversed this life without you?"

"Doc, there's—" A Rubensesque woman paused in her entry from the kitchen. Her hair was cropped short; her calico dress a conservative departure from the rustling taffeta frock Megan remembered so vividly.

"Aren't you Kate Elder?" she blurted.

The woman's dour expression relented to quizzical, but she neither confirmed nor denied it.

"We met on the train to San Francisco. Glory, that was clear back in '69. I'm sure you don't remember me."

A madonna's smile warmed Kate's round face. "You were a sassy child as a recall, and now a woman grown.

Makes me feel overdue for turning up my toes at Boot Hill."

As the cardplayer rose from his chair, a strangling cough burbled from his throat. He spit into a silk handkerchief, tucked it back in his pocket, and reached for a cane hooked on the adjacent sideboard.

"I'll absent myself from this joyous reunion," he said, adding to Kate, "You know where I can be found."

After tipping the brim of his gray hat at Megan, his cane and boot heels beat a three-quarter-time cadence as he left the lodging house.

"How sad to see a man so young in ill health."

"There's harder ways to die than from consumption," Kate retorted. "I suspect one of those will kill him before it does."

"But your husband's a doctor, isn't he? Surely—"

"Doc's neither my husband nor a sawbones. He's a dentist, but only jaw-smiths when Lady Luck abandons him too long. Which isn't nearly as often as I do."

Kate's bluntness fascinated me before, Megan thought, but then it held a rebellious flirt that eased the cut of her words. Now they're hard-honed, just as she is ...

Like a ball clattering into a roulette wheel's wedge, fact and observation clicked together in her mind, particularly, a glimpse of Doc's cartridge belt and holstered revolver.

"Holliday's his last name, isn't it," she stated rather than asked.

"That's right, child. You were face-to-face with a killer outlaw and lived to tell of it." Kate chuckled sardonically. "When Doc's not spitting up his lungs, his Colt's spitting lead at poor innocents' hearts."

"Reputations are often more smoke than mirror," Megan replied. "If he's the monster he's made out to be, I can't imagine why you're with him."

"Perhaps I have a weakness for dentists. Even married one in St. Louis shortly after the war—not due to starry eyes, but to escape the convent."

"You're Catholic, too?"

"My faith and my profession are at discord. Yet I believe the blessed Virgin hears my nightly prayers to keep my son's soul at rest."

Megan could think of no adequate reply. Street noise filtered into the silent room, then Kate continued, "It was shortly after I buried Melvin and my baby that I met you on the train. Doc and I paired up in Dodge, in '77. We need each other; no one else'd have us. Sometimes, we even like each other."

"I read about the shoot-out in the San Francisco *Examiner*. It didn't treat your . . . Doc or the Earp brothers kindly."

Kate waved a hand dismissively. "There are as many versions of who fired first and why, as there are citizens in this fair city. Naturally, most also claim to have witnessed that corpse and cartridge occasion. I'm surprised accounts of October's murderous rampage didn't discourage you from coming here."

"Truth to tell, it sounded like the plot of a dime novel to me. It's not Tombstone's scandals that interest me, it's the millions in silver bullion. I'll be gettin' what I can, while the gettin's good."

"Ah, forever the money-hungry vixen. I admire ambition and would enjoy hearing where yours has taken you. Will you pleasure me by sitting a spell?" Kate hesitated, then added, "I'll not be insulted if you decline."

"You may wish you'd never asked before I'm done," Megan warned with a smile. At times, even to her, the tumble of trials, travels, and travail sounded like bunkum—too audacious for a Mick whose boat docked in Boston but thirteen years earlier.

"Then you've come to prize a silver hoard from Mother Nature's craw?"

"No, gold's my lucky charm. Far as minin' silver's concerned, I learned my lesson in Pioche, but I'll be glad to collect it in the Russ House's cash drawer."

"You'll not serve those saucy French dishes like so many, I hope. Doc and his friends say good steaks and chops are the easiest things to cook and the hardest to find in this town."

"They won't be once my restaurant's open. It's a fact, not brag, that snitching the last of my buttermilk biscuits has caused fistfights in many a minin' camp."

Kate patted her ample hips. "Oh, but it's sweets that put the strain on my corsets."

Megan grinned. "Even Frances's bony frame blossomed with my cookin', so count on loosenin' those stays a tad.

Come openin' day, there'll be a table set aside for you, Doc, and all your friends, and supper's on the house."

For an instant, like a cloud skimming past the sun, Kate's eyes lost their luster. With the dispassionate tone of a teacher calling roll, she said, "Some would question your judgment, but the offer's very generous. I'm sure the men will be delighted to accept your hospitality."

Before Megan could ask why she was subtly declining, Barlow P. sauntered in. After introductions were made, Kate mumbled something about sewing she must finish and excused herself.

Once she was out of earshot, Barlow P. thundered, "Jehosophat, gal. You'd palaver with Lucifer himself if he'd sit still long enough."

"What's that supposed to mean?"

"I ain't been gone more'n an hour or three, and what do I find when I get back? You cozied up in the parlor with not jes' *any* ol' Jezebel—it's Doc goddamn Holliday's Jezebel yer havin' a chin session with."

Heaven help me if he finds out who my first customers may be, she thought. I'd be plumb crazy to slam the door on Doc and the Earps if they moseyed in under any circumstances, but if he knew I'd invited them outright, he'd tan my hide with a dull dubber. Of course, he won't flinch a *minute* to pour 'em all the Three Roses they can swallow.

"Like it or not, Barlow P., Kate Elder is an old friend. Respect that, and don't call her names."

His expression had argument written all over it, but he scratched his salty stubble before replying, "Can't divine how that come to pass, but fair 'nough."

"We met on the train—"

"Hush. I weren't through speechifyin' yet. You gotta understand somethin': Them jaspers she runs with *ain't* yer friends. And if'n you get crosswise with 'em, she can't protect ya. To save her own skin, she prob'ly wouldn't try."

Megan waggled a finger at him. "And you're preachin' to the choir, Father Bainbridge. Now let's go see Mister Shapiro and hustle us a couple of businesses."

He hesitated, then shook his head, reached for her shawl to drape across her shoulders.

Strolling along Fourth Street, no sooner than she caught a whiff of the infamous O.K. Corral's primordial pungency,

Barlow P. steered her into the neighboring Can Can Restaurant.

"I'm not hungry—" she started.

"Me neither, but that don't matter. We ain't stoppin' here to eat."

Nevertheless, he proceeded to order coffee and lunch specials for two. Megan was so mystified, she could only sit and ponder how he'd lost his mind between Fly's Boardinghouse and the Can Can.

After scooting his chair catawampus to rafter a knee with his ankle, he folded his hands in his lap. "I brung ya here 'cause yer a lady, and ladies don't haul off'n polt a feller in public."

"Oh?" The tap of her toes on hardwood was as steady as a Regulator's tick. "What've you done? Lost our stake at a faro table?"

"Well, it's gone, that's a fact," he drawled, patting his coat pocket. "Traded a passel of it fer a coupla deeds this mornin'."

"What!" She glanced around, then lowered her voice. "We were supposed to meet Shapiro together. We're supposed to be partners —"

"Bank that Irish fire and listen: Fer all yer smarts, which are considerable, mind ya, you'd make a damn poor poker player. You was grinnin' like a coon in a tall cottonwood yesterday, and that old dodger was layin' fer ya."

"I was not. I simply inquired about the properties he had for sale."

Barlow P. grunted. "The hell ya did. 'Twas clear as the nose on yer face, you was plannin' the Russ House's daycor in yer head. Get wrathy if'n ya want, but that's 'bout as sensical as holdin' four cards, drawin' back one, then bettin' ever' dime ya got *and* grandpa's pocket watch."

Megan's mouth puckered ruefully at a corner. The old coot's right, she admitted. It wasn't an oversight that Shapiro didn't include Barlow P. in the conversation. He already had an easy mark pegged in the crosshairs.

The waiter returned brandishing an array of chef Quong Kee's mouthwatering delectables. But for all the attention his customers paid, it might as well have been hog snouts and fillet of snail.

"So how'd ya jake around my damfoolishness?"

"Used it. Told Shapiro ya'd flightied a diff'rent direction, already. We jawed awhile about how women oughta stick to their knittin', then come to terms on the Russ House and the One-Eyed Jack."

While he explained the whys and wherefores, Megan's considerable admiration for him increased enormously. Regardless of his "aw, shucks" demeanor, the man was as sly as a panther on the prowl.

"We got 'bout three hunnert apiece left over fer seed money. I'm takin' over the Jack tonight—it's already rollin'. The eatin' house's been locked up since Shapiro's cook quit on him, so it needs some scrubbin' up."

With every word, Megan's heart thrubbed faster. She could hardly keep her seat for wanting to dash over and tour the place herself.

"I know yer fit ta bust 'cause yer face's redder'n strawberry jam," he teased with a wicked grin. "Jes' bear with me a minute so's we can get this all settled legal-like."

As he pulled the folded foolscaps and two thick envelopes from his pocket, she squared her shoulders and primly sipped water from a crystal goblet; its rim adorned with a paper-thin lemon slice. Although its aroma was delightful, she decided such flummery was just a waste of good fruit.

Barlow P. returned his chair to its proper position and edged toward her conspiratorily. "Since I let on that you weren't part of the transactin', the deeds is made out to me."

He handed her an envelope. "That's yer half of the stake we got left, less a dollar. Next day or two, I'm hirin' a lawyer to draw up new papers deedin' both places to ya. That's what the eight bits is fer—somethin' them shysters call 'consideration.' "

"Uh-uh, Barlow P. The saloon's yours, lock, stock—"

"Shore is, and I'll run it like I see fit. Which means, I'd by God better never catch you within a rock-throw of them batwings. 'Cept for the record, I want yer name signed and sealed as the legal owner."

"But why?"

"I ain't been hearin' harp music, but I got a lot more miles on me than you do. If somethin' was to happen to me, this'll leave ya clear to keep it, sell it, or even burn the sumbitch if'n ya care to."

Megan quickly swept any thought of Barlow P.'s passing from her mind. Instead, she contemplated alternatives.

"All right, so you're closer to three-score-and-ten than I am. Neither of us'll hit the pillow tonight guaranteed we'll see daylight again. Why not affix both our names to the papers?"

"Gal, Arizona's a territory, not a state. God only knows what kinda foofaraw the court'd tangle ya up in and how long it'd take to get the knots out. Do this my way, will ya?"

Solemnly she nodded while saying a silent prayer that she'd never have reason to appreciate his farsightedness.

"Tarnation, Megan! Coupla high-rollin' tycoons like us oughta be celebratin', but yer as peaked as a calf with the scours. Perk up, or I ain't gonna tell ya yer surprise."

"Don't you think I've had enough surprises for one afternoon? I'm just realizin' that I've got five years' wages sunk into a piece of property I haven't even seen yet."

"That's not all you got, gal."

"So, are you gonna tell me, or just sit there smirkin' like a fox locked in a chicken coop?"

Rather than answer, he jutted his jaw sideward and lazily etched a doodle on the tablecloth with his butter knife.

"Barlow P. Bainbridge—I swear, I'm 'bout to forget I'm a lady."

Without taking his eyes off his artwork, he drawled, "Ya best study that Russ House deed a mite closer, gal."

She snatched the tri-folded paper and flattened its creases. The first paragraphs of the document took several readings before she believed their content.

"A house?" she whispered. "Of my very own?"

"Well, it ain't a palace by no means—jes' a one-room adobe hunkered behind the restaurant. But it's yers."

Megan stared at the deed, scarcely breathing. I'm the first of the O'Malleys to own the roof over their heads, she thought. Jesus, Mary, and Joseph . . . I'm a *squire*.

# Chapter Thirty-seven

Megan stretched, then groaned when sore muscles complained of their rude awakening. Gloomy skies made the sun little more than a feeble intruder in the barren, cold room.

She heard men's garbled voices and stifled laughter, but paid it no mind. The corner of Fifth and Tough Nut streets was only a block removed from notorious, ever-raucous Allen Street where saloons, gambling houses, and lustier pastimes were available twenty-four hours a day.

After pulling the blankets up to her chin, she found there was nowhere to lay her arms other than crossed over her chest. The canvas cot's middle sagged around her like a sling from shoulders to knees, offering cruel succor to a body aching from a week's scrubbing and whitewashing.

Flailing as awkwardly as an upended turtle, she struggled from its confines, then kicked its wooden frame with the ball of her foot. "If it weren't for rats and spiders, I'd burn you for firewood and throw a pallet on the damned floor."

She bowled her hands, dipped them into a bucket of water resting on an upturned crate, and splashed her face. Sputtering and gasping from the frigid ablutions, she peered through dripping eyelashes trying to find a scrap of flour sacking to dry off with.

When someone fairly beat a fist through her door, Megan almost jumped out of her socks. "Rise 'n shine, gal," Barlow P. bellowed from the other side. "Saint Nick's come to call."

"Saint John Barleycorn's more like it," she shouted back. "Go home and sleep off that load of belt-warmer you're sloshin'."

"Me-gan. Open—the—goddamned—door!"

Lest he use his boot for a key, she complied. Swinging

it wide, the ear-blistering what-for she planned to deliver died in her throat.

Wearing a liquor-stupid grin with half his shirttail flapping beneath his mackintosh and his hat anti-goggled over one ear, Barlow P. stood on the stoop either holding up a towering oak bedstead or being held up by it.

Behind him, three red-faced Mexicans balanced its footboard, sides, and a droopy husk mattress.

"Season's greetin's, gal," he slurred, maneuvering himself and the headboard across the threshold. "I'd brung ya this sooner 'cept Leo Goldschmidt didn't run outta cash to ante up with 'til late last night."

The Mexicans nodded "hallo" as they filed past, then the wobbling quartet slung her cot aside and started setting up the gorgeous tiger's eye-grained furnishings.

Two more olive-skinned porters ambled by bearing a splasher-backed commode and a small, two-drawer dresser. A final trip outside brought forth a white ceramic pitcher and basin and the dresser's beveled glass mirror.

"You won all this playin' cards? Why, these pieces must be worth twenty dollars or more."

"Leo's got a store chock-fulla this stuff over on Fremont. The sledgehammers in his head's gonna pain 'im longer than what my three kings did to his two ladies."

He tottered backward to admire his handiwork. Megan rushed over, stretched, and kissed him square on the lips.

"I take back all the hateful things I've said about you the last few days for not pitchin' in a lick to help me get the restaurant ready for business."

"Been takin' my good name in vain, huh?" He reached into his pocket for a silver dollar to pay his helpers. They beamed their thanks and scuttled out the door.

"Well, it ain't like I've been sittin' on my tailbone watchin' the grass grow, gal."

She used a side rail to leg-up on the mattress, then let her hand glide over its ticking cover. To her callused palm, the nubby cotton was as soft as velvet's nap.

"Oh, Barlow P., I feel like a fairy princess. You truly are the dearest friend anyone's ever had."

He stared at her; his eyes as misty blue as a glacier. He turned toward the window. A ragged patch of vapor billowed and ebbed on the glass in time with his breathing.

"Did I say something wrong?" she asked, scooting forward to slip off the bed.

"Nah," he answered gruffly. "Ain't slept since Monday afternoon. Guess it's catchin' up with me."

She curled an arm around his waist and hugged him tight. "I've got to put the finishin' touches on the Russ today, and the waiters and cook China Mary's sendin' are supposed to drift by later for a look-see. Why don't you pile down on my beautiful new bed and saw logs for a while?"

He ducked his head and worried an earlobe between thumb and forefinger. "Best not, gal. May Fly charges board by the night whether them sheets gets wrinkled or not. Besides, Missouri's tendin' bar and won't know where to find me if'n some dead-eye Dick starts hurrahin' the place or somethin'."

"Missouri? I s'pose that's a person?"

"Hell, I guess I ain't talked to ya since he loped into town. His right name's Homer Coulter. 'Missouri' got stuck on him 'cause he's stubborn as a goddamn mule."

Megan laughed up at him. "Now if that isn't the pot callin' the kettle black, I don't know what is."

"There's a mite bit of hard-tail in me, but nothin' like Missouri's got 'twixt his ears. One time, we was deep in Reb territory when the lieutenant sent us out foragin'. He told us there was a farm 'bout three or four miles east, 'cept it was likely swarmin' with Johnnies and to ab-solutely not get anywheres near it.

"Damned if Missouri didn't light out straight fer it. Said farms had cows and cows had steaks and that he'd et all the roots, berries, and jackrabbits he was gonna.

"Lo and behold, the place looked like a whole regiment on bivouac. Beechnut ever'where. And the only meat in sight was the scrawniest excuse fer a whiteface I ever seen.

"But Missouri was by God gonna get him some beef or die tryin'. He proceeded to belly crawl 'round the encampment, aimin' fer that bone-butted old cow. Then he cinched his belt around a hoof and sorta encouraged her to sidle where he wanted her to go. Musta taken a coupla hours, yankin' her along, 'bout six inches at a whack.

"He finally got ol' bossy into the woods slick enough, but I reckon she weren't accustomed to much travelin'. Dropped deader'n a wagon tire, smack-dab in a brier patch."

"Poor Missouri, after all that—"

"Poor Missouri, my sweet Astoria. Who do ya think helped that mule-brained sumbitch drag his supper home by the hooves, a couple-three miles?"

The mental image of Barlow P. towing a dead cow cross-country got Megan laughing so hard that tears rimmed her eyes. "And you stayed friends after that?"

"That, and 'bout a hunnert more like it. Missouri's a stubby, walleyed ol' jackanapes with more *cojones* than good sense, but he'll do to ride the river with."

"Then I can hardly wait to meet him." She tucked her hand in his arm as he shuffled toward the door. "Why don't you bring him by later this evenin'? Say, ten o'clock? I'll give you both a private tour of Tombstone's larrupin' new chophouse."

"Throw in some free samples and we jes' might get interested."

"Done. And glory be, I may even take a bath before you get here."

Barlow P. sniffed at the air like a bloodhound. "Don't know how yer gonna fold up into that bowl yonder, but ya are gettin' a tad ripe, gal."

"For all the silly capers they cut, not a man alive would hook himself into a rig with bones and steels nippin' him at every breath," Megan muttered.

Through the fabric of her smart, splatter-print shirtwaist, she tried to adjust the corset stay that was gouging her skin.

It was after eight before she convinced Lee Ho that he was the finest cook the world had ever known, and that customers denied his talent would be so overwhelmed by remorse that they'd certainly shoot themselves.

After several hours of Lee Ho's frantic dithering, despite her swearing to every deity she could think of that the food he'd prepared was the best she'd ever tasted, Megan was sorely tempted to hang the little man by his own pigtail.

Thankfully, Wang and Chin, the waiters she hired, seemed more confident of their ability and hadn't required constant smiling reassurance.

Before they left, the three lined up brigade style between the restaurant's back door and her adobe's front, passing bucket after bucket of steaming water, which she poured into a wood-bottomed plunge bathtub graciously abandoned by a former owner.

With her hair piled atop her head, she settled back against the tub's high, slanted end and luxuriated in the camomile soap-scented water. Before climbing out, she ducked down to lather her wet mane, then rinsed it until it squeaked.

Now, waiting for Barlow P.'s and Missouri's imminent arrival, she drowsily surveyed the Russ House's dining room.

Three triple-globed, gilt-finished ceiling fixtures had cost dear, but gave the room a cheery, welcoming glow. Tables for four and eight were laid with blue-and-white-checkered shirting cloths and bleached muslin napkins; all turned and neatly machine-hemmed by Wyatt Earp's industrious common law wife, Mattie. She'd also stitched the short, gathered curtains spanning the bottom halves of the windows—an idea copied from the Virginia Belle.

Ten-inch "True Blue" enameled tinware plates were large enough to satisfy the heartiest appetite. Cocobolo-handled table cutlery would efficiently dissect and deliver bite-sized portions to hungry mouths.

A satisfied sigh escaped Megan's lips. From its spotless white walls to its scrubbed plank floor, the restaurant was as clean, inviting, and attractive as imagination and elbow grease could make it.

The cherry-cased Waterbury on the far wall told her she'd wool-gathered longer than she'd thought. "The men are almost an hour and a half late," she said pensively. "I wonder what could have happened. It's not like Barlow P. to simply not show up."

Without bothering to douse the lights, she snatched her raglan off the brass tree and whisked out the door. Walking briskly up Fifth Street, she thought, late or not, Barlow P.'ll thrash me if I sashay into the saloon. Surely I can find someone who'd favor me by taking him a message.

She slowed her pace when she saw a tall, barrel-chested man wearing a slouch hat cross Fifth from the other side of Allen. Suddenly shots rang out from behind her and to her right.

The man spun in the intersection. Bullets peppered the adjacent Oriental Saloon's side and awnings. Megan backtracked a few steps and flattened herself against a building.

Blood streamed down the man's jacket sleeve and splattered his trousers. A shotgun boomed, then another. The man reeled, grabbing at his elbow.

She heard running footsteps head east down Allen. Peering around the corner of the building, she glimpsed several fast-moving shadows before darkness swallowed them.

Megan picked up her skirts and ran to help the wounded man. His sandy, handlebar mustaches seemed to stand out a foot from his ashen face. Wedging a shoulder beneath his uninjured arm, she said, "Lean on me. I'll take you to Doctor Goodfellow."

"Kind of you," he wheezed. "Just get me back to the Oriental. My brother's there."

She nodded and eased an arm around his back. She felt a warm, sticky ooze at the same time he groaned in pain. Swallowing hard, she snaked her hand back to grab a handful of his trousers' waistband and cartridge belt.

Gray plumes of cigar smoke, cheap toilet water, and whiskey roiled out from above the Oriental's batwings. Megan pushed one side open and sidled through with the bleeding man as close beside her as a Siamese twin.

As if a gong had sounded, the piano player's hands hung suspended above the keys. Laughter and shouts from the game tables quieted to whispers. In seconds, the riotous room became as quiet as a chapel.

"Get out of my way," barked a blond, mustachioed gent as he pushed through the crowd. Attired in a starched white shirt, silk cravat, and tailored black suit, Megan assumed him to be the saloon's owner.

"Good God, Virge," he said. "Where are you hit?"

"Left side. Elbow's shot up bad. Hell, Wyatt, I'm attracting lead like lodestone these days."

Wyatt Earp's icy blue eyes flicked to Megan. "Would you kindly help me take my brother to his room at the Cosmopolitan? He's in a bad way, and I'll not risk him to a drunkard's handling."

"Yes, of course," she replied in a quavering voice. After all, she added silently, how would one go about saying "No" to the Lion of Tombstone?

# Chapter Thirty-eight

Despite the night's excitement, Megan slept like a stone and awakened before sunrise. While pinning her hair into a neat chignon, she bobbed up on her tiptoes, then crouched on bent knees in front of the dresser mirror.

The mellow light cast by the oil lamp revealed a slim, perhaps pretty woman wearing a navy poplin dress as severe as a nun's habit.

"Neither madame nor matron am I," she told her reflection. "It's a businesswoman I see, and proud of it."

The timid rap at her door was not unexpected. She ushered in Barlow P. and a shorter but equally sheepish-looking, stocky gent.

"You must be Missouri Coulter," she intoned. "Where have you two been? Ridin' the river together?"

"I'm powerful sorry, Megan. The Jack was hoppin' with customers last night. We was busier than one-armed carpenters 'til long past midnight."

"Uh-huh. From the smell of you, I'll wager there was a bottle of mash and a deck of fifty-two in your toolbox, too."

"She always talk to ye like that?" Missouri whispered.

"Yep. 'Specially when I deserves it."

"What would you have me do, Mister Coulter? Wring my hands and sob into a lace handkerchief?"

His chuckle faded as he grimaced, then rubbed a hand across his brow. "You're a frisky wench, just like ol' Barlow P. said ye was." He stuck out a grubby paw. "Pleased to make your acquaintance, ma'am."

Megan grinned and shook it firmly. "Pleasure's mine, Missouri. Will you be stayin' in town awhile, or just passin' through?"

"This slat-sided galoot's done hired me to tend bar, so I reckon I'm pitchin' my tent for a spell. Gotta tell ye, it's been like old times."

Megan started to respond, but Barlow P. interjected, "I know what yer thinkin', gal. No lie, me and him's cut the wolf loose real regular. Man's gotta do that now and then, long as he's sensible enough to quit when his tail's draggin' the dirt."

"And Lordy, ma'am, we're draggin' so, ye could plant string beans in the furrows. Reckon it's time we got respectable."

"That bad, eh?"

"Yep. Me and Missouri figger we've spent all the evenin's sluggin' throat paint that a coupla grissel-heels like us can stand." He frowned, adding, "A'course, we ain't the only ones strayed from the straight and narrow. 'Bout time you got a gust of preachifyin' yer own self."

"Oh?" she said innocently. "Are you accusin' me of nippin' at the cookin' sherry on the sly?"

"That'd be better than the company yer keepin'—"

"Lordy, Miss Megan, everybody's talkin' about how you ran out in a hail of bullets to put yerself 'twixt Virgil Earp and them ambushin' sidewinders 'cross the street, then tore into the Oriental to get Wyatt, then ye half carried the jake—bleedin' like a stuck hog, mind ye—to the hotel and saved his life. Damnedest thing I ever heard."

"And most of it, pure-dee-old horse apples," she scoffed. "No wonder Tombstone's got a worse reputation than a Blondined strumpet. The true cake's grainy enough before everyone and their dog lays on the icin'."

Barlow P. looked grim as a widower fresh from the cemetery. "Hmmmph. So which parts is gospel?"

She recounted the shooting in a decidedly matter-of-fact tone. "Truth to tell, if you hadn't been busy drinkin' the One-Eyed Jack dry, I needn't have ventured out a'tall."

"Now, how is it a female can forever twist things to come out a feller's fault?" Missouri grumbled. "Been a puzzlement to me since I was in knee pants."

"I'm not twistin' anything, Missouri."

"Fact remains, gal, yer wadin' muddy water havin' truck with them Earp boys. They've been in the Jack a few times, and acted like gentlemen—I'll say that for 'em. 'Cept shootists draw trouble like a carcass draws flies. There's always somebody hopin' to make a name by puttin' a gunman in the ground."

"You old coot! Are you ever gonna give me credit for havin' a brain under my hairpins?"

"Damn it, Megan, yer the smartest woman I ever knowed—told ya that lots of times."

"Then stop thinkin' I don't know the lay of the land until you draw the map for me. I didn't know whose blood it was wettin' down the dust last night. Didn't give a care. He was hurt, I was there, and that's the end of it."

"The—"

"I *said,* that's the end of it."

Barlow P. glowered like a rabid dog, but kept his peace. Patting her hair, she glided to the door and opened it.

"I've got an eatin' house to manage," she said with a sweet smile. "If you're hungry, Lee Ho'll rustle up the best steak and eggs this side of the Pecos."

Missouri clamped a hand over his belly and groaned. "Please, ma'am. I'd druther take a bullet than stare down a coupla sunny-sides at the moment."

"Later, then?"

Barlow P. bent and pecked her cheek, then settled his Stetson atop his balding dome. "Hope yer apron pockets get so heavy ya can't walk, gal. After a pillow session and a mite of sprucin' up, we'll mosey on back."

It was midafternoon before Megan's behind touched a chair seat. She motioned for Lee Ho, Wang, and Chin to join her at a back table.

"I'm pleased—more than pleased with our grand openin'," she said. "Wang, Chin, I never saw a coffee cup empty or customers waitin' for a clean table. That does an owner proud, and I thank you for it.

"And, Lee Ho, folks looked fit to bust when they waddled out the door." She chuckled when his eyes angled in his beaming face. "I figure when word spreads—and Lord knows, whether good or bad, it races through this town like a prairie fire—we'll be busier than bees in a hive."

"Bzzz-bzzzz. Ah, yes. That be good, Missy Megan," Lee Ho giggled. "China Mary be happy her boys do fine."

With that, the trio stood, bowed so energetically that their pigtails slashed the air like whips, then scuttled back to work.

Megan indulged herself by sliding her feet onto a vacated chair, while contemplating China Town's undisputed queen.

She recollected the day she was painting the Russ House's interior walls—and a goodly portion of herself—when Mattie Earp delivered the linens she'd hemmed. The seamstress was aghast that Megan was doing such chores herself.

"Go to China Mary; anyone in China Town can direct you to her. She'll get you all the help you need—cheap."

Expecting a dainty, petite woman, China Mary's roly-poly body was draped in yards of rich primrose silk and a veritable ransom in jewels. "You need cook? Houseboy?" she'd chirped in pidgin English.

In minutes, not only was Megan's staff taken care of, the celestial sovereign had waggled a plump, ringed finger and assured, "They steal, me pay. They no steal. They bad, they leave. Right away. They not be bad."

Hearing the Russ House door's squeaky hinges signal a customer entering behind her, Megan eased her feet to the floor and licked her lips to ready herself for hostess duties.

She rose from the chair and turned to greet the new arrival. Her breath caught in her throat. She clutched the table's edge for support.

His hair was shot with white, though his mustaches were black as stove polish. Time's passage wasn't fully responsible for the fine lines graven on his face, but those eyes, she thought silently. *Those unforgettable, quick-silver eyes still threaten to engulf me, even after nine long years.*

"Hallo, David," she whispered.

He seemed paralyzed for a moment; his hat gripped in bleached-knuckled fingers. "I can hardly believe it's really you." Tossing the black felt on the table, he held out his arms. "For old times' sake?"

Megan hesitated, then stepped into his embrace as if she'd never left it. Burying her face in his coat, she breathed in the familiar aromas of expensive cigars, printer's ink, and shaving soap.

When they parted, she was trembling like an oak leaf in a breeze. "Let's, uh, sit down, shall we?"

David leaned back in the chair, staring at her unabashedly. "I hope it hasn't upset you, my just appearing out of nowhere."

"No, of course not. Though it's true, you're the last person I expected to see."

"Had you forgotten me, then?"

She shook her head. "That I'll never do. Oh, I've tried.

Sometimes wished I could." A smile flirted with her mouth. "I reckon you made a powerful impression on this little Bridget."

His expression remained solemn. "Then why did you leave me?

From the kitchen, Lee Ho's high-pitched, unintelligible chatter preceded the thunk of tinware plates being dumped into the kitchen's stoneware sink.

"Please, David. Let's talk of what's happened since Pioche; not resurrect it."

He glanced down at the table linen, then nodded slowly. "For my part, there isn't much to tell. Father died a few years after the fire, leaving me at the *Record*'s helm. The town never really recovered from the fire, so when the widow, Artemus Rath, and his cronies packed their grips, I realized that if the rats were deserting, our ship really was sinking."

Megan's ears burned at the mention of the wretched names that had caused her such misery. "Then you knew they were in league together?"

"There'd been rumors to that effect for years. Why else would a comely magnolia like Delia venture to a coarse place like Pioche, unless she'd somehow profit by it?"

"But you told me that she was the one folks called on when they were troubled."

David shrugged. "Black widow spiders spin the most beautiful, gossamer webs. To be fair, she was a godsend for any number of down-and-outers. Her way, perhaps, of doing penance."

Memories flashed in Megan's mind like a kaleidoscope. How different things might have been if I'd known he was privy to the widow's duplicity. If I'd gone to him instead of running away ...

Never look back, she warned herself. You can't change anything, and you don't have a future as long as you're living in the past.

Noting his cock-browed curiosity, she chuckled. "Sorry, woolgatherin's one of my hobbies. What then became of Miracle? I wonder about her often."

"She left with Delia for parts unknown, I guess. I can think of no better companion for that Southern shrew than a deaf-mute."

"Delia said that very—uh, never mind. Go on, please."

"That's about it, really. I sold the *Record* to a crochety old sailor from Massachusetts. Said he'd had ink running in his veins for years."

He curried his mustaches, snickering. "What Percival Phelps Dearborn is full of isn't ink, but his money was good. I quoted him an obscene price for the paper and by God, he paid it without a flinch.

"Last summer, I visited Tombstone and, believe it or not, liked its attitude. The fascinating blend of class and brass appealed to me. I heard John Clum at the *Epitaph* might sell, but he wasn't in the mood when I approached him. Neither was Artemus Fay at the *Nugget*. So, I sank every nickel I had into *The Cochise County Chronicle* and went into competition with both of 'em."

"Mayor Clum may well be regrettin' his decision not to sell."

"Because of that supposed assassination attempt a couple of weeks ago?" David laughed. "Fay did such a thorough job of skewering Clum in the *Nugget,* I didn't even cover the incident. But in all seriousness, the political climate has gotten hotter since the Earp-Clanton imbroglio. Witness last night, for example."

"As I did, which you already undoubtedly know," she replied dryly.

"Which is how I found you."

"I'm glad for that, anyhow. And that you're not lambastin' me for helpin' Virgil Earp like Barlow P. did."

"Bainbridge? He's here, too?" David snorted; a sardonic edge to his voice when he quipped, "Well, of course he is, if you are."

She bowed her lips into a catty smirk. "And how is your lovely wife Amanda?"

An angry flush played across his cheekbones. He reached for his hat, then sagged back in the chair. "She's devoted, loyal, and good-hearted to a fault," he answered. "A man couldn't ask for a more loving companion."

Megan's eyes lowered contritely. "I'm sorry. That was uncalled for."

"No more so than my remark about Barlow P."

"I reckon old wounds never completely heal."

"Maybe not, but can old friends put aside the scars and start fresh?" He laid his hand over her clasped ones. "I've missed you, Megan. It's no coincidence that we're here, together, again. I need a friend. I sorely do."

His touch set her heart pounding furiously. *What do I do? Tell him to stay to his side of Tombstone and leave me be? I can't. God help me, I just can't.*

"I am your friend, David. Always have been. Always will be."

# Chapter Thirty-nine

The hair on the back of Megan's neck bristled when a towering, powerfully built man swaggered into the restaurant. His rolly gait and the musky odor of horse lather tagged him as a cowhand. Leering blue eyes and a mop of curly black hair was as subtle as wearing a signboard with "ladies' man" painted on it.

She was not prone to instant dislike, but this hombre was an exception. "May I help you?" she asked coldly.

"This here's a eatin' house, ain't it?"

"Yes."

"Well then, are you gonna show me to a table or do ya expect me to chew standin' up?"

What I'd like to show you is the door, she thought, leading him to an empty table. He mounted the chair seat like a saddle while ogling her bodice. "Yep, I'd heard your chops was first rate. Can almost taste them, just sittin' here."

Megan started to walk away in a huff, then stubborn pride rooted her to the spot. "And what do you want to drink? Coffee, tea—"

"Gimme a beer."

"The Russ House doesn't serve beer or hard liquor."

"So, scurry your ass up to the Eagle Brewery and fetch me some."

She gritted her teeth to keep her temper in check. "Mister, if anyone's ass scurries anywhere, it'll be the one you rode in on."

His booming laugh momentarily halted other diners' conversations. " 'Ey, that's a good 'un, honey. All right, Miss Temperance, bring me a cuppa Arbuckle's, and get them chops to cookin'."

Because of the sudden rush of customers eager to pay their checks and leave, Chin served the bounder his coffee.

Though the two waiters remained in the room clearing tables, Megan was quite aware that she was now virtually alone with the obnoxious man.

When his food was ready, she plunked the plate and a bread basket on the table without even a glance in his direction. Turning on one heel, she'd hardly taken a step when viselike fingers cuffed her wrist and spun her around.

"You ain't gonna be in business long less'n you act more friendly to your customers. Word does get around, ya know. About all sorts of things."

Megan stalked toward the front of the restaurant holding her back stiff to hide the shudder tracing her spine. She'd hardly crossed the kitchen's threshold when another tall man entered the restaurant. Recognition brought an inexplicable sense of relief.

"Good afternoon, Miss O'Malley."

"And to you, Mister Earp." Her arm swept the room dramatically. "As you can see, you have your pick of most any table in the house."

"Actually, I—" He paused, squinting in the direction of the cowhand, who saluted with an upraised fork. Without taking his eyes off him, Earp continued flatly, "I plan to sample your fare in the near future, ma'am. I only stopped by to thank you again for assisting my brother the other night."

"How is he doin'? Well, I hope."

He returned his attention to Megan. "His elbow was shattered. He'll be crippled the rest of his life. Yet he is still with us, and for that we can be grateful."

Movement within a cloth bag tucked beneath his arm caught Megan's eye. the fabric bunched and writhed like a sack full of snakes.

"I don't mean to be rude, Mister Earp, but whatever it is you're totin' doesn't seem partial to the idea."

His bushy mustaches wriggled when he smiled. "Call me Wyatt, please. I think the events of Wednesday night lends pardon to the formalities.

"As for this," he added, extracting the bag and loosening its drawstring, "it's a token of my appreciation."

An orange-and-white-striped ball of fur emerged, blinking against the sudden intrusion of light. Irritable yowls and bared claws expressed its displeasure with the world in general.

"A kitten? What a wonderful surprise," she squealed, snuggling it to her chest.

"You'd best guard it close. Tombstone's crawling with rats—" he jerked his head toward the cowhand—"of the four-legged variety, as well. Miners have a habit of liberating prowling tabbies to ensure a decent night's sleep."

"'Ey, yer ladyship. This slop you brung me ain't fit for hogs."

"You've eaten well over half of it," Megan snapped. "Funny you should complain now."

"Well, since I'm the one payin' for this pile a shit, I don't think it's very goddamn funny."

"If you don't mind, Megan, I'll handle this." Wyatt flipped his coat back, exposing a long-barreled pistol cozied in its holster. His boots rumbled like thunder when he crossed the length of the room.

"You're out of line, Curly Bill."

"That so? I believe you're breakin' the law wearin' that cannon on yer hip. It's against the city ordinance to be heeled."

"That statute does not apply to a deputy United States marshal, Brocius."

"Marshal? Since when?"

"Since Federal Marshal Crawley Dake telegraphed my appointment this morning. Now why don't you just simmer down and finish your meal, nice and politelike."

Curly Bill rasped his knife blade up and down his whiskers, studying Wyatt, then Megan, then Wyatt again. "Why's my gut your concern all of a sudden? Or is ridin' two saddle-broke mares like Mattie and Josie Marcus already not enough for ya?"

A muscle twitched in Wyatt's jaw. He very deliberately pulled his gun, thumbed the hammer, and pegged the temporal bone beside Curly Bill's left ear.

"I'm only going to tell you this once, boy. If you're not finished with that food in thirty seconds, we'll have us an Arizona-style Last Supper. And if I ever hear of you coming within a half mile of that lady ever again, there won't be enough left of you to bury in a Bull Durham pouch."

Sweat trickled down Curly Bill's face. A part of Megan wasn't pleased with Wyatt's malevolent intervention; the other part desperately wanted rid of the infamous outlaw.

Curly Bill raised up off the chair and kicked it backward.

After tossing a few coins on the table, he stomped out, glaring hatefully at Megan. The kitten mewed pitifully. She realized she was clutching it so tightly, she'd almost strangled it.

Wyatt loomed over her. "Before you curse me for being the short trigger-man I'm made out to be, I believe Brocius came here intentionally to intimidate you."

"Why? I've never seen him before in my life."

"I can't prove it, but I'd bet good money he feared you had—behind the butt end of a Colt last Wednesday night."

"You think he shot Virgil?"

"I suspect he was one of the bushwhackers, yes. We found Ike Clanton's sombrero near the Huachuca Water Company building; there were at least three others involved, most likely Frank Stilwell, Hank Swilling, or Johnny Ringo. I figure any one or all may come calling eventually."

Confusion, fright, and anger collided in her mind. "But I'm not involved in your feud with the Clantons. The so-called Cowboy Gang and the Earp Gang can damn well blow each other to smithereens, for all I care."

Wyatt chuckled good-naturedly. "A prevalent attitude, to be sure, though not a popular one with the members of either faction. However, dear lady, there is such a thing as guilt by association. That you helped Virgil is plenty enough 'association' to gain the attention of our enemies."

"That's ridiculous—"

"Maybe, but better you're safe than sorry. My brothers, Doc Holliday, and other friends will watch over you as best we can. I'm not trying to worry you; just make you aware that Tombstone is a town divided. And whether you like it or not, or agree with it or not, you've chosen to side with the Earps."

# Chapter Forty

Megan stood dead-center in the middle of the Russ House's back room. It was musty from being shut up for so long and empty, save for the rat droppings rimming its perimeter.

Faro wound between her legs, butting and rubbing his striped head against her calf; his tail aloft and crooked like a shepherd's staff. She bent down and lifted his purring body to her chest.

"New huntin' grounds to prowl," she said, scratching him behind the ears. "The way you're growin', varmints'll skedaddle instead of buckin' Megan's tiger, eh?"

She stroked the animal draped bonelessly over her arm. A lot more than Faro's size has changed in the six weeks he's been with me, she thought. So far, 1882 has given equal shares of high times and nerve-janglin' frights. It's no wonder I jump every time the wind blows.

Because the Russ House was within spitting distance of the miners' shantytown, its convenience and reputation for good food at a reasonable price brought a handful, then a roomful, of Tombstone's rugged workingmen through the restaurant's door every night.

"Megan O'Malley . . ." one overalled pickswinger had mused aloud. "Irish, to be sure, and could you be the Angel of the Cassiar as well?"

"There are some who've called me Angel," she answered in surprise. "But that was years ago and thousands of miles from here."

"Aye, but a lady of your luck, pluck, and heart is toasted and told about 'round campfires near and far. Blackie Hoolihan's the name, but it's a hooligan I am, to be sure."

That the Cornish Jacks and Irish "moles" chose her company over slaking their parched throats with soothing, cold beer at the Eagle or any other watering hole in town pleased her enormously.

Later, when they elected her treasurer of the Red Path Branch Irish National Land League, a loquacious moniker for the miner's aid organization, she was so honored, she cried.

Barlow P. or Missouri, whoever won the high-card draw for a few hours leave, started dropping in more regularly, too.

"Makes a man feel at home jawin' with them that speaks his lingo," Barlow P. remarked. "Didn't know how much I'd missed it 'til I found it agin'. And damned if the cookin's not passable fair, to boot."

Besides satisfying miners' and prospectors' appetites whether their pockets were silver-lined or held nothing but lint, she matched them story for story.

After one miner's lengthy tale describing the hellish heat suffered in the tunnels, Megan climbed up on a tabletop and countered, "I'll warrant a body could fry eggs on the boardwalks here, but you won't lose toes to it like you can at fifty below. And snow? Why, the snow up in the Cassiars can swallow you whole.

"One night, Barlow P. and I made camp on the side of a steep hill. The snow was ten feet deep—truly it was. We tossed a pail of water down to freeze solid for a tent floor, then I cut me fir boughs to lay atop it for warmth, crawled inside my fly, and slept like the dead.

"Next mornin', Barlow P. rousted out early, looked all around, and couldn't find my tent. It'd snowed during the night, but not enough to bury it. Scared him so, he started hollerin' and hoppin' around like a jackrabbit with a scorched tail.

"All the while, I was diggin' myself out a half mile down the hill. A snowslide'd commenced durin' the night and, slick as a whistle, took me, my tent, and all my belongin's whooshin' right along with it. The ride didn't wake me up, nor hurt much beyond my pride, but damned if I didn't have to start the day climbin' all the way back up that blasted mountain."

While her audience knee-slapped and hooted in delight, Megan spied two gents, seated at a corner table, watching her with rapt admiration. By the tailored cut of their clothes, they were neither prospectors nor miners, but she recalled them taking their evening meal at the Russ House for several consecutive nights.

One was a strapping bull of a man with an easy smile and an ornery twinkle in his eyes. The other would likely never be arrested for committing a crime; he was one of a million average Joes that couldn't be picked from a crowd. Megan strolled to their table and they exchanged introductions. "Since you gentlemen have come in so often lately, I reckon the food's to your likin'."

"Delicious, stick-to-the-ribs fare," Milt Joyce agreed. "However, it's the stories of derring-do I can't find elsewhere—most especially at the Oriental."

Marc Smith cocked a thumb at his companion. "Milt's saloon is one of the finest in the West, and his clientele's exploits positively mesmerize the clodhoppers that swarm in like flies. But if you've heard of one shootist's dead-eyed dare-deviling, you've heard them all."

"Then, it's gold fever and not hunger pangs you're sufferin' from," she said. "Aye, glitter dust does have a way of gettin' in your blood and stickin' there. Truth to tell, there's days I'd trade my fryin' pans for a gold pan in a finger snap."

"And I'd abandon my legal practice for a chance to go with you. How about you, Milt? We've talked about trying our luck God knows how many times."

"Oh, I'm game. Only why would Miss O'Malley want to partner with two velvet-handed greenhorns itching for a last, grand adventure before they turn up their toes? She's an expert, judging by what I've heard."

"Tell you what, lads. If the fever hits me hard one of these day, we'll strike out and see where it takes us. I'll put up the experience, and you two can finance the grubstake."

Handshakes all around sealed the "someday, maybe" agreement.

The miners and their listeners made her feel like the belle of the town, but it was small comfort for the unrelenting tension that kept her insides tied in knots.

About two weeks after Wyatt named the men he believed responsible for Virgil's injuries, David arrived for his now-customary midafternoon visit brimming with news of another near shooting spree.

"Supposedly, Johnny Ringo was riding out of town when he spotted Doc Holliday and Wyatt Earp talking in front of the Crystal Palace.

"I guess Ringo decided that a gun battle with Doc was

a brilliant idea. That it would settle the Cowboy-Earp wars once and for all—which proves that good old Johnny's not the brightest star in the night sky.

"Doc's skill with a pistol is legendary, and threatening a man who already knows he's dying is like prodding a coiled rattler with a toothpick."

"I hadn't thought of it that way before," Megan mused aloud. "Standing in Saint Peter's shadow could make a man fearless."

"It must, because it surely looked like a coroner's carnival was bound to commence until Billy Breakenridge stepped in and arrested the lot for carrying concealed weapons."

Megan snorted. "Too bad the deputy didn't think of that last October."

"The whole fracas turned out kind of funny," David continued, chuckling. "Instead of killing each other, Ringo and Holliday had to pay a thirty-dollar fine—the going rate for shooting off your mouth with a gun cocked under your coat."

Then, no sooner than Wyatt and Morgan Earp, Doc, and other posse members rode out on official business, Curly Bill and his cronies started appearing outside the restaurant's front windows once or twice a week.

They neither peered in nor made threatening movements. Their very presence served the intended purpose. And there was nothing Megan could do about it.

When David noticed the boardwalk stalkers, she dismissed his concern with a casual, "I guess they've nothin' better to do than hold up my buildin' with their backsides."

Bad enough she'd unwittingly gotten crosswise with the Clantons, et al.; she refused to ensnare David in the escalating intrigue.

"Glory be, Faro," she muttered, her arm muscles aching from cradling his weight. "You're gettin' heavier with every snore."

The cat stretched his front legs, yawned dramatically, then nestled again in his bosomy bed.

"Oh, no, you don't. I've got better things to do than be your pillow." Pitching him gently to the floor, she took a pad and stub pencil from her apron pocket to list cleaning chores for Chin and Wang to do after the Russ House closed for the evening.

"Once my miners' boardinghouse gets goin', the boys'll get clean beds and three squares a day for their dollar, and I'll sleep better just knowin' there's someone to hear if I scream bloody murder durin' the night."

She looked down into a slanted pair of amber eyes. "Someone besides a furry, four-legged rat trap, that is."

As they buggied west toward the San Pedro River on the first sunny day March had seen fit to offer, Megan wriggled sideways for a better view of the driver.

David winked at her, then eased back the reins to set a more sedate pace. "Having fun?"

"Oh, it's wondrous to breathe in the cool country air. I've been cooped up with cookin' pots far too long."

"I know what you mean. The *Chronicle* closes in like a jail cell at times. You have no idea how much I look forward to seeing you every afternoon."

"I think I do. The clock ticks ever so slowly when I'm watchin' it, but my eyes ramble that way hard as I try to keep 'em on what I'm doin'."

He transferred the trace to one hand and laid his arm across the back of the seat. "How different you are, and yet the same."

"How so?"

"Sometimes, I think back to that gorgeous girl who dressed in dungarees and a man's shirt. The sight of her could take my breath away . . . or make me want to lay an ash shovel across her back pockets."

"An ash shovel? Why, it's a brute you are. I'm half your size and a lady, to boot."

"And tough as two-penny nails. I've never known anyone with your stamina or stubbornness. You were a willful little wench, then."

"Still am. I've just been on my best behavior so as not to scare you away."

He grinned, and pulled her next to him on the seat. "I don't scare that easy, Megan." He took a deep breath and shouted to the distant Huachuca Mountains, "God, how *wonderful* it is to be together again."

More quietly he added, "I feel like a kid again. Like the calendar's rolled back a decade."

"So do I, and that scares me."

"Really? I can't imagine why. We talk and laugh and

confide in each other. I was beginning to act and think like a man Barlow P.'s age. Too serious about everything. Becoming convinced that the best part of life was behind me, not ahead."

"And that's what scares me."

He shook his head in exasperation. "Would you mind forgoing the riddles and speak your peace?"

"Will you pull over so I can talk to your eyes and not your side-whiskers?"

For several minutes after the rig halted, Megan toyed with her fingers, arranging her thoughts. David took her hand in his and gave it a reassuring squeeze.

She raised her head, then whispered, "Those feelings you spoke of. I have them, too. They frighten me because I think we're fallin' in love all over again."

"I never stopped loving you. Your ghost has haunted me since the day I received that letter, telling me you were gone for good."

"Just listen, please? You remember my tellin' you about The North Nevada—how Pete Vladislov saved Barlow P.'s life? Well, he said something to me the day he left camp that's nagged like a splinter ever since.

"Pete said if I ever found what I wanted, to grab it with both hands and not let go, no matter what happened. I've pondered that a lot and it bothers me that I really don't know what I want anymore."

"Back in Pioche, you wanted enough money that you'd never be dependent on anyone. I didn't understand it then—even resented it. I came to realize that's only natural for a girl practically fresh off the boat who never owned more than she could carry."

She smiled, a chuckle rumbling in her throat. " 'Hush' is one four-letter word you don't know the meanin' of, Mister Jacobs."

Settling back in the corner of seat, he replied, "All right, I'm hushed. You have the floor, madam."

She fidgeted, putting her train of thought back on track. "When Milt and Marc started talking about a gold expedition, I was *shiverin'* I wanted to go so badly. Except, I really don't want to leave you and Barlow P. or the restaurant, either . . .

"Oh, damn it to hell, David, I'll just say it: I wanted you in Pioche. I wanted you badly, but I guess not badly enough. And I'm beginnin' to want you again, or at least I think I do, and that's impossible, but sometimes bein' with you is torture . . ."

His lips covered hers. She curled her arms around his neck and let herself fall against his chest.

The world, and all its worries, disappeared like smoke in a gale.

# Chapter Forty-one

The wind bullied Megan's cheeks when she turned at the corner onto Fourth Street. A chilling mist had already seeped through to her bones, making spring seem more rumor than fact.

The Miners' and Merchants' steamy storefront beckoned like an old friend. Head down, one hand bunching her raglan at its second button, she pushed the door open and whisked inside.

Yancy Bogart was dusting the display case with his elbows while his lips kept pace with the *Epitaph*'s headline story. Peering over the half glasses that bridged his snout, he gruffed, "Need help?" obviously hoping she did not.

"I'll just gander awhile, Yancy. Thank you."

"Suit yourself."

She started down the center aisle, drinking in the heady aromas of fine-cut tobacco, fresh lemons and limes, vinegar, chocolate, and a thousand other scents that made mercantiles a paradise for the nose.

Her supply list was short, but she dawdled along, fingering a rack of men's dress suits, then inspecting a hundred-piece dinner set's pink, green, and blue floral pattern, concluding it was the gaudiest thing she'd ever seen.

Drifting to the drug department to snicker at the array of potions and lotions guaranteed to cure everything from female weakness to drunkenness, she bumped into a woman stooping to reach an elixir stocked on the bottom shelf.

"Goodness, excuse me, ma'am. I was watchin' where I'd been instead of where . . . I was . . . goin'."

Amanda Jacobs's pale, gaunt face broke into a winsome smile. "It's Megan, isn't it? You used to work for Daddy at the mine?"

She fumbled with a sizable brown bottle labeled "Dr.

Pinkney's Miracle Cure" before giving Megan's wrist a friendly pat.

Two plump dowagers eavesdropping nearby were introduced as Missus Josiah Neeglefester and Missus Charles Albert Moody of the Episcopalian Ladies' Study Group and Enlightenment Society. They nodded a greeting in tandem like pigeons billing on a window ledge.

"David told me you were managing a restaurant here—" She jerked away and coughed so hard it was painful to hear. "I do beg your pardon. Deliver me from this horrid weather. To think we moved here hoping the dry climate would be good for my health."

"I'm sorry you're feelin' poorly. May I see you home?"

"It's all right, dear, really. David calls it 'a delicate constitution.'" Her shoulders heaved with a resigned sigh. "It's just something one learns to live with, like a wart on the nose or club foot."

How awful to be so frail and afflicted, Megan thought. I've never been sick a day in my life, and I don't think Amanda's ever spent one well.

"It's been lovely seeing you again. I could talk the afternoon away, but my poor husband will be dragging home soon, exhausted from putting together the 'Extra' on that Earp killing—"

"Killing? Who? Which one?"

Amanda edged closer. "Haven't you heard? Someone shot Morgan Earp in the back last night while he was out carousing. That's one less cutthroat to walk the streets, I'd say."

Megan stiffened, scarcely breathing. Won't the murderin' ever stop? Wyatt must be devastated ... and readying to exact an eye for an eye.

She hardly heard Amanda and her friends say their goodbyes. Summoning her wits, Megan started to follow them out, then remembered she hadn't ordered the supplies. Lee Ho needed most of the items for the evening menu.

Yancy scrawled out an invoice, giving the pencil lead a lazy lick about every third letter. Megan could hardly keep herself from snatching the implement away from him and writing her own order.

"Can you deliver the goods to the Russ House by three?"

"Well, now, I s'pose I can, Miss O'Malley," he drawled. "But I'll have to charge ya extree."

"How mu— Never mind. Just put it on my account."

"Sure thing. Soon's ya tell me what account ta charge it to."

"*The Russ House, Yancy,*" Megan said through gritted teeth, then dashed out the door.

Mindful of mud holes, cobbled dung piles, and the mounts that made them, she traipsed through the O.K. Corral to the back of Fly's Boardinghouse. With a hasty wave at May Fly, who was up to her elbows in suds washing lunch dishes, Megan went directly to Doc and Kate's room and knocked.

A clicking sound was followed by a slurred male voice. "Whoever the hell you are, *go away.*"

Megan stared at the door's alligatored shellac, deliberating whether to do as she was told or risk being caught in a scattergun blast.

"Mister Holliday, it's Megan O'Malley."

"I am in no mood for a social call."

"I'm sorry to disturb you. I'm looking for Kate."

"Sportin' house. Titty pink one on Sixth Street."

Was he joking? she asked herself. A heaviness in the pit of her stomach said he wasn't. Somehow, she couldn't bring herself to thank him for the information.

She stayed on Fremont Street, a relatively sedate thoroughfare dedicated more to business ventures than vice, until it intersected with Sixth Street.

The red-light district seemed infinitely more sinister than Allen's row of saloons and gambling halls, although many of the houses were well maintained and rather stately in appearance.

"Doc's description was shamefully accurate," she muttered, spying the two-story, rosy pink clapboard structure located midblock. Rickety steps led to a sagging porch and a garish, red-enameled door.

It swung open before she had time to knock. A frowzy brunette in a gaping, threadbare wrapper slouched against the facing. "Yeah?" she rasped, her voice like coffee beans clashing in a grinder.

"May I speak with Kate Elder, please?"

"Law, ain't you just the little lady, sayin' 'may I' and

'pretty please.' Sure, honey, come right on in. We'll have us some tea and crumpets in the parlor."

The broad-beamed tommy scratched a haunch as Megan followed her down a dim hallway. When she turned and pointed at Kate's room, one pendulous breast escaped its flimsy restraint.

She flopped it back behind the fabric while screeching through the curtained opening, "Hey, Kate! The queen's handmaiden's here to see ya."

A hand eased the portiere aside a fraction and a brown eye peered out. "Megan? What—? Hell, long as you're here, *entrez-vous, madame.*"

She shuffled to the iron bedstead's footboard and bent over it to continue stuffing clothes into a tattered cabinet bag. "If you'd been an hour later, you'd have missed me. I wish you had."

"Where are you going?"

"To Globe. They say the, uh, climate's cooler there. I'll likely be back, eventually."

Megan watched the muscles ruckus beneath Kate's tight cotton dress. The bedsprings squeaked as she crammed her belongings into the suitcase.

"I heard about Morgan's death."

"Is that why you're here? To offer condolences?" She laughed and started to turn, then plainly thought better of it. "Guess you'd have no way of knowing how much I despise the Earps. Every goddamned one of them. Doc worships the ground Wyatt walks on, assuming he touches it with his sainted feet. It'll get Doc's brains splattered one of these days. Damned if I'll stay around here to see it."

"Look at me, Kate."

"I'm busy. Got a stage to catch."

Megan sidled between the mattress and the grimy plaster wall. As she'd suspected, her friend's face was battered; her right eye all but swollen shut.

"Did Doc do that?"

"I could claim an overly amorous customer chastised me for dropping my drawers too slow . . . but lying's a sin, now, isn't it. Yes, Doc returned from the Cosmopolitan in a rage over Morgan's being shot in the back 'like a fice dog.' He had to expend it somewhere."

"Kate, you're welcome to stay with me. I've got a nice little place behind the Russ—"

"Thank you, and I really mean that. You've seen me at my worst and know what I am. Still, you don't judge me." She stepped around the corner of the bed and laid her hands on Megan's shoulders. "I can't accept your offer, but I love you dearly for making it."

Megan hugged her close, then kissed her cheek. "Be well, and come back, please. Long as I have a roof over my head, you do, too."

She hastened from the brothel, lost in thought. It occurred to her as she passed Varina Gautier's Millinery, tucked between the Fitzroy Brothers' Realty and the Russ House, that she had no recollection of the route she'd traveled.

When she crossed the restaurant's threshold, Barlow P. was sprawled in a chair, waiting for her. "Afternoon, gal. 'Bout to give up on ya."

"I had shoppin', and other errands to do," she hedged.

"You know about last night's dispatch, then."

"The outcome. Not the details."

"They ain't purty. The short and sweet of it is, some chickenshit shot Morgan through a window whilst he was playin' billiards at Hatch's saloon. Bullet went clean through his spine and into another feller's leg. A second came inches from puttin' a new part in Wyatt's hair."

"Do they know who did it?"

"The shooter got clean away, like with Virge, but Wyatt fer sure has prime prospects."

Megan crossed her arms and regarded him curiously. "Why are you tellin' me this?"

"Fact is, the whole time I been a'waitin', I was askin' myself the same thing. Reckon it shuffles thusly: Wyatt's been decent to us both. He's a killer, no doubt of it, but he don't shoot fer sport like Ben Thompson or even Doc Holliday. 'Cept right now, he's just a man that had to watch his baby brother die stretched out on a whiskey mill's dirty floor."

He looked up at her, his expression speaking volumes. "Yeah, I been in Wyatt's boots. Frankie, my kid brother, tried to nudge his dinner pail from the edge of a hoist. Got a leg caught. Tore off a'fore he reached topside. That's why I was so fractious about you goin' below at Sanders and Meredith."

"I wish you'd told me before," she said softly.

"Couldn't. Hard enough to, now."

After giving him pause to collect himself, she asked, "Is it proper for us to call on the bereaved family?"

"That's why I'm here. To see if'n ya'd want to go with me."

The Earps and their friends were gathered in Virgil and Allie's room at the Cosmopolitan. Grief and tension were thick enough to cut with a butter knife.

"Mattie, Wyatt," Megan said. "We're so sorry about Morgan. Is there anything we can do?"

"Pray that the rest of us get out of here before another coffin's measured," Mattie replied cryptically. "I told the marshal that this was going to happen, but he wouldn't listen to a silly female, even if she is his wife!"

"That's enough," Wyatt growled. "Go see to Louisa. She's the one that's lost a husband."

As Mattie stalked away, he said, "You've done plenty just by coming here. It's appreciated more than I can say."

To Megan, he added, "I hope your kindness isn't costly. I don't doubt this hotel's being watched."

"You have enough worries without shoulderin' mine."

"Will there be a service?" Barlow P. asked.

"Not here." In an instant, Wyatt's eyes hardened like blue diamonds. "Morgan will be buried at our parents' home in Colton, California. We're taking his body to Tucson to meet the train."

In a flat, malignant tone Megan would never forget, he explained, "We have family business to conduct there before we head west."

Graciously, but as quickly as possible, the partners said their farewells and left the Earp quarters and the hotel.

Each knew what the other was thinking: The death toll was sure to rise, inside or outside Tombstone's municipal boundaries.

Ahead, Megan saw David weaving through the clumps of pedestrians strolling along the south side of Allen Street. He grinned and waved at them. Barlow P.'s back straightened ever so slightly.

"Lee Ho didn't know where you'd gone," he panted when he caught up with them. "It's pure luck I spotted you."

"Yep, just pure-de-old luck," Barlow P. drawled, then grunted when Megan jabbed him lightly in the ribs.

David winked at her and teased, "I was afraid I'd have to find another restaurant for my afternoon coffee break."

"The cook bust the tureen or somethin'? Ol' Buck-Tooth didn't have no problem a'pourin' mine a while ago."

"Now, how would you like it if I called Missouri, 'Ol' Dough Belly'?" Megan snapped.

"No skin off'n my nose, though he might not be real partial to it."

"Damned if you two aren't still goin' at it just like you always did," David said, chuckling.

From the corner of her eye, Megan saw Barlow P. arch an eyebrow and cast a knowing glare in the editor's direction.

# Chapter Forty-two

Megan rooted her head into the pillow, her eyelids too leaden to raise. She smacked her lips, muzzily aware that sleep was seconds away from seducing her again.

A cat's mournful yowl denied that surrender. Squalls marked the animal's obsessive pacing as clearly as splattered flour marks a trail.

"Damn it, Faro, shut up. You're not goin' out tommin'."

The mattress shuddered beneath the animal's weight. Megan kicked at him. Then, she smelled smoke.

Whipping back the bedclothes, she padded to the window and nudged aside the woven Mexican rug that served as a curtain. To the north, buildings seemed to be cowering before the wall of ragged orange flames licking at the sky.

In almost a single movement, Megan yanked on a wrapper, grabbed Faro, and ran from the house. Outside, acrid smoke stung her nose and eyes. Disembodied shouts pierced the inky fog. With one arm outstretched, she groped for the Russ House's rear entrance.

It's Pioche all over again, her mind screamed silently. A corner of the kitchen's worktable clipped her hipbone. In the dining room, fiendish chair legs lurked, waiting to mangle bare toes.

"Fire! Get out! It's a'comin' straight for us!"

Babbled curses erupted from the lodging room. Then came the thud of heels hitting the board floor as men jumped down from the higher bunks.

"Smoke—I kin smell it! Jim—Nate—all o' ya! Git yer asses outta here!"

Shadowy figures clad in baggy undershirts and drawers darted past Megan and out the front door. Goggle-eyed with confusion and fear, they pulled up short at the boardwalk and milled together, unsure of what to do next.

Bare-chested, with braces flapping against his trousers,

Barlow P. dogtrotted across the street. "Thank God, yer all right," he bellowed over the inferno's roar. "Whole sumbitchin' town's burnin' down."

"Where's Missouri?" Megan shouted.

"Bucket brigade." He turned to the boarders. "Charlie, take her to the flats and stay with 'er. The rest o' ya come with me."

Megan and the hunchbacked old prospector picked their way across the rocky ground until they were at least a hundred yards from the town's southernmost boundary.

She stared at the flames, hardly aware of her cut, stone-bruised feet. Faro struggled in her arms, but she held him fast.

Blessed Mary, she prayed, keep David safe . . . and Amanda . . . and everyone.

Sunrise found much of Tombstone's business district in ashes. Miraculously, only one charred casualty was discovered in the Cosmopolitan Hotel's rubble.

Hindsighted prophets sagely opined that Allen Street's nigh total destruction evinced an angry God's wrath. Yet, the pious had no explanation for why establishments dedicated to less sinful pursuits were also in smoldering ruins.

Along every street where fire had taken its toll, business owners and hired guards protected property from thieves and lot jumpers eager to test the theory that possession equals nine tenths of the law.

An industrious young gent strolled up and down like a census taker offering to ride to nearby Fairbank's Western Union office and send "All's well" messages to distant loved ones. The cost of such reassurance was a silver dollar, plus five cents per word.

Megan hailed the bowlered messenger, giving him a curt note to dispatch to Frances. He scanned it, verified the address, and said, "That'll be one dollar and forty cents, ma'am."

She frowned and snatched the paper from his grasp, reading aloud: " 'Russ, Bainbridge, and me undamaged. Love, Megan.' Now, son, I'm not so addled that I can't count. That's seven words—thirty-five cents."

"But don't you think 'not damaged' is a better way of puttin' it?"

Megan placed one dollar and thirty-five cents in his outstretched palm. "Me boyo, I'd say it doesn't make a nickel's worth of difference."

Despite grinding exhaustion borne of battling an inferno with nothing more than water buckets and hope, the miners left for work as usual. Missing a day meant missing a day's pay, which none of them could afford.

She'd scrawled a "Closed" sign for the Russ House's window, though no one but Barlow P. had peeked through the glass all morning. The soot-streaked, grim-faced partners sat hunched over a table, nursing cups of coffee neither of them wanted.

"Aren't tinderbox minin' towns ever goin' to learn that a tiny spark means disaster?"

"Kinda makes ya wonder, don't it? Every camp I ever heard of's been rebuilt at least onc't. And damned if they ain't thrown up the same jake-leg way the old one was."

"Worse, even afterward, the fire department's nothin' more than a wagon with a bunch of buckets rattlin' in the bed."

"Yep, jes' like candles on a birthday cake, ore towns get blowed out 'bout every year."

Creases in his wattled neck were black with dirt; his weather-beaten face as grainy as oak planks. Megan noticed that his gnarled, liver-spotted hand trembled when he reached for his coffee cup.

"It breaks my heart that the Jack's gone."

"I ain't frettin'. No cause fer you to. If'n ya hadn't pestered me into gettin' insurance writ on the place, I'd be cryin' into this Arbuckle's like a whole lotta folks is right now."

"You are plannin' to rebuild?"

"Missouri's over to Fly's, draftin' it out and orderin' the lumber. We was wonderin' though, if'n you'd mind a couple more boarders while the hammerin's goin' on. Ain't many places left where a man can lollygag. Figger we'll be hangin' around here like stray pups for a week or two, anyhow."

She hesitated, thinking that Barlow P. and Missouri would surely disapprove of David's daily visits. That conclusion had no more than flashed through her mind when she felt ashamed for even having it.

"Of course, you can bunk here. Told you that when I decided to open the boardin'house."

"Hmmph." He scrutinized her for a long, discomfiting

moment. "Nah. Mebbe we oughta stay at Fly's. Coupla ol' grissel-heels'll jes' be in yer way."

She challenged his gaze with one of her own. "You're known for dealin' a straight game, Barlow P. Don't sleeve the aces."

"All right. It's took me a passel of years, but I finally figgered out that I ain't yer pa, nor yer brother, nor yer beau. I'm yer friend, true enough, 'cept that don't give me the right ta act like none of them other things.

"Ya own yer own life, gal. Gotta pick yer own roads. I'm here to help direct ya, if ya ask. If ya don't, all I can do is hope ya don't choose the one the cows used first. But I won't stop ya, even if ya do. It ain't my place."

That night, Megan lay in her bed, stroking Faro's sleek fur and brooding. Around four-thirty that afternoon, David had popped in to let her know he, Amanda, and the *Chronicle*'s office had survived the fire unscathed.

Similarities to Pioche were hashed over again, but Barlow P. hadn't been amused by the newspaperman's aside that "Strange how things start sizzling when the three of us land in the same place."

For the duration of his short visit, David didn't appear to have noticed Barlow P.'s reticence. But Megan did.

*Da once told me, if you don't know what to do, don't do anything,* she mused, staring into the darkness. *That's easier said than done. And doin's have a way of goin' on without you, I warrant.*

*My mind's so befoggled, I can't think straight. The restaurant, frettin' about Curly Bill and his confederates, Kate, what Hoolihan said about the Grand Central's tunnels startin' to flood, Barlow P., the fire ... David. Maybe if I went away for a spell.*

Faro's soothing purr sounded like confirmation. Scrap by scrap, an idea started stitching itself together.

"The One-Eyed Jack's out of business for a while," she murmured aloud to the dozing cat. "Lee Ho can manage the Russ House by himself. Practically does, anyway. But surely if I wasn't here, Barlow P. and Missouri would move in and supervise, as needed. A smidge of bookkeepin's all they'd have to keep the boardin'house goin'.

"The Oriental's in ashes, too, but Milt's got Frank Leslie to manage things—others for all I know. I think Marc

Smith's takin' an unexpected holiday, too, thanks to the fire.

"And swear and be damned if Barlow P. didn't tell me about some Mexican, older'n Moses, he said, that tried to pay for his whiskey with gold nuggets back a week or so ago."

She knit her brows together, trying to remember the story. "Barlow P. said the codger couldn't speak American. At least, not much. Kept goin' on about Santa ... Rosalia? And a Holo Valle.

"In Mexican, that'd be what, Golo Valley? Well, whatever he was tryin' to spill, he had enough nuggets on him to buy a barrel of John Barleycorn. Poor old fella was found later, behind the Alhambra, with his head caved in.

"Santa Rosalia. Never heard of it, but it's an awful pretty name. Bet if I told Milt and Marc that story, they'd be droolin' to help me find it."

She wallowed down in the pillow, a grin teasing at her lips. "Know somethin', Faro? I always have done my best thinkin' with a pick in my hands."

# Chapter Forty-three

As the driver tossed her gear atop the Modoc stage, Megan turned toward the two men standing side by side on the boardwalk. It infuriated her that neither Barlow P. nor David acted as if the other existed.

"We'll be back in three months—four at the outside," she said cheerfully. "I'll wire you from Tucson and let you know which stage we'll be on."

Milt and Marc stuck their heads out their respective windows. "Bring a crew of strong-arms to meet us," the latter advised. "There'll be more gold aboard than we can carry ourselves."

"Uh-huh. If'n ya had a brain betwixt ya, ya'd hie outta there whilst ya can. *Baja.* Hell, it even sounds downright direful."

"Oh, you're just jealous 'cause you're not goin' with us," Megan teased.

"I can't speak for Barlow P., but I'm concerned for your safety," David stated. "That's cruel country you're headed for."

She laughed and waggled her head. "Aye, what manner of fool must I be, for leavin' this peaceable haven of liquor-brave gunmen, tarantulas, fires, floods, snakes, and warpathin' Apaches?"

The coach squawled and rattled as the driver ascended his seat. "Best you board or wave us off, lady. I've got a schedule to keep."

Hastily, Megan hugged Barlow P. and kissed his cheek, then flew to David with the same farewell.

"I'll be back before you know I'm gone," she called, stooping to enter the coach. It lurched forward; the door swinging shut with a smart spank to the seat of her dungarees.

Sitting down beside Milt, she leaned out the window and waved. Barlow P. and David responded listlessly, wearing expressions so similarly dour they could be mistaken for a father and son.

"How long will it take us to get there, Irish?" Marc asked before they were fifty feet from the depot.

She grinned at the huge, sandy-haired man. His mustaches were so full and droopy it appeared a small animal was nesting on his upper lip. "With six-horse teams—which we're not likely to have past the border—sturdy axles, and no mishaps slowin' us down, we'll make Guaymas in about ten days."

"And then?"

"For heaven's sake, Marc, it's not as if you haven't traced the route on that map so many times, you've worn it through."

"That's why I need reminding."

"Then listen good, 'cause I'll not hash it again," she warned with mock-seriousness. "We'll hire a boat in Guaymas to take us across the Gulf of California. That's another two days, I reckon, dependin' on whether the water's calm or stormy. Then, from Mulege, we'll hike about forty miles up the coast to Santa Rosalia."

"And head inland."

"Yep."

"For the Golo Valley."

"Uh-huh."

He sidled sideways in the corner, his trunklike legs stretching to bump Megan's shins. Sighing like a boy who knows a hot, dusty ride to town portends a penny's worth of stick candy, he closed his eyes; probably imagining his reward awaiting at the end of the road.

Megan watched Milt from the corner of her eye. He was engrossed in a book entitled *Sixteen Months at the Gold Diggings*. She couldn't imagine how he kept his place with his chin dandling with the movement of the coach.

He was much less flamboyant in appearance, word, and deed than the lumberjack-sized lawyer, yet she'd liked the stoic saloonkeeper at first meeting.

She smiled to herself, thinking what an odd-looking group they must make. *The way I figure it,* she mused,

Milt's as dependable as daylight, and Marc's a Goliath if muscle's needed ... or shade.

I don't think either one's accustomed to takin' orders from a female, but they don't seem opposed to it either.

Boom or bust, this ought to be quite an adventure.

# Chapter Forty-four

The village of Santa Rosalia hovered on a coastal plain between the Gulf of California and Cuesta del Infiernillo, which Milt roughly translated as Hill of Hell.

Marc took one look at the bleak wall of rock—its face scarred and cracked by eons of cold nights and blistering days—and renamed it a "Helluva Goddamn Hill."

Nevertheless, he was determined to start the ascent that afternoon instead of staying overnight in Santa Rosalia.

Milt wisely kept quiet, watching his two partners cuss and discuss the situation, smack-dab in the middle of the hamlet's only street.

"So, it's a jackass you want to make of yourself, is it? Then grab a'holt of your pointy-eared cousin there, and be off with you. Swear and be damned, if I'll fall in behind you!"

Marc froze like a statue, his chin nearly touching his chest.

"I've heard the Irish in your voice before," he said, scarcely louder than a whisper, "but that gust of pure brogue sounded so much like my grandma ... well, I like to dropped my britches for a whippin'."

Megan threw back her head and laughed at his bumfuzzled expression. "Now you know what it *means* to get a gal's Irish up, eh, me boyo? And if I had me a fair switch, I'd give you that hidin', too. Maybe it'd knock some sense into that thick head of yours."

He clucked his tongue. "I'll declare you the winner of this round, if you'll agree to a compromise."

Narrowing her eyes suspiciously, she said, "I don't agree to anythin', before I've heard the terms."

"Smart, especially when an attorney's involved. All right, me and Brother Burro will cool our hooves until dawn, *if* we get everything arranged and ready before we hit the blankets tonight."

"That agreeable to you, Milt?" she asked.

"Makes me no difference. I only stuck around to fetch the undertaker if the need arose."

"It's a deal, then. Let's get to it."

A toothless crone directed them to Galeano Quinones's stable just beyond the village's western bounds. Megan was impressed by recent rake marks criss crossing the dirt inside the corral. Obviously, Senor Quinones did more than provide his animals with food and water when the spirit moved him.

Marc went to roust the owner from his siesta, while Milt and Megan leaned against the topmost rail watching the small herd.

"A lot of the old-timers in Nevada chose burros over mules," she said. "They're just as surefooted and sturdy, go farther without water, and eat about anything that doesn't eat them first."

"Stubborn cusses, though. If they get it in their noggins not to move, there's no moving them until they're good and ready."

"That is true, but there is often good reason," replied an elderly man whose snow-white hair and goatee contrasted handsomely with his reddish-brown skin. "I am Galeano Quinones. What may I do to assist you?"

"We need three trail-broke burros to pack equipment and supplies," Megan answered.

Quinones's black eyes gleamed as he rubbed his chin-whiskers thoughtfully. "It is almost thirty miles to the Golo Valle. If it were me, I would purchase four animals to be sure of sufficient water."

She shot Marc a scathing glare. "So much for keepin' our destination a secret."

Before he could respond, Quinones replied, "Your *compadre* disclosed nothing, senorita. A man cannot live in Santa Rosalia for seventy years and not recognize gold hunters when he sees them."

He swept an arm across his chest dramatically. "After all, why else would so many Anglos visit our humble village? For the luxury it affords?"

Megan grunted. "I guess we are a mite conspicuous."

"And no wonder the villagers speak English so fluently," Milt commented.

"Senor Quinones," Marc piped up, "all this talk's getting

me a little gun-shy. What's the chance of being followed and robbed of our gold—if not worse?"

The older man shrugged. "First, you must have something worth stealing, senor." He turned to wink slyly at Megan. "A fourth burro would be useful for transporting the treasure you seek."

"Three will do just fine, Senor Quinones."

"As you wish. Come, let me show you the stock."

The animals skittered away from the strangers in their midst, but gathered around their owner like overgrown, doe-eyed dogs.

"These are wild burros, which I capture and tame." He nudged one sideward, indicating a dark marking on its withers. "Notice the cross? It is said to be a sign of divine protection, honoring the burro for carrying Mary and the Christ child on their flight from Egypt."

The buyers eyed each other, then Milt, who was more familiar with the exchange rate, stepped forward to discuss price. Soon, a handshake informed the silent partners that a deal had been struck.

Buyer and seller rejoined Marc and Megan. "If you desire," Quinones offered, "Frederico can be instructed to deliver your supplies to me. I will pack the animals and have them ready whenever you wish."

"Frederico?"

"The village grocer. You will buy what you need there, yes?"

The three Tombstoners laughed, realizing that nothing they'd do in Santa Rosalia would escape notice.

"Do you already know what time we'll be hitting the hay, too, Senor Quinones?" Marc teased.

The corners of his eyes creased good-naturedly. "Perhaps not, but you will rest well at Senora Manzanilla's boardinghouse."

Once the details were agreed upon, they bid the stablemaster adios and headed back to town to buy supplies, let rooms for the night, and enjoy the last proper meal they'd have for weeks.

"I can't shake my worry that everyone in this town knows our business," Marc grumbled.

"Like Senor Quinones said, why fret before we've got anything to fret about?" Megan asked. But Marc's scowl only deepened.

# Chapter Forty-five

"And a little burro shall lead us," Marc replied in response to Megan's suggestion.

The party had been zigzagging up the mountain for three back-breaking days. All too often, what appeared to be a natural trail ended abruptly in either a sheer drop or a vertical wall of granite.

"Well, the jacks are more familiar with the terrain than we are," she shot back defensively.

"Makes sense to me," Milt agreed.

Marc raised his hands as if surrendering. "Hey, I'm not arguing. I wouldn't care if the devil himself lent us a leg up. I'd just like to get on the sky side of this rock pile before the year's out."

Wearily she nodded and snatched up her burro's lead, preparing to fall in behind Marc. I've never seen country like this, she thought. Jagged cliffs, flat ridges, peaks, arroyos; their faces pocked, shattered, and striated in rose, mauve, green, blue—some even mellowed like hammered gold. It's a jumble, like God gathered every kind of sediment on earth, crushed them to stone, and hurled them down from the heavens.

Canvas packs lashed to her burro's back scraped the ragged rock with every step. The ledge they followed was hardly wider than a bedroll, but the animal didn't behave as if it knew one misplaced hoof meant certain death two hundred feet below on the arroyo's boulder-strewn floor.

Megan willed herself to keep her eyes pegged on the burro's rump—which was easier said than done. The outcropping was a maze of twists and switchbacks; each bend inviting a glimpse at the eerie, awe-striking panorama carved by ancient seas.

Over the clatter of rocks skittering off the edge as they passed, her stomach growled like thunder. Goatskin water bags sloshing against the burro's ribs teased Megan's parched throat mercilessly.

We'll come to a plateau soon enough, she speculated silently.

Darkness and its chill steadily crept into the canyon. The party had no choice but go on. Shivering inside her sweaty clothes, Megan groped for her burro's tail and clutched it along with the ropes secured to its halter. She could no longer see where the ledge ended and black oblivion began.

The animals slowed to a trudging pace, their necks bowed from exhaustion.

"Camp ho," Marc croaked out from several yards ahead of her.

Megan thought she'd swoon with relief. As if it understood the lawyer's words, her burro's head snapped up and it eased into a smarter gait.

Behind her, the third jack brayed in terror. Flailing hooves scrabbled against rock. Then came a thud, and the animal's bloodcurdling bleats fading in the darkness.

All was still, but for a trickle of sediment pecking off the ledge.

"Milt!" she screamed. "Are you all right?"

Interminable seconds passed before a strangled voice answered, "Yeah ... shakin' like wheat in a field, though."

She flattened herself against the cliff's face. Cold sweat drenched her from brow to boots.

"Megan ... Milt ... what's going on?"

"Milt's burro fell," she shouted. "Thank God, he didn't go with it."

"Need help?"

"Lead my jack out and tie it with yours. Stay with them. Don't try comin' back for us. It's too dark."

The spectral blur of the saloonkeeper's white shirt shimmered against the murrey cliff. "Catch your breath yet, Milt?"

"I guess. Said a couple of prayers, too, I don't mind telling you."

"Can you tell whether the ledge broke off, or did the burro just lose its footin'?"

"Don't know for sure. Can't see past my braces."

"That's all right. Stay still, but stretch your left arm out against the bluff. I'll do the same with my right. I'm goin' to sidle your way real slow. When our fingers touch, we'll know the ledge is solid between us."

"What if they don't?"

She closed her eyes as a shudder ratcheted down her spine. "Don't borrow trouble, Milt."

"I can't let you—"

"You're not lettin' me do anything. Get that arm stuck out like a signpost. You hear?"

Swallowing hard, she eased a boot scant inches to her right and pressed down with the ball of her foot before shifting her weight to it. Bringing the left to its mate, she repeated the process with methodical precision.

Midway into the tenth sliding step, her temple bashed against a crag. Tiny amber lights danced in her eyes. A rush of dizziness threatened her balance.

"What is it, Megan? Is the ledge gone?"

"Everything's . . . fine. We oughta be playin' patty-fingers any second."

Snaking sideward again, her prediction soon proved correct. When they touched, Milt's fingers were as clammy as her own.

"To be sure, slide your foot over 'til it bumps into mine . . . there."

"Uh, Megan?"

"Yes?"

"Thanks. More than I can say, thank you. If you hadn't come after me, I'd have been plastered to this mountain until the Lord called me home."

"Aw, you'd do the same for me, no doubt of it," she assured, squeezing his sweaty hand. "Now, as Barlow P. would say, 'How 'bout we get the hell off'n this sumbitch?' "

"My feelings exactly."

The next day, with astounding abruptness, mountains and arroyos fanned out to table-flat desert. Despite Marc's repeated objections, Megan tied a bandana at the base of a cactus.

"We're a burro short on supplies already, boys. We can't risk another trial-and-error wander through the mountains."

"I'm telling you, Irish. I've been hearing things since we

left Santa Rosalia. Shoot, why not paint red arrows pointing which way we've gone to make it easier for the banditos."

"I don't doubt for a minute that you're hearin' things," she replied sarcastically. "Just make sure you sign our trail or all those cutthroats'll find is our bones."

As Senor Quinones had told them, a straight track was clearly visible in the sand. But after following it for several hours, the trail forked sharply.

"I say we go right," Megan adjudged, taking the opportunity to slake her raging thirst.

Marc wiped his chin with his sleeve. "As usual, I disagree. Milt?"

"Wonders never cease. For once, I'm with you, Marc. Left appears to head toward those hills, yonder. More likely to be a 'Golo Valley' there."

The sun was copper-plating the grainy expanse when the trail ended at an abandoned settlement.

"May as well pitch camp and get an early start tomorrow," Megan said. Noticing Marc's dejected expression, she added, "Aw, buck up, shyster. If Senor Quinones had bothered mentionin' that the trail branched out, we wouldn't have had to pick one in the first place, right?"

To make up for lost time, they headed out the next morning before dawn, reaching the fork just as the sun's fiery wrath blazed above the horizon.

Lacking both the wind and the spit for conversation, they marched single file along the original trail, pausing only for sips of water and chunks of rubbery goat cheese to keep up their strength.

At midday, the trail branched in three directions. Unanimously, they agreed to take the center fork. While they were resting, Megan studied her partners closely.

They're both already as red as scalded lobsters, she thought. Of course, I probably am, too. It must be a hundred and twenty degrees out here—or hotter.

Farther on, wind had sculpted the sand into dunes, yet thankfully had not obliterated the deep-cut trail. Heat shimmers swam before Megan's eyes. The desert's eerie silence made her acutely aware of her own breathing and the swush of her boots against the sand.

That stillness was more frightening than the unrelenting heat and dryness. For all the bleak, empty space, stretching as far as she could see, she felt as if she were entombed.

Over the next three days, the trail branched and re-branched so many times, Megan lost count. Whether they had stopped to rest or to camp for the night, the partners hardly spoke to each other; not from anger, but from an increasing lethargy.

Little by little, the heat and slogging onward from dawn to dusk sapped their stamina as well as their water supply.

After dark, the desert came alive with all manner of creatures too wise to challenge the sun's heat. Megan lay awake a long time, listening to the nocturnal meanderings and pondering.

We must turn back, she thought. There's no other choice. We've been taking this fork and that, for five—or is it six?—days. Rationing hasn't done much good. We're running out of food and water.

She rolled over on her side and punched the pack beneath her head with her fist. This is all my fault. If only I'd taken Senor Quinones's advice about that extra burro. And I should've checked to make sure Marc was signing our trail. I knew he was dead-set against it, but I never once looked back. I'm supposed to be the veteran prospector, not Milt or Marc.

Thanks to me, we're adrift in a vast sea of sand.

# Chapter Forty-six

"Marc, c'mon, wake up," Megan said, shaking the big man's shoulder. The back side of her hand grazed his forehead and cheeks. His skin felt unnaturally cool and dry as foolscap.

"He's babbled some, but hasn't stirred for hours," Milt rasped. "I don't have the wherewithall to put the ground under my feet, either." Lying back on the blanket, he sighed, "We're done in, Megan. Done for."

She sat back on her heels, gazing south across the undulating, honey-colored barrens. I could wheel east or north or west, she thought, and it'd look the same.

One half-full water bag sat enthroned atop a mound of gear like a precious jewel on a velvet pillow. At most, a quart remained. A goodly portion of that would evaporate before sundown even if no lips touched its neck.

"I'm goin' for help, Milt," she said quietly. "I can't just sit here and wait to die."

"Weak as you are, you won't get a mile."

"Maybe not, but that's a lot farther than I'll get sittin' here and prayin' for rain."

After checking the burros' tethers, she rummaged around until she found the forked sticks they'd used for a pot rack. There'd been no fire built the last two nights, but she'd insisted they pack them, anyway.

Twisting their ends into the sand at an angle back from Marc's shoulders, she then slit two corners of a blanket with her knife and poked one prong through each opening.

"It doesn't throw much shade, but it'll have to do. Scoot over and share what there is, Milt. If you can swing it around with the sun, it'll give some relief."

The saloonkeeper rolled over and up on all fours. "You stay with Marc," he wheezed, "I'll go."

He struggled to his feet and staggered a step. His knees

buckled, and he sank like a trapdoor had opened under his boots. "No use. Too weak."

"My legs've got the wobbles, too," she said. "But maybe they'll carry me far enough to find water."

"There's no shame in admitting when you're licked."

"No, there isn't. Only difference between you and me is that I'm a mite younger and stronger—no insult intended."

"None taken, dear lady."

"While I'm gone, force Marc's lips apart if you must, but make him drink now and then. You do the same. What food we've got's in that knapsack."

Hope sparked in Milt's sunken, bloodshot eyes. "I do believe, if anyone can get us through this, you can."

Glancing up at the cerulean sky, she replied, "If somebody up there'll help me, I will."

Keeping the sun at her right shoulder, she struck off due north. Higher-elevated mountain peaks bordered the desert in that direction, and on the east. To the west, untold miles away, the Pacific lapped ashore.

"Stands to reason," she cogitated, "when snowmelt and rain run off those peaks, most of the streams cut ought to wash pretty well due west, toward the ocean.

"If I'm right and the bed hasn't parched again by now, I ought to find me one, eventually. If I'm wrong . . . well, then, I'm wrong."

As the day wore on, she got the strangest feeling that she hadn't traveled farther than a few yards from the campsite. Each dune surmounted gave way to its twin, and then another, and another.

She tried singing songs to divert her mind from its wily tricks, but that only dried her tongue and mouth more quickly. When sucking at her fingers failed to bring saliva, she'd tip up one of the six flattened water bags she carried and licked greedily at meager droplets formed around its rim.

The sun was scorching her left arm through the fabric of her shirt when she saw David beckoning to her from the next dune. Trying to run to him, her boots sank ankledeep in the loose sand.

Waving madly, she laughed with joy. Her lips cracked, stinging like wasps were attacking them.

David held out his arms, just as he had that day at the

Russ House. Scrabbling atop the mound, she threw herself into them, tightly wrapping her own around his waist.

She fell to her knees in the burning sand, clutching nothing but air. Dry sobs wracked her chest; there was no moisture for tears.

A tickling sensation meandered down her chin. She touched her fingertips to her mouth. They came away bloody; grains of sand sticking to the splits in her lips.

Curling up into a ball, rage and despair bombarded her like clubs wielded by invisible assailants. "I hate you, David. I hate you ... hate you," she shrieked, her lungs searing with every word.

Another voice, louder than her own, boomed in her mind. "Damn it, gal, yer burnin' daylight. Best get to gittin'."

With a ragged sigh, Megan raised her head, almost expecting to see a mangled Stetson eclipsing the sun. She climbed to her feet, set her jaw defiantly, and stumbled down the dune's far side.

No longer trusting her eyes, when the grotesquely writhing branches of an elephant tree appeared in the distance, she looked away.

Yet, time and time again, glimpsing in that direction, the spindly branches loomed closer and more distinct. "Please," she whispered, "let it be *real*."

Marching like a battle-hardened soldier, she scaled the drift sheltering the tiny-leaved plant. A few feet from its base, a slender stream gurgled along its rocky bed.

She knelt and scooped at the water, marveling as drops flipped from her fingertips. Bowling her hands, she gulped the cold sweetness, then rubbed her blistered cheeks with her wet palms.

Handful after handful of glorious, life-giving water spilled down Megan's throat, inside and out. She splashed in the riffles, giggling like a child, then ducked her whole face in the shallows.

Two goatskins were already filled, with bubbles rising from the mouth of a third when she noticed that many of the pebbles lining the creek bed were a dull yellowish color.

Turning a few over in her hand, she tossed down the bag to snatch up more stones. A sliver scraped away when she scratched one with a fingernail.

"This isn't iron pyrite. It's gold. It's truly *gold*."

Megan untied her neckerchief and spread it over the sand. She started panning by scraping the stream bottom, using her fingers as a shovel.

Intently extracting nuggets from worthless sediment, she froze when a shadow bridged the water from the adjacent bank. Her eyes rambled upward from a pair of bare feet wearing leather sandals to a rope-belted, coarse woven robe, a large, hammered gold cross, and a massive head arbored by curly, iron-gray hair.

"I did not mean to frighten you, my child. I am Padre Hidalgo Miguel Cavillo of the Mission de la Santa Isabel."

Megan introduced herself, surreptitiously wadding the kerchief around her find. "Are you lost, too, Father?"

He clasped his hands in front of him and chuckled. "No, Senorita O'Malley. My mission is nearby. Come, tell me of your plight as we go there. Perhaps I can help you."

"Oh, but I must take this water back to my friends."

The priest looked up and shook his head gravely. "The sun is setting. You are tired and certain to lose your way. There is food at the mission and plenty of water. Rest for the night as my guest."

Scanning the stark landscape behind her, she nodded. "I s'pose you're right. This water won't do Milt or Marc any good if I'm tumblin' around in the dark unable to find them."

En route to the mission, she told him everything, from the old Mexican's references to the Golo Valley to their camp's dire need of supplies. The only thing she failed to mention was the cache of gold nuggets bulging her dungarees pocket.

Through the mission's guest room's slit window, stars were still visible in the silvery sky when Megan eased from beneath the coverlet.

Shivering, she donned her stiffened clothing as quickly as she could. Holding her boots by the heels, she tapped them against the bed frame just in case a scorpion had taken up residence during the night.

She found Padre Cavillo seated on the terrace, cradling a cup of tea with both hands. He poured her a cup from a carafe and invited her to help herself from a heaping tray of fresh breads, fruit, and cheeses.

"I must be on my way soon, Father. It's grateful I am

for your kindness, but I feel guilty partakin' of it while my partners are swelterin' out there."

"When you are ready, Juarez Santoya will guide you and a supply burro back to your *compadres* and on to Santa Rosalia. Juarez knows a less harrowing trail through the mountains than the one you traveled."

"I don't know what to say. Just thankin' you doesn't seem nearly enough. I'm promisin', we'll find some way of repayin' you and your parish."

He smiled over his teacup, then swallowed a sip. The four-noted songs and trills of desert wrens warbled from the orchard. Their music only emphasized the terrace's sudden and uneasy silence.

Keeping his eyes locked on a tub of geraniums near the flagstones' border, he asked quietly, "That repayment you speak of? Will it come, perhaps, from the gold you'll sluice from the riverbed?"

She tried stammering a reply, then her lips closed in a taut line.

"What you found is only a portion of what washes down from the mountain every spring," he continued. "It has been this mission's only means of support for over a century. My people never glean more than enough to meet one year's need, and send couriers to various cities to exchange it for currency. To return again to the same place would raise suspicions of a strike. When the hordes descended, our way of life would be destroyed."

"So that's why the old man came to Tombstone? To get cash for the gold?"

"And buy supplies with it on his way back. It is sad that Norteno's family must mourn him because of his thirst for whiskey. There is not time to send another man before snow comes to the mountains. Belts will be tighter by spring, but it is God's will."

For a moment Megan felt light-headed. The gold field he alluded to was undoubtedly large enough to be the bonanza she'd dreamed of for so many years.

She tugged the knotted kerchief from her pocket and wedged it beside her cup on the tray. "Gold, you say? Why, my partners and I have wandered all over this godforsaken desert. There's no gold here, Father. I'd swear to it."

When he rose from his chair, she knelt at his feet. Laying a hand gently on her head, he gave his blessing for a safe journey, then intoned, "*In nomine Patris et Filii et Spiritus Sancti.*"

Megan crossed herself with the Holy Trinity and stood. "Again, thank you, Father."

He closed his fingers over the knotted, lumpy cloth. "I will take you to your guide, Miss O'Malley. May God be with you and your *compadres.*"

# Chapter Forty-seven

Mindful of an army of insects scaling its trunk, Megan leaned against a palm tree watching stevedores load the steamer's hold.

Her partners squatted near the water's edge, talking quietly. Though they'd enjoyed two weeks of Senora Manzanilla's motherly care at the boardinghouse in Santa Rosalia, Marc's face was still drawn. He hadn't regained the nigh twenty-five pounds he'd lost on their "adventure."

Milt had fared somewhat better, but the haunted dullness of his eyes concerned her, as did his sudden, temperamental flare-ups.

A few nights earlier, when Senor Quinones entered the cantina, Milt accosted him angrily, accusing him of "sending us on a goose chase that damned near got us all killed."

With calm dignity, the stable master listened to Milt's account of their trek through the mountains and the crazy-quilted path across the desert.

"With all due respect, Senor Joyce, you did not follow the mountain trail I described to you. That it did not lead to the correct desert track, which I also described, comes as no surprise, now does it?"

Milt released his grip on Quinones's arm. "No, sir. I guess it doesn't. I'm very sorry."

"*De nada,* senor. No harm has been done, to any of us, eh?"

A half-dozen goats and innumerable stacks of woven baskets remained on the wharf. Megan shut her eyes, thinking, how grand it will be to get home to David and Barlow P., the restaurant, good old Faro ... and the world's longest, hottest soak in my lovely, deep tub.

Three tepid bathings in the skimpy receptacle Senora Manzanilla provided had finally rinsed the grit and grime from her skin, but it was the luxury of peace and privacy she craved.

"Hey, Irish—"

"Shhh, Marc," Milt hissed. "Can't you see the lady's dozing? God, for what she did, she deserves better'n a tree for a bed."

She edged one eye open and grinned at him. "Feathers, Milt. Pile me feathers up ten feet high and toss me right in the middle of 'em."

"Dear heart, when we get back to Arizona, by God, I just might do it."

Marc rose and stretched for the sky. "Looks like it's time to board that old bucket and head for home."

The steamer was several miles out in the gulf when a sudden lurch slammed Milt into the railing. "What the hell'd we do? Hit a whale?"

An immediate tilt to starboard sent crates sliding madly across the deck. Though the water appeared relatively calm, Capitan Bustamente steered his craft side to side as if avoiding a maze of floating obstacles.

Megan wobbled aft, clutching her abdomen. "Swear and be damned. The *Wardlow* never heaved and hoed this bad all the way across the Atlantic."

Pale blotches formed on Marc's sun-pinked cheekbones. He craned his neck toward the glass pilothouse high above the deck. "You think he's doing that on purpose? But why would he?"

The craft wallowed in the waves. Seawater swooshed across the deck when it keeled sharply.

"The son of a bitch is insane," Milt snarled. "He's going to swamp the boat."

Megan pointed at Tomas Bustamente's lithe figure clambering up a metal ladder to the pilothouse. "Maybe the captain's son'll get things righted again. Can you imagine what this swayin's like in the hold?"

No sooner than her words blew out to sea, the steamer spilled violently left, then reeled the opposite direction.

"That's it. Come on, Marc. We're going to pay *el capitan* a visit."

"You're not leavin' me to pitch and toss. I want to give that fool a piece of my mind, too."

They staggered forward, their boots slipping and sliding on the slick, planked decking. Scaling the ladder between her partners, Megan gripped the iron bars with all her strength when the boat listed as if it would roll over on her.

For all the creaking, scraping, and waves crashing over the bow, she could hear Capitan Bustamente's off-key tenor wailing a Mexican ballad.

"That bastard's booze blind," Milt growled from behind her.

Marc yanked open the hatch and stepped inside, then pulled in Megan and Milt. The screeching opera was so loud, she clapped her hands over her ears.

Tomas was gesturing wildly and by his expression was imploring his father to let him take over the wheel. He scowled at the new arrivals and pointed at the door.

"*En sequida omitir! Consegur hacia fuera aqui!*"

"Get out, my ass," Milt snarled. "Marc, grab the captain. I'm takin' over this tub."

"What? You don't know how to steer a boat."

"I can damn well do a better job sober than that sorry greaser's doing drunk."

Megan sidled into a corner when Marc grabbed Bustamente by the shoulders and jerked him off his feet. Tomas lunged for the attorney and caught a solid elbow under the chin for his trouble. The younger Bustamente crumpled to the floor like a rotted scarecrow.

The wheel spun demonically. With a horrendous groan, the steamer veered starboard. Milt clamped the wooden sprockets in both hands. Spinning the wheel the opposite direction, he paused, then caught and held it steady.

Sweat veed the back of his shirt and wet pools spread beneath his arms. But the steamer's dizzy rocking slowly stopped.

Until it burst past her lips, Megan hadn't realized she'd been holding her breath. Or that the captain's serenade had changed to a litany of unquestionably obscene Spanish epithets.

"Hand me that length of rope behind you, Irish," Marc instructed. "I'm not going to bear hug this rummy all the way to Guaymas."

He bound the captain's arms and legs like a calf on branding day and eased him to the floor on his side. Waggling a handkerchief in the Bustamente's face must have gotten the point across that he could either keep his mouth shut or gnaw cotton. It wasn't long before grating snores thundered through the cramped space.

"Where's Tomas?" Megan asked.

"Slunk off while Marc was hog-tying his daddy. I'll bet that kid's teeth are still rattling from that clop in the jaw."

"That better be a sure thing. My elbow hurts like hell. So, now that we've taken charge of this tub, how in God's name are you going to find Guaymas?"

"You two are going to use that sextant and the map to figure out where we are, where it is, and head me straight for it."

"I can read a ground map fine," Megan argued, "but I don't know a thing about sextants or sea maps."

"Then I'd advise you to learn how pretty quick. Either it's getting dark awfully early today, or there's a storm blowing in behind us."

Night passed with neither sleep nor squall. Groggily Milt declared that they'd outrun the storm or that it had dissipated over the gulf.

They cheered when a land mass came into view on the horizon. More whoops filled the pilothouse when they sailed close enough to see wooden structures rambling up the low hills.

"By my reckonin', I can't swear that's Guaymas," Megan hedged. "But it's a seaport and that's good enough for me."

Nosing through the coastal currents revealed the village to be their desired port of call. Milt, however, almost waited too long to disengage the paddle wheel.

For a moment, it appeared they were going to plow through the wharf and dry dock on the beach. The steamer did scrape the wooden pier a bit sharply, but no real damage was done to it or the boat's sidewall.

Marc pumped the grinning skipper's hand while Megan slapped him on the shoulder. Through the glass she saw Tomas Bustamente sprint down the pier.

When she mentioned it, Milt said, "If the boy's got any smarts, he's tearing after the same thing I want—the biggest beer the cantina can tap."

"I don't know . . . he had a mighty mean look on his face. I think the faster we find a stage goin' north, the better."

"What about him?" Marc asked, jerking a thumb at the still-slumbering captain.

"No use waking him up by untying him. His swabbies'll find him soon enough."

As they descended the ladder, crewmen were unloading the steamer as if nothing unusual had transpired. The Tombstonians hurdled over the rail and struck out toward Guaymas.

They'd hardly set foot on the street when Tomas reappeared with a burly, sombreroed man huffing at his heels.

"*Senorita y senores,*" he gasped, then swallowed, trying to catch his breath. "Is it true that you relieved Capitan Bustamente of the wheel? Of his command?"

"Damned right, we did," Milt shot back. "*El capitan* was drunk as a lord and would have drowned us all."

"As that is the case, senor, you are all under arrest. Come with me, *por favor.*"

"Arrest?" Megan cried. "For what?"

"Mutiny, senorita," he answered curtly. "A very serious offense in my country."

Behind him, Tomas massaged his chin, a satisfied smirk spreading across his face.

# Chapter Forty-eight

"You've conceded that Bustamente was unfit for command." Marc's fist slammed on the police chief's desk. "How in God's name can our relieving him of it constitute mutiny? Hell, our *lives* were at stake out there."

Cristobal de Anda steepled his fingers and regarded Marc complacently. "Your courtroom dramatics are quite impressive, Senor Smith, but premature."

A steely shimmer flickered in his eyes. "Able-bodied seamen were aboard, including *el capitan*'s son. It is not as if you had no alternatives."

Megan's eyes averted to the dirty, rough cedar floor. He's right, in a way. Maybe we did act impulsively. Except at the time, it surely didn't seem like it.

"Senor de Anda," she said, "does it really matter so much *who* brought the boat into port? We all got here alive. Doesn't that count for anything?"

"The grace of God, perhaps." The policeman chuckled without humor. "The charge has been leveled, senorita. You have admitted your guilt."

He stood and reached to open the top desk drawer. "There is nothing further to discuss."

"Then I *demand* to see the American consul," Marc bellowed.

"That is your right. I will telegraph Senor Hartman at the consulate in Mexico City."

"Mexico City?" Milt growled. "Christ, it'll take a week or more for him to get here." Stepping forward, he prodded de Anda's chest with his finger. "Look, Pedro, or whatever your name is, you don't know who you're dealing with. We've got powerful friends in Arizona. If you think you're locking us up in this two-bit hoosegow—"

The policeman eased a revolver from the drawer and

thumbed the hammer. He jabbed the barrel beneath Milt's ribs. "As you can see, I have a powerful friend, too."

The saloonkeeper grunted and backed up.

"Senor Smith, unbar the cell doors."

When Marc hesitated, de Anda sneered, "Do not make it any easier for me to pull the trigger."

The attorney glanced at Milt's sweat-shiny face, then edged toward the first of two, tombstone-shaped, solid oak slabs set in deep, adobe archways. Iron bars cradled in mortared brackets were more formidable deterrents to escape than locks. The rusty strap hinges squalled when he yanked the door open.

The stench gusting from the cell was almost visible. As he broached the second cell, a rat darted across the floor and into the street.

"Your cellmate must not have liked your looks, Senorita O'Malley," de Anda smirked.

Marc whirled to face the policeman. "I'll be damned if I'll let you put her in there. She had nothing to do with what happened on the boat."

De Anda waggled the revolver between the two men. "The lovely lady is an accessory to a crime. I will do with her as I wish."

Megan's blood turned cold at the tone of his voice. His officious demeanor had obviously been an act. She surveyed the wide, dusty thoroughfare, an enticing fifteen feet away.

No, he'd put a bullet in my back before I made it to the threshold, she warned herself. Or worse, he'd kill Milt.

"Drop your wallets on the floor, senores—very slowly. Ah, *gracias*." A vicious thrust with the pistol sent Milt careening backward into the cell. He swung the barrel at Marc. "*Entrar el carcel, amigo*."

The big man's eyes probed Megan's for a long moment. "We'll get out of here somehow, Irish. And if this animal so much as—"

De Anda's revolver hammered Marc's jawline. The skin split wide, like a bloody mouth, from cheekbone to chin. He staggered and crashed into the adobe wall.

Cocking his knee upward, de Anda rammed a boot into Marc's groin. He retched and bent double. The policeman shoved him into the cell.

"*Animale*, eh?" de Anda shouted over the clang of the

bar sliding in place. "It is not I who is caged, *se bastardo pendejo.*"

White-hot rage coursed through Megan. She lunged for the gun dangling in de Anda's hand. He spun on one heel, bracing his elbow against his side. "You are a pretty *mujer,* but a stupid one."

"I s'pose pistol-whippin' an unarmed man and fendin' off a woman takes brains? If you had one, you'd let us go before the consul—or a search party—arrives."

Pushing her roughly into her cell, he taunted, "And who can prove any of you were ever here? Ah, you'll pull in your claws soon enough, *gato bonita.* Then we will ... negotiate."

His mocking laughter ceased with the door's thudding closure.

Meager light from a tiny, barred window cut high on the wall was enough to expose the horrors of the stifling, empty cubicle.

In the corners, horseflies swarmed and maggots writhed in feces and puddled urine. Splattered, dried blood, like starbursts with rivulets drizzling down from their centers, defiled its grimy walls.

"A week, maybe more, before the consul can arrive?" she whispered. "What if de Anda doesn't send the wire?"

She sucked in tiny gasps, trying to breathe without choking. A rat's bewhiskered, feral nose probed a crack in the adobe wall. Panic clutched at her throat.

"Why *should* he send it? He's stolen all our money. Like he said, even if someone does come lookin' for us, those that know we're here won't talk."

Her head swam. The cell glowed greenish-yellow. There was nowhere to sit or lie but on the filthy floor. Gnats hectored her eyelids. She had no strength, no desire, to swat them away.

A strangely comforting sense of calm engulfed her. "I'm goin' to die here. I know that, just as surely as I know my name."

Her knees buckled, and she pitched forward into a lush, velvety blackness.

Megan flinched at the irritating buzz pestering her ears and face. She brushed a hand at the noise and squinted through her eyelashes. For all its squalor, the stone floor was cool against her cheek. She pushed up on her elbows, swinging her legs around to sit Indian style.

The cell was silent but for insect and rodent sounds, and her own shallow breathing. Two earthenware bowls had been left near the door. One contained a putty-colored gruel teeming with flies; the other held water.

Her cottony mouth pleaded for moisture. "I won't touch those slops," she rasped, licking her dry lips. Yet, she couldn't take her eyes off the glazed clay container.

The water drew her like the flies to the food. Cupping the bowl in her hands, she sniffed and wrinkled her nose at its stale, fishy odor. It tasted oily and flat, but she drank greedily until the bowl was half empty.

Her stomach lurched. She clenched her teeth, willing herself not to vomit.

Hugging the water bowl like an heirloom vase, Megan crawled back to the center of the room and curled around it protectively. She closed her eyes, denying the horrors she couldn't bear to see, and beckoned dreams of David and a world that might have been.

An unfamiliar voice reverberated faintly in her mind like footfalls in a dark tunnel. Hands clawed at her shirt. She brought her knees tighter to her chest.

"Why do you cower like a fawn, *puta*?" de Anda crooned as he bent over her. "I am not a heartless man. I have waited for four days." He fondled himself obscenely. "It is time I took my reward."

"No! Please, no!" she sobbed, scooting into a mucky corner.

"I will shackle your wrists if you fight," he warned as he unbuttoned his trousers. "That will not lessen my pleasure. Only yours."

De Anda stepped toward her. Megan panted like a trapped dog, her head pivoting, frantically seeking some kind of weapon.

The cell door burst open. A blond man flanked by two uniformed soldiers filled the archway. Marc loomed behind them, with Milt craning his neck to see into the cell.

The soldiers dropped to one knee, elbows propping their rifles in firing position. "Get away from her, de Anda," the blond commanded.

The police chief's arm halted in midstrike. He whirled,

then lowered it casually. "Ah, *Embajador* Hartman. I did not expect you so soon."

Hartman's malevolent glower was as deadly as the carbines leveled at de Anda's heart. "Obviously not. The consulate telegraphed me in Chihuahua. They had already received several inquiries from Arizona regarding the whereabouts of Smith, Joyce, and Miss O'Malley."

The policeman adopted an informal slouch. "The men, they have been no trouble, but this one"—he gestured toward the corner—"she is loco, *Embajador*. I bring her food and water and she pounces to scratch my eyes out."

Megan tried to shake her head. Her pulse throbbed inside her skull like a sledge on an anvil. She slumped sideways. Dry heaves tore at her chest and bile scalded her throat.

The next thing she knew, Marc had scooped her up in his arms. He groaned; his steps short and faltering when he started carrying her out of the cell.

"Put your hands on top of your head, de Anda," Hartman barked. "Dearborne, strip him. Mancini, if he so much as sneezes, shoot the son of a bitch."

"Wait—what have I done?" the police chief shrieked. "I sent for you as my prisoners asked. And you're *norte americano*. You have no authority in—"

"You only wired me to cover your butt in case of an inquiry," Hartman shot back. "Had I been detained, there'd have been nothing here but a pretty story and three unmarked graves."

"Oh, no, senor—*no lo comprende*—"

"I understand perfectly and assure you the Mexican government will be notified of your conduct . . . eventually."

Marc wobbled out the door into the brightness of the front office. Megan peered up at the man cuddling her to his chest like an infant. Tears washed pale swaths down his battered face. Both eyes were purpled and swollen; the gash on his cheek oozed pus.

"Dear God, de Anda was about to—" Milt said, nearby. "I'll kill that—"

"No, you won't," Marc mumbled. "Hartman's got the right idea. Let de Anda wallow in his own shit until he begs for a bullet in his brain."

"I'd still like a crack at him. Why he thought we'd found us a gold mine, I don't know. But I guess if he hadn't, he'd of killed us outright days ago instead of trying to torture us into talking."

Megan kneaded her trousers pockets. They were empty. *Mary, mother of God,* she said silently. *The little nugget Father Cavillo blessed and gave me for a keepsake is gone. De Anda said he'd watched me. He must have found it . . .*

As if from a great distance, she heard the cell door slam and the bar rattle in its brackets.

"My guards are posted. Gentlemen, take Miss O'Malley to the hotel, *pronto.* I'll fetch a doctor."

"No," Megan moaned through swollen lips. "Go home."

"Honey, we've got to get you cleaned up and let a doctor look you over first," Milt said.

She wriggled in Marc's grasp. "Bath and . . . home. Please?"

The attorney nodded toward the street. "Milt, Mister Hartman, we'll be along in a few minutes." He shuffled to a disjointed chair, which threatened to collapse beneath their weight.

Propping her back on his knee, he said, "You've always been straight with us, Irish. I'll not insult you by candy-coating anything.

"The fact of the matter is, you're not fit to travel. I don't need a medical degree to know you've got a fever, and your mouth's swollen twice-sized. Rat and fly bites have welted you up pretty good, too, and they're festering bad."

Dazed, she raised her arm and squinted at the sores smattering her skin like angry freckles. *Was I so addled that I didn't even feel varmints gnawin' on me?*

Starting to touch her face, she grimaced at the revolting muck caked between her fingers. "Nasty. I'm nasty and ugly."

Her head lolled and she glimpsed her private hell's arched, oaken portal and the stern-expressioned sentry guarding it. Hazy recollections whirled in her mind. With them came a revelation: *I almost died in there. I wanted to, desperately. Inventing and clinging to a time and place where David and I were together is all that kept me alive.*

*For days, I've dreamed of him, yet I never really told him how much I love him. And I came so close to never having the chance.*

# Chapter Forty-nine

Megan brushed trail grit from the lace-trimmed, white dress Marc bought in Tucson for her homecoming. He'd laughed and said it'd turn dust brown long before they reached Tombstone, but the voluminous skirt gleamed as snowy as it had in the dress shop's window.

She studied her partners; both dozing with their chins sagging to their chests. They're not the same men they were when we left almost five months ago, she mused.

Marc's quieted some; he's more pensive. Milt's tougher for havin' seen the elephant. As am I, in ways I can't see in the mirror, but feel inside.

As they had a hundred times since Marc carried her from the jail, tears rolled unbidden down her cheeks. When the coach rumbled onto Allen Street, she wiped them away hastily, then finger-combed her earlobe-length hair.

Guadalupe, the *niñera* who'd cared for her in Guaymas, had tried vainly to brush out the mass of matted tangles.

Megan told her to cut it off, but Guadalupe wailed, "No, Senorita Megan. *No es tu muchacho. Tu est muchacha.*"

"Well, if folks can't tell I'm a girl, there's more lackin' than a hank of hair. Besides, it'll grow back."

She was finishing her sprucing up when Marc roared a leonine yawn and stretched lazily. "You look beautiful, Irish."

She could only smile back at him. Much as she'd longed to be home, she felt a sudden irrational impulse to leap from the stage before it pulled up at the depot. It was as befuddling as it was frightening.

Gooseflesh crawled up her arms. She glanced down, terrified that welts were rising on her skin again. In the blink of an eye, her hands and her beautiful dress were smeared with slimy muck. Then the taint vanished without a trace.

Megan startled violently at a tap on her knee. "Honey?

What's wrong? You're white as that gown you're wearing,"
Milt asked in a sleep-slurred voice.

She looked down at her lap again, then at Milt. "Uh, I'm
just excited about coming home, I guess. Aren't you?"

"For all its hooraws and hombres, I think Tombstone'll
seem pretty tame after what we've been through," Marc
replied, chuckling. "I'm going to miss you, Irish."

"Yeah, that goes double for me."

Her heart tugged a bit. "It's not as if we're partin' ways,
boys. This ol' town isn't so big that we're gonna lose each
other in it."

Milt fairly hollered as the stage lurched to a halt beside
the boardwalk, "Well, hallelujah. That sounded more like
the Megan we rode out with than I've heard in weeks."

The door yanked open. David reached inside, inquiring
huskily, "May I assist you, ma'am?"

"David! How did you know . . . .?"

Marc cleared his throat. "I sent a telegraph from Tucson.
Hope that wasn't out of line."

"Do you think it is?" she countered evenly.

"If I did, I wouldn't have done it."

Crooking a finger for him to bend closer, she kissed him
on the cheek. "Thank you."

"Aw, don't mention it. Now how's about getting your
behind off that bench and saying 'Hullo' to the poor man."

Megan slipped her hand into David's and stepped down
from the stage. Looking up into his eyes, she murmured,
"I want to go home. With you."

Not another word was spoken until after they reached
the adobe cottage behind the Russ House. David closed
the door behind them and bolted it. She raised her arms
and whispered, "Hold me. Tight. Ever so tight."

With her face nestled in his chest, she felt safe; as if
the shelter of his embrace vanquished all the horrors and
heartaches—diminished them to nothing more than dregs
of a nightmare.

He stroked her hair tenderly. "I missed you. I felt hollow,
empty, the instant that stage spirited you away. Tell me
you won't ever leave me again."

"David, I've fought lovin' you for half my life. I almost
left this world regretful and mournin'. That was harder to
bear than anything else I've suffered."

She eased from his arms and gazed up at him. "I realized

that time has healed my regrets for those things I wish I hadn't done. It's forgiven or almost forgotten them. But those things I *wished* I'd done? There was no forgiving or forgetting. Just achin' regret for what might have been, and what I thought never would be."

He drew her to him, and kissed her long and gently. The sweetness of his lips fired a passion too long denied. She arched her back, molding her body to his.

The room swirled as his tongue sought and found hers. He cupped her buttocks, crushing her to him. Megan tore her mouth from his, panting from the heat and lust threatening to suffocate her.

Laying her hand over his, she slid it upward to her breast, nearly swooning at his touch.

"Oh, I've wanted you for so long. Make love to me, David. Make love to me, now."

White cotton and lace jumbled with black broadcloth in a heap on the floor. With no shame or shyness, she stood naked before him.

"You're more beautiful than I ever imagined," he whispered.

Her eyes roamed the vee of thick black hair covering his chest; its point narrowing to a line, then tufting lushly at his groin.

As if in a trance, she knelt and touched him, marveling at the satiny tautness. No one ever told her that a woman surrenders; she does not seize. Stroking, and caressing him with her cheek, she kissed his thighs, reveling in his musky, erotic aroma.

He trembled, groaning with pleasure as her lips traced the length of him, parted, and claimed him. Capturing and savoring him only heightened her own arousal.

"Oh, God, darlin' ... I can't take much of ... won't be able to stop myself ...."

He eased his hands beneath her arms and raised her to her feet. Stretching out beside her on the bed, his tongue teased her nipples, while his soft hands explored every inch of her. Fingers sought and delved the core of her as his lips rambled languidly down her belly, and beyond.

His glorious, sensual seduction sent wave after wave of rapture shuddering through her until she almost screamed with its crest.

Rising to his knees, he eased inside her; the swollen hard-

ness of him bringing another delirious, delicious surge of
carnal pleasure.

She raised her hips to take all of him. With a final thrust,
his body quaked and he reared his head back like a stallion.

They slept in each other's arms, sating their passion again
and again whenever it awakened them. For a dozen hours,
Megan's dreams became reality.

She squinted when a ray of sunlight glanced off the mirror and probed her eyelids. David cuddled against her; one
arm snuggled beneath her breasts. Snoring softly, his warm
breath feathered across her neck.

There are those who'd call me a whore now, she thought.
I'm supposed to feel guilty—remorseful, for lyin' with a
man who's not my husband.

Worse than that, I reckon I should feel powerfully guilty
about *not* feeling guilty. If it's a mortal sin to love a man,
body and soul, then sinner I'll have to be.

She reached back to caress the contour of his muscular
thigh. He stirred, rasping a stubbled chin on her shoulder,
then drowsily fondled her breast.

Fairly purring with the wonder of his touch, she swiveled
her hips until the object of her desire responded as she'd
hoped it would.

"I must say, you're a randy little Colleen," he whispered huskily.

"Never was until last night."

He propped his head with one elbow and she wriggled
around to gaze at his beloved, handsome face. "Darlin', it
wouldn't have mattered if I hadn't been the first, but it's
very special to me that I was."

She hesitated, unsure of how to respond. "It's silly, I
guess, but I can't help wishin' I'd been yours, too."

A wistful smile played across his lips. Stroking her cheek,
he murmured, "In a way, you are. At least, I haven't been
with another woman since I met you."

"But what about—"

"Our marriage was never consummated, Megan.
Amanda and I love each other, very much, but what we
share is companionship, not passion. I knew from the beginning that she was repulsed by the physical side of marriage,
but I thought, in time, she'd feel differently."

"That's why there've been no children."

He bowed his head and nodded. "Shortly after we were

married, a doctor told her she'd never survive a pregnancy. That risk is the main reason we haven't been together as man and wife. Truthfully, I've missed not having children much more than the other."

Megan pulled him to her and held him close. "I don't know what to say, except that I love you more than anything in the world. What we have is private. It's between the two of us, alone."

"Then you understand that I can't leave Amanda, regardless of how I feel about you?"

"Amanda and I aren't competin', and you're not the prize. It's not a case of 'either or,' and especially not 'or else.' "

His eyes searched her face intently. "Are you being honest with me? With yourself?"

"Yes, I am. I can't live with you. I'm not sure I'd want to, if I could. I've been on my own a long time, David, and I'm right fond of my own company—of privacy. But I don't want to live entirely *without* you, either."

Shaking his head, a low whistle breezed past his lips. "You're a helluva woman, Megan, and a wondrously natural lover. Why you chose me to fall in love with, I'll never know."

"Now that ya mention it," she drawled, "I'm kinda wonderin' myself. Maybe you'd better do somethin' to remind me, eh?"

It was nearly noon before he kissed her good-bye. "I'm not sure when I can see you again."

She laid her fingers on his lips to shush him. "I'll not pine and peer out the window lookin' for you, but I'll be here. Whenever."

Closing the door behind him, she leaned against it. Part of her wanted very much to crawl back into the tousled bed and sleep the day away.

She sighed, and chastised herself. "There's a restaurant and a boardin'house needin' your attention, a couple of old codgers you're hankerin' to see, and a cat ... Glory be, I haven't given a thought to Faro. I wonder where he is?"

After promising herself a luxurious hot soak later, she poured a measure of tepid water into the basin and shivered through a spit bath. A red tattersall-print shirtwaist enhanced the roses in her cheeks, and with a good brushing, her hair curled under into a becoming pageboy.

She stripped the bed, carrying the bundle to the Russ House's rear entrance and adding it to the pile already in place. Sometime before the restaurant closed for the night, Won Gee's Laundry would whisk everything away, leaving behind a string-tied, brown paper-wrapped bundle of clean linens.

When she stepped into the kitchen, Lee Ho cried, "Missy Megan! Missy Megan!" swinging a cleaver so wildly she didn't know whether to duck or disarm him.

"For heaven's sake, Lee Ho, put that thing down before you fricassee the both of us."

"You back now? You stay now?"

"I'm back, and I'm stayin'. I s'pose that's all right with you? After all, you've been the boss man for quite a while."

He looked over his shoulder and murmured, "Not me, boss, uh-uhhh. Bar-row P., *he* boss. He very loud boss man. He say, Ree Ho, goddamn this, and Ree Ho, summabit-cha that."

"That's right," bellowed a voice from the dining room's door.

"Bar-row P.!" She giggled, racing into his outstretched arms. He hugged her so tight she thought her ribs would crack.

Grinning up at him, she started to tell him how much she'd missed him when she saw two fat tears squeeze from the corners of his eyes.

He passed a sleeve across his face. "Goddamn fumes. If his cookin' don't rot a man's gut, it'll blind 'im jes' smellin' it. C'mon, let's pull up to a table and sit a spell."

Sliding her chair back with uncustomary courtliness, he sauntered off to fetch them some coffee. Megan sipped the steaming, aromatic brew, declaring it the first decent cup she'd had since she left.

Barlow P. extended a work-callused hand, beckoning her small, softer one. "I ain't gonna ask ya about yer trip, gal. Don't need to, and I reckon yer still too raw to be a'tell-in' it."

She smiled wanly. "Then you've already seen Milt or Marc?"

"Nope." He hesitated, scratching his stubble with a fin-gernail. "I guess it ain't no secret: Marc writ me a letter whilst you were recuperatin' at the hotel. Told me what that sumbitchin' greaser done to ya, and what he tried a'doin' to ya. Missouri pert near had to cinch me to a post to keep me from goin' down there and killin' the bastard."

"This'd be a perfect time to say, 'I told you so.'"

"What do ya mean?"

"You tried six ways of Sunday to talk me out of goin'. Warned me that Mexicans can be contrary, even cruel to each other, let alone foreigners."

"No different from us, im that respect, gal. Naw, I was jes' frothy 'cause you didn't ask me to go with ya. Felt like a spavined horse gettin' put out to pasture."

She chuckled and laced her fingers in his. "We've been double-yoked for a lot of years, partner, and will be for a lot more. Like I told you, I just needed to get away from everything familiar and think."

"Well, it appears to me ya cogitated so hard, yer hair shrunk up ta yer ears."

She grinned and stuck her tongue out at him. "When the snaggles wouldn't comb out, I asked Guadalupe, the maid, to whack it off. The way she acted, you'd a thought I'd told her to dance down Main Street naked. She swore and be damned folks'd think I was a boy."

His eyes drifted downward and a blush flamed his cheekbones. "Anyone what can't tell you ain't must hang by his toenails in a cave."

"Does that mean you like it cut this way?"

"Hell, no."

"So, you think I look awful?"

"Tar-nation, woman. Ain't there no choices betwixt likin' it and awful? You'd be purtier than a sunrise if'n you was bald as a eagle. Hmmmph. Now I reckon yer head's gonna swell too big fer what hair ya got left."

"No, it won't, and thank you for the lovely compliment," she replied. "At least I think that's what it was."

"Hmmmph."

"Oh, stop your gruntin' and tell me what's gone on here while I was gone."

Barlow P. took a long drag on his coffee cup. "Well, the silver minin's saggin' a mite, but the lead minin's 'bout the same. Back in July, they found Johnny Ringo agin' a tree trunk with the wind whistlin' through a hole in his head. Coroner decided he'd kilt hisself."

"Why would he do that?"

"Coroners don't hafta explain them kinda details. Or

why the fool's cartridge belt was buckled on upside down. Buckskin Frank Leslie's aired Billy Claiborne out permanent, too."

"What about the Earps and Doc?"

"If Wyatt's manufacturin' all the corpses they're sayin' he is, he's either got the world's fastest horse or a rifle with a three-hunnert-mile range to it. Don't really know what's become of Holliday. Last I heard, he was bunkin' behind bars in Colorado."

"How about Missouri and the One-Eyed Jack? And where's Faro?"

"Whoa, now. We hired Faro—temporary—to keep four-legged rats outta the saloon, which is hootin' and hollerin' along jes' fine.

"Missouri's practically run it single-handed whilst you was gone. Had to. Hell, ever' time I turned my back, that Chinaman was slippin' oysters or eel nuts or some such inta the stew."

"Barlow P.!"

"Well, damn it. I ain't eatin' no offal, and no pigtailed feller's gonna sneak it inta my supper, neither."

"See, Missy Megan?" came a shrill, disembodied voice from the kitchen. "Bar-row P., he very loud boss man."

# Chapter Fifty

Megan strolled among the tables ready to fill a cup, fetch a condiment, or roll her eyes at a bawdy joke. Patting a familiar, steel-muscled shoulder, she asked, "Things to your likin', Hoolihan?"

"Aye, the food and the company's splendid as always, malvoreen."

"But you and the rest of the boys get quieter every week. If I slapped bookshelves upside my walls, folks'd think this was a library."

"Oh, would they, now. And is this the same Megan who once threatened our manhoods for rowdyin' to wake the dead?"

She winked at Seamus Heaney, gobbling his dinner across the table. "It is. As I recall, that was the night I caught you rascals sneakin' splashes of whiskey into your Arbuckle's."

"A tonic, 'twas, malvoreen. Lo, can it be a mite more'n a year ago we was frolickin' like lambs in sweet clover? Eighty-three, it's been a boggy year, that it has, and I warrant the mines'll pare wages a'fore we're deep in the next."

"I hear tell those big, fancy pumps were suckin' the tunnels dry again," she countered, adding to herself, according to David, they'd cost over a hundred thousand dollars each. At that price, they should be turning those floodwaters to wine.

"Well now, they are, and then again, they ain't," Seamus remarked around a mouthful of buttery, baked tatie. "the Contention, Grand Central—don't matter who owns 'em, them tunnels is mazed like gopher runs. If the boys down the road's gettin' their socks wet, we starts cuffin' our britches."

"Mark me words, lass: This camp's a'fadin' like a poor woman's charms," Hoolihan mourned with typically Irish fatalism. "If tumblin' silver prices don't do it in, the gushin' will. It's only an eejit that fights God or the gov'ment and expects to win."

Later, Megan pondered the miners' grim predictions while tidying the cottage. Faro's brawny twenty-five-pound physique festooned the rocker's cushion he allowed her to occupy on rare occasion.

Swiping an oiled rag tacked to a stick across the wooden floor, she grumbled, "Lord, do I hanker sometimes for somebody to fret with." She glanced at the cat, whose glassy stare was profoundly bored. "Might as well be prattlin' to myself. Which I reckon I am."

Snaring the feather duster holstered in her apron's waistband, she mused, I don't think Barlow P.'s set foot inside that threshold since the mornin' the Russ House opened. He's common as a salt cellar at the restaurant, but shies from here like it was strung with barbed wire.

Megan regarded the sad, puckery face reflected in the mirror. I miss the old coot. We don't spend nearly as much time together as we once did. But Barlow P.'s got a business to run and Missouri keepin' him company. I have the Russ House, and David.

"Can it be nigh on a year since we became ... uh, you know?" she asked the cat, who merely creviced an eyelid in response. "Wonder where David's been keepin' himself the last few days. Not here, eh?"

Sharply flicking her wrists made the dresser scarf snap like a bullwhip. "Glory be, will you listen to me, carpin' like a fishwife? Considerin' my disposition of late, it's no surprise we're hermits, Faro."

She gently patted the fringed rectangle into place as if apologizing for treating it so roughly. "Wouldn't relish a man underfoot all the time, anyhow. Truth to tell, I'm happy as a bee in a hive. Don't even have nightmares anymore. Hardly ever."

She'd never forget that rainy June afternoon when Barlow P. was barking out a supply list while she jotted the items on a scrap of butcher paper. Suddenly, from the corner of her eye, she saw a portly mouse waddle across the kitchen's floor.

Her vision narrowed to pinpoints, centering on the rodent. Then, like a candle being thrust into a cave, the spectrum enlarged to illuminate bloodstained walls, mounds and pools of human waste, and thousands of horseflies and rats swarming her face and scurrying maniacally around her feet.

Hysterical screams echoed faintly, like a foghorn trumpeting from miles offshore. With the sensation of fingers digging into her shoulders and her head jerking backward came a realization that the screams were her own.

"Megan . . . *Megan.* C'mon now, baby gal, simmer down. Ever'thin's gonna be all right. Ol' Barlow P.'s done scared away the haints that was pesterin' ya."

She clung to him, acrid sweat seeping from every pore. He rocked her gently from side to side, his cheek nestled against the top of her head.

"I—I don't know what came over me."

"Yeah, you do, gal," he replied solemnly. "And it ain't the first time it's happened. I have 'em, too."

When Megan kept silent, he continued, "I calls 'em the war willies. Used to have 'em bad. Still get 'em some. I'd be mindin' my own business and hear, or smell, or see somethin' and *rattlety-bang*—my mind sent me back smack-dab in the middle of every gruesome memory a man'd sooner forget.

"Fought more battles wrasslin' in my bunk after the war than I ever did durin' it, too. Smelt gunpowder and fresh-spilt blood. Heard horses and men scream. For a lotta years, I thought whiskey'd bury 'em once and for all and let me sleep in peace. It didn't. Jes' made the haints worse, and the mornin's hard to welcome."

"But I wasn't in a war, Barlow P."

"The hell you weren't. Think I didn't know 'bout Curly Bill harryin' ya? Then came the fire, which sent ya south more ways than one. Damn near dyin' in the desert, takin' over that boat and frettin' all night whether you'd see dry land agin', and then that greaser jail? If them ain't battles ya waged, I don't know what is."

"So you don't think I'm goin' crazy?"

He drew back his chin, nudging her forehead with it. She looked up into his searching, sky-blue eyes. "Well, if ya are, that's jes' another thing we got in common."

"I'm not the same Megan I used to be. It befuddles me, now and then."

"Baby gal, the onliest thing that never stops is time and change. There's good and bad in both. Jes' 'cause things

get diff'rent, don't mean it's bad. Nor good. It's jes' dif-
f'rent, and ya gotta keep goin'."

He leaned closer. She thought, for an instant, that he was
going to kiss her. Their lips almost met, but he turned away,
burying his face in her hair and hugging her close.

Megan smiled at the bittersweet recollection. Barlow P.
was, and always had been, the best kind of friend: constant,
strong when she was weak, and proud of her, right or
wrong. Mostly, *he lets me* be.

A thunderous pounding at the door jarred her from her
reverie. Faro hissed and scrambled to his feet, ears pricked
and foreclaws primed to punish whoever had dared inter-
rupt his nap.

"You Megan O'Malley?" wheezed the pock-faced lad
poised on the stoop as if rogues were close at his heels.

"Who wants to know?"

"Western Union, ma'am. Got an express wire for her."

She extended her hand for the missive. "I'm grateful for
you bringin' it so late. Wish I had a bit to give for your
trouble."

The boy blurted, " 'Sall right, ma'am," and sprinted into
the darkness.

Ripping the envelope at its seams, she extracted the
folded sheet inside. The message originated from Tucson,
dated 11 October. "Two days ago," she muttered. "So
much for 'Express.' "

Megan's eyes scanned the lines:

Amanda seriously ill Stop En route to San Francisco Stop
fastest means Stop Will send word as able Stop Love
Stop David Stop

# Chapter Fifty-one

Though the first Saturday in December had brought a larger than usual crowd of shoppers to Bisbee's business district, Megan was hardly aware of the throngs strolling and laughing along the boardwalk.

Over and over, Doctor Phineas Ahern's verdict parroted in her ears: "Congratulations, Missus Dannelly. I'm sure the proud papa—Oran, was it?—will say such news is the best Christmas present a man can receive."

"But, Doctor, uh, we haven't been married long," Megan stammered. "We took precautions—wanted to be better established before . . ."

Ahern nodded understandingly. "I admire you for wanting to feather a nest before filling it. However, but such, shall we say, devices are far from dependable."

Patting her gently on the hand, he added, "Bringing a child into the world is truly a blessed event, my dear. And at twenty-nine, perhaps it's best it's happening sooner than you wished. You're healthy, and I'm not implying there's any cause for alarm, but the older the mother, the higher the chance of complications."

Mary, Mother of God, she thought, as scurrying townsfolk jostled her this way and that. How will I tell David? When will I tell him? His last letter said Amanda was slowly improving, yet still too sick for him to risk a trip back to Tombstone.

Suddenly a hand clamped around her wrist. Her arm was nearly jerked from its socket. "Get down, lady! Get down!" a raspy male voice bellowed in her ear.

At the same time her knees slammed onto the planks, she heard gunshots, running feet, and terrified screams.

Two mounted men with bandannas bridging their noses were firing at random from the middle of the street. Hud-

dled against a building as tightly as cheap paint, she winced
at each concussion.

Their rearing, skittering horses kicked dirt in the face of
a woman sprawled near their hooves. A few feet away a
man writhed in agony, a scarlet stain spreading rapidly
across his flannel shirt.

With bulging bags clenched in their fists, three more
masked bandits loped into view from the direction of Gold-
water & Castenada's mercantile. Its plate windows exploded
as the shooters covered their confederates' escape.

Once mounted, all five geed their horses in circles. Bullets tattooed posts and storefronts in all directions.
Whooping like Apaches, the robbers set spurs and galloped
hell-bent-for-leather into the night.

Megan ran to help the fallen woman. Kneeling beside
her, she slid one hand beneath her cheek and gently raised
the woman's head.

Beneath a perfect widow's peak, a trickle of blood had
meandered from a small, dark-ringed hole. Enormous doe-
brown eyes stared fixedly, a surprised expression etched for
all eternity. Even in death, she was holding her high-
mounded belly protectively.

"Missus Dannelly," a voice called from behind her. It
was a moment before, remembering her alias, she recognized it as Doctor Ahern's. "Missus Dannelly, come with
me, please. This is no place for a woman in your
condition."

Megan glared at him, then she reached to close the young
mother's eyes. "It's a shame no one told *her* that ten
minutes ago."

News of the "Bisbee Massacre" spread through the entire territory, long before Megan returned to Tombstone
by stage. Barlow P. and virtually every able-bodied male
who owned a horse or could borrow one had lit out to
track down the killers.

After ordering Lee Ho to either take charge of the restaurant for the day or lock it up—whichever he chose—she
stumbled to the cottage cabin and fell into bed without
bothering to undress.

The room was dark as pitch when she awakened, head-
achy and stiff. "What'll I do?" she whispered, caressing her
swollen abdomen. "If anyone looks close enough, they'll

see I'm already showin'. Loose stays and aprons won't hide it much longer.

"I can't run away and never tell David. Raising the baby by myself or givin' it up for adoption is worse than cruel: it cheats him of the fatherhood he's yearned for, and denies the child one or both of its parents.

"But if I stay, folks will guess sooner or later who its father is. Amanda would certainly hear of it, and be heart-broken and publicly humiliated. I don't give a fat damn what they'd say about me, but I won't have this innocent little lamb known as 'David Jacobs's bastard.'"

Megan tossed and turned, mulling questions with no an-swers. By the time dawn filtered through the window shade, she'd made the two most agonizing decisions of her life.

With calm deliberation, she stripped to the skin and donned fresh clothing. Clutching her reticule, stuffed with the savings she'd stashed away under the mattress, she started out north along a deserted Fifth Street.

At Safford, she hastened east to the corner, only pausing to knot a scarf over her head before entering the Sacred Heart Catholic Church's central portal. Kneeling before the life-size statue of the Madonna, Megan crossed herself and clasped her hands together until her knuckles blanched.

Her heart felt leaden when she emerged an hour later. Tears blurred her vision as she made her way down Sixth. She didn't bother knocking on the bordello's crimson door, but let herself in and went directly to Kate Elder's room.

She brushed the ratty curtain aside. Kate whirled, corset lacings gripped in her fists and petticoats swishing.

"Jee-sus Chri—" she gasped. "You scared the liver out of me, Megan." Cocking an eyebrow in puzzled concern, she deftly bow-tied the strings as she stepped nearer. "What is it? What's wrong?"

"I'm with child, Kate."

Her old friend crossed her arms under her tightly harn-essed bosoms. "The father?"

Megan's lips compressed to a thin line. She shook her head, averting her eyes.

"Another Immaculate Conception, I suppose?" Kate snorted derisively. "Takes two to make a baby, honey. It's bad enough you'll have to carry it alone."

When Megan kept silent, she observed, "That stone face tells me you didn't come here to cry on my shoulder. Your mind's made up about something, and I'm afraid I know what."

Megan swallowed hard, then replied, "I can't have this baby, Kate. Too many people would be hurt and the child would suffer for it all its life."

She nodded sagely. "Folks'll tar and feather the mother, but only shrug their shoulders at the man, whoever they guess him to be. Been that way since the dawn of time."

"You don't understand. It's not me I'm protectin'. I don't care a'tall what names I'd be called. Never have. I can't tell you the whys and whos—you'll just have to trust that my reasons are sound."

"I don't doubt they are. but I can't help you. I won't."

Megan's chin quivered and tears rimmed her lower lashes.

"Come here," Kate murmured, spreading her arms wide.

Wracking sobs echoed off the room's dingy walls. Megan felt as if hands were wringing her heart like a sodden cloth. She cried for David, who'd never know why she'd left him, for the faith she'd never be able to take solace in again, and the beautiful, young mother shot down in a dusty street whose baby, like Megan's own, would never be born.

"What I have to say might not make a lick of sense to you," Kate soothed. "Just hear me out, please. You've asked me for the only thing in this world I can't give.

"I'll not send you to a butcher, and that's the only kind of doctor that cures this kind of trouble. I've seen too many girls bleed to death to let you risk being one of them.

"And I may be a whore, but that doesn't mean I've turned my back on the Church, though it's likely turned its back on me. Doesn't matter. The way we were raised and what we believe are as much a part of us as brown eyes. Stretching those canons is one thing. Living outside the faith, with no hope of redemption, would leave your soul—your spirit—empty as air."

Kate eased her grasp. Her eyes bore into Megan's. "If you need anything: money, a place to go, a friend who'll see you through this, I'm here. Always will be. Just don't ask me again for the one thing I love you far too much to give."

A wan smile curled the corners of Megan's lips. She wiped away her tears. "Bless you, Kate."

"I didn't do anything but deny what you wanted most from me."

"Anyone on Sixth Street could have given me that. You cared enough to give me what I *needed* most: a conscience I couldn't shut out like I did my own. That's a far more precious gift."

"What will you do now?"

Megan turned toward the door. "Truly, I don't know. But I've got a clearer head for ponderin' it."

"The father can't, or won't, marry you?"

She hesitated, then replied softly, "Can't."

Kate kissed her cheek as she pulled the drape aside. As Megan started down the hall, she heard her mutter, "If only that mousey wife of his'd breathe her last ..."

Three days later Barlow P. shuffled into the Russ House and collapsed in a chair. Tossing his hat on the table sent clouds of dust wafting toward the ceiling.

"Lawsy, you look tireder than me, gal," he mumbled, massaging his creased brow.

"Have the killers been caught?"

"Yep. One of the posse riders, saloonkeeper name of John Heath, sent ever'body tearin' this a way and that 'til the rest of us started suspicionin' why ever'thang he said held water like a sieve."

"So ... ?" Megan prompted impatiently.

"Some of the boys encouraged Heath to explain hisself a mite better. A'fore ya know it, he'd spilt that he'd planned the robbery and sang out the names of the five shooters what actually done it."

"They'll hang, won't they?"

"When we caught up with them bastards, we'd sure like to of saved the territory the price of a trial, right then and there. But we locked 'em up in the Cochise County jail."

"Just so justice is served." She sighed morosely. "Too bad it won't bring back those they slaughtered."

Barlow P. brushed trail grit from his dungarees while scrutinizing her intently. "Hmmmph. What else's frettin' ya, gal? Yer mouth's kinda pickly. And why's that apron flappin' 'round yer bootlaces?"

"I'm wearin' it to protect my dress, like I always do, you old coot."

"Well, for God's sake hitch the thang up so's you don't trip over it. Looks plumb silly like that."

Feeling tension cord her neck, she flounced over and started smoothing wrinkles from an adjacent tablecloth.

"Gal?" he said softly. "Is you feelin' poorly or somethin'? You ain't been actin' right for weeks, now."

"Jesus, Mary, and Joseph! I'm not sick, Barlow P. Quit fussin' over me like a mamma hen, all right?"

Diligently she tugged the cloth a fraction until it centered perfectly on the tabletop. She risked a backward glance. His squinted eyes caught hers and held them for a long, discomfiting moment.

He knows, she stated silently. There's no way he possibly could, but he knows all the same.

# Chapter Fifty-two

Megan turned side to side, eyeing her mirrored profile. The navy shirtwaist was a somber choice for such a festive occasion, but what few nice dresses she owned were already binding her waist and bust.

She splayed her fingers over her abdomen, pulling the fabric taut. "If I was a strappin' lass," she mused aloud, "there'd be more room in there to hide."

After finger-creasing the yoked gathers back in place, she brushed her hair until it fell in glossy waves to her shoulder blades. A wide crimson ribbon bowed jauntily off center added a hint of Christmas cheer.

"Glory, I wish Barlow P.'d hurry up and get here," she muttered, grinning. "In all the Christmases we've spent together, we've never given each other presents before. Most times, we hardly knew it *was* Christmas."

For nearly an hour that afternoon, she'd prowled Norton, Woolley and Company, ruminating over, then rejecting everything from intricately carved pipes to watch fobs. Missus Woolley bustled along beside her, chirping comments and questions about the recipient and offering up all manner of goods.

When the final selection was made, the shopkeeper wrapped its box in layered tissue paper and tied it with gold cord. "No charge," she insisted. "It's Christmas."

Now it lay, fairly glowing, atop the upturned, half whiskey barrel draped with her mother's shawl, beside the cushioned rocker. Two flickering tapers, a small decanter of brandy and snifters, and a plate of fresh-made divinity surrounded the gift.

Faro wound in and out between her legs while she stood admiring the table's setting. With one lithe stretch, he rested his forepaws on the barrel's lip. Whiskers twitching, he sniffed at the walnut-studded confections.

"Skedaddle, you varmint. That's Barlow P.'s favorite, and I'll skin you alive if you smirch it."

He pranced away, tail aloft, obviously delighted he'd captured her notice. A scant second later he froze in his tracks and cocked his head.

Megan's heart soared when she heard a knock, and rushed over to throw the door open wide.

"Evenin', gal," Barlow P. drawled, "an' merry Christmas to ya. Almost, anyhow."

He was decked out in his handsome "city suit," holding his hat in one hand and a box of chocolates in the other. His thinning hair sported a die-straight part, with his mustaches trimmed and their tips waxed to sharp points.

"Lawsy, Barlow P. I look like a mussy charwoman beside such splendor."

He winked as he stepped inside. "A feller's gotta take a bath onc't in a while, jes' to keep 'im civilized."

After taking his hat and thanking him for the candy, she led him to the rocker. Clasping her hands together at her chin, she babbled, "I hope that divinity's fit to eat. I never made it before. Or maybe you'd rather have some brandy? Yancy said it was the best they had in stock. No, how about you open your present. Please?"

"Yer flitterin' like a butterfly in wildflowers, gal," he said, chuckling. "Land yerself in that chair yonder a'fore ya tucker yerself out."

"Oh, grumbly old coot, I can't help myself. I've never had a true Christmas with company comin' and presents . . ."

"Never? Not even when you was little?"

She shook her head. "But 'twas a grand time, nonetheless. Our whole parish'd turn out to sing carols and hymns, then we'd go home and Momma'd sprinkle a pinch of real sugar on thick pieces of bread all slathered with butter—lard, after Pa's barrows got swapped for rent. If I close my eyes, I can still taste that wondrous, sweet treat. I wanted to gobble it quick, but made myself savor it 'cause I knew it'd be a year 'til the next."

Smiling at the memory, she leaned her elbows on her knees. "I s'pose I did have presents then, didn't I? Mama and Da gave us the best they had, and somethin' to remember, after."

Barlow P. sniffed and sawed a finger under his nose. "Reckon so, baby gal."

She scooted the chair closer and snatched the white and gold package from the table. "Da always told me that two shortened the road. This is for you, dearest friend, who's always shortened mine."

Barlow P. cradled it for a moment before slowly drawing on the cord and unwrapping the filmy paper. Upon removing the box's lid, his eyes fairly goggled at the pair of black gallowses with shiny brass clasps folded inside. "Heavenly days," he murmured. "Them's the purtiest riggin's I ever did see."

She grinned from ear to ear. "You really like 'em? Missus Woolley said they came all the way from England."

"Ain't never got a finer present. Might'n jes' buy me some o' them fussy-front shirts to show 'em off proper."

Gnawing her lip expectantly, she watched as he returned the parcel to the table, then patted his coat pocket. His knees crackled when he stood up and reached out his hands. "I know how a man's s'posed to do such a thang, 'cept I'm a'feared I'll air my britches if'n I try bendin' so fer down."

"What in the world are you ramblin' about, Barlow P.?" she asked, giggling as she rose from the chair.

Holding her hands in his, he cleared his throat and said, "Yer the best woman God ever put on this earth. I sure ain't good enough to be askin' ya, but I'm gonna do it anyhow. I love ya, gal, and I want ya for my wife."

Megan's mind swirled with emotions. She could not speak; only stared into his soft blue eyes as he continued, "I know I ain't the one that holds yer heart, and I won't oblige ya to any of them 'conjugal' duties. But Bainbridge is a respectable handle for a child to wear, and I'd be right proud fer yer baby to have it."

"It's a name I'd be proud to have, too, Barlow P.," she whispered. "But I'm not deservin' of it if I can't be a real wife to you."

"Would ya stand by me if'n I needed ya to?"

"Of course—"

"And take care of me if'n I got sick?"

"Yes, Barlow P., but—"

"Will ya smile at me first thang in the mornin' and maybe gimme a peck on the cheek a'fore ya turn in at night?"

Her chin quivered and a knot sealed her throat. She nodded.

"Then I reckon that's plenty enough for me. I reckon that oughta be enough for any man."

He reached into his coat pocket and brought out a small black velvet box. Beneath its hinged lid lay a narrow gold band. "Will ya marry me, Megan?"

Swallowing hard, she squeezed his hand. "Yes, Barlow P. I will."

# Chapter Fifty-three

The stage was still rocking slightly when David pushed the door open and stepped onto the boardwalk. Planting his palms against the small of his back, he groaned as he stretched the knotty trail kinks from his spine.

"Jacobs?" came a raspy voice from behind the stage. "Haven't seen you in these parts for a coon's age."

David extended his hand cordially. "It's been a while, for sure, Missouri. My wife was taken ill several months ago and I've been in San Francisco attending to her."

"She's all right now, I hope . . . ."

Before David could respond, the grizzled barkeep looked up and shouted at the driver, " 'Ey there, Bert. Don'tcha dare toss off that crate of French horse-water. Paid too much for it, plus the special freightin' to get it here."

"Champagne?" David queried. "Well, the One-Eyed Jack must be going all out for New Year's Eve."

"Hell, our regulars'd druther stay dry than paint their tonsils with spoilt grape squeezin's. That high-falutin' stuff's fer the weddin' next Friday."

"Oh? Who's getting married?"

"A couple a folks what shoulda been a long time ago: my old buddy, Barlow P., and Miss Megan O'Malley."

David felt the blood drain from his face. Goddamn you, Bainbridge, his mind thundered silently. I'll bet you started making up to her the minute I left town.

". . . get this crate stashed over to Fly's. Good day to you, Jacobs. Glad you're back."

As Missouri struggled across the street with his cumbersome freight, David started off down the boardwalk.

"Whoa, Mister Jacobs," Bert hollered, "you're forgettin' your bags."

"Leave them," he snarled over his shoulder. "I'll pick them up later."

The Russ House's darkened windows reflected his scowl as he passed by them to the tidy cottage behind it. After pounding on its door, he was wiping the sweat from his brow when Megan opened it a crack and peered out.

"David? Is it truly you?"

He strode over the threshold and quickly surveyed the room. "You're alone, I see."

"What? Well, yes, I—"

"Will your fiancé be dropping by later?"

Megan raised her chin defiantly. "You got my letter, then."

"No, Missouri shared the glad tidings down at the depot." He snorted derisively. "So you wrote me another 'I'm sorry, David' letter, eh? It appears you'll have to tell me why to my face this time, doesn't it?"

"Not 'til you sit down and calm yourself, I won't."

When she turned away from him, her body seemed fuller, more rounded than he remembered. She settled into the rocking chair, the waistband of her dress rucking tightly beneath her bosom.

Joy and fury collided in his brain. "You're pregnant. And it's my baby you're carrying."

She looked down at her hands folded in her lap, then up at him. "Yes, David. I am, and it is."

He paced the floor. "Why in God's name didn't you tell me? You had to have known for months."

"I wasn't sure until a few weeks ago, when I went to a doctor in Bisbee."

"Bullshit. How many bleedings had you missed by then? Three? Four? And you went sobbing to Bainbridge just like you always have. Naturally, he said he'd marry you to salvage your good name. Damn you for that, Megan. Damn you and him to hell."

She smiled and chuckled mirthlessly. "It's harsh, cruel words you're speakin'. Hard to believe there was once such love and tenderness between us."

"How would you have me act? What would you have me do? I've thought of nothing else but coming home to you for months. The minute I step off the stage, I'm told you're betrothed to another man.

"Oh, but that's not the half of it. I get *here* only to find out you've decided, without ever even telling me, that in the eyes of the world, Barlow P. will be *my baby's* father."

"And if you'd never left, what would you have done? Told Amanda that you'd sired a bastard? Packed up and left that poor woman to wed your lover? I hardly think so."

"I don't know what I'd have done," he shot back. "But I'll be goddamned if I'll let Bainbridge take you and my child away from me."

Icy rage surged through him. He stalked toward the door.

"David, wait. Where are you goin'?"

He let the resounding slam serve as his answer.

Hazy, crimson haloes encircled the faces of everyone he passed along Fifth Street. He ignored familiar voices and hands raised in greeting.

That son of a bitch has wanted her for years, he seethed. Megan doesn't love him. Never has. She loves *me*. Only me. Saved herself for me. Gave herself to me. He'll never touch her, by God. *Never*.

David slapped open the One-Eyed Jack's batwing doors and walked straight to the bar. Barlow P. glanced up from the glass he was drying with a rag.

"Missouri tol' me you'd hit town. Ain't never had the pleasure of servin' ya, boy. What'll it be?"

"Whiskey. Leave the bottle. And don't call me 'boy.'"

The other customers bellied against the rail fell silent. Barlow P. plunked a glass and a bottle in front of David.

Missouri eased around the corner of the mahogany bar and edged near his boss. "Ain't gonna be no fracas, is there?"

"Nah. Me and Jacobs is old friends. Reckon he's jes' tuckered out and plumb parched from eatin' dust alla way from Californee."

David never took his eyes off Barlow P. as he drained the jigger. Liquid fire scorched the length of his throat and burned in his gut. He licked his lips and poured a second shot.

"There's not going to be a wedding, *old friend*." He cocked his head back to toss down another mouthful.

"Whether there is or ain't's betwixt Megan and me," Barlow P. replied evenly, while buttoning a cuff. "She's done accepted and I ain't heard nothin' 'bout her changin' her mind."

David's entire body chilled; his muscles stony and taut. "Well, I'm changing it for her." His eyes flicked to the waist of the man beside him. A gun butt jutted from his holster.

David yanked it free, thumbed the hammer, and aimed it at Bainbridge. The pistol bucked in his hand. He hardly heard the powder explode.

The silk gallows over Bainbridge's heart split; the upper half snapped upward. Blood spread across his shirtfront. He slammed against the back bar. Glasses and bottles shattered on impact. He slid to the floor.

What have I done? David screamed silently. He heard a bellow, like a gored bull, and whirled toward the sound.

Missouri pulled a pistol from under the bar. He leveled it and fired. The slug cleaved David's ribs like a knife.

The gaslight dangling from the ceiling twirled crazily. Its flames dimmed to silver flecks. A warm stream trickled down David's thigh. The world faded to blackness.

# Chapter Fifty-four

Just as he'd promised, Marc Smith was leaning against his carriage, a few yards beyond the cemetery. Megan lifted her veil and draped it over the crown of her hat.

She felt ancient, as brittle as sun bleached bones.

"I'm sorry if I kept you waitin' overlong, Marc. Barlow P., David, and me had matters to discuss before I left town."

He cradled her thickened waist in his hands and helped her into the buggy. Settling in beside her, he clucked his tongue at the matching sorrels. As they whisked away, Megan looked back at the gravediggers shoveling dirt into the fresh graves.

"What manner of woman am I?" she asked quietly. "I loved those men more than life itself, but I can't cry for them. The tears won't fall."

He reached and laced his fingers with hers. "It's not right for you to be alone at a time like this. Let me take you to your sister's."

"Oh, no, Marc. We need you here. There's headstones to be set and paid for from the proceeds of the Russ House's sale. Did I tell you how happy Barlow P. is that I've deeded the One-Eyed Jack to Missouri? Soon as he sobers up, there's that transaction to finish. And Faro. Please see that Missouri takes proper care of Faro."

"Please, Irish. You're not—"

"If only I could help Amanda somehow. David's frettin' for her. She's bedfast; her heart's givin' out slow but sure. It's a pity, her bein' so young and all."

"For God's sake! How can you speak of these things with such an air of . . . detachment?"

"My head still thinks and ponders and worries," she answered. "It's my heart that's dead. I can feel it beatin', but it's a hollow thump, like bangin' a stick on a rotted log."

She knew by his expression that he didn't understand, and was glad he didn't. To do so would mean he'd known the same emptiness, she thought. I wouldn't wish that on an enemy, much less a friend.

Patting her rounded belly, she smiled reassuringly at him. "I'm not alone, Marc. And Barlow P. and David will always be with me, long as I'm able to visit them in my mind."

"You can't live in the past, Irish."

"Not tryin' to. Our child is yesterday, today, and tomorrow combined. But rememberin' its fathers, tellin' it what kind of men they were, and raisin' it to be the best of both of them . . . well, I think that's what's meant by everlastin' life. Folks don't truly die when their spirit leaves 'em. Only when they're forgotten by the livin'."

# Chapter Fifty-five

"Momma said to bring you this, Auntie Megan," Ellen said, holding out a frosty glass of lemonade. At almost thirteen, the auburn-haired, blue-eyed beauty held promise that her father would suffer many a sleepless night when she was old enough to entertain suitors in the parlor.

Megan smiled wanly, reaching to grasp the beaded container. "Oh—damn," she gasped when it crashed to the floor. Writhing in the chair, she dug her fingernails into its slubby upholstered arms.

"Momma, bring a towel, please," Ellen shouted out the door, then added, giggling, "And some soap."

In seconds, Frances Dannelly's distinctive clackety tread pecked along the hallway. "What's happened?"

"Didn't mean to frighten you, Momma. there's a spill that needs sopping, that's all."

"And the soap?"

"Well, you'd be makin' me eat it if I said what Auntie Megan's been sayin'."

Despite daggerlike stabs in her back and groin, Megan grinned at Ellen's orneriness. Frances's lean form loomed above, knuckles on her hips and bony elbows jutting like plucked wings.

"Hardly a sound's come from you for all the months you've perched there starin' out the window," she chided. "Now, it's blasphemy you're sayin', and to my daughter, no less."

Squatting down to eye level, she added, "Praise be, how much lovelier the cussin' is than the quiet. That reposeful woman was like a stranger wearin' your skin."

Megan exhaled slowly and relaxed. "I didn't realize I'd vexed you so. Mostly, I kept to myself so I wouldn't trouble you for anything. Lord knows, with five children and a hus-

band, you've got plenty enough to do without me addin'
to it.''

Frances peered at her quizzically and laughed. "Full circle, lass. We've come a full circle."

"Whatever do you mean?"

"Don't you remember? After Oran was burnt and we
were livin' like hobo dogs, who came and sailed into me
for not lettin' you help when we needed you most?"

"That seems so far past to be another lifetime, but yes, I
do remember. I reckon I'm better at givin'—ah ... thunder-
damn-nation."

Frances clapped a palm over Megan's taut, contorting
abdomen. "Let's get you to bed, quicklike. Why didn't you
tell me you were laborin'?"

"Not," she groaned through gritted teeth. "Twinges.
Couple of days. Water's not broken."

"Ellen, scat to Doctor Glazier. Tell him my sister's strain-
in' fierce." To Megan, she continued in a more soothing
tone, "Lean on me, and I'll help you to the bed."

"You're frightenin' me, Frances. First babies—are always—a trial. Slow to be—born—aren't they?"

"True enough. And yours isn't a wee bairn, unless I miss
my guess."

She fluffed a sheet and laid it loosely over Megan, then
sat on the edge of the mattress and gently chafed her wrist.

"I'll not leave you, hear? Not for an instant."

Through the night and most of the next day, Megan
pitched and tossed as waves of agony tore at her like starving wolves at a carcass. Frances's croons of encouragement
belied Doc Glazier's rigid expression.

"Push, lass. Push *hard,*" Frances cried. "It's comin'. the
baby's comin'. I can see it."

Megan screamed. It felt as if her body were being turned
inside out.

"God be praised, it's a boy. A fine, strappin' son."

The grinding pain ebbed to a dull ache. Megan's head
lolled to one side. Her eyelids were heavy as stone, but she
forced them open, trying to see through the haze of sweat,
tears, and exhaustion. "Cryin'? I don't hear cryin'."

The smart slap of skin on skin was followed by a lusty,
angry bellow. Don't blame you a bit, darlin' bairn, she said
to herself. 'Tis a surly welcome the world gives its babes.

Megan thrust her fists into the mattress, inching her back

up the headboard. Warm blood oozed from between her legs, soaking the wadded sheet.

"No, no, you've gotta lay flat 'til the bleedin's done," Frances cried.

"Please, I want to see my son."

"There'll be time for that later, when—"

*"Give me my baby."*

Cradling the naked infant, Megan dampened a corner of the sheet with her tongue to gently wipe his face.

"Barlow David O'Malley," she whispered. Tears splashed on his ruddy skin, glistening like tiny diamonds on his long, curling lashes. "The love and strength of three is within you, as it always will be."

She kissed his plump, warm cheek, then nestled it to hers.

# Chapter Fifty-six

Megan watched Frances pace the small bedchamber, remembering that long-ago day when a similar sisterly confrontation had taken place in Missus Braggonier's boardinghouse.

"I'm sending for Doctor Glazier," Frances fumed. "It's childbed fever you're sufferin'—it must be. There's been pirates and priests, farmers and gypsies in the O'Malley line, but nary a lunatic until now."

"It's not me pitching a fair conniption." Megan looked down and smiled at her son, sleeping peacefully in her arms. "I'll thank you not to wake Barlow David with it."

Frances whirled, her narrow face ablaze with anger. "And how, blessed Madonna, do you propose he'll rest while you're trudgin' afoot to Alaska? It's insanity, I tell you. Oran's beside himself with worry."

Megan snorted. "Beside himself from listenin' to your ravin's, I'll warrant. Oh, yes, and surely it must be me that's driven him out to the pubs most every night of late."

Frances hugged herself tightly and strode over to stand at the window. "It's union meetin's he's goin' to . . ." Her shoulders shook a fraction. "He's a captain now and—"

"Please don't cry, Frances. I'm sorry I said that, truly I am. Devil take me and my temper, too."

Other than quiet sniffles, it was as if her sister had turned to stone.

"For heaven's sake, wouldn't it be lovely if we could just talk like neighbor ladies—or even friends?" Megan asked.

Frances wiped her eyes, then smoothed the wrinkles from her skirts. "Yes, it would." She fetched a ladderback, set it adjacent to Megan's rocker, and sat down.

Folding her hands in her lap primly, she chirped, "And isn't this just the balmiest weather we're havin', Miss

O'Malley? It's got the daffodils sproutin' and the roses to bloomin' in your cheeks, to be sure."

"Aye, and it's full of beans you are, Missus Dannelly."

Frances burst into giggles, rising to laughter. "Miss Bossy Britches came calling again, didn't she?"

"I reckon, but I know it's only because you care so much."

Frances nodded. "That I do, and I know above all others how strong your wanderlust is. But there'll be time for that again, once Barlow David's grown, and he will be, faster than you can imagine."

"True enough, which means I've got two mouths to feed, the only way I know how. The placer Joe Juneau discovered a couple of years ago isn't the only gold in that territory. I've panned enough on the British Columbian side of the mountains to know there's a bonanza waiting to be found, and I aim to do it."

"With a month-old baby to tend?" Frances said, her eyes softly pleading. "You've said yourself, prospecting's a harsh life and dangerous to boot. What if something happened to you? That precious bairn'd be left a foundling."

Megan stroked her son's downy black hair with a gentle fingertip. "You and Oran wouldn't take him in? Raise him as your own?"

"Of course, we would. But if you were hurt or sick and needed help, or, God forbid, the worst happened, how would we ever know? How would we find him, so far away?"

Megan shook her head. "It's a grim picture you're paintin'. A freight wagon could run me down right outside the door, just as easy."

"Maybe so, but—"

"I'm not a greenhorn, Frances. I know the country and besides, I'd winter in town, like I used to in Victoria—manage a restaurant for our keep while the snow's flyin'."

Her sister grinned slyly. "Then gold diggin's not all you know how to do, now is it?"

Before Megan could reply, she continued, "A man by the name of Halbert Rodgers owns a restaurant not a block from the firehouse. Sad it is that he's failing from the consumption, but Rodgers is needin' to sell out and Oran's struck a bargain for the place. It's bringing a fair profit now, but with a good scrub, a dab of whitewash, and a pretty Irish lass wearin' the apron, the cash box is sure to spill over."

Dazed by the announcement, Megan stammered, "I—I don't know what to say."

Frances looked as happy as a child in front of a candy counter with a shiny dime in her pocket. "Say it's a *grand* idea. Say you'll let us—your family—help you the same way you did us. I'll care for Barlow David while you're workin'. If I don't spoil him proper, he's got five cousins that'll ruin him sure as the world."

Memories, questions, and confusion tumbled together in Megan's mind. "Has money been put down on the property?" she asked meekly, almost dreading the answer she feared was inevitable.

"Well, if I'd had my way, it would have been," Frances retorted. "But Oran said we must discuss it with you first instead of surprising you with the deed. He'll be home at shift change to give you the particulars, though, because Rodgers has another party interested and wants an answer by tonight."

Megan glanced at the chifforobe, her beaming sister, and the infant puckering his tiny lips. Her mother used to say when a baby did that, he's kissing the angels that watch over him.

"It's a fine scarf you could knit with all that wool you're gatherin'."

"And more to be done before Oran gets here. Don't think I'm not grateful—I am, more than I can say—"

"I'll leave you to it, then," Frances said. She caressed Megan's cheek, adding, "You've always been wise beyond your years. There's no doubt you'll do what you know in your heart's best for you and your child."

# Chapter Fifty-seven

"What's the future a'holdin' for us, Barlow David O'Malley?" Megan asked for the dozenth time in the last hour. He scowled, his slate-blue eyes studying her intently.

"Ah, me boyo, you're the spittin' image of David, yet there's a fair shake of Barlow P. in you, I see," she crooned, chuckling. "I'll teach you to love and respect the power of words as your father did. But you'll have Barlow P.'s horse sense, too, I'll warrant; judgment that came from livin' life, not just endurin' it."

At her touch, the infant's strong, delicate fingers curled tightly around her own. "Before I ever saw you, I dreamed of you taking your first steps in soft, cool grass; heard you laugh when the blades tickled between your toes.

"The city's not much for glades, though is it? Nor quiet nooks to lay and gander at the bears and elephants in the clouds. It's got other wonders to share, though ... it must have, to keep so many folks cooped in it.

"But can you imagine runnin' through a wildflowered meadow as high as your waist and laid at the foot of a crystal blue glacier?

"That's not a storybook place, Barlow David, I've seen it; listened to that mountain of ice shudder and crack like cannons. I'll take you there ... someday, I'm a'promisin'.

"And to the desert—to Baja where you can stand and look west over the Pacific Ocean, then east at the Gulf of California. It feels like the top of the world; like you could reach up and snatch a piece of cloud and keep it for your very own."

Megan rested her head on the chair back. David would have jumped at the chance to settle in San Francisco with a ready-made business, a profitable one, too, it seems, all wrapped and bowed like a present. He loved the hustle-bustle, the noise, the stinks—"the aroma of commerce," he called it.

Her son gurgled happily and suckled at her fingertip. "Your Auntie Frances is right, you'll be a strappin' lad before I can count three, but one of these days, I'll take you to Pioche, and Tombstone, and . . ."

Lips parted, and eyes wide and glistening like sapphires, Barlow David drew up his knees and started kicking like a frog. She stared at him a long moment. In an instant she felt as if anvils had been lifted from her shoulders.

Slipping her arms under him, she kissed the baby's forehead and rose to her feet. When she laid him on the bed, Barlow David cooed and kicked harder. She patted his plump belly, strode to the chifforobe, and threw open the doors.

Megan smiled at the scratched leather satchel waiting patiently on the top shelf. She cuddled it like an old friend before unlatching its hasp and setting it on the foot of the bed.

"There's three ways of doing things, son. The right way, the wrong way, and my way, and mine's served me well enough for many a year. I can't be what I'm not and won't promise you somedays we might never get."

Shirts, socks, an extra pair of trousers, and other necessaries were soon piled beside it. Megan rolled the garments into tight bundles to fit the bag's confines.

"If Barlow P. were here, he'd tell me to quit cussin' my mule and wishin' it was a horse. He'd say, 'Either saddle the damned thing, or sell it.' "

She nodded her head curtly. "Barlow David O'Malley, I'd say it's time we saddled ours and see where it takes us."

# Author's Note

Megan O'Malley is a figment of my imagination. The adventures she thrived on and survived, however, were based on those of Irish immigrant, prospector, and entrepreneur Nellie Cashman.

The Civil War and its aftermath had a profound (and many of that era would add "negative") effect on the labor market. Because of the scarcity of hale, hearty men to fill positions, women were given employment opportunities they would have never been considered for otherwise.

Similar to the fictional Megan O'Malley, Nellie Cashman operated an elevator at a Boston hotel and did make the acquaintance of newly sworn in President Ulysses S. Grant.

Shortly thereafter, Nellie went west on one of the transcontinental railway's hellish immigrant cars and worked as a mining camp cook in Pioche, Nevada Territory.

The fictional account of Megan necking a supply sled from Wrangel, Alaska Territory to her scurvy-suffering partners' claim was inspired by a lifesaving mission Nellie Cashman undertook in 1877.

According to the Victoria [British Columbia] *Daily Colonist* "Her [Nellie's] extraordinary freak of attempting to reach the diggings in midwinter and in the face of dangers and obstacles . . . is attributed by her friends as insanity."

Obviously, lunacy is in the eye of the beholder for the miners whose lives Nellie saved not only nicknamed her the "Angel of the Cassiar," but years later one survivor said on his death bed, "If Nellie Cashman were only here, I'd get well."

At the height of Tombstone, Arizona Territory's rootin'-tootin' heyday, Nellie managed the Russ House restaurant (among other business concerns), was acquainted with the Earp brothers, revered by *Tombstone Epitaph* owner/

publisher John Clum, and was by many accounts, the belle of the town.

Nellie's expedition to Baja's Golo Valle with Tombstone attorney [and later, first Arizona senator] Marc Smith and Oriental Saloon owner Milt Joyce is part of historic record.

The inebriated steamer captain's "joy ride" across the Gulf of California and the party's subsequent arrest and jailing in Mulege, Mexico, for committing mutiny was probably the most nightmarish experience of Nellie's life.

Whether or not she literally stumbled upon that gold-laden stream in Baja, encountered its guardian Jesuit padre, and assured him that his secret was safe with her is more the stuff of legend.

It is intriguing to note that despite numerous newspaper interviews where Nellie told and retold sundry gold mining adventures, she seldom referred to and never expanded upon what has come to be known as "The Lost Cashman Mine."

Nellie never married. As she told a curious *Arizona Star* reporter, "Why, child, I haven't had time for marriage. Men are a nuisance anyhow, now aren't they? They're just boys grown up. I've nursed them, embalmed them, fed them and scolded them, acted as mother confessor and fought my own with them and you have to treat them just like boys."

The indomitable Miss Cashman never bore a child, although she was a foster mother to her sister's five children after tuberculosis claimed the lives of both parents.

Everyone has heroes; at least, I hope that's true, for as Louis L'Amour said via one of his fictional voices, "A (wo)man needs heroes. (S)He needs to believe in strength, nobility, and courage."

Nellie Cashman is my hero. Yet, like many, I'd never heard of her until I happened upon an article about her in "*The Women*," one volume of *Time/Life*'s "*The Old West*" series.

I soon learned no book-length biography of Nellie Cashman existed. It astonished, then aggravated me enormously that such a fabulous Western frontier-tamer had all but fallen into obscurity.

Taking her maxim, "When I saw something needed doing, I did it" to heart, *Nellie Cashman, Prospector & Trailblazer* was published (Texas Western Press) in 1993. It is a "just the facts, ma'am" account of which I am very proud, but by nature, can only present a singularly-dimensioned view of Miss Cashman's accomplishments.

*Trinity Strike* is my three-dimensional interpretation of Nellie's fierce determination, lust for adventure, and child-like sense of wonder—the intuitive myth behind a Western legend.

It's not through death that pioneers such as Nellie Cashman almost vanish into history's black hole, but from the livings' tendency toward "forgetfulness."

May Nellie Cashman and the hundreds of others like her never vanish from memory. How infinitely poorer we would become for never having known them.

*Wednesday, April 10th, 1861*

*Snowed all night and still snowing now, but I started for
Denver City, wind right in my face and the snow blinds
me. Almost hard to keep road at all. I got down to Steels
Hotel and there I stopped. Could not go any further.
Snowed all day, snow in places is two feet deep, six inches
on level.*

I awakened with my belly rumbling like an ore wagon.
When I'd blown in the night before with a blizzard at my
back and not a nickel to my name, the hotel's wizened desk
clerk had taken pity on me. The storeroom's cot proved a
rickety affair, but its blankets smelled of lye soap and sunshine. I slept as cozy as a cradled infant.

The ecstasy of stretching sore limbs into usefulness
brought vapors puffing forth like a fairy-tale dragon girding
for battle. Draughts seeped through hasty chinks, stirring
scents of lemon rind, onions, and salt meat.

Hunger gnawed at my backbone. I recalled Sunday's
greasy, spit-cooked rabbit and a half-frozen biscuit; a meager repast, and a fatal one for my beloved father. That
Maximilian Roswell Tremain Fiske choked to death on a
sliver of lodged bone was too ironic for a playwright's plot.

"You were a dashing dreamer, a drunk, and a conniver,
Papa," I whispered to the log walls. "And the best, most
loving father a motherless little girl could hope to have."

Night after night, posturing on the tailgate of our garishly
painted wagon, Doctor Maximilian R.T. Fiske cured me of
a horrendous palsy with a scant teaspoon of his eighty-
proof Miracle Nerve & Brain Elixir. Astounded audiences

all but stampeded to buy those gilt-embossed pint bottles for a mere dollar each.

As Reverend M.R.T. Fiske, he restored my sight, my hearing or straightened my twisted clubfoot, fervently assuring the multitudes that such Divine Intervention would be visited upon all true—and generously tithing—believers.

And though the clouds rarely cooperated, famous meteorologist Professor M.R. Tremain Fiske, *Esq.* soaked every drought-stricken community in Iowa for the services of his roaring, guaranteed-within-two-weeks, rain-making machine.

Tears rose, and spilled over. "Colorado was to be our Promised Land, Papa. Our golden opportunity to settle and be respectable. A hundred times, I could've lost you to a bullet or the noose, only for you to strangle on your damned dinner."

I swiped my streaming face with the scratchy covers and threw them aside. Cringing when my socked feet met the cold floorboards, I snatched the hand-me-down, four-buckle gaiters from beneath the cot frame.

"He called me tougher'n post oak, smarter by half than most men he ever knew. Guess the time's come to prove it."

From my pack, I tugged out a high-collared, gun-metal gray suit—the kind one buys for its durability, later praying for a tragedy like a stove-black stain so it can be scrapped for rug braids.

Slipping the voluminous creation over my cotton scout shirt and denims, I vowed to torch the godly frock at the first opportunity and never repeat the error.

The fabric was as creased as a farmer's brow, but the worst offenders smoothed out with the flat of my hand. I pretended the scuffed, stubby-toed boots peeking beyond the hem were black kid oxfords with ribbon laces.

Careful not to let the screen door slam behind me, I departed through the trade entrance as the desk clerk had advised and hastened around the building to the street. I startled when what I thought was a bundle of rags stuffed in a packing case, moved. A gurgling cough echoed from within as a filthy moccasin emerged.

Hundreds of destitute emigrants rambled the city's treeless streets trying to survive the winter months on scraps, handouts, and hope. It frightened me to admit the only thing separating me from them was a nameless hotel clerk's compassion.

It seemed every member of Denver City's colorful and varied population chose this morning to brave the elements. Miners, merchants, buffalo-robed Indians, gamblers, and silk-hatted lawyers jostled their way past. None were old, in fact few had reached middle-life, and I appeared to be the only one wearing a chemise beneath my shirt.

I asked a Bible-clutching parson for directions to the El Dorado Parlor-Saloon. His bulbous nose wrinkled as if a foul odor invaded it. He pointed westward, and failed to bid me a good day.

By its posh name, I expected to find a smoke-hazy gentleman's club with a potted fern or two, brass cuspidors, and a number of antlered trophies peering blindly from their mahogany mountings.

Instead, the decor was one of pink, flocked wallpaper and a life-sized portrait of a reposed, bovine brunette wearing nothing but a string of pearls, several strategically-placed feathers and an unChristian leer.

Movement on the stairway caught my eye. A Negro boy tiptoed down the creaky runners like a burglar. "Can I do ya fer somethin', ma'am?"

"Is there a Garrett Collingsworth on the premises?"

He chewed a knuckle thoughtfully. "Uh, no ma'am. He done come in, and gone inta the parlor over yonder."

I thanked him and whisked through the portiered doorway he'd indicated. The room's roughly ten-by-ten dimensions contained enough furniture and bric-a-brac for three its size, which gave it all the gentility of a train wreck. Amid the jumble, a great bear of a man sat at a table reading a newspaper.

Quietly slipping out of my pack and mackinaw, I laid them and my rifle on an ugly, horsehair settee. A hammering heart made an aura of supreme confidence all the more difficult to attain.

"Excuse me, sir, I'm Abigail Fiske. I believe you're expecting me?"

Dusky, long-lashed eyes glanced up, over his shoulder, and back again. "I'm waiting for a man by that name—"

"My father was called to Glory on Sunday instant, Mister Collingsworth. It's left to me to tend his share of the prospecting partnership."

He nodded, motioning to an adjacent chair. Rather than object at his assessing my charms as I settled in it, I returned the scrutiny in kind.

The jut of his ears held back waves of shoulder-length dark hair, framing a neatly-trimmed beard and moustaches. He was twenty-five if he was a day; twenty-seven, at most and while his hands bore the scars and callouses of a common laborer, his fingernails were clean as a banker's.

"Well now I feel kind of cheated by destiny, Miss Fiske. From our correspondence, I looked forward to meeting your father. I'm real sorry I'll not be getting the chance."

My chin trembled and I stiffened, fighting for composure. On the mantle, a Waterbury's pendulum switched as loud as a ballpeen on tin. "I may be a poor second to the arrangement, but have no doubt that I'll earn my share of its bounty."

His brows collided above the bridge of his nose. "There's no earning to be done, ma'am. Mister Fiske wired his hundred dollar grubstake weeks ago. You have my word that a quarter of any gold we find is yours."

"Such trust will come easy since I'll be there helping divide the spoils."

"What do you mean, *be* there?"

"At the diggings, of course." Steel edged my voice, though he didn't seem particularly cowed by it. "As I said, I fully intend to fulfill Papa's share of the bargain."

Collingsworth shook his head. "No way, no how, little lady. I admire your gumption, but a miners' camp's no fit place for a woman."

"Oh, bullfeathers."

"Miss Fiske—"

"Abigail's my given name. I'll thank you to use it." Planting a forearm on the table, I leaned toward him like a guard dog on a short lead. "Gender has nothing to do with the business at hand, Mister Collingsworth. I can work as hard as any man, draw down on our supper, skin it, and cook it.

"I've ledgered accounts since the age of six, drove a team at eight, have more medical know-how than a lot of sawbones with shingles swinging from their awnings, and as Papa'd tell you if he were here, I don't need anyone to take care of me, tell me what to do, or how to do it."

The prospector's cheeks flushed as rosy as Rome apples.

He reached for his coffee cup and took a long pull at the contents.

I clenched my fists so tightly the knuckles blanched. In my mind, I heard Papa cluck his tongue and say, "Confrontation only heightens a disagreement; it rarely lessens one. Finesse, Abigail. Will you ever learn the fine art of finesse?"

Collingsworth cleared his throat. "There's probably lots of men in Denver City that'll appreciate those talents." Chair legs puckered the flowered rug as he scooted back from the table. "Unfortunately, I'm not one of them."

He stood at least six feet four inches; shoulders wide as an ox yoke. Looking up at his rock-solid frame, I felt the same sense of abandonment I had when Papa breathed his last.

"Forgive me, please, for my rudeness," I said softly.

Hazel eyes pegged my brown ones. "Rudeness nothing. A gal's gotta have sand to get by in these parts. Never have understood how the meek propose to inherit the earth or how'd they'll manage if they do."

"Then why are you so angry with me?"

A smile widened the part in his moustaches. "I'm not angry. We just don't have anything else to talk about and there's chores to do before we leave out tomorrow."

"What time shall I be ready?"

Instantly, his expression rivaled a hanging judge's. "You're not going, Miss Fiske. Raise all the hell you want, but that's the way of it." He took a step toward the door.

I leaped after him, tugging at his sleeve. "No, I'll tell *you* the way of it. If I'm not fit for this expedition, Papa's money isn't either. I demand its return."

"It's already spent for provisions and supplies. I doubt if me and the boys could raise six bits between us."

The emotional toll of the last two days squeezed my heart like a cider press. I bowed my head, speaking more to myself than the man staring at me irritably.

"I don't have anywhere else to go; no money to stay here. Being Maximilian Fiske's daughter is all I know how to do ... and I guess I'm not really that, anymore."

All that'd kept me going since I buried my father in a half-caved, shallow mine shaft was fulfilling his dream—a last, grand adventure, he called it. We'd sold everything to meet that hundred-dollar stake, with just enough left over to keep body and soul together for the long march from Topeka.

Nobody knew us in Colorado. Hard times and all those warrants—with Papa's name misspelled but the charges clear as branch water—that haunted us the last few years were supposed to vanish at the borderline.

A rough finger slid beneath my chin. Collingsworth raised my eyes to his, obviously searching for a trace of guile.

"Traipsing about with the likes of me, Ransom Halsey, and Dick Curtis'll ruin your good name, Abigail."

"Why? Because I choose to work for my keep rather than beg for it? I don't need your protection. I need a partner . . . and maybe a friend."

A heavy sigh brushed my face. By the vein pulsing at his temple, conscience must be waging a silent war with good judgment.

"I reckon my sister Lillith can put you up here for the night," he said. "We'll light out at midday, but I'll caution you here and now: pull your weight and hold that temper or I'll send you packing."

My spirits soared; I could have helped roosters rouse the town but curled my toes inside my boots to stifle the urge. "Bless you, Mister Collingsworth."

"Garrett's my given name and I'll thank you to use it." A lopsided grin belied his mockery. "And I don't know what you're blessing me for, unless it's plumb taking leave of my senses."